DANNY COLMENARES

The Flame of Niradim

FLAMESTRIKER
BOOKS

First published by Flamestriker Books 2024

This novel is entirely a work of fiction. The names, characters, and incidents portrayed in it are the work of the author's imagination. Any resemblance to actual persons, living or dead, events, or localities is entirely coincidental.

Second edition

ISBN (paperback): 979-8-9905667-1-2
ISBN (hardcover): 979-8-9905667-2-9

This book was professionally typeset on Reedsy.
Find out more at reedsy.com

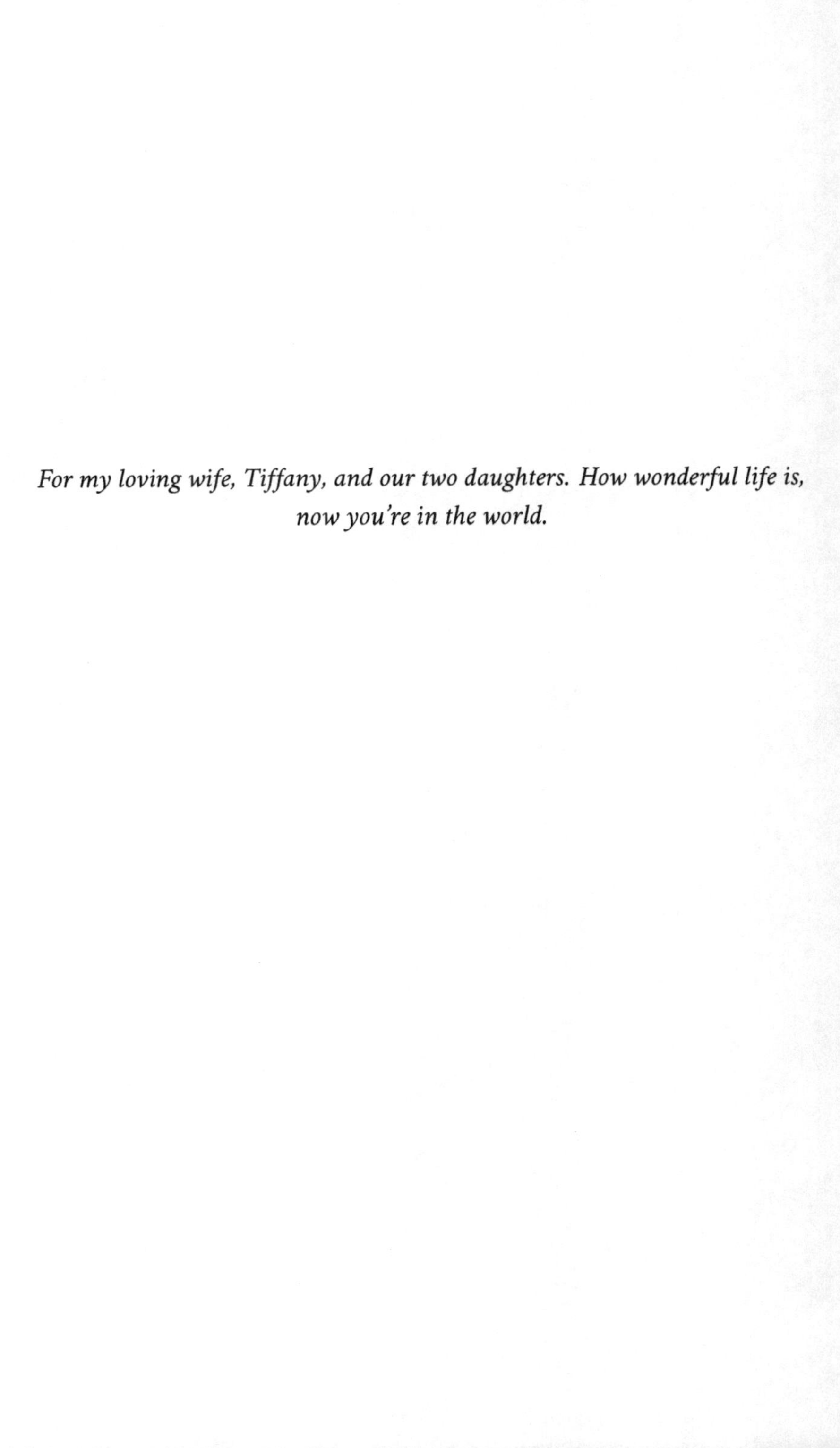

For my loving wife, Tiffany, and our two daughters. How wonderful life is, now you're in the world.

1

Ronan

Seven days ago

"Astoro, they're summoning something!" Ronan yelled over his shoulder as he cut down another cultist. He slid his short sword into his shield and turned to his friend. "Tell the others we need to move! Now!"

The dense forest canopy barely let shafts of sunlight through, casting dappled shadows over the wooden constructs of the cultist hideout. Ronan skidded to a stop in the loose dirt as he breached the front gates and paused for a moment to gain his bearings. The air was thick with magic and blood. The Cult of the Fallen Star needed to be stopped.

Ronan could see the summoning circle beginning to glow at the far side of the hideout. That was their target. Who knew what monstrosity they'd have to deal with if they didn't disrupt the ritual soon.

Movement grabbed his attention from the left. He raised his shield in time to deflect a crossbow bolt and located the novaborn who fired it. He muttered a quick prayer and touched his necklace to channel Niradim's magic.

His arm tingled at the sensation as a small flicker of holy fire gathered into his hand. He threw the puny ball of fire into the chest of the cultist. It wasn't enough to do much real damage, but his target stumbled back and tumbled off the wall. Cursing his weak magical ability, he broke into a run and drew his short sword from his shield as three more enemies rushed to meet him.

Ronan's muscles tensed with adrenaline, his grip on the sword tightening as he heard the screams of the townspeople. Each cry echoed in his ears, a haunting reminder of the stakes at hand. He couldn't stand hearing them suffer.

Why would Niradim allow this to happen? Didn't he have the power to stop this? Well if Niradim wouldn't do anything, Ronan would.

The cultists moved towards him in a wave, their eyes devoid of humanity, caught up in the frenzy of the ritual. As they rushed towards him, the clashing of steel and the thud of bodies echoed through the grim forest. Cultist after cultist met Ronan's blade and fell still as he focused his entire self on this one goal. He needed to make it to the summoning circle!

He broke through the last of their ranks in time to see the final victim fall to a bloody dagger. Screams of terror turned to pain and then faded into nothing. The limp body slumped to the ground next to the others as the leader finished his dark incantation.

Sigils etched into the ground at the edge of the summoning circle flashed a vibrant purple and the ground morphed into an amoebic fluid. Sacrificed bodies sunk into the pool of liquid, dissolving like ink in water and swirling into the amethyst abyss. As they did, a massive form rose from the center and began to take shape.

Ronan gazed upon the surging fluid, a cold dread settling in his stomach. His surroundings darkened, as if the very essence of the forest was being corrupted by this rising mass.

Come on, Niradim, help me out here! Ronan thought, ripping off his necklace and holding it in his hand. *You have to give me more power!*

A cultist caught Ronan by surprise, tackling him to the ground and knocking the necklace out of his hands. He managed to roll out of the way as a dagger just missed his throat. Ronan unsheathed one of the many knives he had strapped to him and buried it into his attacker's chest. He pushed the man off him and looked back up to the summoning circle.

A terrifying amalgamation of starlight and death towered before Ronan. It held two enormous axes in its hands, radiating and glowing with heat. Its arms were as massive as tree trunks and connected by a broad, muscular chest. Its skin was like a starry night, and its eyes were burning coals of fury locked onto Ronan. The nightmare smiled down at him and prepared to charge.

Ronan's mind raced. Astoro and the others would take too long to get here. And the necklace connecting him to Niradim's power was gone. Fine, he'd have to force Niradim's hand.

He discarded his shield and brought his hands up, index and middle finger of each hand making an 'X' in front of his face. Niradim would lend Ronan his power like he had so long ago. He had to. Sweat beaded on his forehead as he concentrated on channeling Niradim's magic.

Ronan watched as white energy began to rise from his body like smoke. He smirked and returned the beast's glare. Now he'd finally show everyone what he was capable of.

* * *

Present day

Pain

Ronan gasped, eyes flaring open as his body arched and then slammed back down. The pain faded, leaving the dull groan of a body pushed past its limits. He blinked once. Twice. On the third blink, his memory unfolded back into his mind, one image at a time.

Blink

A hulking monster stood before him, revealing a row of pointed teeth behind a sinister, ear-to-ear Cheshire grin. Smooth, purple-black skin broken by freckles of starlight covered its entire muscular body. Starfire eyes filled with blood lust as they focused on Ronan. It charged forward, raising two blazing battle axes from powerful arms.

Blink

Ronan's hands came together in front of him as wisps of white power began to steam from his body. Ten glowing knives slid out from their sheaths and hovered around him. Extending his arms, he sent the knives streaking towards the monster. The knives flickered mid-flight once, twice, and then went dull. He watched as they dropped to the ground before reaching their target. Ronan's eyes went wide as the starlight beast descended upon him.

Blink

One axe sliced deep across his chest, cauterizing his flesh as it tore through him. The second one split his left collarbone like a twig. Suddenly, he was looking up at the creature from his back. Blood coated his hands and his body was torn to shreds. A pool of crimson blossomed on the ground from his center. Ronan watched, vision fading at the edges, as the monster raised a burning axe above its head and slammed it back down into him.

Pain

Blink

Darkness

This is wrong, he thought. *I should be dead.*

Ronan sat up and coughed as he choked on some of the ash that was falling off his body. He wiped the debris from his face and took a deep breath. His lungs filled with the familiar acrid smell of burned air and tortured metal. Looking to his left, he saw a white-hot surge of flames was beginning to simmer back down to its normal flicker.

He was lying on the massive anvil in front of the Soul Forge, covered in a thin layer of ash. He looked down at his body and took a sharp breath. He was adorned in the embellished robes of the Smelting Ceremony. Somehow, his body was completely healed, with no evidence of any of the fatal wounds he now vividly remembered receiving.

He looked over to see his custom-forged sword and shield leaning up against the anvil he rested on. His face reflected back at him on the front of the shield. It was dirty from the ash, but otherwise unblemished by any wounds or scars.

He pulled back the hood over his head and ran a hand through his disheveled red hair. His deep brown eyes struggled to make sense of what he was seeing compared to what his mind remembered. He touched one hand to his chest, where his necklace usually rested, but the familiar metal wasn't there. That's right, he lost it in the fight.

Was he back in Midral? He turned his head to view the aged metal working tools adorning the wood-slatted wall. A soot-stained leather apron hung from a peg next to the iron tools, black scorch marks marred the worn leather from years of use. Thick, heavy gloves rested on the workbench beneath it.

Shadows flickered across the intricate carvings of the cathedral from the magical torchlight. They danced in concert with the Flame of Niradim resting in the depth of the Soul Forge. He could feel the comforting heat of the holy flame deep within him, somehow different than it was before.

He looked up to see the familiar slim form of Elder Oren wearing the white and red robes of Niradim, the dwarven god. Sweat dripped from his brow as he stared at Ronan. Ronan's master, Ginmar, stood beside him. Ronan could tell by the streaks down his face that he'd been crying, but now his eyes were wide in astonishment.

"Ronan?" Ginmar whispered as if his voice might shatter the miracle before him. He took a timid step forward.

Ronan finally noticed they weren't alone. He looked out from the platform and saw that the cathedral was completely packed with dwarves. They all stared at him in hushed awe.

"What's going on here?" Ronan asked, turning back to Master Ginmar. His voice reverberated in the unnatural silence of the packed cathedral.

Ronan heard as the dwarves in the audience began to whisper. He caught fragments of sentences but still struggled to understand what was happening.

"…Reborn from the ash!"

"Like a phoenix…"

"…Niradim's chosen!

He put his hand to his head as the room spun for a moment. Ginmar rushed to his side and steadied him with a strong hand on his shoulder. He took a deep, steadying breath and looked up at Ginmar.

"Welcome home, son." Ginmar's voice broke as he wrapped Ronan in a tight embrace.

* * *

It took a few days for the soreness in his muscles to finally dissipate and for Ronan to start feeling like himself again. At least as much as he could, considering what had happened. Everything was different now, and he couldn't stop wondering why he was here. What purpose could he still serve after failing his last mission and dying in the process?

Being alive was a miracle, there was no doubt about that. The priests believed it was a sign he still had a job to do in this realm before passing to the next. He wasn't so sure.

He found Ginmar exactly where he expected to – hard at work at his personal forge. A wave of nostalgia washed over Ronan as he surveyed the scene. The ringing of hammer on anvil, the glow of superheated metal, the feel of shaping simple metal into something with purpose - he missed this.

He spent so many hours here, sweating in the heat of a roaring forge and working his body to the brink of exhaustion. All to create beautiful works alongside the man who had raised him. The forge was Ronan's safe place. A place he could escape to when he needed to get away.

Ginmar's long white hair and beard dripped with sweat as he hammered a piece of metal against the anvil. Ronan watched as he wiped a muscled forearm across his brow, leaving another black streak across his forehead. He wore nothing to protect his upper body from the sparks that flew with each fall of the hammer, save a worn leather apron, leaving his toned arms bare. Whether it was because of the heat, or to show off his massive biceps, Ronan never knew.

Without a word or so much as a glance, Ginmar gestured toward a familiar apron hanging on the wall. Ronan donned his apron and took his place next to Ginmar. For the next several hours they worked side by side, neither saying a word, melting into the familiar rhythm of creation.

Ronan took some tongs from the wall and used them to pull some metal from the forge for shaping. He held the white-hot metal on the anvil, keeping it still while Ginmar hammered it. He rotated it every few strikes to stretch out the metal and bring out the shape of the weapon they were crafting.

After a few moments, the white glow turned to yellow, and then the yellow turned to orange. Ronan placed the metal back into the forge to return it to the white-hot glow that primed it for shaping. This time Ginmar pulled the metal from the forge and let Ronan take the hammer. They repeated this process, alternating back and forth until the metal resembled the knife it would become. It still needed grinding, sharpening, and polishing, but the shaping was complete.

Ronan cleared the little flakes of hammer scale that accumulated on the anvil from the repeated blows of Ginmar's hammer. Shaping was tough on the metal. It was heated beyond anything reasonable and then hammered into the shape the blacksmith wanted. During the process, pieces of the metal would flake off as the metal molded into shape. These pieces were called hammer scale.

Niradim's faith taught that everything that happened to a person was part of their Shaping. He was molding them into the creation he meant them to be throughout their life. They even had a Shaping Trial that Acolytes who wanted to progress to Disciple had to complete.

Some dwarves would call what had happened to Ronan a part of his life's Shaping. He felt more like the hammer scale that flaked off from the metal in the forging process. As a human, his presence in Niradim's faith was unnatural to begin with. Niradim was the god and creator of the dwarves. Ronan didn't have a piece of Niradim's soul within him like the dwarves did. Maybe it was his time to be removed.

Ginmar inspected the knife they had shaped together.

"Just as fine as ever," Ginmar said, finally breaking the silence between them. "Thought I'd have to teach you from scratch after being gone so long." He chuckled.

"We stopped at several towns with forges," Ronan said. He didn't really want to remember his time on the road leading up to his failure. "I always volunteered to help the local blacksmiths when I could."

"Ha! Never could keep you out of the forge, even when you were a kid," Ginmar said, clapping him on the back. He turned and placed the metal on a nearby bench with a pile of others.

"You haven't touched your sword or shield since you woke up," Ginmar said as he pointed to a corner of the room.

The ornate weapons had been carefully laid on a spare workbench, waiting for their owner to retrieve them. Ronan had created those as a part of his Shaping Trial. He had been the first human Niradim had ever accepted into his ranks.

Despite never being great at channeling Niradim's magic, the fact he'd been able to do so at all as a human had been a point of pride for Ronan. Until Ronan came along, that power had always been reserved for Niradim's people. He believed he'd been special to Niradim, to be granted that ability. But it hadn't been enough. Not when he needed it most.

That sword and shield were Ronan's entire faith, forged into a symbol of protection that he could carry into battle wherever he went. It was his finest work as a master blacksmith. And he was, indeed, a master blacksmith. That was one area of Niradim's realm Ronan never had trouble with.

He had poured himself into those magical items, and he thought they would be enough to stand out as a Disciple of Niradim. Now those creations were a sour reminder of a god who abandoned him in his most crucial time of need. Maybe it was time for him to go back to being just a blacksmith.

He looked away. "I guess I just don't see the point," he said with a shrug, not meeting Ginmar's eyes. "I'm best utilized here at the forge where my work can make a difference."

Ginmar frowned and started to say something, but stopped himself. He knew Ronan well enough to know he didn't want to talk about it any further. Instead, he walked to the side of the room to hang up his apron.

"It's about time for dinner. Let's both get cleaned up and get something warm to eat."

* * *

After dinner, Ronan made his way to the Crucible Gate to get some fresh air in the Sky Sector. Being under the mountain for so long in the Earth Sector was starting to make him stir-crazy. Besides, he needed some time alone and he missed his city.

He crossed through the Crucible Gate into the Sky Sector. The Crucible Gate was Midral's last line of defense, and had never fallen in its history. As the massive stone doors parted, the bustling marketplace in the Court of Fire greeted him on the other side. The massive courtyard was an open place where vendors could come and sell their wares in Midral. It was also the location of the Festival of Fire that was always held after an Acolyte attempted the Shaping Trial.

Ronan closed his eyes and took a deep breath of the crisp air of early winter. A wave of familiar sounds and smells washed over him, and a tightness in his chest loosened as he soaked in his home.

A year had passed since he left on his mission, but he could tell as he wandered that not much had changed. Each street was as he remembered. He listened as the vendors in the market heralded their wares to passers-by. This time of year, they were selling furs and warm clothing as the cold season was fast approaching.

Now that he was out in the Sky Sector, he started seeing the other peoples that lived in the city. Except for Ronan, only dwarves had permission to roam the Earth Sector, but anyone was free to come and go in the Sky Sector. It was refreshing to see the diversity that had made its way into the open part of Midral.

Dwarves and humans made up the greater population of the Sky Sector, but other races were beginning to call Midral their home as well. He watched as a few novaborn children played in the street, their parents struggling to keep up. Their star-like freckles were beginning to glow as the sun descended in the sky. Usually, novaborn skin was a shade of red or orange, but he'd also seen those with shades of blue or purple in his travels.

A couple of florians made their way from stall to stall, buying anything that would help them keep warm in the chilly air. Their plant-like features stood out in a city like Midral - it was rare to see them this far north. They usually preferred the warmer parts of the continent closer to their home forest. His best friend had told him florians could go weeks on water alone as long as the weather was sunny.

He even spotted a green-scaled draken selling hot food and drinks from her homeland. She made a show of heating the delicacies with flames she expelled from her mouth. The smell made his mouth water as he passed by. He'd have to remember to come back and try the food when he hadn't just eaten.

Even though the fresh air was relaxing, something still felt off to Ronan. After a few minutes, Ronan noticed people reacting strangely to his presence. People were stealing glances his way and he caught whispers of his name as he passed. They parted when he approached, and a vendor even refused payment from him when he ordered a warm drink. He said it was an honor to serve Niradim's chosen. The rumors of his resurrection had clearly spread beyond the border of the Crucible Gate.

Tired of the attention he was drawing, Ronan took his drink and made his way back to the Court of Fire. It was time to head back to his home. As he entered the Earth Sector, the familiar musty scents filled his lungs. It had taken time to get used to living in a place that was completely surrounded by earth, but he'd grown accustomed to it over the years.

The Earth Sector was perhaps the only place of its kind in the world. At about a quarter the size of the Sky Sector, this part of the city resided within the Midral mountain. Dwarves were allowed free passage in and out, and followers of Niradim were even allowed residence in the Earth Sector. This was where the Flame of Niradim rested - inside the Soul Forge at the heart of the mountain.

Niradim's Flame powered the forges within the Earth Sector and allowed blacksmiths to create amazing works of metal. The most gifted Disciples of Niradim were even able to craft magical items. Ronan counted himself among those. Though he wasn't able to channel Niradim's magic very well, even he could craft magical items at a forge powered by the Flame of Niradim.

Magical torchlight replaced natural light as he made his way deeper inside the mountain. Finally, the massive cavern of the Earth Sector opened before him and he paused to take in the spectacular sight of the city inside the mountain. He didn't feel the same comfort he normally did.

He took a deep breath and continued to wander with no real destination in mind. He just needed to walk. But as he did, the questions he'd been fighting to keep at bay began to plague his mind once more.

This whole thing seemed like a cruel joke. He'd devoted his life to Niradim and defended his city and people on many occasions. Didn't he deserve to access Niradim's magic in the same way the dwarves did? Couldn't Niradim at least lend him a burst of magic when faced with certain death? He'd done it once before when his master's life was at stake. Was his own life not worth it? And why let him die just to bring him back? The questions were eating at him.

After about half an hour of walking, he stopped and noticed he'd made his way to the Cathedral of Niradim. Home of the Soul Forge, and the place of his rebirth. It was late, and the Cathedral was empty, but he knew that Niradim's doors were never locked. Anyone could enter and pray at any time.

He slowly lifted a hand towards the heavy wooden door and let it hang in the air for a moment. He didn't know what had compelled him to come here. What did Niradim even want from him? What was his purpose? And why had Niradim abandoned him?

The mounting questions were finally too much. Anger surged through him and he threw the doors open with a shove. His footsteps echoed in the empty chamber as he strode through the middle of the aisle towards the Soul Forge. His breath caught in his throat at the sight of the large anvil before him. The same anvil he had risen from a few days before.

The Flame of Niradim blazed behind the anvil in an ornate forge, casting the entire sanctuary in cool, white light and dancing shadows. The eerie silence broken by his footfalls made the hairs on his neck stand on end. He came to a halt a step in front of the anvil and stared deep into the holy Flame behind it.

"Why am I here?" Ronan demanded. "I pledged my life to your service, and in return, you cast me aside when I needed you most! You let me die!"

He waited, but no voice, no sign, no fire answered him.

He was tired of giving everything and receiving so little in return. He was tired of being the weakest Disciple. He was tired of Niradim. If Niradim could cast him aside, then he could do the same to Niradim.

"I'm done," Ronan said, rounding the anvil towards the Soul Forge. "You can take that sword and shield I made you. And that necklace that's gone missing, you can have that back too. I won't be needing them anymore."

Ronan ripped the cloth free from his waist marking him as a Disciple of Niradim and threw it into the forge. It blackened and curled at the edges before catching fire and becoming one with the Flame.

"I pledged my life to you, and gave it in service," Ronan said, his voice quiet and somber. "My oath is complete. I don't care if you brought me back, you only get one life from me, and you wasted it."

With that, Ronan turned his back on Niradim and left.

2

Kyros

Well, that was a voiding nightmare. Kyros cursed to himself as he hiked through the mountains. *The next mission better be easier, or I'm going to start regretting this deal, no matter the power I've attained.*

The fresh snow crunched beneath his feet, breaking the muffled silence of the snowy peaks. He took a deep breath as he stepped to the edge of a cliff overlooking the great dwarven city of Midral. Surveying the city from this distance was fine, but he preferred another method. A small brown owl perched on his shoulder, jerking its head left and right before stopping to focus on Kyros. He closed his eyes and felt the spark of his magic activate. The crystal embedded into his forehead flashed purple and he felt his perspective change. When he opened his eyes again, he was looking directly at the side of his own face, from his owl's eyes.

It was always unnerving to see his own eyes glazed over with the violet glow that indicated he was using his owl's sight. He'd tied his long white hair back to keep it out of his face for the multi-day trip through the mountains. The sun was beginning to peek over the horizon, so the starlight freckles dotting his purple skin - a trait shared by all novaborn - were beginning to dim. They'd be invisible during the day, just like the stars in the sky.

"Come on, Noct" He saw himself say through Noct's eyes. "Let's get a better view of the city."

Noct's head turned back to view the city far below, and he took flight from Kyros' shoulder. Kyros would be vulnerable while looking through Noct's eyes, but he wasn't worried about any danger this high up in the mountains. He was certain there wasn't anything alive up here that could threaten him.

From where they were, it was a several-minute flight to the city and Kyros couldn't help but reflect on the circumstances that brought him here. The rough path behind him led back to an ancient city that had been long forgotten until about a week ago. He rediscovered it with a group of mercenaries he hired to help him traverse the massive forest and mountain range that hid the city from the world. Fortunately, he knew the path they needed to take. Unfortunately, it was incredibly dangerous.

The majority of his party had either died on the way or after they'd reached the city, including his own brother. It was fine, his brother would have tried to find a way to stab Kyros in the back at some point and take the power Kyros had attained for himself. There had been no love lost between them.

The losses were acceptable since he accomplished the task he'd been assigned. In fact, the fewer people that knew about the city, the better. He'd still need to track down the ones that got away at some point, but he had a plan for that already in motion.

The city was coming into view and he directed Noct on a path straight over the main gates. The city of Midral was impressive. A normal assault on the city would be difficult. It was built at the base of an enormous mountain and surrounded by impenetrable walls. It would take a massive assault to breach the front gates. Fortunately, he'd be walking right in and conducting his business from the inside.

Noct flew over the different areas of the city and Kyros noted some points of interest. There was a large plaza in front of massive stone doors that led into the city. That must be the Court of Fire. The vendors were beginning to set up their shops and getting ready for the day. He located the main living areas of the city, and more importantly, he found an area of the city that looked like it was more run down.

He watched as a couple drunken dwarves were tossed out of a tavern, too inebriated to stand back up. In an alley nearby, a draken and a novaborn were fighting over what looked like a game of dice. He would definitely have some business on that side of town.

Satisfied he'd seen enough to get his bearings, he closed Noct's eyes and shifted back to his perspective on the cliffside. He opened his eyes, once again overlooking the city of Midral from a distance. The normal route would take several hours of hiking, but his new staff would help him cross most of the distance instantly.

He unlatched the staff from his back and held it in his hands in front of him. The smooth crystal vibrated with power at his touch, begging to be released. The Crystalline Staff was the reason for his visit to the ancient city, and it acted as an amplifier for his own magical ability. A massive amplifier.

He could see the edge of a forest to the west that was only a short distance away from the city on foot. That would work. He focused on a spot among the trees and muttered an incantation under his breath. The crystal on his forehead glowed a bright purple, and the staff in his hands lit up like a beacon with the same light.

He tapped the staff to the ground and his body exploded into a cloud of mist. With a flash, he reappeared in the forest near the city, behind the tree line where he wouldn't be spotted. The Crystalline Staff faded a little and the vibration died down to a small hum. It would gain its power back over time and return to its normal brilliance. Without the staff, that mist jump would have had a max distance of only a few dozen feet.

He took a moment to wrap the staff in leather so it wouldn't attract attention once he was in the city. It was time to get moving. He didn't know the details of his new mission yet, but once he found a place to stay, his Patron would contact him and give him his new assignment. He shuddered despite himself. He couldn't wait to be free of this contract.

He stepped out of the trees and made his way towards the main road that would take him to the front gates of the city. The sun crested the horizon, and he could see as the people traveling the roads were beginning to take off their thickest layers of clothing. Kyros smirked and glanced at the dark ring on his finger - another trophy from his recent trip to the ancient city.

The black ring had a faint, almost imperceptible pale blue glow, and looked as if a thin layer of frost coated it. The ring was an Artifact thought to be lost to history, destroyed by Niradim's own flames as the stories put it. Yet here it was, adorning his finger and keeping him comfortable in his elegant clothing despite the frigid air. He still needed to learn the depths of its abilities, but from his limited understanding, he knew it was extremely powerful.

And now that power was in Kyros' hands. Between the ring and the staff, Kyros may actually be one of the most powerful individuals on the continent, and he absolutely loved it. And as soon as he'd completed his contract, he'd be free to wield that power however he saw fit. For now, it was time to enter the city and find out exactly why he was here.

* * *

"Are you here for business or pleasure?"

"Oh, pleasure of course," Kyros said with a smile. "Always pleasure."

The guard waved him in. Using the knowledge of his earlier surveillance, he made his way to the nicer part of the city to find some lodging. He preferred to stay in only the finest establishments, a leftover habit from his lavish upbringing. This meant he had to visit a few in person before he judged one worthy enough of his patronage. After camping out in a danger-filled city, he was looking forward to relaxing, even if for a moment.

"Niradim's Greatest Blessing," Kyros said out loud as he read the sign in front of the nicest inn he'd seen. "Wow, now *that's* pretentious, don't you think, Noct?" The owl tilted its head as it regarded him from his shoulder and ruffled its feathers. "Let's have a nice chat with the innkeeper about a free room. I'm sure the fanciest suite in this place is about to have a vacancy."

He strode through the gaudy entrance and located the innkeeper behind the bar. He was laughing as he spoke with a beautiful woman with long hair and a bright smile holding a small baby. The woman handed the innkeeper a key and turned to a little girl in a bright dress decorated with flowers. She was in the middle of chasing a small gray dog that had only one ear that stood up properly.

"Julia, let's get going," the woman called after her. "Cecilia is about ready for her nap, and your father is waiting for us in the carriage outside."

"Yay!" the girl squealed as she ran out ahead through the open door. The dog followed close behind but stopped and growled at Kyros as he passed. Kyros sneered in return.

"Maverick, be nice!" the woman said as she followed her daughter outside. She snapped her fingers and the dog turned and followed at a comfortable trot. Kyros turned and approached the innkeeper.

"Welcome, valued guest, and Niradim's Greatest Blessings on you!" the dwarven man said as Kyros approached. "My name is Travier, how can I assist you today, my lord?"

"Travier, I'll be taking your finest room for the foreseeable future," Kyros said.

"Our finest room is currently occupied. Fortunately, each of our rooms is finer than any other you'll find in Midral!" Travier replied in a practiced cadence. "I'm sure you'll be more than pleased with what we have available."

"No, your finest room will do. I'm sure the current occupants are unfit to stay here anyway." Kyros' crystal glowed a subtle violet as he spoke, and he saw the magical charm settle into Travier's eyes.

"Yes, of course, my lord, what was I thinking," Travier said. "I'll have them right out and get the room cleaned up for you."

"Please be quick about it," Kyros said.

"Of course, my lord."

A few minutes later, Kyros watched as Travier ushered out a very angry Elven couple and then returned to lead Kyros to his room. He had Travier draw him a warm bath and bring him some fine food and even finer alcohol. He had to remove his ring to enjoy the bath's warm temperature, but it was worth it. Only the best for their most esteemed guest.

He wasn't looking forward to meeting with his Patron tonight. He knew tomorrow would mark the start of another, likely unpleasant, mission. But for now, he indulged in the finer things as he settled into the warm bath and let his muscles release.

* * *

As always, Kyros felt himself flying through the void of space towards the familiar purple star. He hovered in the air in front of it, suspended in the cosmos. The Star Prison stretched out like a pulsating sea of amoebic fluid, its hues swirling like a cosmic storm. Each pulse sent shimmering waves of light across its vast, nebulous expanse. The orb of energy before him kept his Patron trapped and unable to return to the mortal realm.

Kyros didn't know all the details, only that other gods had banished his Patron and encased him in a star-like prison made of pure violet energy. If he squinted, he could make out what almost looked like a webbing of runes surrounding the energy, keeping it contained. The Star Prison was visible in the night sky as a faint purple star. If you looked at it for long enough, you could barely make out the pulsing light.

As Kyros gazed upon it, a faint hum vibrated through his being, resonating with the star's rhythmic pulsing. The space around him seemed charged with a palpable energy, tingling against his skin and filling his nostrils with the scent of ozone. This is where he always came in his dreams when his Patron needed to talk to him.

He remembered the first time he visited The Star Prison. He'd been searching for a way to access stronger magic than his measly abilities allowed him. One night, the opportunity presented itself and Kyros used the only real power he had in his arsenal - negotiation. So he and his new Patron had come to an agreement that granted Kyros exactly what he wanted, in exchange for his service. Unfortunately, he wasn't sure if this agreement was going to be in his favor as much as he once thought.

IT IS TIME TO DISCUSS YOUR NEXT TARGET.

His Patron's voice boomed in his mind as it always did.

"That first mission was a voiding mess," Kyros cursed, ignoring the topic. "You didn't tell me how dangerous the ancient city would be. I'm lucky I made it out of there at all!"

Dangerous was putting it mildly. The city, and the route to it, had been a deathtrap. He should have expected that his Patron would only be as forthcoming as needed. It was always in one's best interests to keep as much information to oneself as possible. His brother never got it through his thick skull, but there were many forms of power, and information was a big one.

THE DANGER DOES NOT MATTER. THIS IS WHAT YOU AGREED TO.

"Yeah, well I didn't see any of that in the fine print," Kyros replied, crossing his arms. Lesson learned, and two can play at that game. Perhaps it was time to start keeping secrets of his own. "Anyways, I made out with the staff as you required."

YES, BUT YOU SHOULD HAVE LEFT NO SURVIVORS. SOME OF THE MERCENARIES WHO REDISCOVERED IT WITH YOU STILL LIVE.

The pulses of light emanating from the Star Prison undulated in sync with his words.

THE CITY NEEDS TO REMAIN HIDDEN UNTIL YOU'VE COMPLETED YOUR TASKS AND EVERYTHING IS GATHERED.

"The survivors will be dealt with," Kyros replied, brushing off the concern. "I have instructed one of my subordinates to revive two individuals that were turned to stone. They will help us locate the missing mercenaries."

MAKE SURE YOU FIND THEM ALL OR THERE WILL BE CONSEQUENCES.

A cold sweat broke out across Kyros' forehead, betraying a hint of fear at the threat. He wasn't sure exactly what the limits were to his Patron's power, but he didn't want to find out. For now, he needed to remain on his good side.

"So, about that next target," Kyros said, moving on. "What exactly will I be collecting this time?"

Immediately, a vision snapped into his head. He found himself in the middle of what looked like a Cathedral. The vision moved him over the empty pews towards what looked to be a large anvil at the front of the room. Behind that, a white fire roared in what looked like an ornate blacksmith forge. He could almost feel the heat emanating from the heart of the forge as the vision took him closer. After a moment of focusing on the fire, the vision faded.

YOUR NEXT TARGET IS THE FLAME OF NIRADIM, THE SOURCE OF POWER AT THE HEART OF MIDRAL. PLUNGE THE STAFF INTO THE FLAMES AND IT WILL DRAW THE FLAME INTO ITSELF.

"I need to steal the whole Flame?" Kyros asked.

ONLY A SLIVER OF ITS POWER IS REQUIRED FOR MY RETURN, BUT I WANT TO MAKE MY OLD FRIEND SUFFER.

Kyros wasn't sure he liked where this was headed.

BRING ME THE FLAME AND PLUNGE MIDRAL INTO DARKNESS AND DESPAIR!

* * *

Kyros jolted awake, drenched in sweat. He was never able to sleep in after speaking with his Patron. As he thought, this deal kept getting worse and worse for him. Stealing the Flame of Niradim was going to be next to impossible. He'd have to start planning right away.

He muttered an arcane incantation under his breath as his fingers wove through a simple gesture. A faint shimmer of amethyst light traced a path from his head to his feet, leaving his skin and attire pristine. The simple spell drastically cut back the time it used to take him to get ready for the day. Magic truly was wonderful.

After a quick visit to Travier to refresh the charm spell on him and grab some breakfast, Kyros set out to get to work. Moving through the streets, he began to feel the pulse of the city. Unlike most cities he visited, the majority of the people here seemed genuinely happy. They lived good lives, for the most part, and were well protected.

But every city had those that moved in the shadows. Those were the connections he needed to make if he was going to succeed. That task would be easier to accomplish at night when those types of people usually stirred. For now, he needed to scope out the Crucible Gate and figure out how to get to the Flame.

He made his way through the Court of Fire, keeping track of the number of guards he saw and where they were stationed. He also took note of the different ways in and out of the Court. Several streets led to the Court of Fire, which would give him plenty of options to get in and get out when the time came.

Kyros found a tavern close to the Crucible Gate so he could sit and study the procedures at the entrance. A barmaid walked up to him.

"Niradim's Blessings, my lord," she said with a practiced smile. "What can I get ya?"

"Something I can drink slowly," Kyros said. "Surprise me."

"Coming right up!"

As she walked away to get him something he was sure was going to be beneath his expensive tastes, he turned back to study his target. There were four guards posted at the gates, split two and two at the entrance and exit. A simple distraction might be enough to get them to leave their posts and allow him to sneak in.

He took a closer look at the crowd around the Court of Fire and began to notice guards mixed in with the general populace patrolling around. They weren't wearing uniforms, but their posture was too straight and their weapons were too polished. After a few moments, he noticed they patrolled in a regular pattern. Yes, it was simple to pick them out now that he knew what to look for. No doubt they were around to make sure the guards at the gates never left their posts, even in the case of a disturbance. Causing a distraction by itself was unlikely to work to get him inside.

He turned his attention back to the gates. Each person entering had to provide some paperwork to be allowed through. If he could get his hands on one of those documents, he could forge some for himself. Then a magical disguise would make sure nobody would recognize him. As he considered it, the barmaid returned with his drink.

"So, I haven't seen you around here before, handsome." She leaned over strategically to expose a fair amount of skin. "You new in town?"

"Yes," he replied without taking his eyes off the gates.

"Well, what brings you in?" She leaned a little closer. "Going to attend the Festival of Fire?"

"Actually, I was thinking about doing some sightseeing," Kyros said, finally turning to look at her. His eyes ignored the not-so-subtle invitation to drop below her neckline. "Tell me, do you know how I can get documentation to visit the Earth Sector? I've just been dying to see it."

"Oh." She frowned, leaning back as she realized her attempts at seduction weren't working. "You *are* from out of town. I'm afraid you're out of luck, the only people allowed into the Earth Sector are the dwarves that live and work in the city of Midral. It's not open to visitors except with very special permission."

Voids above, Kyros cursed to himself as the barmaid continued to blather on. He could magically change his appearance, but not his height. He was easily a foot or two taller than most dwarves, so that wasn't going to work. As he began to consider alternative strategies, he watched as a red-haired human walked up to the gates and was allowed through.

"Wait," he said, interrupting her in the middle of what he was sure was a riveting story. "I thought you said only dwarves were allowed through the gates. What about that man with the red hair?"

"Oh, that's Ronan Flamestriker!" she said with a hint of admiration. "Well of course he's also allowed in. He's the only human ever to complete the Trial of Niradim, so he gets special permission. Why, just the other day, he…"

"Thank you, that will be all," Kyros said, dismissing her with a wave of his hand. She frowned, but got the message and left with a huff.

So maybe the disguise could still work. He could easily disguise himself as this Ronan fellow and forge some documentation to get himself in. Another thought occurred to him.

Let's take a more detailed look at that paperwork… He thought.

He muttered some words under his breath and made a symbol with his hand. His pupils flashed violet and he looked closer at the papers passing between the dwarves and the guards. He saw a faint glow stamped on each document.

Magic. Of course. All of those documents had some kind of magical seal on them, probably to prevent simple forgeries. Well, that meant paying someone for a forgery was likely out. He'd have to get his hands dirty and steal one or coerce someone into validating a forgery he made. Engrossed in his scheming, Kyros almost missed the 2 pairs of guards that had diverted from their normal patrols. They were closing in on his location.

Voids, He cursed to himself. *I should have known that with this much security, they'd be on the lookout for anyone using magic.*

It was time to leave. He left some money on the table and exited out the back of the tavern. He needed to get back to his room and prepare anyway. He had a busy night ahead of him.

* * *

A couple more days of scoping the Crucible Gate would be needed, but there was new work to do now that the sun had set. This was the fun part of his job.

After cleansing himself from the grime of the day, he slipped into the embrace of a stark white shirt. He felt the crisp, pressed fabric against his skin like a second, more refined armor. Some black pants tucked into black leather boots and his purple coat with silver embroidery finished the ensemble. He exited into the brisk night air, starlight freckles glowing against his violet skin, adding an otherworldly air to his persona. He made sure that his heavy coin pouch hung on his waist, visible to any passers-by. It was time to draw out the rodents of the city.

He set out towards the shadow-laced alleys of the city, where the roads stayed dark when the sun went down. The area he had in mind wasn't as well patrolled as the rest of Midral, perfect for making connections in the city's underground population. There were a couple different strategies one could employ on a mission like this.

The first was to find the most run-down bar in the area, sit down with some drinks, and wait for individuals to meet together to discuss business. Then the tough part was finding a way to engage the individuals without spooking them. But that strategy required a different wardrobe more fit to blend into a crowd like that, and more time than he had available. No, he needed to have some fun and blow off some steam tonight after having been gone from decent civilization for quite some time. And the truth was, he did so love to dress up.

So instead, he found his way to the rowdiest bar he could find - The Braided Maiden. It was filled to the brim with drunkards, gamblers, and gang members who needed vices to distract them from their worthless little lives. This time of night, it was full to the brim with patrons. He elbowed his way to the bar to get a drink of what they called their finest liquor and then scoped out the bar to pick his target.

He needed something flashy and visible, so he could make a proper scene and attract the attention he wanted. His eyes located a dwarf with a deep black beard, braided with gaudy jewelry woven throughout. The dwarves around him sported matching tattoos on their arms and jumped at his every demand. Perfect.

It looked like they were setting up to do a little gambling and there were still a few open seats at the table. Taking his drink, he approached and casually sat down as if they had been saving that seat especially for him.

"Oy, whaddaya think you're doin'?" Black Beard said. "Game's full. Take yer girly clothes elsewhere." A few chuckles arose from the other dwarves at and around the table.

"What, afraid of a little real gambling?" Kyros replied, casually laying out 100 gold on the table. These fleas probably didn't make as much in a year. "Someone told me this was the high rollers table, but I guess I can find someone else with deeper pockets to play with." He rose as if to leave.

"Well, I guess we have room for one more at the table if ya got the coin ta spare," the dwarf said. "Might even give ya a few lessons while yer here."

"Sure, that sounds like fun," Kyros said with a sly smile. "I feel like doing some learning tonight."

Kyros played each hand with a nobleman's confidence, dropping large amounts of coin early and often, drawing a large crowd of onlookers. He lost a few early hands to lower his opponents' defenses and used those rounds to learn each of their tells. Reading people was a special talent of his, and these weren't the brightest stars in the sky compared to the people he usually dealt with.

Once they had dismissed him as a threat, Kyros pounced. His game changed dramatically, becoming more and more aggressive with each hand. He threw around large amounts of money to bait the others into playing losing hands again and again. After taking a particularly large pot from the table, he stood to leave.

"Thanks for the easy money," Kyros said. "I would say it was a pleasure, but I've had more exciting games from children."

That ought to seal the deal. He could see Black Beard's face turn red with anger as he scooped all of their money into his pouch. He made sure they could see how full it was as he got up from his seat and left the table.

As he left the bar and started down the street, a small owl took flight gliding far above him. It didn't take long before he noticed several shadows tailing him, darting from alley to alley. After a few blocks, he finally decided to spring the trap and made his way down a dark alley that had a dead end. Four men made their way in after him, and once they had proceeded about halfway down, Kyros turned to meet them.

"Well, it took you all long enough," Kyros said. He noticed their leader wasn't among them. Good, they'd have to deliver the money to him to prove they had it. "I've got a job for you and your leader, take me to him"

"You ain't goin' nowhere," the brute in the front said, holding a knife out in front of him. "Hand over your coin nice and easy, and we promise to make it quick."

Kyros smiled. Just as he'd hoped. He'd get to have a little fun after all.

"Oh, but I'd rather take my time," Kyros sneered.

As Kyros spoke, the alleyway grew darker and colder. Soon, the thugs' breath was a visible fog in the air. Kyros smiled as he saw they finally began to understand this encounter would not go exactly as they originally planned. The crystal on Kyros' forehead began to glow a deep violet, and the ring on his hand frosted over with ice and pulsed with pale blue light. That same frost from the ring began to crawl like vines outward from Kyros, across the ground and walls toward the prey at the other end of the alley.

Having seen enough, the two thugs in the back dropped their knives and started to make a run for it. But Kyros wasn't letting anyone escape until he had his fun. He raised his ringed hand and the ice that had been creeping out from him shot across the surface of the alley, ahead of the 2 runners. A barrier of ice rose and shut off any chance they had of escape. Sharp spikes protruded from its surface.

The two thugs slid to a stop before colliding with the spiked wall. As the two thugs in front watched their comrades try to flee, two dark purple-black bolts of energy streaked by them and hit their allies. The force of the blasts flung the cowards the last few feet and impaled them on the jagged, icy teeth.

The two remaining thugs turned back to Kyros who was holding his hand up in front of him, palm extended. It was still smoking from hurling the bolts of energy. A deadly smirk crept across his face. Killing them was so easy. One of the thugs found his courage and ran straight at Kyros, dagger striking out towards him.

The crystal on Kyros' head flashed violet, and a pool of darkness washed out across the ground in front of him, obscuring the ice that had been forming. As if out of a nightmare, a dozen inky tendrils dotted with specks of light reached up out of the darkness. The starlit tendrils seized the thug as he was reaching Kyros, stopping him in his tracks. It was as if the night sky itself had wrapped its arms around his appendages and held him aloft.

"You should really be more careful," Kyros taunted. "you could seriously injure someone running around with something so sharp."

Kyros plucked the dagger out of the man's hand and plunged it into his stomach. As the man gasped, his flesh turned to ice around the wound and began to spread across his body. Kyros held on to the knife and reveled in his newfound power as the ice entombed his victim. He'd never known power like this. It was glorious.

Once the ice had completely spread, he let go of the knife. The inky arms released what was now an ice sculpture of a man with a knife in his stomach standing in an alley. Kyros stood back and admired his art. That was fun, he'd need to look for more opportunities to play. For now, it was time to get back to business.

The glow in his crystal subsided and the darkness on the ground faded, revealing the frosted ground beneath. He stepped around the alley's newest ice sculpture and turned his attention to the last man standing in the alley.

"P-p-please don't k-kill me, sir. I was just doin' what I was t-told!" he stammered and dropped to his knees, discarding his knife.

Kyros rolled his eyes. "Hold on and keep quiet, I need to check on something."

He closed his eyes and opened them in the sky. Noct was keeping watch, and he hadn't heard any signal that anyone was around, but he wanted to make sure. After giving the area a once-over, he was satisfied that his playtime in the alley hadn't alerted anyone. Shifting back into himself, he turned to the lone survivor.

"Now, let's discuss a wonderful new business opportunity I have for your boss…"

3

Val'ran

"Hey Val, think they'll feed us anytime soon? I'm getting pretty hungry."

"Shut up, Bogg."

Val'ran's joints were still stiff from being turned to stone for a month - the result of a trap that her idiot companion had set off. And now his incessant talking almost made her wish she was a statue again. They'd already been in this prison for a few days, and she still didn't know why. Why would these people rescue them just to keep them imprisoned?

The cell itself was a cold, damp chamber, its air thick with the earthy odor of dirt and mud. Faint drips echoed in the silence, at least whenever Bogg wasn't running his mouth. A sliver of light crept through a small opening high above, casting long shadows across the dirt floor.

Vertical iron bars extended from floor to ceiling. Hinges allowed the entire front of the cells to swing open, and there was a heavy metal lock ensuring they couldn't leave. Rusty chains and manacles hung from a simple stone wall across from the doors, but their captors hadn't bothered locking the two of them in those. At least not yet. It was a simple prison, but effective.

The memory of her petrification haunted her – a sensation of numbing cold and helpless immobility. She could almost hear her father's deep, resonant voice chastising her carelessness. But Bogg's persistent bragging got under her skin, and she was too competitive for her own good. A simple race to a crystal staff set off the magical trap, and who knows what had happened to the rest of their party. Maybe once they were out she could track one of the other members down if they were still alive. If they could get out.

She tore off a thin piece of cloth from her shirt and swept her long brown hair back over her pointed ears, tying it back into a simple ponytail. She was still wearing her brown and green leather armor, but her longbow and her father's scimitar were missing. She glanced at a puddle of water on the ground next to her to regard her physical state.

Val'ran's emerald eyes flickered with a mix of frustration and determination in the reflection of the murky water. It was a sharp contrast against her pale, elven skin. With her hair out of the way, she could see the elegant contours of her face a little more sharply due to the lack of food and water they'd been given.

Across the iron bars from her sat Bogg, with his unkempt beard and a short stubble beginning to fill in the top of his normally bald head. He still wore his sleeveless leather armor, fashioned to show off his battle-toned arms, but had also been stripped of his weapons. His large hands fidgeted with the rusty manacles hanging beside him.

She crossed her legs and rested her elbows on them, bringing the tips of her fingers together in front of her face. She didn't know why, but she always thought better while sitting like this. Her father used to joke that it looked like she was saying a prayer, but for her it was a battle meditation. She shook away the memory of her father and took a deep breath, closing her eyes. It was time to focus on analyzing her present situation and figure out a solution.

She decided they must still be in the ancient city. She'd been healed inside her cell and watched as they'd healed Bogg in his. It was unlikely someone moved their heavy stone bodies through the treacherous forest and mountain paths first. So if they were still in the ancient city, then that meant that someone in their party had betrayed them.

She shook her head, chiding herself for falling into the trap of trusting people again. There was no other explanation for them being prisoners. Only the people in her adventuring party had known the location of this city, so one of them must have come back for her and Bogg and imprisoned them. Probably so they couldn't leave and tell others about this city's location.

That made the most sense. She could see why someone might want to keep the location of this city quiet. That person would be able to come and go as they pleased to find out what secrets and treasures this city held. She knew that people were selfish by nature, but after a couple months of traveling with the party, she'd let her guard down. Now she was learning the same painful lesson she should have already taken to heart.

So, who was the most likely in their party to set them up like this? It obviously wasn't Bogg - even if he hadn't been sitting in the cell next to her, she knew he wasn't smart enough to pull anything like this off. No, he'd only been in this for the adventure. Landren wasn't likely either. The emotionless monk didn't seem like the greedy type.

That left either Frederick or one of the novaborn twins - Falrose or their leader Kyros. Frederick was one of Bogg's friends. He wasn't nearly as dumb, but she also didn't think he'd do something like this to his friend. Though she'd been wrong about that before. Nevertheless, she thought Falrose or Kyros was the most likely culprit - possibly both. Falrose was cocky about his magical ability, rightfully so from what she'd seen him do. Would he be willing to go to these lengths to keep the secret of the city to himself? It was definitely possible.

Kyros was their charismatic leader, quite different from his twin brother, Falrose. He had a silver tongue, but she hadn't seen any displays from him that hinted he was as gifted with magic as his brother. She had seen the way Kyros looked at Falrose from time to time, especially when he used powerful spells. It was jealousy.

Kyros had the look in his eye of someone who wasn't satisfied with the amount of power they had. She could see Kyros being behind this betrayal in the pursuit of more power. Not to mention he'd been the one who chartered this mission in the first place. She'd never thought to ask where he'd gotten his intel about the location of the city.

Stupid, Val! She thought to herself. *Stupid stupid stupid!*

She'd gotten rusty since her time in the Arcane Knights. And now she found herself trapped in a city nobody knew about with one of the most annoying people she'd ever had the misfortune of meeting. She needed to get out of here.

She was still trying to work out exactly how she'd be able to accomplish that. She and Bogg were weaponless. She could do some minimal magic, but she couldn't think of any spells that would get them out of this predicament. And she didn't bother bringing Bogg into her planning. Bogg was too impulsive to trust with any plan, so she'd have to do this herself.

Even though he wouldn't be included in the planning, she would get Bogg out as well. Despite her well-founded trust issues, she wasn't the type to leave a comrade behind. So whatever she decided to do, she'd at least do Bogg the professional courtesy of breaking him out with her. Then they could go their separate ways.

"So what do you think?" Bogg said, trying to pick some rust off the manacles. "You think they wanna eat us or somethin? Maybe they're cannibals. I've heard of people like that. Seems kinda gross if you ask me."

"Nobody asked you, Bogg." Her eyes were still closed as she tried to work out a plan. "Seriously, shut up so I can figure out a way to get us out of here."

"Bet I can get us outta here before you can," he said. He just couldn't help but make everything a competition.

"Fine, if you can get us out of here before I can, I'll buy you a nice new bow," she said. There was no way he would be able to get them out before she did. "But If I get us out of here first, you stay quiet for one whole night so I can get some damn sleep for once!"

She finally opened her eyes and turned to look at him through the bars. He was smiling like an idiot.

"Deal"

* * *

Bogg's first attempt went as poorly as she imagined it would. He tried to lure one of the guards close by saying "Hey, come here real quick" to try to grab the key from his belt, like it would be that easy. He earned a nice beating from that one, though it likely didn't knock any sense into him. They'd also decided to go ahead and put those manacles hanging at the back of his cell to use to restrain him. That would be a new problem they'd have to deal with whenever she figured out how to get them out. At least they hadn't put her in manacles too.

"Ok, so I got another idea," Bogg said. "I'm going to steal a knife so that way when I tell them to come here real quick, I can gut em and then just walk out."

"And how exactly are you going to get the knife?" Val asked.

"Well, I'm..." Bogg stopped and began to consider the question.

That simple question should keep him quiet for a few minutes so she could think. Not that it would do her much good. She'd hit a dead end trying to think of a way out. She had never been very good at picking locks, and even if she were, she didn't have the necessary tools to give that a real try. Plus, without any weapons, it would be difficult for either of them to get far even if they did figure a way out of the cells. This was starting to look more and more hopeless.

No, she told herself, *this is exactly what you trained for back in the Arcane Knights. Think of it like a mission. Figure out what tools you have at your disposal and solve the puzzle before you.*

Shoot, if Bogg did have a way to get a knife, she'd be able to get them out in no time. Most of her magic was only good for fighting because she needed to draw blood from her target to activate her spells. But she *could* create some minor visual and auditory illusionary effects without needing to draw blood. Maybe she could use that to create a distraction and build off that. Finally, a plan started forming in her mind.

She'd have to wait for the perfect set of circumstances. She couldn't risk Bogg screwing something up while she was in the middle of executing her plan, so she needed to ensure he couldn't interfere. And there was only one guard who had what she needed, so she'd have to wait until he was on duty. But with some patience, she was sure she could get what she needed to break them both out.

A couple nights later, her target rounded the corner, patrolling with another guard she'd seen a few times before. Bogg was snoring in his manacles against the back wall of his cell, fresh off his latest beating. Val leaned into position with her back against the door to her own cell as the guards passed by. She turned her head and opened one of her eyes to watch as they came closer. Tonight would be the night.

She waited until the guards were walking by her cell, and then focused her mind on the torch across the hall. Quietly, she muttered under her breath and closed her open hand quickly into a fist. As she did so, the burning torch immediately went out and plunged the hallway into darkness.

The guards jumped away from the torch by instinct, maneuvering them a hair closer to her cell. It was all she needed. Before their eyes could adjust to the sudden darkness, she reached through the bars and swiped the item she needed. After tucking away her new trophy, she re-positioned herself.

"Ashes!" One of the guards cursed. "What happened to the light?" He reached into his pouch to get something to relight the torch on the wall. She saw the other guard check his belt to make sure the keys were still there. Satisfied they were, he tucked them away again.

"Well hey, now that it's out, can you just leave it like that the rest of the night?" Bogg asked, having woken up by the disturbance. "It's tough to get decent sleep with that stupid thing flickerin' all night."

"Shut up, Bogg, you were sleeping just fine when it was lit a few minutes ago," Val said, rubbing her eyes. "Besides, the less you sleep, the less I have to deal with your annoying snoring."

Once the torch was lit again, one of the guards turned to Bogg.

"If I were you, I wouldn't be wastin' my time sleepin' anyhow," he said. "The boss will be here in a few days to deal with you two personally."

"Yeah," the second guard said. "None of the other prisoners ever came out alive after meetin' with him. Scariest florian I ever met."

"Wait, did you say florian?" Val asked. There hadn't been any florians in their adventuring party. "Who's your boss?"

"Oh, you'll see soon enough, sweetheart. Sweet dreams," he said, chuckling to himself as he walked away.

* * *

Now that Val had a knife, she could work on the next step of breaking out. If she'd been able to, she would have used that knife immediately after stealing it to get herself out. Unfortunately, it took Val a little time when she acquired a new weapon before she could use it for her blood magic.

The next time Bogg fell asleep, she got to work on preparing. She used the knife to give herself a small cut and smeared some of her blood on the blade. She then meditated and concentrated on the knife. After some time, the blood marking sunk into the surface of the blade and disappeared.

There we go. Val thought. *This blade is mine now.*

Val started to get an uneasy feeling about this unknown florian. She didn't know who it was, but she knew they had to escape before he arrived. They said he'd be there in a few days, which was a little vague, but gave her 24-48 hours to figure out the rest of her escape plan.

She didn't know the layout of the prison, but she was sure the floor they were on had to be a large circle. The guards always came from her left and disappeared to her right and never backtracked. That meant they could get back to their starting point by walking in the same direction the whole time. When she broke out, she'd go to the right to avoid running into any guards. With luck, she and Bogg could escape before any other patrols noticed they were gone.

She knew they were underground, but figured they couldn't be more than a couple levels down. It would have been pretty difficult to move the two of them very far while they were still statues. Then they just needed to escape from the city after they got to ground level.

The city was a mere shadow of its former glory, with ivy-clad ruins and streets silent but for the whisper of the wind. But its dangers were not just of the architectural kind. Monsters prowled in the shadows of once-grand buildings. Their lairs hid among the forgotten splendors of a lost civilization. Getting out of the city would be dangerous even after they escaped the prison. She hoped they could at least get some weapons on their way out.

She was still puzzled about who the florian was and how he fit into the picture. Even if he wasn't one of their original party, he had to be working with one of them. There was no other way someone could have found the city and moved in a whole group of people so quickly.

Tomorrow night, she thought. Tomorrow night is when we're going to escape.

It had already been a full day since the guards had tipped her off about the upcoming meeting, and she couldn't wait any longer to make her attempt. She still decided not to tell Bogg about her plan. He'd probably find some way to mess everything up. She'd wait until the guards walked by and figure out a way to draw them close. Now that she had a knife, her magic was back in play, but she'd have to surprise and incapacitate them quickly to make sure they couldn't signal for help. Good thing she had spent the better part of her life training for exactly this kind of situation.

She checked again that her knife was tucked into her waist and settled down into her normal position up against the bars of her cell. As always, the guards came from left to right. She turned her head as she normally did and…

Something's different. She thought. Adrenaline pulsed through her body, sharpening her senses to a razor's edge.

The two guards were escorting a cloaked figure she hadn't seen before. The hood was up, so she couldn't see their face, but she couldn't help but feel there was something familiar about how they carried themselves. They looked casual but somehow also poised and ready to strike, always on guard. They stepped up to her cell and paused.

"Well, well, well," a familiar deep voice said. Her blood ran cold. Of all the people, she never thought she'd hear his voice in this place. "What a pleasant surprise, you're alive after all!"

She rose and spun. Before she could think, her hand had thrown the hidden dagger at her waist directly at the chest of the man she most despised in the world. As if he expected it, and he probably had, his right hand reached up and snatched the dagger out of the air. He was careful not to let it draw any blood to activate the magic she had poured into it. The two guards jumped back.

"How did she get that?!" One of them said, at the same time Bogg yelled, "Slag and ashes!"

"Your skills haven't dulled a bit, my dear" The cloaked man said jovially. He reached up and lowered his hood to reveal the face of the florian that haunted her nightmares.

He stood tall and menacing, his presence as commanding as ever. The smile across the green skin of his face was interrupted by a gruesome burn that continued up the side of his head and into the curled, blackened leaves of his hair that had never recovered. His eyes, cold and calculating, surveyed Val with a mix of amusement and disdain.

"But never forget, V, I taught you everything you know," he said, tossing the knife aside.

This was the man the guards had warned her about, but even they probably didn't know just how dangerous he really was. The florian standing before her was the former captain of the Arcane Knights. He had been her teacher and mentor.

He was also the man responsible for taking away everything she had ever loved.

"Zandro Nerivyre." She practically growled his name. "What are you doing here?"

"Oh, that's none of your concern," he replied with a smile. "Now, I do wish I could stay and chat, but I have an errand to run taking me away from the city for the moment. But don't worry, I'll be back so we can truly catch up."

With that, he turned and left her to her thoughts. She couldn't believe he was really here, after all her searching. They needed to escape, and soon.

She had a florian to kill.

4

Brand

The icy mountain wind stung Brand's face as he picked his way down the sheer cliff face. Loose rocks skittered under his feet and fell into the misty abyss below without a sound. He pressed his body against the rock wall to brace against the relentless gusts which occasionally hammered him. Years had passed since he'd been outside the comfort of the mountain's solitude. It was only his warden's urgent summons that compelled him to leave for the first time since he was a boy.

He'd reached the bottom of the cliff, so with no more room to descend, he took a look around. On the other side of a fifty-foot gap of open air was a ledge that would let him take the rest of the trip on foot. Focusing inward, he pushed away all thought and emotion to open up a clear path to access the Chi at his core. With emotions out of the way, he opened the gate to his Chi and felt his body awaken with energy.

With a shove, he heaved himself away from the rocks into the open air. As he flew, he twisted his body and landed safely on the other side of the large crevice. Brand closed the inner gate and let his Chi rest back at his center. He relaxed the minimal effort of restraining his emotions, and the Path closed back up. The rest of the trip would be a simple walk.

He only had the worn, dusty cloak on his back and simple brown trousers to keep him warm, but it was enough for him. Monastery life taught simplicity. Worldly possessions would only burden him in the mountains, where he had roamed for some time. Being back among normal people would be strange, but also a little exciting if he were being honest with himself.

The letter from his warden contained scant details, only insisting Brand meet him immediately. Pathwarden Landren must have discovered something extraordinary to call Brand out of solitude. He hadn't even notified any of the sages of the Open Path, the leaders among their monastery. It was a curious decision, but Brand trusted Landren's wisdom in the matter. If anything, it made him more eager to meet his warden again.

Rock turned to grass, and grass to road as Brand approached the first signs of humanity he'd seen since he was a boy, fending for himself on the streets. Pathwarden Landren had saved him from that life and given him purpose and direction, so if Landren called, Brand would answer. He owed his warden his life.

The bustling sounds of the town punctured Brand's idle musings on his past. The scraping of wagon wheels and merchants' bright shouts greeted him as he walked deeper into the crowded streets. It was time to find a place for the night. He had another early morning of travel ahead of him.

* * *

When Brand stepped through the weathered door frame of The Saucy Siren, he stopped short as a wall of sound crashed over him. Raucous laughter, bawdy singing, and the constant clink of glasses colliding in a toast assaulted his senses. The inn's fiery glow enveloped him along with the tart smells of ale and roasted meats. He adjusted his cloak, acutely aware of how his dust-laden boots and plain tunic marked him an outsider among the sea of patrons.

As he pushed through the crowd, he saw farmers regaling stories over dice. Armored mercenaries laughed into their cups, and traders gambled their day's earnings away. The patrons were diverse, but then again he'd expected nothing less from a town that served as a crossroads of several trade routes. Brand didn't have much to compare it to, but he did know that Spine's Crossing was larger than the average town. Still, it paled in comparison to his final destination.

At the center, atop a crude wooden stage, a dwarf woman danced - her provocative moves eliciting catcalls from the crowd. She seemed to revel in the attention, winking at onlookers as she drained another flagon of ale. Her revealing leather bodice left little to the imagination, and Brand felt his cheeks flush as he swiftly averted his gaze. While he was still getting his bearings, something slammed into Brand from behind. He felt a wave of warm liquid splash down his neck and back, soaking his ragged clothes.

"Hey, watch where you're going, slaghead! You made me spill my drink!" A large drunk man said as he waved his now-empty tankard around in the air. He turned to the nearest barmaid walking by. "Another for me, and put it on slaghead's tab over here - he spilled my drink."

"Sorry," Brand said quietly. His training at the monastery kicked in and he pushed down a sudden spike of anger. He spotted someone he hoped was the innkeeper behind the bar and turned to head that way. Before he took a step, a large hand landed on his shoulder and spun him back around.

"Hey! You hear what I said, slaghead? This dr-"

By instinct, Brand reached up to the hand on his shoulder. He used the momentum from the man's pull to turn him around and give him a gentle push in the opposite direction, causing him to stumble. Brand felt uncomfortable as he started feeling people's eyes focus on him. Again, he reached for his training to help him push down the emotions threatening to bubble up.

"Listen, I'm happy to pay for your drink. I don't want any trouble," Brand said, pulling some money out of his pouch to hand to the barmaid. Before he could gather any coins, the drunkard turned back to Brand.

"You're gonna pay for that!" he said, taking a couple steps forward. As the drunkard lunged forward, a short man stepped between them, holding up his hands. His long, pointed ears peeked out from a tangle of long brown leaves that made up his hair. Brand noted the man's emerald-green skin and realized he must be a florian. The plant-like people rarely needed to travel as far as the Silverspine mountains, so Brand had never met one in person before. An easy smile belied the daggers hanging casually from his belt.

"Calm down, Frederick, you're just drunk. Maybe it's time to call it a night, eh?" the florian said.

"But he spilled my drink!"

"You ran into him and spilled your own drink, you stupid ragweed!"

"Oh, right," Frederick said, grabbing another drink from a passing barmaid and taking a long swig. He turned back to Brand. "No hard feelings, eh slaghead?"

"Uh, no I guess not," Brand said, watching the man turn around and stumble towards another barmaid.

"Don't drink too much Frederick, we have an early morning tomorrow!" the florian called out to him, shaking his head.

"Sorry about that, my friend. Frederick didn't mean anything, he just gets a little rowdy sometimes when he's been drinking too much. Thanks for taking it easy on him back there," the florian said, holding out a hand towards Brand. "My name's Astoro. What's your name?"

"Brand," he said, shaking Astoro's hand. "Thanks, I'm a bit new here. This place is very different than what I'm used to."

"Yeah, I can imagine," Astoro said, looking him up and down and noticing Brand's worn clothes. "But don't worry about it! Here, let me pay for your room tonight for the trouble my drunken associate caused."

"Oh, no that's ok I-"

"Nonsense! It's the least I could do after Frederick spilled ale all over your clothes," he said. Before Brand could respond further, Astoro took his arm and wove them through the crowd to the relative quiet of the bar.

"One room for the night, and a drink for my new friend here," Astoro said, placing some coins on the bar and sliding them across.

"Oh, actually, I don't drink," Brand said. His warden had always warned him against substances that would make it more difficult to keep emotions in check.

An amused twinkle danced in Astoro's eyes. "Well, that's the first bloomin' time I've heard that!" he said with a laugh, turning to the innkeeper. "Alright, just the room then."

He turned back to Brand, key in hand. "Enjoy the room, my new friend." Astoro handed Brand the key from the innkeeper and turned to go. "Wish I could stay and chat, but I really do have an early morning tomorrow."

"Me too, actually. Thank you very much Astoro, it was nice to make your acquaintance."

With that, Brand retired to his room and settled in for the night.

* * *

98…99…100

Brand picked himself up off the floor after completing his morning pushups. He may be in an unfamiliar place, but working up a light sweat helped put his mind at ease. It was important to keep up his routine, especially in unfamiliar territory. He still had plenty of traveling to do, so he put on a clean pair of clothes and went downstairs to get an early start.

Descending the creaky wooden stairs, Brand picked up the muted sounds of a tense conversation drifting up from the empty common room. Astoro's irritated tone cut through the quiet morning air, punctuated by the innkeeper's timid protests.

"What do you mean he bloomin' left?" Astoro snapped, his fist cracking against the splintered wood of the bartop. His half-drained ale sloshed over the rim of his glass, foaming across the scratched surface.

The barkeeper wrung his hands on a grimy rag, ignoring Astoro's accusatory glare. "I already told ya, he left in the middle of the night," the barkeeper repeated. His thin hair clung to his scalp with sweat from working in the kitchen, and his apron sported several fresh grease stains.

"Well isn't that just a bloomin' storm on a sunny day," Astoro said, sulking away from the bar. "How am I going to find someone to replace him on such short notice..."

Brand approached the bar to turn in his key and could see that Astoro was already pacing on the far side of the room.

"Excuse me," Brand said to the barkeeper. "What's wrong with Astoro?"

"Oh, that ruffian he was traveling with, Frederick, just up and left last night," the innkeeper said, cleaning some glasses behind the bar. "Guess Astoro needed him for something, though I don't know what Frederick was good for besides being a goon."

Brand stole a glance at Astoro, taking in the florian's disheveled appearance. He noticed Astoro's nervous movements and the dark hollows under his eyes. There was an air of anxiety over his companion's unexpected disappearance. Astoro raked a hand through his leafy hair, muttering curses under his breath as he downed the rest of his ale. Though they were no more than strangers, Astoro had shown Brand genuine kindness. Brand had a mission of his own, but he decided he wouldn't leave this new friend of his in need.

"Hey Astoro, I hear you're in need of a little help," Brand said as he approached the frustrated florian. "I'm not sure exactly what you need, but I'd be happy to help if I can."

"Oh, hi Brand," Astoro said. "Yeah, I'm stuck in a field of weeds right now, but I can't ask you to help. It's too dangerous, and I need someone like Frederick who's good in a fight."

"Oh, fighting won't be a problem," Brand said with a slight smile, a glint shining in his eyes. He pushed down the excitement he felt at the prospect of a fight. Positive emotions could be just as bad as negative ones when it came to following the Open Path. "I have some time before I need to be on my way. Why don't you tell me a little more about this fight."

* * *

Astoro filled Brand in on the way. Astoro had been traveling with his best friend, Ronan, and a small adventuring group. Their mission was to investigate a string of kidnappings that had taken place over a few months in a nearby town and try to stop those responsible. The investigation led them to a fortress deep in the nearby woods occupied by a novaborn cult.

The novaborn were said to be a cursed race, created by a god banished long ago to confinement within an Amethyst Star known as the Violet Prison. Most of the novaborn lived normal lives, but this group of fanatics dedicated themselves to freeing their deity. Rumors were spreading that the Cult of the Fallen Star was planning on summoning powerful monsters known as Starspawn. Their goal was to build a sacrifice large enough to break their god out of the Violet Prison and bring him back to their world.

Unfortunately, Astoro's party hadn't realized what they were dealing with before it was too late. They found themselves surrounded by the cult with a massive Starspawn at their command. Three of Astoro's party had fallen in battle before they were able to kill the Starspawn and several members of the cult. Ronan had been one of the casualties. Astoro and his allies finished off several of the cultists as they gathered the bodies of their friends before they needed to retreat. Unfortunately, Ronan's necklace - an item Astoro knew to be of great personal value to Ronan - had been left behind in the chaos. Astoro vowed to retrieve it and deliver it to his best friend's home and final resting place.

Astoro led Brand to a hideout deep in the shadowy woods - terrain that would play to Astoro's strengths as a florian with his affinity for nature magic. He knew that several cultists still lurked within those wooden walls. He needed another ally at his side to take down the fanatical remnants of this dangerous group and recover the necklace. Brand could see that Astoro was nervous about bringing him along, but there was no other option. According to Astoro, the cultists were going to be abandoning their hideout soon. Astoro couldn't afford to wait any longer to put his plan into action.

As dusk bled across the sky, they approached the cult's camp, moving silently through a stand of dense pines. Astoro led the way, his footsteps ghosting over the forest floor, avoiding any stray twig or leaf that might betray their presence. They wanted to observe the camp's layout before the darkness of night concealed the details from view.

The Cult of the Fallen Star occupied this remote patch of woods for months. They'd hacked down trees to create a clearing where they could erect their timber fortifications. The stumps still dotted the periphery, like amputated limbs strewn about a bloody battleground. They'd used many of those trees to form a simple wooden palisade around the perimeter of their camp. Astoro noted that the main gated entrance had been repaired since his last visit. Two guards stood in small towers at either side of the gate. After spending a few minutes watching, they saw two more guards patrolling the top of the wall.

Inside the wooden palisade, a large two-story lodge loomed over the smaller structures around it. This grand building clearly served as the central hub for the star-worshiping cultists. Flickering torchlight spilled from its narrow windows, casting an eerie glow on the packed earth below. All around the perimeter of the main building, small ramshackle huts clustered like toadstools. Astoro mentioned these crude shelters normally housed the lowest-ranked cultists. Those that were unworthy of a room in the grand lodge at the heart of the camp. They stood empty now that their numbers had dwindled.

To one side of the camp, a large clearing marred the lush forest ground. Dark blood had soaked into the dirt, leaving a blackened scar of earth. Etched around its edges, a sinister summoning sigil marked the spot where countless innocents had lost their lives. They were sacrificial lambs slaughtered by the cult to achieve their dark purpose. The air felt heavier here, weighed down by the echoes of suffering and screams.

"There are significantly fewer of them remaining after our battle," Astoro said. "I intercepted a communication from their leader that said they had plans to vacate this location tomorrow morning at first light. They've been packing up their camp over the past few days."

"So then we need to do this tonight." Brand kept his voice low. "What's your plan of attack?"

"Well, the original plan was to take out both patrols at the same time and then scale the walls. But I don't see how that's possible now."

"Why not?"

"Well, for starters, you don't even have a weapon! How are you going to take out a guard twenty feet up on the wall without a bow, or at least some throwing knives or something?" Astoro said, eyes flickering uneasily to the hulking silhouette of the guard pacing the wooden ramparts. "We'll have to think of another way."

"No, your original plan sounds good," Brand said. "Trust me, I can handle the guy up on the wall. You just take care of the other guard."

* * *

It took a little more convincing, but Astoro finally agreed. They took their places on opposite sides of the wall and waited until the patrols reached their designated spots. Brand took a couple steps back and quieted his mind, pushing his emotions aside to open up the Path. He could feel the Chi coursing through his body and enhancing the strength of his muscles. He dashed forward silently. About five feet before he hit the wall, he pushed off the ground, took two huge steps up the side of the wall, and pulled himself up the rest of the way. He didn't make a noise as he landed behind the guard.

Brand kicked the back of the guard's legs to bring him to his knees, and snapped his neck before he could make a sound. He glanced across the camp to see Astoro cleaning off a bloody dagger over a motionless body. Astoro looked up at him and surprise flicked across his face for a moment as he saw Brand had already taken out his target. Then he gave Brand a quick nod and smirk of approval before he started lowering himself down the inner side of the wall into the camp.

Brand descended the wall and clung to the shadows behind the main building. A flicker of movement made him flinch before he recognized Astoro's small form slipping out from the darkness. They exchanged terse nods as they gathered at the door.

"Thorns!" Astoro cursed under his breath. "This door is a lot more reinforced than I thought. Do you know how to pick locks?"

"No." Brand shook his head. "What's the problem, weren't you going to use your magic to get us in?"

"Well yes, but I thought we'd be dealing with a wooden door. My magic doesn't allow me to manipulate metal in the same way as wood."

Brand stopped to consider. The original plan had called for covertness. They were hoping to be in and out of this place quickly and quietly, only fighting when necessary. There was another way they could play this, and Brand was confident he had the skills for it, but it would still be dangerous.

"How important is this necklace to you?" Brand asked Astoro.

Astoro met Brand's eyes. "Extremely. These people murdered my best friend. This necklace was precious to him, and I can't let them have something that meant so much to him. That and…" Astoro's eyes darkened a little. "I'm going to make them pay."

Brand nodded, seeing the determination and pain in Astoro's eyes. "I understand. Stand back and get ready, this is going to be a little louder than the original plan."

Shutting his eyes, Brand emptied his mind and let his training take over. He once again pushed aside emotion to open the Path for his Chi. For some reason, he found it more difficult than normal. Living in solitude meant he rarely had to deal with emotions. Here among civilization, it took a little more effort to bottle things up and make a way for the Path.

Now that the Path was open, he turned his focus further inward, feeling for the reservoir of Chi coiled tight in his core. With a gentle exhale, he released the gates. The energy surged through him, setting his nerves alight and honing his senses to razor sharpness. He could feel each gentle tickle of the wind. He smelled the dirt and aging blood from the sacrificial circle. He heard the whispers of the night around them. As he opened his eyes, Brand's eyes glowed with flecks of orange.

Brand centered his mind, calling upon the countless hours spent practicing under his master's discerning eye. Moving through memories, his body responded automatically. He slid his right foot back, heel planting firmly into the hard-packed dirt. Pivoting, he angled it just so, rooting himself solidly to the earth. His left foot edged forward, poised and ready.

Hands rising, he inhaled the night air, tasting hints of dirt and iron. His left palm hovered before him, fingers loosely curled, prepared to divert anything that might come. He drew his right hand back to his waist, knuckles white from the tight clench of his fist.

Though it was the very first stance his warden had engraved into his bones, it was no less powerful. His whole being was anchored in this pose - body, mind, and spirit aligned and grounded. With another deep breath, Brand began to shut off the flow of Chi to parts of his body. He envisioned a series of gates at each of his joints, slowly closing to lock the energy within his core, leaving only the gates to his right arm open. Chi rushed eagerly down through his shoulder and elbow, converging with tremendous power into his clenched fist. Wisps of orange mist began to rise from Brand's right arm as his body struggled to maintain so much Chi in one spot. He turned his head to Astoro.

"Astoro?" Brand's voice came out monotonous and free from any emotion or inflection. "Are you ready?"

Astoro took a small step back, eyes widening at the display of raw power. Goosebumps rippled across his skin from the energy pulsing through the air. He steadied himself and lifted his hands, emerald light swirling around his fingers. He brought his right hand to his chest and his eyes flashed green with magic. Brand watched as hardened bark grew across Astoro's body, covering him with protective wooden armor. Astoro crouched, glowing hands up and at his sides.

"Ready."

With a thunderous crack, the heavy door shattered free of its iron hinges at Brand's Chi-enhanced punch. It tumbled down the shadowy hallway, crashing into a cultist partway down the hall. Another person further down the hall stood frozen, eyes wide with shock. A second later he found his voice and shouted "Intruders!" His cry echoed down the wooden corridors like an alarm and his hand reached for the sword at his waist.

Brand raced down the hall, his boots pounding urgently on the clay ground. Though the man's panicked shouts echoed ahead, Brand's reflexes were faster. In a flash, he was upon the cultist, grabbing his arm before his fingers could close around the hilt of his sword. Three quick strikes were enough to down him, but he had no time to stop before more people came pouring into the hallway.

A wave of fear tried to spill onto the Path, but Brand held his emotions at bay to allow his body constant access to the store of energy at his core. He let his Chi flow freely, directing his body like a deadly puppeteer. He didn't have time to count the number of people who filled the small space, but it didn't matter - none would leave this place alive.

He began a dance of destruction and his victims accompanied him with a chorus of pain and death. He progressed down the busy hallway, stepping over each new victim as he felled them one by one. Each of Brand's movements was as precise and lethal as a viper's strike. Every punch and kick found its mark with cruel efficiency. And as abruptly as the chaos began, it was over. No more targets stood between him and the oak door at the end of the hall.

"Brand?" A distant voice echoed in Brand's ears as if from the far end of a tunnel. "Can you hear me?" The words sounded muffled and unfamiliar to Brand's flickering consciousness.

Brand shut his eyes tightly and began to close the Chi gates in his body, one by one until his Chi rested back in his center. Finally, he willed his consciousness to take control again and opened his eyes. He identified the source of the voice as Astoro, who he now realized sounded concerned.

"Brand, can you hear me?" Astoro repeated, waving a hand in Brand's direction. "Are you alright?

"Yes. Sorry," Brand replied, shaking off his momentary confusion. He didn't realize he'd been concentrating so hard on keeping the Path open. "I'm alright, are you ok?"

"Well, yeah, I barely had to do anything!" Astoro said. "One last guy came out of that first room after you'd made most of the way down the hall, so I took care of him. But Brand, that was amazing!" He turned for a moment to count the bodies. "You took out 12 people in like 15 seconds!"

15 seconds? It felt like it had taken longer than that. Time was hard to gauge while he was concentrating, but he rarely had to struggle so hard to keep the Path open. Maybe things were different because he was no longer in solitude? He would ask Master Landren to help him figure that out later. For now, it was time to focus on the matter at hand.

"Well," Brand said, turning back to Astoro, "do any of these guys have the necklace you're looking for?"

"Oh, right!" Astoro began walking back down the hall, checking the faces and pockets. "I recognize a couple of these guys from our previous fight."

"What does it look like, maybe I can help find…" Before Brand could finish his sentence, he saw a flash of movement from one of the bodies on the floor. His honed instincts were all that saved him from taking the spinning knife directly in the chest. Instead, it lodged itself firmly into his shoulder.

Brand grunted in pain as the knife pulsed with sickly green energy once after piercing him and then faded. A man sprung to his feet and fled down the hall back towards the open entrance before they could make a move to stop him.

"Brand!" Astoro yelled, running towards him.

"I'm fine," Brand said, standing up. "I've had worse than this, it's not that…"

The stone floor swayed and tilted beneath his feet, and his vision narrowed to a dim tunnel. He fell back to the floor.

"…bad."

And then he spun into darkness.

5

Ronan

"There you go." Ronan handed a newly forged blade to a dwarf he was sure had never used a sword before. "Make sure you take good care of that blade, and it will take care of you."

"Thank you, Ronan!" the dwarf said. "This is amazing. I see you still have Niradim's blessing!"

"No. That one's all me." Ronan turned and walked back into his forge.

He was getting tired of people coming by and making subtle remarks about his faith like this. It wasn't a secret that he no longer wore the mark of Niradim around his waist. He had also made it abundantly clear that it wasn't because he lost it when he died.

The mark of Niradim, a red swallowtail flag edged in gold, was more than a mere symbol; it was a badge of faith. Most followers of Niradim wore it at their waist, but he had seen others attach it to one of their shoulders, hanging behind them like a small cape. For the first few days after he began forging again, people would come by and offer him new marks for him to wear. They'd even leave them on the counter when he wouldn't take them out of their hands.

After the third day, he took an old anvil that had a slot in the middle that fit an old sword of his and placed it outside the doors of his forge. He gently laid the whole stack of marks on top of some hay over the slot and went back inside. He returned a few minutes later holding a large sword he had just pulled from the flames, still glowing orange-hot.

A crowd had gathered, curious to see if he was finally announcing his return to Niradim's faith. They watched in stunned silence as he drove the glowing sword through the marks of Niradim, pinning them to the anvil and scorching the pile of cloth. Nobody brought any more marks after that, but they still made comments.

At least business had slowed a little after the stunt with the anvil. At first, he'd been inundated with people wanting to get something metal worked by the man Niradim brought back to life. Being alive again was great, but he was not a fan of all the attention it brought him. Hopefully, the novelty would wear off soon and he could live his life in relative peace.

The one thing he was still getting used to was life without his magic, even if he had only been a novice compared to other Disciples. Severing his ties with Niradim had left him back where he started before joining the faith. He was still an amazing blacksmith, but one who was unable to infuse magic into his creations. His old sword and shield were still propped up in the corner of his forge as a reminder of how great he used to be at creating magical items. Sure, it was hard work, but he had been the best at it, and nothing compared to the items he'd created in his Shaping Trial.

Despite leaving the faith, he couldn't get rid of them for some reason. He couldn't help feeling he still needed them in some way. If nothing else, they served as an important reminder of Niradim's abandonment. He wouldn't soon forget that Niradim had let him die.

There was a knock at his counter, and he tore his eyes away from the old relic to see what job awaited him next. Smiling up at him was a young dwarven woman, probably in her early 20s with dark brown hair twisted into two thick braids that fell past her shoulders.

She stood a little over 4 feet tall, pretty standard for most dwarves, and was bouncing with excitement, and maybe some nervousness. The white robes she was wearing marked her as an Acolyte of Niradim, someone who hadn't undergone the Shaping Trial to ascend to the rank of Disciple. She held a pouch of gold and a piece of parchment that looked like it had descriptions and measurements all over it.

"Oh hello Master Ronan, sorry to bother you! Niradim's bless..." She caught herself before saying the full phrase, realizing who she was talking to. At least she was trying to be polite. "Uh, I mean, good day to you!"

"Good day to you, and you can just call me Ronan," he replied. "How can I help you?"

"Well," she began, holding up the parchment in her hands. "I just got measured for my first set of armor, and I was hoping..."

Her first set of armor? She must be new as an Acolyte if she hadn't been fitted for armor yet.

"Sure, let me see the measurements," he said.

He took the parchment from her and gave it a look. He was surprised to see much more detail in the measurements than he usually got from his customers. There were unique designs and details on the different pieces that he'd never seen before. It even had annotations with thoughts about how different structural choices might allow for more mobility without losing protective strength. This was entirely different than anything he'd made before, and definitely not the standard armor for the Niradim Protectors. That being said, it was very impressive.

"Who made these?" Ronan said as he studied the unfamiliar design. "If one of the other masters came up with a new design, they should be the first to try it out."

It was important for the person who came up with a new design to be the one to work through the forging process. Only the original designer could confirm the piece functioned as they intended it. It wouldn't be right for him to take another person's design and be the first to try it out.

"I don't know why they'd send you to me," he continued as he held the parchment back out to her. "The only person fit to forge this armor is the person who designed it."

"About that," she said, blushing. "I was the one who designed the armor."

"No, sorry, this is a very nice drawing, but I mean the person who actually designed the structure of it, which master helped you with this?" He looked down at the paper to see who signed the design notes. "Brin Dawnstar. Take it back to Master Brin and have him help you with it."

"*I'm* Brin. It's short for Brillenia," she said as her bright eyes morphed into a glare. "Look, the Niradim Protectors use outdated armor without any desire to improve the functionality. This design will keep them safer so less of them die…"

She trailed off, realizing who she was talking to.

"Well, you've come to the wrong place then, have one of the other masters help you with this. I don't serve your god anymore in case you hadn't heard," Ronan said, nodding towards the scorched cloth on the anvil. "Besides, no armor will help if your god deserts you in the middle of a fight." She winced as he said it.

He hadn't spoken much about what happened to him, but enough people knew that his magic had failed in the battle. Most people didn't know what to make of it, Ronan included, but of course, there were plenty of opinions on the matter.

"Even if I wanted their help, they wouldn't agree to it," she said, under control of herself again. "They care more about the traditional uniform than their own protection, so I want to forge my design in my Shaping Trial. If I forge it as a part of my Trial, it'll have Niradim's blessing and they'll have to accept it."

Ronan was impressed by her determination, but he didn't want any part of Niradim or his followers. It wasn't his place anymore.

"Then have the masters teach you the traditional way, and forge this yourself when you've learned the proper techniques," he said.

"No," she said, bluntly. "I don't care who you serve or don't serve, I don't care about your past or your relationship with Niradim. That has nothing to do with your skill as a blacksmith." She paused and her voice quieted. "I just want them to be protected, even if I have to learn from someone outside the faith to do it."

She looked up at him again and met his eyes. "If I'm going to learn how to forge something like this, then I need to learn from the best, and that's you."

Ronan stopped and considered the request. She was the first person since his revival who had made a request of him without trying to coerce him in one way or another back into the faith. Sure, she was a follower of Niradim, and working her way toward the Shaping Trial, but she was treating him as a person instead of a prize to re-convert. He hadn't realized it, but it was actually refreshing.

He could also tell this was very personal to her. Most people who took on the Shaping Trial attempted to create some kind of amazing magical weapon or shield - he was no exception. When someone created something different, it usually had some deeper personal meaning to them. He didn't know what exactly made Brin want to improve the armor of the Protectors, but he suspected it was something specific.

"Fine. I'll teach you," Ronan said as Brin's face lit up with a huge smile. "But listen, I'm not going easy on you. Also, aside from teaching you what you'll need to know for the Shaping Trial, we're not going to be talking about your god while we're in my forge, got it?"

"Yes! Anything you say, Master Ronan!" She hopped with excitement.

"Besides," he said with his first real smile since his fiery resurrection.

"Training you to forge better armor than theirs will drive the other masters crazy."

He took off his apron and hung it on the wall next to a table and spread out her notes. "Now, grab something to write with, Brin. Some of your designs need a little tweaking."

* * *

"It's a common misconception, but female armor doesn't need to be fundamentally different from male armor," Ronan said. "Just give a little more room in some places to account for anatomy when taking measurements. If you've done your job correctly, it should be very difficult to tell a man from a woman on the battlefield."

Brin was fiercely taking notes while Ronan spoke. She was actually very gifted, and someone had already taught her a lot of the basics before she came to him. He found her a quick study in everything he showed her, just like he used to be when first learning from a master.

Ronan demonstrated a hammering technique for her to try. His arms moved in a rhythmic dance, each strike shaping the metal as if he were a sculptor crafting art. She absorbed everything he taught her, usually on the first attempt. Her instincts for forging techniques were great, especially when it came to armor.

Weapons, however, were a different story. For some reason, she had a bit of a block when it came to forging weapons. She made mistakes anytime she tried forging even the simplest of blades. That's something they'd have to work on at some point, but for now, she was absorbed in finalizing the details of her custom armor.

Ronan continued. "I like the ideas you have with the pauldrons, but you need to leave a little more room for the rotation of the arms. And the torso piece needs to be deconstructed into at least 2 separate pieces that move independently. Most of your power and movement comes from your core during a fight. You need to be able to bend, twist, roll, or any other movement you can think of without sacrificing protection."

"What if we double that to give maximum room for movement, but overlap them so there aren't any gaps?" Brin asked.

"It's possible, but we'll have to make sure it doesn't cause any pinching underneath…"

They carried on like this for hours, meticulously going over her design until it was drastically different from the standard armor of the Niradim Protectors. But if forged correctly, it would be an enormous upgrade.

"Now, about the magic…" Brin said, trying to carefully broach what she knew was a sore subject for Ronan.

"You'll have to get one of the other masters to show you those techniques. I can explain them, but I can't demonstrate them for you," Ronan said, and then added quietly, "Not anymore…"

"Ahem…" They both stopped and turned to look at the source of the noise from the front of the shop. Master Ginmar leaned against the door frame with his arms crossed, a twinkle of amusement in his eye.

"Oh, my goodness, Master Ginmar!" Brin said, giving a short bow. "Niradim's Blessings."

"Niradim's blessings, Acolyte Brillenia," Ginmar said. "Isn't it a bit late to be working? Don't you have studying to do before lessons tomorrow?"

Ronan looked past Ginmar to see it had indeed grown dark. The magical flames that illuminated the Earth Sector mimicked the sunlight outside the mountain. When the sun would set, the flames would dim as well. It was a lot later than they both had realized.

"Y-yes, Master Ginmar, you're absolutely right." She turned to Ronan and bowed. "Thank you, Master Ronan. Umm, we didn't discuss anything formally, but shall I come back tomorrow at the same time."

"Yes, that sounds fine," Ronan said with a nod. "Thanks, Brin."

Brin rushed to gather her things and made her way towards the door. Before she exited, she turned one last time and gave a small bow.

"Niradim's blessings, Master Ginmar. Niradi... I mean... Good night, Master Ronan." With that, she turned and hurried away.

After watching her go, Ginmar turned back to Ronan, eyebrows raised as if in question.

"Hello, Master Ginmar," Ronan said as he turned to arrange the notes on his table. It looked like Brin had forgotten a few things, so he moved them to the side. He'd give them back to her tomorrow. "What brings you to my forge this evening?"

"So..." Ginmar said, ignoring the question. "We've taken on an apprentice, have we? You know she's an Acolyte, yes? Does that mean..."

"No, Ginmar," Ronan said, cutting him off. "My feelings have not changed about your god."

"Ah, yes, my god," Ginmar said. "You know, until recently, he was your god too."

"Let's not get into this again, Ginmar," Ronan said, rubbing his head.

Ginmar sighed. "Fair enough. I actually came to talk to you about something else," he said, starting to look a little concerned. "There's been... a disturbing event in the Sky Sector."

Ronan looked up and crossed his arms. Whatever had happened worried Ginmar quite a bit. He seemed shaken.

"A few nights ago, someone murdered a couple of thugs in an

alleyway," Ginmar explained. "Now, normally this wouldn't have caused much of a stir, but the circumstances of the murder are very strange. It's hard to describe, you have to see it for yourself."

"Why can't the normal guard take care of it? I'm not a Disciple or Protector anymore, Ginmar. This has nothing to do with me, I'm just a blacksmith now."

"You have more experience than the rest of the guard," Ginmar said. "I fear this may be something beyond their capabilities."

"I'm sure they can handle…" Ronan started.

"Ronan, please," Ginmar interrupted, taking on a serious tone. "For me."

Ronan started to get anxious. Ginmar had raised Ronan since he was a young child, and he had never seen Ginmar like this. He may not believe in Niradim anymore, but he still felt the pull of wanting to protect his adopted people.

"Ok Ginmar, I'll come take a look. Lead the way."

* * *

Ginmar led Ronan to a part of Midral he had only visited a few times when he was on patrol as a part of the Protectors. Midral was a beautiful city, but it still had its darker parts. He was guiding Ronan towards a reflective black wall that was blocking an alleyway. A few guards stood watch outside it.

As they got closer, Ronan was surprised to discover that the reflective wall was actually ice. It was as black as obsidian and had a large hole chiseled through the center of it for passage. A chill pierced Ronan's cloak as he stepped up to the unnatural entrance. The air was a sharp, biting cold that seemed to seep into his bones, a stark contrast to the street's milder temperature.

As he stepped through, a horror story unfolded around him. Two dwarven corpses, frozen solid, hung from the spikes on either side of him as he crossed the threshold of the icy scene. Their faces contorted in eternal, silent screams. The narrow alleyway was cloaked in shadows, its cobblestones slick with frost. Distant echoes of the bustling city faded, swallowed by a heavy silence that clung to the icy walls.

"Careful now," Ginmar said to Ronan. "The ground in this alleyway is patchy with ice. We were able to carve out a safe space to walk through the center, but we had some guards take a rough tumble when we first breached the wall."

Ronan walked forward toward another humanoid shape at the end of the alley. Getting closer, he was increasingly confused by what he saw. A man hung suspended in the air by what at first glance looked to be cords of ice wrapped around his wrists and ankles. Like the others, he was frozen solid.

A dagger protruded from his stomach, which had also frozen to the corpse. But what unsettled Ronan the most was the man's face, which was twisted with a look of intense horror and pain. Ronan tore his gaze from the frozen visage and turned back to Ginmar.

"Wait, if this happened a few nights ago, why hasn't any of the ice melted yet?" he asked Ginmar. "And why is it black?"

"We don't know anything for certain except that the ice is clearly magical," Ginmar replied.

"Yes, but magical ice melts the exact same way as normal ice. The weather has been cold, but well above freezing," Ronan said, talking things out as he continued to study the scene. "This ice on the ground and corpses should be completely gone by now, and the wall should be much smaller. There's no water in this alley or anything else that would indicate the ice has even begun to melt."

"Ronan, come take a closer look at this one with me." Ginmar gestured to the body Ronan had just examined. "Do you notice anything inconsistent about the ice on this man compared to the ice in the rest of the alley?"

Ronan returned to the suspended body. At first, he wasn't able to determine that anything was different about it compared to what he'd already seen. He knelt down to get a closer look at the ice holding the man aloft.

"The cords. Everything here is frozen completely solid except these. They're hollow," Ronan said, and then added. "Whatever these cords were, they froze at the same time as the body. Then somehow, they disappeared, leaving space in the middle."

"Ronan, I know you don't like to think about your time serving Niradim," Ginmar said. "But there are stories about a certain Artifact created long ago by the dark god that had powers similar to what we're seeing here. Do you remember?"

"The Black Frost Ring. Yes, I remember," Ronan replied, turning to face Ginmar. "But I also remember that those stories went on to say the ring was destroyed along with the lost city, did they not?"

"What if those stories had it wrong?" Ginmar said.

Ronan scoffed, looking away. "Then it wouldn't be the first lie Niradim told."

"Ronan, don't make this about that," Ginmar pleaded.

"He betrayed me and left me to die, Ginmar," Ronan said.

"Ronan, I've seen many followers fall in battle," Ginmar said gently. "He didn't betray you. He doesn't promise to protect us from death."

"He took away my magic, Ginmar!" Ronan spun on Ginmar so quickly that Ginmar took a step back. "Right in the middle of a fight! I was channeling his magic and I felt him pull it away from me when I needed it most. That's how I died! If that's not a betrayal, then what is?"

"Ronan, I…" Ginmar started.

"I don't want to hear it, Ginmar," Ronan said, cutting him off. "Look, if this is what you think it is, then I'm useless against it anyway."

Ronan took one last look at the poor soul dangling before him. "Your god is going to have to find some other fool to clean up this mess."

Ronan walked back toward the entrance of the alley. Before turning the corner, he took one last look back at his old master. Ginmar was staring at the ground in defeat. Ronan knew that Ginmar wanted to recruit Ronan to help him get to the bottom of this mystery, but that wasn't his life anymore. He just wished everyone else would realize it too. Ronan shook his head and then continued home.

6

Kyros

The last rays of the sunset bled into a deep indigo sky, casting long shadows over the cobblestone streets. As the night started to settle in, Kyros donned a dark purple cloak that he could use to hide his face if needed. Not that his face looked like his own at the moment. He couldn't risk being identified, especially if he was going to continue doing some of the activities he'd been up to a few nights ago.

Perhaps I should have done a better job of cleaning up that mess. Kyros thought.

It was unlikely anything would be traced back to him, but he had started hearing rumors about a strange murder that occurred a few nights ago. The unusual circumstances and black ice had been a real talking point.

He'd have to be careful about using the ring too much - for a couple reasons. First, his left hand had gone completely numb after so much use in the alleyway, to the point he couldn't use it at all the following day. Apparently, there was at least some danger to the user of the ring as a tradeoff for the amount of power the user could wield. At least the tingling sensation had finally worn off.

Second, he had received intel from one of his lieutenants, Agent Crimson, who was able to do a little digging into the history of the ring. He learned that certain entities could sense the ring if it was used too much. Repeated use in the same location could draw them in like moths to a flame. If he could time it correctly, he could unleash chaos on the city to draw attention away from himself at just the right time. He needed to start sending Noct to monitor the surrounding area for signs of them.

For now, he really needed to get moving on his next step. He had some muscle he could exploit after speaking with the leader of the Blood Forge. It was easy enough to strike a mutually beneficial deal. In exchange for their help in his heist, he would thin out some rival gangs and consolidate their power to grow their ranks. They already secured some forged documents that were required to get past the guards to the Earth Sector. Unfortunately, the simple forgery wasn't enough. It needed the magic of one of the followers of Niradim to certify its authenticity.

Coercing someone into validating his credentials would be straightforward enough. Especially for someone with his particular talents. Tonight he'd stake out the Crucible Gate and wait for someone who looked like a good target to come out. He'd follow them until an opportunity presented itself and then use a magical charm to get them to do his bidding. Any weak-willed individual would do, but to avoid attention, he'd need to wait for someone to come out alone. He also knew he needed to be cautious about using magic too close to the Earth Sector. He wasn't sure how far from the gates they could sense magic, but he didn't want to take too big of a risk.

He made his way to a tavern a few blocks away from the Court of Fire and ordered a drink. After settling into a dark corner, he sent a mental command to Noct to circle above the Court and wait for a proper target. After a few moments, he felt a mental alert from Noct that someone had exited the Earth Sector. Kyros pulled his hood over his head and shifted into Noct's eyes.

Noct perched on a nearby rooftop looking at the center of the Court of Fire where a small dwarven woman was walking alone. It looked like she was heading in his direction. Perfect. He shifted back to his own senses and made his way out of the tavern.

It was time to hunt.

** * **

The night was cold and damp as Kyros made his way through the streets. The smell of oncoming winter mingled in the air with burning wood as the town's residents heated their homes. Kyros was again glad for the Ring's ability to combat extreme temperatures. Even though he could feel the cold in the air, it was somehow still comfortable for him. As the sun descended, the magical lamps began to burn and light up the darkening streets. Kyros moved like a shadow, carefully avoiding the pools of light from the magical lamps. His footsteps were a mere whisper against the cobblestones as he kept an ear out for the clinks of armor that signaled the presence of guard patrols.

The trouble with being out at night this close to the Court of Fire was that you couldn't hang around unless you had a good reason for doing so. The shops had closed for the day, so anyone loitering about would catch the attention of any patrolling guards. He had spent a few nights memorizing the routes the guards took - they were far too consistent for their own good. It was easy for him to figure out where the best place to intercept the girl's path would be.

He picked a good spot to set up his ambush and waited. A moment later, a young female dwarf with brown hair pulled back in twin braids appeared around a corner. His target had arrived.

Kyros waited in the shadows as she slowed and began rummaging through her pack. After rifling through loose parchment a few times, she stopped in the middle of the road and put a hand up to her head. Kyros watched with frustration as she turned around and hurried back the way she came.

At first, Kyros thought she might have noticed him, but that was impossible. From the way she had been digging into her satchel, Kyros figured she must have left something behind. Using magic this close to the Court was risky, but he didn't want to let this opportunity escape, it was too perfect. He'd have to take the risk.

Retreating into the inky darkness between two buildings, Kyros gripped his staff. Its surface was cool to the touch and pulsing with latent energy. His eyes narrowed in concentration, silent communion with Noct taking place in the realm of his mind.

Usually, he wouldn't be able to do much through Noct at this distance except see through his eyes, but the staff amplified his abilities. He shifted into Noct's eyes and saw the girl's braids lightly bouncing as she made her way back towards the Crucible Gate. She would be there in less than a minute. He had no time to lose.

To a casual observer, the sky offered only the mundane sight of an owl, its wings slicing through the starlit canvas in pursuit of its nightly prey. But beneath the mundane, a dance of predator and magic played out. Kyros had a first-person view as he directed Noct into a steep dive. Silent as the wind, he descended toward the unknowing girl.

Just as Noct was closing in - Kyros muttered some arcane words and a pulse of violet light flashed from the crystal on his head and through the staff. In unison, as Kyros released a spell, Noct's eyes flashed with the same violet light as Kyros channeled the spell through him. The light from Noct's eyes alerted his prey to the attack, but it was too late. She spun and raised her arm in a futile act of defense as she saw the bird.

Noct's talons sliced across her forearm, a flash of dark amethyst energy leaping from his claws to her skin. The girl's gasp was lost in the night, a brief cry of pain and surprise. When the girl opened her eyes, they faintly shone with an amethyst glow - proof the spell had taken effect. She slowly lowered her bleeding arm back to her side.

Kyros could see from Noct's eyes that she was standing motionless in the middle of the street, awaiting Kyros' command. Fortunately, there was nobody around who could have seen the flash of light from the attack. After circling for a moment just to be sure his magic hadn't been detected by any nearby guards, Kyros was satisfied the coast was clear.

A sinister smile unfurled across Kyros' lips as he anchored his consciousness back into his own body. The cold night air felt even more alive with the thrill of his success. That was close, but his improvised plan had worked perfectly. He took a moment to look down at the staff in his hands. Using it in this way hadn't depleted nearly the same amount of its power as when he had mist-jumped before entering the city. Good, he needed it at full power when he enacted his plan to steal the Flame. For now, it was time to get what he needed from the girl.

* * *

Fortunately, the girl had been pretty close to her home before she had turned around to go back to the Earth Sector. In less than 10 minutes they had made their way back to her place, which he had confirmed with her was vacant. And "vacant" was definitely the best word to describe the shack she called her home.

The one-room domicile was sparsely furnished. An ancient mattress, its fabric thin and frayed, lay on the ground in the far-left corner. A desk was sitting across from the mattress with a three-legged stool that looked like it was ready to crumble under the slightest weight.

On the left wall, there was a simple chimney area with a small iron pot, rusted with age, hanging over some charred wood. And to his right was a small, wooden chair with discarded clothes draped over it.

The floor was littered with discarded parchment adorned with sketches of armor he had never seen before. He kicked aside some of the parchment, watching as a swirl of dust rose into the dim light. His eyes scanned the unfamiliar designs sketched on them, but he couldn't make any sense of the drawings.

"Gods, how does anyone live like this?" He said, squirming and trying not to let his clothes touch anything. "I don't want to be here any longer than I have to."

He handed her the forged identity he had received from one of his new contacts.

"I need you to give me a detailed sketch of the Earth Sector, and then make this official with your god's magic so I can get past the guards," he ordered her. "Once you've done that, I'll do you a favor and burn this place down.

"Yes, of course," she obliged, sitting down at the desk and taking out some paper and a pencil.

"People will probably be surprised it didn't burn down sooner with all this kindling on the ground," he said, kicking away some more crumpled parchment. "Besides, I need this to look like an accident so nobody thinks it's another murder."

"This will take a few moments, the Earth Sector is very large," she said.

"I just need enough information to get around. Be sure to include any places guards regularly patrol. It doesn't need to be a work of art."

Kyros picked the dirty clothes off the lone chair with his fingertips and sat down to let her get to work. The rickety chair protested under his weight, its discomfort a sharp contrast to the opulence he was accustomed to.

This stupid thing better not fall apart while I'm sitting in it. He thought. *Time to check in with Noct.*

He closed his eyes and opened them in the air above the city. It was getting late and most of the city had settled down into a quiet and chilly night. He could see the familiar guards on patrol exactly as every other night he'd checked on them. Most in this part of the city were casually chatting, barely paying attention to anything around them. He decided to do a circle around the other side of town to see what had changed since his night of fun a few days ago.

The guard patrols near his first victims had definitely changed. There were more guards, and they were definitely still on high alert from his activities the other night. None were casually chatting, and most seemed quite on edge. He guided Noct toward the familiar alleyway and had him land on one of the nearby buildings. One of the guards looked up as he landed, but all he saw was an ordinary owl in the night and he went back to his duty.

They had almost finished clearing the area from all the ice. He supposed they needed Niradim's Disciples to clear the ice with their magic, as he knew the Black Frost didn't melt like normal ice. The ice sculptures he'd created from the bodies had been removed and the blood had been cleared away. It looked like they'd probably be able to finish cleaning the area up by the end of the next day. Perhaps the gossip would die down a bit shortly after the evidence was all cleared. It wasn't good to have guards on alert. He much preferred the aloof guards that patrolled the nicer part of town.

Satisfied with the recon, he returned to his own senses. The girl looked like she was finishing up the map she was drawing, so he stood over her shoulder to get a look at the layout of the Earth Sector. It was bigger on the inside than he thought, and he hadn't realized there was a residential sector on the inside as well. There was a complete, functional city on the other side of those gates. He almost began to worry that it would be too large an area to explore, but his fears abated as he watched her write the words "Soul Forge" over one of the buildings.

"This building here in the center," Kyros said, interrupting her. "What is its purpose?"

"This is the Soul Forge, where Niradim's Flame resides and provides the magic for the items that come out of the Earth Sector of Midral," she said, the reverence clear in her voice even through his spell. "Many of us worship Niradim at the Soul Forge. It is the place where Acolytes must undergo the Shaping Trial to earn the rank of Disciple."

Kyros rolled his eyes. All of that just to be in service to something for the rest of your life? At least *his* contract had an achievable end and he got to keep his magic when it was complete. Some people really needed to learn to work smarter, not harder - his brother's face came to mind and he shook his head to rid himself of the mental image.

"Well, I think this map is good enough." He snatched the map from the desk and folded it into his pocket. "Now, how about we prepare for the bonfire before you complete your final task."

Once she swept the loose parchment into the fireplace, he had her pour lantern oil over all the firewood she had lying around. He took a lantern and held it over her desk so she could cast her spell to authenticate his forged documentation.

She touched her left hand to a pendant that was pinned to the center of her chest and her right hand to the document Kyros had placed on the desk. She began to mutter some words that sounded like a prayer under her breath and the pendant began to glow with a faint white light from behind her fingers. Once she finished her prayer, a pulse of white light traveled from the pendant, through her body, and out of her hand onto the forged documents. A dwarven rune settled on the parchment, flashed once, and then faded as it sank in. Just as she finished, a knock at the door broke the silence of the night.

"Hello, Brin? It's Ronan," the voice at the door said. "Sorry, I know it's late, but I figured you'd still be up - you forgot your notes at the forge. Also, Master Ginmar said we should all go get a drink after a tough week of training for your Trial. His treat."

A second voice chimed in. "My treat? I said no such thing!"

"What…" Brin started, as she slowly reached toward her head. "Master Ronan…"

"Damn it, Kyros, you're better than this," he muttered to himself. He had let down his guard and the sudden noise had startled him and broken his concentration. The girl was beginning to come out of her trance and now Ronan and another master at the door had ruined any chance he had of making this look like an accident.

Why didn't Noct notify me there were people... Ashes! He cursed to himself.

He'd left Noct on the rooftops of the alleyway from the other night. He was getting overconfident and sloppy. He needed Ronan alive so he could disguise himself to get through the Crucible Gate. The other two were expendable. He sent a mental command to Noct to return to him quickly.

He quickly whispered an incantation under his breath and touched the crystal on his forehead. Crystalline fractals rippled out from his touch as a magical barrier formed around him, shimmering with an ethereal light. Confident with his defenses now in place, he drew his staff from his back and picked the lantern back up. Brin was starting to come to her senses, and just as she began to yell, he smashed the lantern over her head, knocking her out and setting her and the room ablaze.

"What was that? Brin, are you alright in there?" Ronan asked from the door. "Ginmar, I think I see fire, help me break down the door!"

Before they could come barging in, Kyros unleashed a large staff-enhanced energy blast at the door. It shattered at the blast and threw the two masters fifteen feet back into the darkness. Satisfied that Brin would burn with the house, he turned his full attention to Ronan and his friend.

"Ronan, are you alright?" The dwarf said, picking himself up from the ground.

"I'm ok, Ginmar." Ronan groaned as he stood "Ashes, Ginmar, I can see Brin in there!" He looked back to Kyros, who was calmly walking out through the shattered door frame. "Who are you, what have you done with Brin?"

Kyros smiled back at the crimson-haired human in front of him. "Oh, I wouldn't worry too much about her right now." The surrounding air around them began to chill, and he swung his left arm out in front of him. A dark lance of energy shot forward and slammed Ronan square in the chest, sending him flying once again.

"Ronan!" Screamed the dwarf, as he dashed forward to engage Kyros with his mace and shield. Ginmar's first swing hit Kyros right in the chest, and the arcane armor he'd prepared before flashed and cracked as it absorbed most of the blow. He dodged backward, regaining his balance, and fired another enhanced bolt of dark energy at the dwarf. Ginmar was able to get his shield up in time, but the force of the blow wrenched the shield from his grasp and flung it into the night.

The dwarf leapt unnaturally high in the air and his mace began to glow with divine energy as he brought it down to bear on Kyros. He swung his staff to meet the glowing mace's blow in the air. As he blocked the attack, the mace's energy surged down into the staff and then detonated back out at the dwarf. Ginmar went sprawling across the ground, unconscious. It was time to finish him off and be on his way.

Kyros formed a javelin of ice in the air above the prone form of Ginmar and drove it down towards Ginmar's chest to impale him. As it was about to find its mark, Ronan dove over Ginmar and blocked the attack with Ginmar's discarded shield, shattering the ice on impact. Kyros could see Ronan was struggling from the hits he had already taken, but Kyros had expected that last energy blast to do more damage. Strange. No matter, Ronan was clearly in dire straits.

The crystal on Kyros' forehead flashed a deep violet, almost black, and his eyes inked over as dark tendrils snaked out from him along the ground. Kyros saw confusion flash across Ronan's face as the dark pool broke into shadowy tendrils that seized him and Ginmar and hoisted them into the air. Ginmar's shield clattered back down to the ground as Ronan struggled against the bonds. Kyros felt an alert in his mind from Noct that signaled a warning. He was running out of time.

"I don't know how you're still conscious, but you should have played dead." Kyros raised his arm and formed a dagger of ice in his hand as he walked over to Ginmar who hung limply in the air by his arms. "Now you'll have to watch as I kill your friend."

"No, don't!" Ronan yelled as Kyros swung his arm for the killing blow.

Just before the dagger found its mark, Ginmar's shield shot straight up from the ground, hitting Kyros' arm and breaking through the arcane armor. The dagger of ice flew through the air, as Kyros screamed in pain, grabbing his arm where the shield had hit. The blow broke his concentration on the spell that was keeping Ronan and Ginmar aloft and they crashed to the ground below in a heap. The inky tendrils melted back into shadows.

Kyros saw Ronan looking past him to the building that was now fully ablaze. Turning to look, the dwarven girl - Brin - was standing in the fire. She brought her hands up, index and middle finger of each hand making an 'X' in front of her face. Kyros actually took a step back in fear as he regarded her fiery appearance. She was completely engulfed in flames, but also burned with a radiant holy energy as

Ginmar's shield came to hover in the air in front of her. The flames on her body began to die down as the energy around her intensified.

She stepped out of the flames, clothes still smoldering from the fire, and then she fell to her knees, exhausted. The shield stopped glowing and clattered to the ground for the third time in the fight.

He began to hear yelling from down the street and he cursed under his breath. He was really out of time now, not to mention injured from the fight. He was lucky his magic had blocked enough of the blow to his arm that it hadn't broken, but he would be sporting a nasty bruise in the morning. He looked up and directed Noct to find him a clear path, and then turned back to Ronan.

"Consider yourself extremely lucky," he said.

Kyros slammed the bottom of his staff into the ground, creating a shockwave that threw Ginmar and Ronan sprawling across the street. Cursing under his breath, he disappeared into the night.

7

Val'ran

"I still can't believe you got rid of your knife."

"Shut up, Bogg."

"That was pretty cool the way he caught it, though."

"I said, shut up."

Several days had passed since Val's misguided assassination attempt on Zandro. She should have kept her cool. She'd been trained better than that, ironically, by Zandro himself. Val's grip tightened around the bars, her knuckles whitening. A surge of anger spread through her veins like wildfire. She couldn't stand the thought of that man walking around free.

I'm going to hunt him down as soon as I get out of here. She thought. *He'll pay for what he did.*

So, the knife idea was out, but she had another thought brewing that she already hated. It had nothing to do with her former Captain and everything to do with relying on her annoying prison mate. Regardless, it wouldn't work if she couldn't use her magic, and she couldn't use her magic unless she had a weapon that could draw blood. She needed something sharp. All she had access to were a few tiny pebbles littering the ground of her cell, but they were too small to do

81

any damage.

"So, I think I got another plan," Bogg said, interrupting her thoughts.

"Is it the same as your last two plans?" she said. "Piss off the guards and take a beating? Because that might actually lift my spirits a little."

"No, this one's good!" Bogg protested.

"So you admit the others were bad," she fired back.

"No, I didn't say that! They were good too but… just let me tell you!" He continued. "I'm gonna tell 'em I'm feelin' all sick so they come in here and unlock my arms, and then I'm gonna surprise 'em!"

"You're going to tell them you're sick…" she started.

"Uh-huh," he replied.

"And then you're going to… surprise them," she finished.

"Exactly!" he said as if the plan were as rock solid as the prison they were in.

"And you don't think they'll see right through that?" she asked.

"Of course not! Cause I'll act all sick and stuff!" he said, puffing up his chest.

Good. Gods. That man was so dumb. Yeah, there's no way she could trust him with any part of the plan. She'd have to rethink things again.

The next time the guards passed by, it went down pretty much exactly how she expected it to. Now Bogg was sporting a new head injury to match the cuts and bruises from his previous beatings. At least it had been entertaining. She was starting to become a little impressed with how much of a beating Bogg could take.

"Well, I'm surprised that didn't work. It was an airtight plan," she taunted.

"Shut up, Val," Bogg said. His head hung defeated between his knees as he slumped against the stone wall.

"No, seriously, that was your best plan yet. Real ingenuity went into that. Very original," she went on.

"Hey, I don't see you on the other side of those bars either!" he yelled, looking up at her.

She sighed. He had a point. She had only given it one real attempt, and the only other plan she could think of had too many holes in it. Things were getting pretty desperate - it was time to try another strategy.

"Sorry, Bogg, you're right," she said. "Neither one of us is having any luck on our own. I think we need to work together if we're going to get out of here."

"Really?" Bog asked.

"Yes, really. I have one idea left, but I don't see a way it'll work without a weapon like a knife," Val explained. "You've seen me use magic before, right? Well, I need a weapon to be able to do it."

She took a moment to explain to Bogg how some of her magic worked. She needed to imbue an object with her magic, and then that object needed to penetrate her target enough to draw blood. Once the weapon touched blood, the magic would activate. It didn't take long for Bogg's eyes to glaze over - probably a little to do with the recent beating, but also because he was a moron.

"So, you just need blood?" Bogg finally asked.

"No, I don't *just need blood*, I need to be able to *draw* blood." She was beginning to feel a headache coming on, trying to explain this to him. "To put it another way, I need to make the person I'm attacking bleed."

"Well, I'm bleeding. Why can't you use my blood for your magic?"

"Again, I can't use just anybody's blood, that's not how it works. Sure, if you were the person I was attacking…" She trailed off as an interesting new plan began to form in her mind.

"You know what, Bogg?" She said with a smile. "I'm starting to think you may be more intelligent than you appear."

She had to explain her new plan to Bogg three times in detail before he understood, but he was on board.

* * *

This was it, their last shot at getting out, she hoped she could trust Bogg to hold up his end of the plan. She could hear the guards down the hall, but Bogg was getting restless. He needed to hold out a little longer.

"Val, I'm tired of this. I have to get out!" Bogg yelled, standing up and beginning to struggle against his bonds.

Bogg's muscles bulged as he thrashed against the shackles, his face contorted with a mix of desperation and rage. Val's eyes darted anxiously toward the approaching footsteps.

"Quiet, Bogg!" She yelled at him. "You're going to summon the guards!"

"I don't care!" Bogg yelled back, banging the chains holding him even louder. "I'm getting out of here right now!"

"You're going to ruin our chances of getting out of here!" She said, throwing one of the pebbles at him.

She could already hear the guards running this way to check on the noise. A moment before the guards turned the corner and came into view, a loud boom emanated from Bogg's cell, followed by silence. Val turned back to see Bogg's cell vacant, empty chains clanking against the wall. The guards halted as they realized they were missing their most annoying resident.

"What... Where did he go?" The first guard stammered. He pulled out his short sword and looked around the dimly lit passage.

"He was just here yelling, and all of a sudden, he was gone!" She replied, eyes wide in shock. "I don't know what happened!"

"Slag and ashes!" The guard cursed as he fumbled for the keys on his waist. He identified the correct key, and unlocked Bogg's door to inspect the cell. He ran to the far wall where Bogg had been seconds ago and picked up one of the manacles now dangling freely against the wall. There was no sign of Bogg aside from the spattered blood left behind.

"We've got to alert the boss that one of the prisoners escaped," the second guard said. "At least it wasn't the girl, but maybe someone can get word to him up in Midral."

They must be talking about Zandro. She wasn't sure what business he had in Midral, but she knew exactly where she'd be going next. It was time. As the second guard turned to hurry back down the hall, Val made a symbol with her hand. The fabric of reality seemed to warp as Bogg reappeared in his cell, unchained and with a wide, bloody smile.

Before either guard could process what was happening, Bogg grabbed the guard nearest to him in a chokehold. As he struggled, Bogg slammed the guard against the bars of Val's cell to hold him steady. The second guard yelled 'Hey!' and turned, running at Bogg and drawing his weapon. But Val was too fast.

She relieved the first guard of his dagger while Bogg pinned him to her cell, and flung it at the second guard. The dagger took him in the center of his throat. He grabbed at his neck and crumpled to the ground, gurgling sounds bubbling out of him. While he bled out, she swiped the keys from the guard Bogg was grappling. After a moment, Bogg found the grip he was seeking and twisted. The sickening snap of the guard's neck breaking under Bogg's iron grip echoed off the prison walls.

"That'll teach 'em to put me in jail!" Bogg said, while wiping some of his own blood off his face from his latest beating.

"No time for gloating, Bogg, take whatever weapons he's got on him, and let's go," Val said, opening her cell with the stolen keys. She made her way into Bogg's cell to loot the guard she'd killed.

"So does this count as me getting us out, or you getting us out?" Bogg asked her as he pocketed a knife from the fallen guard.

"What? Why?"

"Well, are you gonna buy me a nice new bow or not?"

Val rolled her eyes. "Come on, you idiot."

They were finally free.

***

Ok, well maybe not completely free. Val thought to herself as they finished cutting down a couple more guards. It was the third pair they'd come across, and pretty soon someone would start wondering where all the guards were disappearing off to.

Val knew they couldn't go on like this forever. Her breath came in ragged gasps, and her limbs felt weighed down by the weapons she carried. She could maybe use her magic one more time before she'd be too exhausted to continue. Bogg was in even worse shape after the repeated beatings he'd been taking.

After climbing one floor, they had come across a few rooms, but no exit. Val whipped open another door, scanning the dark scene before her. The room reeked of iron and fear, its walls smeared with dried blood. In the center, a lone chair with frayed ropes spoke of countless unspeakable horrors.

That's probably where she'd find herself dealing with Zandro if they didn't get out of here tonight. Or today. Come to think of it, Val had no way of knowing whether it was even day or night outside, they had been underground so long.

She shook off the thought and joined Bogg across the hall in another room. This was the last room before the next set of stairs leading up to where they'd hopefully find fresh air. They took a moment to catch their breath before proceeding. It looked to be a large storage room, filled with crates. Glancing around, she saw something familiar catch her eye.

"Bogg, watch the door in case any more guards show up," she said.

"I need to check something."

She hurried to the back of the room and felt a surge of joy at what she found. Stretching across the top of two crates were her and Bogg's weapons. Both of their bows, Bogg's longsword, and her Flame Scimitar which she had inherited from her father lay untouched. Val's fingers traced the familiar etchings along the blade, a wave of memories flooding back. She thought she'd never see it again.

Sitting next to the crates were their packs, along with all the contents they'd had before being petrified. It was about time they had a stroke of luck. After fastening everything in place, she grabbed Bogg's bow and carried it back to him.

"Here," she said, tossing the bow to him. "The new bow I promised you."

"Hey, this is my old bow, you promised me a brand new one!" Bogg protested.

"I said I'd get you a new bow if you could get us out before I could," said Val. "But if you recall, it was my plan that got us out."

"But you couldn't have done your plan without my help!" Bogg said. "You had to hit my blood with your little magic rock for me to disappear!"

"Which is why I'm giving you anything at all. I could have just left your old bow back there with the rest of your stuff," Val said with a smirk on her face.

"But I really wanted a new one! I've already used this one… Wait a second." She felt like she could literally see the lights go on in his head. "Did you say that all my stuff is back there?"

She raised an eyebrow at him. "See for yourself."

He hurried back to the crate she pointed out and ransacked it like a child who had just received some new toys from their parents. In no time at all, he had put his old stuff on and returned, latching the longsword onto his back in its familiar place. They were still exhausted from being imprisoned for so long without proper nourishment and exercise. Bogg's repeated beatings from trying to escape in increasingly stupid ways didn't help either.

But donning their old gear had given both of them a second wind and the confidence they needed to continue to move forward, so they snuck down the hall towards the stairs leading up to the next level. As they approached, they began to hear voices beyond the top of the staircase.

Val put her back against the wall at the base of the stairs and peeked around the corner. She couldn't see much, but the room above opened up to a much larger room. She was relieved to see a window high on the wall, looking out to a dark and starry night. They were finally near the top.

"Ok," she whispered to Bogg. "I can hear a few voices up there, so we'll have to take them by surprise. If there are too many, we may need to make a run for it. I saw a window to the outside, which means we just have to get past this last room and then we can try to lose these guys in the city. Are you ready?"

Bogg nodded. "Let's do it."

They crept up the stairs and paused before the crest to the room above. It was easier to pick out the voices in the room now that they were so close. She gave Bogg a hand signal to stop and wait for a moment. She wanted to see if there was any intel they could learn before escaping. She could tell he wasn't happy about it, but obeyed the signal and stayed put for the moment.

"...Agent Viridian is still on his way to Midral to meet with Agent Amethyst. He should be arriving in the next day or so."

"What's taking him so long? He should have made it to the city by now."

"He had to make a stop on the way to hand deliver the coordinates to our new base here. Some previous communications were intercepted and he didn't want word of this getting out."

"So, what, we're expecting even more people here?"

"Well that's the thing, we just got a message from Viridian saying they were attacked while he was there a couple days ago. He made it out, but I guess the rest of them weren't so lucky."

"Wonder if he poisoned 'em all because of that failed summoning a while back…"

Looks like Zandro is still using his code name, Agent Viridian. Val thought. *But then who is Agent Amethyst? Was it one of her old party members, or was he still working with Lord Syndalin?*

There wasn't much time to continue that train of thought, as the discussion turned to why it was taking so long for the patrol to get back. She turned to Bogg, who already had his longsword drawn and was waiting to be unleashed. She drew her scimitar and counted down with her hand 3…2…1… And then they burst into the room.

Despite their fatigue, they cut through the four people in the room with ease. Only one had a weapon on them, and he didn't even have time to draw it before Val had hit him with one of the daggers she had on her. They clearly hadn't been expecting to have to defend themselves in this room.

And why should they? We're in the middle of a long-lost city, and we just killed probably half of the people in the world who know its location while breaking out. Val thought to herself.

"Well, that wasn't so bad," Bogg said, as he wiped his longsword off on one of the dead guards' shirts before sheathing it onto his back.

These men hadn't been serving under Zandro for very long if they let their guard down that easily. If he were here, getting out would have been next to impossible.

"So, where to next? Back to that jungle town with the gladiator ring and the great ale?" Bogg said, completely oblivious to the world around him now that there were no enemies left to kill. "Oh boy, I could go for some good ale right now. Ashes, I could go for some *bad* ale right now, it's been so long."

"I'm going north to Midral," Val replied without looking up. "You can do what you want."

Val was scouring the room for any information she could find about the operation these guys were running, or what their ultimate goals were. So far, it seemed like some kind of cult. But at least there had been an updated map of the area with their location. With it, she could find her way to Midral using a new path marked out to the east of the city. It would be better than going back the way they came which would take them south first.

"Midral? That city of dwarves?" Bogg asked. "Why are you going there?"

"Do you remember that man that I threw a knife at a few days ago that you kept reminding me about?" Val said without looking up.

"Yeah, that plant-man? What are they called again, floorans?"

"Florians," Val corrected, still studying the documents strewn about. "Yes, that man. He's in Midral, or heading that way at least, and I have a score to settle with him."

"He's in charge of this group that put us in jail for no reason, yeah?" Bogg asked her.

"No," Val said, holding up a document she'd found signed with a familiar name. She knew it, they'd been betrayed. Her blood began to boil. "Kyros is. Kyros is Agent Amethyst."

Bogg growled. "That stuck-up novaborn is in charge?"

"Yes, and he played me like a fool!" Val crumbled up the paper and threw it across the room. She began to pace. "Zandro probably told him to hire me so he could get to me once we'd reached the city."

"Well, that's it then," Bogg said, crossing his arms.

"What?" Val said, finally stopping to look at him.

"Well, you're chasing after this Zandro guy, and I'm not going to let

Kyros get away with locking me up," Bogg said, stretching his arms. "So we go to Midral together and make them pay."

She hadn't planned on bringing Bogg any further along than necessary. His idiotic demeanor and competitive nature constantly got under her skin, and she'd be happy to be rid of his company as soon as possible. But even she had to admit that he was an amazing fighter and she could use someone like him to help her hunt down Zandro. Plus the road between here and Midral would be dangerous. She knew she couldn't trust anyone anymore, but she at least knew that they had a common enemy.

"Fine," Val said, her voice dark and cold. "But when it comes to Zandro, he's mine."

Bogg smiled.

"Deal."

8

Brand

"Brand. Hey, can you hear me?"

"Ugh, yeah, what happened?" Brand was beginning to come to, but the world was swirling around him as he looked up at Astoro. His shoulder was swathed in hastily-applied bandages and pulsed with a deep, relentless throb. He vaguely remembered a surprise attack from a man on the ground. A knife had hit him in the shoulder, but not very deep, and nowhere critical, yet he felt like he had been hit by a wagon.

"Poison," Astoro answered, his voice steady but eyes betraying a flicker of concern. "One that not a lot of people would have been able to cure. It may not feel like it, but you're very lucky I was here. I was able to remove the poison from your system"

Giving Brand one more glance and satisfied that the immediate danger of Brand's condition had passed, he sat back against the hallway wall. They still sat in the narrow hallway of the cultist fortress. Bodies were still littered about from the night's chaos, but the light pouring in through the cracks in the wood told Brand it was late morning.

"You removed it? Then why do I still feel like death?" Brand asked him.

He struggled to sit up as his strength began to return to him. His left arm, the one attached to his injured shoulder, felt partially numb, and he could tell he didn't have full range of movement at the moment.

"It's a nasty poison derived from a very specific plant only found deep in the forests of Floria. Honestly, most people don't even know it exists because of how rare it is, and even less know how to cure it," Astoro said. "It attacks a person's nervous system and spirit simultaneously. Even if it's removed and the target lives, it can take a while for the person to completely recover from it.

"What do you mean it attacks a person's spirit?" Brand asked.

"It takes away their ability to use magic," Astoro explained. "And it takes a while for a person to fully regain control of their magic if they survive the poison. So you might have the magical ability to cure the poison from someone else. But you wouldn't be able to cure yourself because your magical ability gets shut down while it's in your system."

"Wow, that's awful," Brand said. He couldn't believe his luck that Astoro was able to save him.

"Like I said, it's a particularly nasty poison. And I have no idea how someone in this cult had access to it. I didn't get a good look, but that guy must be a florian like me."

Brand slowly nodded. After a few moments of rest, Astoro helped Brand up to his feet. Brand was surprised to see that the sun was starting to come up, despite knowing they had made their attack in the middle of the night. He must have been out for several hours. That explained why Astoro looked pretty exhausted. Whatever he had done to remove the poison must have taken a lot out of him.

Brand took a few moments to eat some of the rations he always carried on him, and Astoro had given him some water to sip on to help regain his strength. Meanwhile, Astoro took the opportunity to look through the rooms at the end of the hall. He returned, looking at something shiny in his left hand.

He held a necklace, its gold chain glimmering dimly in the morning light. The pendant, a finely wrought sword impaled upon an anvil, shimmered with an almost mystical allure. He closed his eyes and took a deep breath as his fingers wrapped around the pendant. It looked like their mission had been a success.

After a moment, Astoro reverently wrapped the necklace up in some cloth and tucked it away into one of his pouches. He turned to Brand and nodded.

"Thank you Brand, I couldn't have found it without you, I really owe you," Astoro said.

"Oh, I think saving my life was payment enough, my friend." Brand smiled at him. "Well, what will you do now?"

Astoro thought for a moment. "I found some letters in the back room that indicated these guys were about to make their way to a new camp of operations. It's somewhere up in the Midral mountain range. Midral is where I was heading to next, to deliver this item to my friend's old master, and to visit his resting place." Astoro paused. "Maybe I can also alert someone in the city to this cult taking up residence somewhere up there. The Midral mountain range is pretty big, so it may not be close to the city of Midral itself, but they should at least know about it."

"Well then, I think we have our next destination," Brand said, standing up and taking a moment to brush the fresh dirt from his clothes. "When do we leave?"

"No way, Brand, I can't ask you to come with me," Astoro said, putting up his hands. "Don't you have to meet your warden some-where?"

"Funny enough, that will not be an issue." Brand chuckled. "My warden is waiting for me in Midral."

* * *

They had to return to the inn to gather their things and prepare for the journey. Once they had everything together, they left the following morning. The weather was clear, but Brand was still recovering from his injuries so they went at a slower pace than normal. After a day or two of travel, he was regaining some of the movement and feeling in his arm. Nevertheless, there was a weariness about him that continued to linger. He found it difficult to focus on his morning and nightly meditations.

Astoro had mentioned that it would take longer for his spirit to heal from the damage than it would take his body. He figured that must be what was wrong with him. There was no easy way to measure just how healthy a person's spirit was. Either way, Brand didn't have any magical ability, so the aftereffects of the poison shouldn't hinder him much once his body was back to 100%.

Traveling was good for his body and his mind. He began to wonder just what his warden had in store for him in Midral. It had been years since he'd seen him. Brand's final tests had been in his late teens and then he had dedicated himself to helping the remote monasteries in any way he could. He often wandered in the mountains, left to his own thoughts and trying to find enlightenment. The solitary had been good for him at first, but he began to miss the connection to the civilized world. The letter from his old warden had come unexpectedly, and he hoped the old man had something for him that he could use to figure out just where he belonged.

As twilight draped the sky in a tapestry of purples and golds, they settled down on a grassy knoll beside the cobblestone road. The distant murmur of a brook and the rustle of leaves in the gentle evening breeze created a tranquil atmosphere. At first, Brand worried that traveling with Astoro would be awkward for him. He and Astoro had only known each other a short time, and Brand didn't get a lot of practice with social interactions up in the mountains. Fortunately, the two of them got along very well, despite their obviously different upbringings.

Astoro grew up in Gladen, the capital grove of Floria. Most florians had some magical capability, but some truly excelled, and Astoro found himself a part of the latter group. Astoro told Brand that traveling with someone was the best way to get to know them. It was how he and his late friend, Ronan, had gotten to become such close friends. He enjoyed talking about their adventures on the road together and reminiscing about his old friend.

"Any time we stopped in a town for the night, Ronan would break off from the rest of the group and go work at the local forge," Astoro was saying. "I found out it was part of his religion. He'd go find a blacksmith, pray over their forge, and restore their tools back to new with the little magic he had. Then he'd work with them for a few hours." Astoro smiled. "And he'd teach them a thing or two - Ronan was the best of the best when it came to working the forge."

"He sounds like he was a very kind person," Brand replied. "Sorry, I was under the impression that Ronan was a human, but you said he was a follower of Niradim, the dwarven god? So he was a dwarf?"

"No, he was a human. Ronan told me he was the only human Niradim ever accepted into his faith," Astoro said. "Ronan was dedicated to the dwarves - they basically raised him."

"That's... amazing. What an honor," Brand said. "I'm sorry for your loss, Astoro. Men with that kind of faith and heart are rare in this world."

Astoro nodded as he settled into his sleeping bag. "Right you are, my friend. Right you are."

The next day, Brand woke before the sun. Astoro wasn't up yet, so he let the florian continue to rest and he walked a small way away from their camp. The darkness of the night slowly retreated across the sky as the orange rays of the sun began to pierce through the horizon.

There was a sprinkling of dew on the grass that kicked up on Brand's heels with each step as he opened his senses to the nature around him. He could smell the bittersweet fragrances of the grass beneath his feet mingling with the sparse trees around him. He already missed the comforting solitude of the hermit lifestyle he'd adopted.

The calls of songbirds interrupted the calm quiet of the fleeting night, ushering in a new day. The stars retreated as the rising sun morphed the muted scenery into a field of color.

Though there was still a dull, throbbing pain in Brand's shoulder, he took a deep breath and felt refreshed as he stretched his limbs. He ran through his morning exercise routine and was happy to find that his arm was beginning to regain some of its strength. By the time they reached their destination, he was sure his arm would be back in fighting shape.

Blood pumping from the warm-up, Brand sat in the open area he had found close to their camp and crossed his legs to begin his meditation. He waded into his Inner Path into the emotions that flowed through him and started to notice that the river of emotions was larger than it normally was. It must be because of his injury.

Shrugging it off, he got to work on clearing the Path. Brand found that the early morning was usually the easiest time for this mental exercise. Brand envisioned each emotion as a stream of different colored liquid, all coming together into a vibrant rainbow wave. He took any emotions he could identify and bottled them up one by one, setting them aside on a shelf away from the Path.

The fogginess of his head over the past few days had finally begun to subside. Even so, he found it more difficult than normal to complete his meditation due to the larger range of emotions he had to bottle up. It was like there was still some kind of static pulsing through him that he couldn't clear. It stayed at the edges of his mind and prevented him from focusing. After a few frustrating minutes of being unable to bottle everything, he gave up and started back towards the camp. He needed to begin packing for the next leg of their journey.

Astoro had just begun to stir as Brand returned, and together they packed up the camp. They planned on making it far enough to stay in an actual inn that night, and it looked like the weather would cooperate. Astoro took the time to fill Brand in on the little he knew about the city of Midral. Brand couldn't help but feel a little apprehensive about being in such a large city after his time in solitude.

Astoro had never met Ginmar, so he wasn't exactly sure how to contact him, but he hoped that he'd find out a way once they got there. Brand also didn't know how he was supposed to contact his warden in Midral either. The letter had only told Brand to meet him in Midral at a specific Inn without a date or time. He would have to trust that his warden would know how to contact him once he'd arrived.

Hopefully, they could both accomplish their goals. If Astoro could get in contact with Ginmar, he could warn him of the cult taking up residence in the mountain range. He was sure that was something Ginmar would want to know about, considering this was the cult that had killed his student. In any case, they had time to think about things since they were still several days' journey from Midral.

* * *

At last, the outlines of a small town emerged, bathed in the warm, golden hues of the setting sun. Long shadows stretched across cobblestone streets, and the fading light cast a serene glow on the town's rustic buildings. This would be the last time they got to sleep comfortably until they arrived in Midral. Astoro said he'd take care of finding them a room at the inn if Brand wanted to get them some more provisions. After asking around, he was able to procure some more food for the road ahead.

That task done, he began to explore the rest of the small town. He even went into a local forge to get a better idea of what Astoro had told him about Ronan. After turning down what the blacksmith claimed were "the best weapons south of Midral", Brand thanked the man for his time and went on his way. Weapons weren't really his thing.

Brand slowed his pace as he realized that his path had taken him to the edge of the village; he must have made a wrong turn while he was lost in thought. As he turned around to retrace his steps, he noticed three masked men emerging from the shadows armed with knives and clubs.

"Looks like someone's lost their way." The leader's voice dripped with mock concern. "I'm sure we'd be able to point you back in the right direction for a small payment, friend. Go ahead and empty those pockets of any coin you have."

"Apologies," Brand said, pulling three copper coins and his rations out of his pockets. "I travel pretty light, and just spent most of what I had, but you're free to split my remaining copper and I'll just be on my way."

"Sorry if I don't take your word for it," the leader said with a fake smile. "Maybe my associates here will be able to find a little more in those pockets if we search ourselves."

"Listen, I don't want any trouble, and I don't want to hurt you all." Brand was beginning to get irritated. He tried to use his training to push away the anger, but he was struggling. "This is all I have on me, and you're welcome to it."

"Oh, you hear that, fellas? He doesn't want to hurt us!" The two others who had now circled him began to chuckle. "One more chance, tough guy."

"I told you, I don't have…" The thug on his right swung his knife, but Brand was able to dodge and knock the blade free. He kicked out and hit the man right in the sternum, knocking the breath out of him. Anticipating the next attack, Brand focused inward and began to release the gates to his chi, when he noticed something was terribly wrong.

Why can't I unlock any gates?! Brand thought.

His mind raced in panic. The familiar pathways of his Chi felt like muddied rivers, clogged and unyielding. The startling realization made him lose focus as one of the other two thugs tackled him to the ground. The thugs began to beat him while he tried his best to defend himself without his Chi. Soon, the third thug had recovered and joined in. Kicks and fists began raining down on him, and he was helpless to stop the onslaught.

After a few moments, the beating stopped as Brand had no energy left to defend himself. The two henchmen patted him down to try and find any hidden treasure Brand had on him.

"Looks like he was telling the truth, boss," one of them said. "Not a copper more on him."

"Slag and ashes, what a waste of time," he said, turning to Brand, who had slowly worked his way to his knees. "What, you haven't had enough yet?"

Brand's head was swimming, but he got back to his feet. His heart was racing, and he was beginning to see red. He didn't know what was going on with his Chi, but he wasn't about to let these thugs get the better of him. He'd tried to be peaceful about it and follow the teachings he'd grown up with. But the ways of the world were beginning to flood back into his memory. Memories that brought back the anger he'd fought a long time to overcome with training. The way he was treated as an orphan on the streets, beaten regularly by those with more power.

He rushed forward, screaming with rage as something broke inside him. A burning sensation ripped through him as his Chi burst through one of his inner gates along a new Path. The burning Chi crashed through his gates one by one until it reached his fist, setting it alight with crimson energy as it found its target.

Brand's fist, enveloped in a crimson aura, connected with a thunderous impact. The henchman's jaw snapped audibly, a shockwave of energy sending him spiraling into a nearby stone wall with a dull thud. Brand felt a surge of satisfaction as he heard the man break.

But that was as far as his adrenaline-fueled rage took him. The shock from using his Chi without clearing the Path overtook him and he felt his inner gates slam back into place, cutting off his Chi once again. As he tried to recover and swing a second time, the leader dodged and landed a solid blow on Brand, sending him back to the pavement.

"Oh, you messed up now," he said, pulling out a knife and holding it over his head. As he swung downward, a mess of vines caught the dagger-wielding arm, mid-swing, and yanked the man backward ten feet.

"Hey!" the second man yelled, turning toward the source of the vines. A loud buzzing filled the air and a swarm of insects descended on him and sent him running away screaming.

"Brand!" Astoro yelled, emerging from the alley, where the leader was tied up in vines and unconscious. "Hold still!"

He ran up and knelt next to Brand. A soft, emerald light radiated from Astoro's outstretched palms, weaving around Brand's bruised form. The soothing energy knitted his wounds, easing the pounding in his head and steadying his breath. He took Brand's arm and threw it over his shoulder.

"Let's get out of here, buddy," Astoro said, and he led them slowly back toward the inn.

9

Ronan

Ronan pulled a superheated piece of metal from the Forge and began to shape it on his anvil. He let his mind wander as the rhythmic clanging of his hammer strikes filled the Forge. The workshop had always been his sanctuary, even before he'd joined Niradim's ranks.

It was a few days after the attack, and Ronan was still sore from the beating he took. Without his normal sword and shield, he was useless in that fight. If he hadn't been wearing his mythril chainmail under his robes, he'd be in far worse shape now. Though Master Ginmar and Brin hadn't fared much better even with their magic.

And the spell Brin had used… That was a spell Ronan had developed on his own, he had no idea how she could have learned it. Well, it didn't matter. He had nothing to do with that old life anymore. Thank goodness he hadn't been killed. He doubted Niradim would have brought him back a second time after the cold shoulder Ronan had been giving him.

After they had all recovered, Brin filled them in on exactly what had happened. Their adversary had used some kind of charm spell to force Brin to do anything he asked. And what he had asked of her had them all very worried. From what they gathered, he was attempting to infiltrate the Earth Sector - the area only accessible to Niradim's dwarves.

Well, and also accessible to Ronan, at least for now. Even though it was widely known Ronan was no longer a Disciple, they hadn't kicked him out. How could you justify kicking someone out who Niradim himself raised from the dead? It's possible with time they'd reconsider and ask him to leave, but for now, those memories were too fresh in everyone's minds.

As his aching muscles warmed up from the blacksmith work, Ronan couldn't help but wonder why this mystery person would want to infiltrate the Earth Sector. Was he a spy from another country? A thief trying to steal something?

He shook his head. The reason didn't matter, because this man was clearly a threat to Midral. After he fled, the soldiers that came to their rescue put out the fire and healed the three of them. By the time everything was under control, it was too late to chase down the individual responsible for all the chaos.

Now that he had seen it up close, Ronan had to admit that Ginmar's theory had to be correct. The Black Frost Ring had resurfaced. And unless he missed his guess, that staff was also a powerful Artifact, though he didn't know which one. Artifacts were incredibly rare, and even one in the hands of the wrong person was extremely dangerous. But two? The novaborn, Kyros, hadn't exaggerated. They were lucky to be alive right now.

He glanced over to the corner of his shop, where his sword and shield were still propped up against the wall. His gaze lingered on them, his brow furrowing in a silent battle of longing and denial before he turned away with a resigned sigh. He wanted nothing more than for things to go back to the way they used to be. But it wasn't possible, not when he could no longer trust the god that he'd worshiped.

"That's not you anymore," he whispered to himself. "Ginmar and the rest of the Disciples will have to take care of this themselves."

He turned back and tried to continue his work, but his mind and heart just weren't in it at the moment.

* * *

Ronan approached Brin's temporary lodgings in the Earth Sector. She'd been allowed some accommodations while she healed and found a new place to live. Hopefully they'd allow her to stay until she completed her Shaping Trial. Once she passed that, she'd be able to live in the Earth Sector permanently.

"Yes, that's right. He asked me to draw him a map of the Earth Sector. Then he forced me to authenticate his forged documents," Ronan heard Brin telling someone inside. She must have told her story a hundred times in the last three days. It was time for the visits to stop.

"Is there anything else you remember that he asked you to do? Any names or places he specifically asked about?"

"I think I remember him saying his name was Kyros, but that's all I..."

"Ok, that's enough for today, don't you think, Lieutenant Vorkin?" Ronan said, entering the room. "Doesn't Niradim have more important tasks for you than pestering Brin day after day?"

"Master Ronan, Niradim's Blessings," he said without missing a beat. "My apologies, I'm just trying to apprehend the man that almost killed you the other day. Or don't you remember that you were assaulted by someone allegedly wielding an Artifact?" He rolled up the parchment he was holding and tucked it away before continuing. "Perhaps you hit your head a little too hard the other day? I would have expected Niradim's Phoenix to put up more of a fight."

"Niradim's what?" Ronan asked.

"Oh, you haven't heard? That's what the people are calling you," he said with a slight smirk.

"That's ridiculous," Ronan said. Niradim's Phoenix? He wasn't even a part of the faith anymore. He wouldn't be Niradim's anything.

"Oh come on, think about it. First, you're brought back to life, then you survive an encounter with the legendary Black Frost Ring? The very ring that was said to have been destroyed by the mythical phoenix?" He stopped to consider that last statement. "Although I guess that story's been proven false by the reappearance of the ring here in Midral. But it does set up for a good nickname, you have to admit."

"Look, I want nothing to do with Niradim. I'm done with him," Ronan said sharply.

He walked to the door, turning one last time to address Ronan before leaving. "But maybe he's not done with you."

Ronan shook his head as the footsteps disappeared down the hall. Niradim's Phoenix… ridiculous. He turned to regard Brin, who had been silently watching the conversation unfold.

"Niradim's Phoenix?" Ronan asked her, raising an eyebrow.

"Hey, there are worse things they could call you. It's a pretty cool nickname," she said with a smile.

"You're the one that was on fire the other day," Ronan pointed out, moving to sit across from her bed in an open chair. "Speaking of, how are you feeling?"

"Better, thanks," she said. She rolled up her sleeves to show Ronan. "The burns are all healed up and I've regained most of my strength. Who knew that being healed could take so much out of you?"

"You think that's bad, try being brought back from the dead," Ronan said with a slight smile.

"Yeah, I bet that's a doozy!" Brin laughed. "But really, I'm feeling a lot better, and I've been thinking a lot more about my designs now that I've been in a real fight, and I have several new ideas…"

"Actually, Brin," Ronan interrupted. He hadn't been looking forward to this. "I wanted to talk to you about that."

"About what?" Brin asked. She sat up, sensing something was wrong.

He couldn't meet her eyes. "I'm leaving the city, Brin. There's nothing left for me here, it's time for me to go."

She stared at him as if he had just slapped her in the face. He knew it would be tough for her to hear this, but it was what was best for everyone. The people loved him right now, but once they finally accepted that he had left the faith, the fallout would be ugly. He couldn't have Brin associated with that. It would tarnish her reputation by association with him, and the work she was doing was for their own good, no matter who her master was. Plus, he had to admit, he cared for her too much. He was afraid of what it meant for her faith if he stayed.

"Ronan, you can't leave!" Brin said, leaning forward on her hands. "I can't do this without you!"

"Yes you can, Brin, there's nothing left for me to teach you to complete your Trial," Ronan said. "You have all the skills you need, your designs are great, and I know you've been working with Master Ginmar on the magic involved. He told me himself that you're ready. You can do it without me from here on out."

"But I need my master to sponsor me for the Trial!" Brin protested. He was ready for that objection.

"Master Ginmar can do that for you, I already spoke to him about it and he said he'd be more than happy to." Ronan had broken the news to Ginmar that morning. Even though Ginmar hadn't tried to dissuade him from leaving, he could tell that his old master had taken the news pretty hard as well.

"No, Ronan," Brin said, straightening up and waiting until Ronan finally met her eyes. "Disciple Ginmar is not my master. You are. I'm not going to do the Trial without my master sponsoring me for it."

"Brin, I'm not a follower…" Ronan started.

"I don't care!" Brin yelled, cutting him off. Her tone softened. "Ronan, I've never cared that you aren't a follower of Niradim anymore. It doesn't matter to me." Tears started to form, but she quickly blinked them away and composed herself. "Please Ronan, I understand that you feel like you have to leave, but at least stay for my Trial. Please."

Ronan could see how much this meant to her, and he felt himself taken back to the time when he had asked Ginmar to sponsor his Trial, even though he was a human. Ginmar had been hesitant at first but could see the faith Ronan had at the time, and just how much it had meant to him. He couldn't help but see that same fire within his apprentice, and he couldn't bear to deny her this request.

"Ok Brin, I'll stay for your Trial," Ronan finally said. "But as soon as it's done, I'm leaving Midral."

"Thank you, Master Ronan," Brin said.

He turned to leave but stopped at the door.

"Also, Brin," he said without looking over his shoulder. "You should be careful with that spell you used to save us."

Images of his last attempt to use the same spell flashed through his mind. Memories of the flickering knives clattering to the ground and axes cutting into his flesh made him flinch.

"It's not always reliable."

With that, he left.

* * *

The Trial would be in one month, and the fact that 'The Phoenix of Niradim' would be sponsoring it had caused quite the stir, much to Ronan's chagrin.

Oh well, he thought. *I'll be gone soon anyway, and then they'll move on with their lives.*

And he would finally move on with his own.

The search for Kyros, the wielder of the Black Frost Ring, hadn't turned up much, but there were reports of black ice being found all around the city. Some were beginning to murmur that the weather was getting colder than usual for this time of year, but Ronan figured that was just superstition.

That being said, Ginmar had confided in him that new Black Frost murders were being discovered nightly. Each kill was of prominent members of different gangs in the city. On the surface, it almost made it seem like Kyros was providing a service to the city by ridding it of crime, but Ronan and Ginmar knew there had to be more to it.

"So all of the gangs have been targeted?" Ronan asked Ginmar over a drink in a tavern bordering the Court of Fire.

"As far as we can tell," Ginmar said. "In the last two weeks, every major gang has been hit. The first murders were members of Blood Forge, then the Orebreakers lost a few of their top men. Then two nights ago, the Stonehammers' leadership was almost totally wiped out."

"What are the Protectors doing to try and put a stop to it?" Ronan asked.

"We've increased patrols in the seedier parts of the Sky Sector, and made sure those men are wearing better armor, but I mean…" Ginmar took a large drink from his mug, "There's not much more we can do, now is there? We only have a limited number of resources to cover such a large area, and we're dealing with someone with an Artifact." He lowered his voice. "Maybe two, if your hunch is correct. Have you learned anything?"

"Not really" Ronan replied "There are a number of staves that are referred to in history books, but all are accounted for in one way or another. Some are in the possession of kingdoms, a couple were said to have been destroyed, and one was buried when the city of Lumenova was lost."

"Yeah, well the Black Frost Ring was said to have been destroyed as well, but that doesn't seem to be the case," Ginmar said. "Maybe one of those that were supposed to be destroyed is the one that he has?"

"Maybe. Or maybe he stole one from somewhere," Ronan said, rubbing his chin. "You should try reaching out to Midral's allies to see if they're missing any Artifacts."

"I can try, but I don't know how forthcoming anyone would be about one of its major weapons going missing."

"That's true."

"Well, at least it's a start and something I can actually do instead of sitting around waiting for the next murder to be reported. The crazy thing is that even though we've increased patrols, it's like this guy knows where we are at all times. Like he's got some kind of eye in the sky or something," Ginmar said, shaking his head before downing the rest of his drink. "Thanks for chatting, Ronan, and I appreciate the help. I know this isn't your fight anymore."

"It's fine, Ginmar. Kyros attacked my apprentice, and you," Ronan said, standing to go. "I'm happy to help where I can while I'm still here."

Ginmar's face fell at that last comment. Ronan knew that Ginmar was still upset that Ronan was leaving.

"Well, I'll take all the help I can get," Ginmar said.

Ronan nodded. "Good luck."

Ginmar reached up and placed a hand on Ronan's shoulder before leaving. "I'll take all of that I can get as well."

10

Kyros

Kyros poured himself a drink and settled down into a chair in his lavish room at the inn. He took a long swig of the expensive liquor, the taste of smoke filling his mouth before the welcome burn traveled down his throat. It was only a couple hours before sunrise, and he was starting to feel the exhaustion of the repeated late nights.

Agent Viridian stood opposite of him, casually leaning against the wall, spinning a knife between his fingers. Even relaxed, Zandro was a dangerous presence in any room he occupied. The burn that climbed up the side of his face only made him look more deadly. Kyros was glad that his family's connections ran deep enough to employ such a weapon as the former leader of the Arcane Knights.

"Viridian, what do you have to report?" Kyros said, pouring himself another drink.

"Well, I can start with the good news, Agent Amethyst," Zandro said. "The hidden base is coming along. We sent coded messages to several of the cultist encampments to let them know to begin making their way to our new headquarters."

"Good, we need to start occupying the city in force," Kyros said. The sooner they could move their operations to the lost city of Lumenova, the better. He didn't know the details, but his Patron made it clear that his old city played a part in his plans to return.

"Despite the dangers we found on arrival, re-discovering Lumenova has proven to be a huge boost to our operations," Zandro continued. "After your successful delve into the Temple of the Fallen Star, we're eager to explore the rest of the holy site and other areas of the city. For now, we occupy only a small area that has been cleared of the more dangerous monstrosities we found."

"The unexplored areas of the temple will be deadly," Kyros said. "Send in some of our more expendable people to explore the areas that I haven't detailed in the map I gave you."

He finished his drink in a large gulp. The memory of his brother falling into a trap and disappearing just steps inside the front doors of the Temple flashed through his mind. They never found out what happened to Falrose, not that Kyros cared all that much. Better that his brother was dead and out of his way.

"What about Val'ran and Bogg?" Kyros asked, pouring another drink. He hoped Zandro would finish his updates soon so he could at least get a couple hours' rest.

"They've been restored and imprisoned," Zandro said. "And I hunted down Bogg's friend, Frederick, before visiting the camp we established to the south of Lumenova."

"Good," Kyros said. "Clean this mess up, Viridian. Did you at least interrogate Frederick before you killed him to make sure he didn't tell anyone about the city?"

"Please don't insult me, I know how to make threads of information disappear, as you well know," Zandro said. He finally stood up straighter and gave Kyros an intense look. "But as we agreed, as soon as that's done, Val goes into my custody. I will kill the others as you requested, but I need her alive."

"And please don't insult *me*, I know how to keep my end of a deal." Kyros returned Zandro's intense gaze. "Now, is that all?"

Kyros was already getting up out of his chair to signal the end of the conversation. He needed to get some sleep soon, and he just hoped his Patron didn't want a spontaneous meeting overnight.

"No, actually. There is one more minor thing," Zandro said, leaning back against the wall. "While I was visiting the fortress camp, it was attacked and wiped out."

"Really?" Kyros said, raising his eyebrows. That was an interesting development. "The same camp that summoned the Starspawn a while back? I thought the town had given up on neutralizing that camp after their heavy losses, did they send a new group?"

"No, it was only two people," Zandro said.

"The entire fortress was eliminated by two people?" Kyros replied. How was that even possible? "Do you care to explain how two individuals were able to wipe out our entire camp while Zandro of the Arcane Knights was present?"

"I'd prefer if we didn't use our real names when discussing our operations if you please, *Agent Amethyst*," Zandro said through gritted teeth. "And most of the carnage was carried out by one of the two - an unarmed monk who moved like an old friend of yours."

"Landren," Kyros guessed, finishing the drink in his hand and setting down his glass.

These problems just kept mounting. Landren was one of the few from his party who had escaped Lumenova before Kyros had obtained the staff. He was one of the several loose ends Zandro needed to tie up. "Was he one of the attackers?"

"No," Zandro shook his head. "But it was clearly someone who studied the same kind of martial arts as he did. I was able to neutralize him, so he won't be a problem any longer. The other was a florian who had some magical ability, but he seemed to be as surprised as I was at the destruction his companion caused."

"Do you at least know what their motivation was?" Kyros asked.

"The florian seemed intent on finding something," Zandro explained. "It was personal in nature, so my theory is that it was simple revenge."

"Be careful, Viridian," Kyros said, turning to look Zandro in the eye. "Revenge can be quite the motivator."

"I can take care of myself," he replied.

"Yes, I'm sure you can," Kyros said. "Even so, I think it's time to bring in Agent Crimson to deal with Landren and anyone from his monastery that he may have informed." He motioned toward the door. "Thank you for the report, Viridian. You are excused."

Zandro disappeared without a word, leaving Kyros with his thoughts and exhaustion. Eventually, he would need to bring Zandro up to speed on his plans, but not tonight. Right now, he was too tired to have that conversation.

The last several days since his encounter with Ronan had been especially busy ones. Through consistent use of his ring, he'd eliminated the leadership of rival gangs. That left the Blood Forge as the sole criminal powerhouse in the city, and their numbers swelled as a result.

He had also found out that the drawbacks of the ring got progressively worse with repeated use. Though he planned on keeping that particular information to himself. He could barely feel the fingers on his left hand anymore, and the numbing sensation was beginning to crawl up his arm to the elbow.

Good thing it's almost time, Kyros thought.

He'd met with the Blood Forge earlier in the night to go over his plan that would get him past the Crucible Gate. The Shaping Trial would begin soon, and he'd learned that they always finished on the night of the third day. There would be a massive celebration, perfect for causing a distraction.

Things had become more complicated now that he had been exposed. There were twice as many guards posted at the gate, and he suspected they knew his target as well. But the celebrations of the end of a Trial would give his makeshift army a chance to get in close and cause the chaos he needed to slip in.

For now, he needed to rest. The sun was about to come up, but he knew he could sleep a few hours and then take a warm bath to get some feeling back into his arm. Barely able to make it to the bed, Kyros was asleep within seconds.

* * *

Kyros found himself pulled through the abyss of space once again, for the first time since he had entered the city. With the amount of times he'd been through this, he should be more used to the sensation. Still, he had to fight down the urge that pushed him to terror as he flew through the darkness at breakneck speed. Straight towards the familiar purple star summoning him.

After what felt both like an eternity and no time at all, he came to an abrupt halt, floating in space before the Star Prison. Unlike the usual steady energy he was used to, the violet energy was chaotic, fighting at the seams of the runes that contained it.

WHY DON'T YOU HAVE THE FLAME YET?

His Patron's voice raged in his mind and he doubled over in pain, curling into himself in agony.

MY PATIENCE IS RUNNING SHORT.

Straight to the point, as always. He'd never heard his Patron this mad before. Kyros' proximity to the Flame must be making his Patron restless.

"I've almost got it!" Kyros screamed back, holding his hands to his head. "I just need a little more time."

I HAVE GIVEN YOU TIME. I NEED THE FLAME NOW!

"I have a plan in place to steal it at the end of the Festival of Fire," Kyros said through gritted teeth. "It's the only time I'll be able to create a distraction big enough to breach the Crucible Gate."

The chaotic energy began to subside until it settled into the normal undulation that Kyros was accustomed to. Now that he knew Kyros had a plan, his Patron had regained control of his temper.

YOU HAVE BEEN USING THE RING TOO MUCH.

Kyros was caught off guard by the abrupt change of subject. At least his Patron's voice had come down to the normal booming volume Kyros was accustomed to, so he relaxed his body into a more natural position.

IT IS DRAWING ATTENTION.

"I have it under control," Kyros said. "I know I have their attention, but the Protectors won't be able to locate me."

YOU MISUNDERSTAND. THE RING DRAWS ATTENTION FROM FAR MORE POWERFUL CREATURES THAN PUNY DWARVES. CREATURES WHO SEEK TO RECLAIM THEIR LOST ARTIFACT.

"Yes, I know that as well, no thanks to you," Kyros said, crossing his arms. It was time to test a theory he'd been wondering about. "They are part of my plan, don't worry."

WHAT DO YOU MEAN, PART OF YOUR PLAN?

Good, at least he could confirm his Patron wasn't all-knowing. He tucked away the knowledge in case he needed it for the future.

"You said you wanted darkness and despair, right?" Kyros said with a sly smile. Yes, revenge could be quite the motivator indeed.

His Patron paused for a moment as if considering.

FINE. I WILL GIVE YOU THE TIME YOU REQUESTED AND CONTACT YOU AGAIN ONCE YOU HAVE THE FLAME IN YOUR POSSESSION. DO NOT DISAPPOINT ME, OR OUR NEXT

MEETING WILL NOT BE PLEASANT.

Before he could reply, Kyros was jolted backward into the darkness of space and back into his own body. He sat up, waking in a sweat and gasping for air. He put a hand to his head to steady himself.

The next meeting won't be pleasant, huh? Kyros thought, catching his breath. *As if any of these meetings are pleasant to begin with.*

Still, he trembled at the thought of what his Patron might do to him. Pain was one thing, but Kyros coveted the power granted to him. He didn't know what he would do if he lost it. He had to admit that he was dealing with an entity he understood frustratingly little about. He was starting to feel like he was in over his head.

He can't take away your power as long as you're keeping up your end of the deal. He reminded himself. *The contract is binding.*

He laid back into bed as fear took root in his mind at the thought of losing his power. He couldn't go back to the way he was. He replayed the words over and over again in his mind.

He can't take away your power.

He just wished he believed it.

11

Val'ran

"It's cold as balls out here. Wait, what do ladies say when it's cold outside? It's cold as boobs?"

"Shut up Bogg."

Even with the map they'd found, they weren't making great time on their path. There wasn't exactly a nice road to lead them to Midral, and a relentless frost had seized the area. The frigid weather turned the barely navigable paths into treacherous trails of deep, crisp snow. Icicles hung like daggers from the bare branches, and each breath turned to mist. It shouldn't be this cold so early in the season.

Zandro had a big head start on them, but she'd overheard those guards saying he had to make a stop on the way, so hopefully they could catch up with him in Midral. She couldn't afford to let this opportunity to settle things pass her by.

So far the travel hadn't been too bad, but it was getting more difficult as they got closer to the city of Midral. They'd only had one dangerous encounter, but it was with monsters that didn't belong to this area. They had clashed with a couple of orcs patrolling with some dire wolves, their fur as white as the snow they prowled. Bogg was keen to find more and "have some more fun" as he'd so eloquently put it, but

Val was too focused on catching up to Zandro for their normal banter.

A few days later, she could tell they were starting to get closer, but the weather conditions hadn't gotten any better. She stopped in the snow as she spotted some large tracks nearby. A cold shudder ran down Val's spine, but this time it wasn't because of the piercing wind. Those were the tracks of giants. A lot of them.

She'd never seen one herself, but ice giants never wandered this far south, and usually traveled alone or only with the orcs and dire wolves that served them. What was going on?

"Are we there yet?" Bogg asked.

"Does it look like we're slaggin' there yet?" Val replied, her annoyance at Bogg was at an all-time high, she usually didn't resort to cursing. "It's going to take us a little while longer, especially with this weather."

"Yeah. What's up with this weather?" Bogg said, oblivious to her tone. "I haven't been outside in a while but I don't think it's supposed to be this cold yet. Shouldn't we go a little slower?"

"If you can't keep up, feel free to turn back," Val spat.

"No, no. I can keep up."

Nothing was going to keep her from getting to Zandro. She almost wished Bogg would just leave so that she could travel as fast as she wanted, and in peaceful silence. Unfortunately, getting a hint was not Bogg's strong suit.

They continued to trudge through the knee-deep snow. Each step was a battle against the biting wind that seemed to cut through the trees, scattering powdery snowflakes like ash. As the sun began to set on the horizon, they saw movement ahead of them.

"Hey, do you see that?" Bogg said.

"Yeah, I see it," Val said. "The tracks we've seen must belong to them."

"You mean those huge feet prints?" Bogg asked.

"Yeah, those huge feet prints." Val rolled her eyes. "Those are ice giants up ahead."

"They look pretty small for giants."

"That's because we're far away, you complete moron," Val snapped, her voice laced with exasperation. Her brain was physically hurting after traveling with Bogg for so long. "They're much larger up close and also deadly. Taking down one would be tough. But from what I can tell, there might be double digits in that group."

"Double what?" He asked with a vacant look on his face.

"Ugh, don't worry about it. The point is, there's a lot of them, and that's extremely dangerous," Val said. She hated to admit it, but even alone she didn't dare get anywhere close to an ice giant camp. Much less so with her loud companion. They would have to go around. "For some reason, they're heading in the same direction we are, but I've never heard of ice giants visiting any of our cities, so it must be a coincidence. Either way, we'll have to go around, but that means we'll need to move faster, I don't want to lose much time." That shiver was climbing up her spine again.

"Whatever you say," Bogg replied. "This is your hunt."

Val took off at a hurried pace in a wide arc around the path of the giants with Bogg keeping pace as best he could. Why did there have to be giants, of all things, in her path? She could just imagine Zandro finishing his business in Midral and leaving before they even arrived, his trail going cold again. She couldn't lose this opportunity, Zandro had to pay for what he'd done to her.

Her focus on catching Zandro propelled her even faster, and after about an hour, Bogg began to lag behind. Somehow, he must have sensed a change in her, because miraculously he kept his mouth shut. She pushed through the snow and trees. Her years of training allowed her to move much faster through the difficult and dangerous terrain than most.

A loud crack and subsequent yell from Bogg eventually broke her out of her dark thoughts. She finally stopped and looked behind her. Bogg was nowhere to be seen.

"Ow!" Val heard Bogg yell from somewhere behind her. "Hey Val! I fell in a hole, can you come help me out?"

Val began to take a step towards his voice and then paused. This was her chance. She could finally leave him behind and continue on without him. Bogg was an idiot, but he was resourceful.

"Val! Hey!" Bogg yelled even louder. "I fell in this hole, can you hear me?"

She had no doubt he'd eventually be able to get himself out of whatever hole he'd fallen into without her help. She'd make much faster time without him and ensure she'd have enough time to find Zandro in Midral. That was the most important thing, she couldn't let someone like Bogg slow her down and keep her from getting her revenge. It would be so easy. All she'd have to do is turn around and keep going as if she hadn't heard him.

So she did.

Step by step, she put distance between herself and Bogg. For some reason each step felt heavier than the last. It wasn't just a physical distance she was increasing, but an emotional one that she hadn't realized was even there.

Zandro had taken everything from her. Her father, her friends, her life. After the loss of her father, she'd joined the Arcane Knights under Zandro's wing, considering him a mentor and even a friend. She'd learned from him as she fought beside him, and she trusted him completely. The pain of that betrayal lingered far longer than the physical wound he'd given her. The pain of being betrayed by someone you trusted.

Val halted, her breaths coming in short gasps, not from the physical exertion but from the sudden, piercing realization of her actions.

What am I doing? She thought to herself.

She'd lost herself in this quest for vengeance, letting it take over her and consume her, preventing her from forming new bonds. And here was someone, as annoying as he was, who was willing to stand and fight by her side despite the walls she'd put up to protect herself. She finally realized those walls were a prison of her own making, and it was time to break out.

Zandro had taken so much from her, but she hadn't realized until now that the scars he'd left had taken away a piece of her humanity. No more. She was done being his victim. She turned back towards where she'd left Bogg and began to sprint back to him.

It took about thirty minutes to backtrack to where she'd left him, but once she got back to the area, it didn't take long to find the hole he'd fallen into. As she got closer, she slowed as she noticed fresh tracks in the ground that didn't belong to her or Bogg.

Oh no. She thought. She didn't see anyone in the immediate vicinity, so she crept up to the edge of the hole and peered in.

It was empty.

* * *

She quickly realized the hole he'd fallen into was a hunting trap. Some of the orcs traveling with the giants must have set it up to capture large animals for the giants to eat. It must have been a surprise for them to find an annoying and fully-armed human at the bottom of the pit. She was now tracking a large hunting party made up of five orcs and five dire wolves that were heading directly toward the giants' camp.

She had finally caught up enough to see that they were dragging Bogg behind them, but they had stopped for a moment to check on another one of their traps. She had to rescue him before they made it back to the camp. She couldn't deal with giants.

Ok, think.

She swept her long brown hair back over her pointed ears and tied it back into a simple ponytail. She cleared some snow and sat down, crossing her legs and resting her elbows on them. Bringing the tips of her fingers together in front of her face, she settled into her battle meditation. It was time to come up with a plan.

There had to be a way to get Bogg out of this mess before they arrived at their destination. The odds weren't in her favor. She couldn't hope to take out the whole party by herself, but trying to rescue him from the middle of a giant's camp would be impossible. That meant she'd have to be a little reckless, and she *hated* being reckless.

That didn't stop you from throwing a knife at Zandro as soon as you saw him and almost ruining your escape. She reminded herself.

But this would be different. This would be *calculated* recklessness, and that was something she could at least pretend to be ok with. She needed to focus.

First, I need to get Bogg away from the group.

She figured Bogg could probably get out of his restraints with a little time and a little help from a knife. She had a good idea of how to get him away from the group, but switching places with him would put her right next to the enemy. Well, actually they were dragging him a few feet behind the pack, so she'd be behind them. That may give her an opportunity to do some damage.

And then what? You can maybe kill or wound three or four of them before the other ones turn around and then it's game over.

There were simply too many of them. And while the orcs were pretty easy for her to take out at close range, that many dire wolves would kill her. Plus, she couldn't fight long enough to give Bogg a chance to escape. She just needed to create some chaos and confusion, and then run. Well, she could at least do that.

The shot to switch places with Bogg would be a tough one, especially with him lying flat. Not to mention, she'd have to draw blood for her magic to work. The arrow placement would have to be precise enough to break skin, but not injure him in a way that would make their escape more difficult. Wonderful, as if this plan needed any more complications.

Well, I have been wanting to shoot an arrow at him for some time. She thought. *Guess I should thank these orcs for the opportunity.*

She chuckled at the thought, pulling a knife out of her boot and laying it on the ground in front of her. Dark humor was a coping mechanism well suited for a battlefield, and this was definitely going to be a battlefield.

The plan was set. She opened her eyes and stood up, focused and ready. She drew an arrow out of her quiver, nocked it into her bow, and took a deep breath. Her emerald eyes sparked with arcane power as she channeled her magic into her weapon. She took aim at her companion on the ground as her arrow began to crackle with energy.

Ok, let's do this.

She let the arrow fly and watched as it seemed to move toward Bogg in slow motion. It cut clean through one of the ropes, pierced the leather armor, and sank about an inch into her friend's left shoulder. Perfect.

As the arrow flew, she'd already begun unsheathing her scimitar in anticipation - years of battle experience flaring back to life inside of her. Her father's blade roared and ignited in a blue inferno as she felt the familiar jolt of the switch. As she swung the blazing scimitar, the two dire wolves who had been tasked with dragging Bogg behind the group burst into blue flame. The fiery explosion drove back the two orcs that had been trudging alongside them. She spared a glance over her shoulder as she re-sheathed her blade. It looked like Bogg had located the knife she left behind and was already working on freeing himself.

Good. Now, work on the remaining wolves while they still don't know what's going on so they can't pursue and then get out of here.

The first two wolves were completely engulfed in flames, and the three in the front had turned at the sounds of combat. In the blink of an eye, her bow was back in her hand. This time she strung up two arrows at the same time and sent them at the remaining dire wolves. One arrow lodged itself into a wolf's shoulder, but it didn't seem to slow the beast down as it started to charge at her. The other arrow bit deeply into the throat of a second wolf, taking it out of the fight.

There were two dire wolves left, but she didn't have time to fire another shot before the orcs would rally. Everything had happened so fast, that they were still trying to process why two of their wolves were on fire. Before they could gather themselves, she took off at a full sprint towards Bogg. He was sitting up and working to cut through the ropes tying his legs.

Three of five wolves down, and Bogg is almost free. She thought as she ran. *The orcs won't be as fast as us, but the wolves will be able to catch up in just a moment.*

She would need to finish off the last two wolves before the orcs caught up, and then she and Bogg could outrun the orcs. It would take another few moments before she could reignite her blade - too long. The wolves would be on her before she could use that ability again. It would be a straight fight then. She looked over her shoulder and saw the two wolves gaining on her.

Wait just a little longer... A little longer... And...

"OH YEAH, TIME FOR SOME FUN!" Bogg screamed as he sprinted past her *towards* the wolves.

"Oh, you have GOT to be KIDDING me!" Val couldn't help but yell back as she slid to a stop in the snow.

By the time she completely stopped, Bogg had rammed his sword deep into the chest of the first dire wolf which still had her arrow lodged in its shoulder. To his credit, the all-out assault confused the second wolf long enough for him to get his blade free. The last dire wolf pounced at him and knocked him on his back, but he'd stopped the deadly bite with his sword and was keeping the beast at bay for the moment.

"What are you doing, you were supposed to run *away*, not back towards them!" Val screamed at him. She nocked another arrow and fired it into the wolf's chest. As it flinched, Bogg wrung his blade free and sliced its neck. He grunted as he pushed the heavy beast off him.

"While you got to do all the cool stuff? No way, we can easily take this group out," he called over his shoulder as he turned to the four orcs that were running straight at them.

He dashed into the middle of the group with blinding speed and took the arm off one of the orcs. Another one of her arrows found the eye socket of an orc trying to attack Bogg from behind, as he engaged the final two. One of them scored a glancing blow that Bogg barely seemed to register as he ducked low and swept the orc's legs out from under him.

While that one was flat on his back and winded, Bogg turned in time to block a heavy blow from a large axe delivered from the fourth orc. He feinted left, getting the orc off balance, and then spun and struck from the right, cutting through a good chunk of the orc's side.

As that one sank to its knees in pain, he brought his sword back above him and swung down in an executioner's blow and severed its head. He turned back as Val was pulling her blade out from the chest of the orc he had tripped a moment ago. She sometimes forgot how fierce of a fighter Bogg was.

"See, I told you! Easy!" Bogg said to her.

"They're not the ones I was worried about," she said back with a glare. "I didn't want to draw the attention of anything bigger." Something was off, and that shiver up her spine was back and stronger than ever.

She looked down at the bodies around them and adrenaline fired in her veins.

"Bogg, where's the fifth orc? I counted five when…"

She wasn't able to finish her thought as enormous meteors of ice and rock began raining down around them. They both turned in time to see a massive ice giant picking up another boulder to throw. This time, at least Bogg had enough sense to run *away* from the danger.

"This is exactly the type of attention I was trying to avoid!" Val yelled as they ran. "Why couldn't you just run as soon as you were free of the ropes?!"

"Well, it's not like you told me the plan!" Bogg replied as another boulder dropped out of the sky a lot closer than Val liked. "How was I supposed to know we were going to take the most boring option? I'm not a mind reader!"

"I… Ok fine, you have a point," she admitted. She turned her head and could see that the giant was about a hundred feet behind them. But now he was in pursuit and closing fast since he was out of large rocks to chuck in their direction. "Pick up the pace, Bogg, he's gaining on us!"

She was pretty tapped out of magic from the rescue, well rescue *attempt* at this point - they still had to get away for it to qualify as a true rescue. She had enough energy for one more magical arrow, but she wasn't sure which one of her abilities could get them out of this mess.

"Any bright ideas?" Bogg yelled.

"I came up with the first rescue plan!" she replied. "Why don't you try coming up with a plan!"

"Well there's a lake over there," Bogg said, pointing to the left as they continued to run. "Do you think he can swim?

Val turned and looked to where he was pointing and shook her head. "Bogg, I can see from here the lake is frozen!"

"Probably just the top though. I've fallen through plenty of frozen lakes!" Bogg replied. "I bet he'll fall right through."

Leave it to Bogg's experience with doing stupid stuff to get them out of this mess. Well, it was a better idea than anything she had. They had to try it.

"Bogg, you continue to both surprise me and not surprise me at the same time," she yelled. "Head for the lake!"

As they neared the lake, Val spared a glance over her shoulder - the giant had closed half the distance to them and was swinging around…

Slag and ashes, is that a tree trunk!? Val thought.

She shook her head - Bogg better be right about this. There was no time to slow down and test whether the ice would hold them, so with a scream they pushed forward at full speed and hoped for the best. To Val's astonishment, the ice held without any issues. She could feel the tremors in the ice when the giant transitioned from running on the ground to the lake's surface.

After a few moments, she looked over her shoulder again. They had gained some separation as the giant got its footing on the ice, but it was beginning to run again. It would catch up to them soon.

"Bogg, I can't help but notice he's not falling through!" she yelled.

"Yeah, uh, the ice is actually a bit thicker than I thought it would be!" Bogg admitted. "I don't think he'll fall through on his own!"

That was going to be a problem. She could tell the ice was pretty thick, but she was fairly certain it wasn't frozen down to the bottom. If she could manage to crack the ice, she thought it might be enough to make the giant fall through the rest of the way.

"Ok Bogg, I have an idea" Val yelled. "It's pretty stupid, so I think you're going to love it. Keep running forward, and don't slow down!"

"Sounds fun!" Bogg yelled back.

Val rolled her eyes as she pulled out her bow, planted her feet on the ice, and began to slide. She pivoted her body so that it was facing back toward the giant - who she noted was only a few strides behind them with the massive trunk raised above its head. She quickly slotted an arrow into the bow and concentrated on sending all of her remaining arcane energy into it.

Here goes nothing.

She aimed down and fired directly into the giant's foot. As soon as the arrow pierced the skin, it detonated and pushed the giant's leg down into the ice, sending the giant sprawling forward. The ice began to spiderweb outward and break apart as the giant broke the surface and plunged into the frozen depths. Val stumbled as she was caught in the wake of the ice quake radiating from the new hole in the ice.

Just as she was about to plunge into the icy waters herself, a strong hand caught her arm and righted her. Bogg held her arm for a moment, oddly surefooted despite the cracking ice, until she'd gotten her feet back under her. She followed his lead the rest of the way to the far shoreline. Both of them collapsed with exhaustion from the adrenaline-fueled sprint as soon as they reached solid ground again.

"Bogg, I thought I told you to keep running," Val said between gulps of air.

"Yeah, well I wasn't just gonna leave you there to take a cold bath," Bogg said. "Besides, you came back for me."

"Bogg, I…" Val started.

"Look, Val, I get it," Bogg interrupted her, holding up his hand. "I'm not the easiest guy to travel with. I get into a lot of trouble, and get a lot of other people into trouble because of it." He turned to look her in the eyes. This was the most serious she'd ever seen him. "But you're the first person to ever come back for me."

Val couldn't lie to him after what she'd done. She had to come clean, even if it meant he hated her for it. "Bogg, I left you in that hole."

"Come on, Val," Bogg said, giving her a knowing look. "I might not be smart, but I am loud. I knew you could hear me when I fell in."

"You knew?" she whispered, averting her eyes.

"Course I knew. I wasn't even mad, more surprised that it took you so long to get rid of me," Bogg said with a chuckle. "But that don't matter. Point is, you came back. Thanks for coming back."

Val smiled, and a small part of her began to heal from the scars Zandro had left on her soul. Maybe she could learn to trust again, in time. For now, she was content with having a new friend by her side, no matter how much he got on her nerves.

"You're welcome, Bogg. Thanks for coming back for me too," Val said, forcing away the tears that were threatening to break free. "Um, I wanted to ask. Why are you so good at running across cracking ice?"

"Oh that's easy, my friends and I used to do that as a game when we were kids," Bogg said. He reached a hand up and rubbed the back of his head. "Like I said, I've fallen in a *lot* of frozen lakes…"

They both laughed until their sides hurt and they couldn't breathe. It was the first time she'd laughed since the Arcane Knights. She hadn't realized how much she missed it.

12

Brand

"I don't know what's wrong with me," Brand said, his eyes downcast, a shadow of frustration crossing his face. "I should have been able to handle those thugs on my own."

"It's alright, Brand," Astoro said. "Thank the sun that I was nearby and heard the commotion. How are you feeling, any better?"

"Physically? Yeah a little bit," Brand replied. "Thanks for healing me. That's twice you've saved my life now. I think I'm back to owing you one."

"Eh, I'll figure out a way you can pay me back," Astoro said with a smile.

The night after his run-in with the thugs was full of tossing and turning. How had things gone so wrong? The past decade of training was swiftly evaporating after coming out of isolation.

But that wasn't the most alarming thing. He'd accessed his Chi *without* clearing his emotions. According to everything Brand had ever been taught at the monastery of the Open Path, that shouldn't be possible. The training to control his focus and emotion during combat had slipped, but he'd accessed his power anyway. He wasn't sure what it meant, but it brought everything he'd learned into question.

Those thugs had brought out the younger, untrained version of himself. The version he was as a kid, freshly kicked out of his 4th orphanage for anger issues. Those issues led to dozens of altercations and other bad decisions over the years. It was the monastery, and more specifically Landren, who had been his savior. Without Landren, Brand's life had been speeding towards a life like those of the thugs he'd fought.

*   *   *

Ten years ago

Brand raced around a dimly lit corner, slipping on the cobblestone street as he struggled to maintain his speed. He could see his breath forming small clouds in the air as the night temperature dropped. The movement kept him warm in a way his tattered clothes couldn't in the cold of night. He listened as the shouting grew closer. He needed to get to his secret spot before the men caught up to him. All this trouble for such a small bracelet.

"Stop that thief!" he heard the shopkeeper yell to the sparse crowd from somewhere behind him.

It was late, and the number of people out shopping had dwindled. Only those who loved to squeeze out lower prices from desperate vendors still roamed the marketplace. They were unlikely to offer any help to someone chasing a boy through the streets.

He took the trinket out of his pocket and studied it as he ran. It was just one little bracelet. There were plenty of others he'd left behind that were bigger, with more shiny rocks on them. Sure, this one had the biggest shiny rock on it, but it only had the one.

Brand was kidding himself, he knew he'd be able to eat for weeks if he could trade this to the right person. He hadn't had a full meal in longer than he cared to think about. The hunger made him desperate enough to steal something a lot more expensive than his usual take. He tucked the bracelet back into his pocket and picked up his pace.

He'd finally accepted this was his lot in life, and so why not lean into it? What else did he have to live for? His anger got him in trouble everywhere he went, and he didn't have a skill to use for work. The best he could hope for is to one day join a gang and try not to get himself killed long enough to make a small living.

He was pretty good at that so far - not getting killed. Despite his smaller size, he was very good in a fight. People always underestimated him, and he was a lot faster than most people realized. He used that to his advantage.

But today, he was trying to avoid the fight. He needed to get to a very specific alley and then he'd be able to lose the men chasing him. Once that was done, he'd trade this ruby bracelet to someone for a nice, thick, stack of gold. Then, after getting the first good meal he'd had in months, he'd get out of this city and make his way to somewhere better.

Engulfed in his frantic thoughts, Brand collided headlong with a figure emerging from the shadows. The impact sent Brand tumbling to the ground. The cloaked figure looked down at him as he gathered himself. The man stood in the street, unfazed by the impact of a young boy slamming into him.

"My apologies," the man said. His voice was completely void of emotion, though he did reach a hand down to Brand to help him up.

"Watch where you're going, old man!" Brand spat at him as he slapped away the man's hand.

The stranger tilted his head as he looked down at Brand. A speck of emotion flashed across his face before the emotionless mask returned. It was unusual to see pity in someone's eyes. Anger or indifference were the most common emotions Brand saw when people regarded him. Not pity. Brand shook the unusual encounter off as he picked himself back up and kept running.

"There he is!" he heard the shopkeeper yell as Brand disappeared into a nearby alley. He turned to look at the far end of the alley, which came to an abrupt halt halfway down with a stone wall. Perfect.

He reached the stone wall at the end of the alley as the shopkeeper and two other men entered, breathing heavily. Brand's eyes went wide at the sight of weapons. That's something he hadn't expected. Maybe he'd stolen from the wrong person this time. The two people on either side of the shopkeeper had long daggers in their hands, and the shopkeeper was drawing a long scimitar from his waist.

"You've got nowhere left to run, boy," the shopkeeper said. "Hand over the bracelet."

Brand inched his way toward a small corner of the wall covered by a wooden board. In just a short moment, he'd be free of this mess and lose these goons for good.

"Sorry, I don't know what you're talking about," Brand said. "Wish I could stick around to help you out!"

He placed his hand on the board leaning up against the stone wall. Behind the board was a small hole, just big enough for him to squeeze through to the other side. He'd used the tiny portal to escape several situations just like this one in the past several weeks. All he needed to do was get through it before the men could run down the alley to get him. Brand threw aside the board and dove for the corner.

The hole was gone.

What! Brand thought with alarm. *No, I know this is the right alley. Where is my escape?*

His hands scrambled over the stones in the low light, searching for any sign of the hole in the wall he knew *had* to be there. After a moment, he heard snickering behind him. He turned to see the three men walking towards him, brandishing their weapons.

"What's wrong, boy?" the shopkeeper asked with a sinister smile.

"You look like you were expecting something different to be behind that board."

"What did you do?" Brand asked, anger and a mounting terror leaking into his voice.

"Oh, I didn't do anything," he said. "But one of the residents here found a small hole in his wall that some rats and other *vermin* kept using to get to the other side. So I loaned him some coin to get it fixed."

He stopped a few feet in front of Brand and pointed his sword. "Now give me back what you stole and I'll make sure all you get is a beating and a nice scar instead of killin' you outright."

Brand swallowed hard and reached into his pocket. This bracelet definitely wasn't worth his life, despite the amount of comfort he could buy with it. He'd have to move to a different part of town and try something different.

He patted one pocket, and then another. Brand's heart began to race. Somehow, the bracelet was missing.

"Come on now, boy," the shopkeeper said. "Hand it over!"

He was within a few steps of Brand now. There was no getting around him to safety.

"I…" Brand started. "I'm sorry, I don't have it! Honest!"

"Oh come on now, you really expect us to believe that?" the shopkeeper said.

"Really, I don't!" Brand said. "I mean, I did, but now I don't! It must have fallen out of my pocket as I was running!

"Fine, we'll do this the hard way," the shopkeeper said, stepping up to Brand. "Maybe I can rattle that head of yours around enough to get the memories flowin'."

The shopkeeper struck out with the hilt of his scimitar faster than Brand could dodge. The blow to the head sent Brand to the cobblestones, his head swimming.

"Please!" Brand tried to say, but a hard kick to the stomach sent all the air out of him and cut off his desperate plea. He doubled over in pain. He was used to fighting with boys his own age, not fully grown adults. Adults could hit much harder. The man picked Brand up by his collar and shook him.

"Remember anything yet? WHERE'S MY BRACELET?" the shopkeeper yelled into Brand's face.

"Please. I don't have it…" Brand whimpered. "I don't have it…"

The shopkeeper was seething. He threw Brand against the stone wall and Brand crumbled to the ground.

"Check the alley," the shopkeeper said, turning to his two companions. "He must have dumped it somewhere before we got here."

The two others turned to look around the few crates and trash heaps that populated the alley. Brand was catching his breath as the shopkeeper put his hand up to his head in frustration. His vision finally focused back in. He needed to escape, and he needed to do it now while they were distracted.

Brand took the opportunity and bolted. He had no other choice, he knew he was dead if he stayed. But he hadn't recovered as much as he thought. He made it about three steps past the shopkeeper before he felt the fire of something cutting across the flesh of his back. He stumbled face-first into the cobblestones and his own blood began to pool around him.

"Not so fast, you slaggin' little thief!" The shopkeeper picked Brand back up and threw him against one of the side walls of the alley. Brand's head slammed backward into the wall and he blacked out for a moment before coming to again. He couldn't see straight.

"That's it, I'm done with you, boy," the shopkeeper said as he raised the bloody scimitar for one final blow.

Brand knew this day was coming. It was only a matter of time when you were an orphan that nobody wanted. He thought he'd be able to last a little longer, but what was the point of existing if this was all it would come to in the end. Better for the end to come sooner than to live day after day in suffering.

Brand thought he believed that. Truly he did. Until the moment was here and he saw the flash of the scimitar above him. Now that it was happening, he wished he had a chance to do something better with his life. And he'd never get to find out if he could. Brand watched in slow motion, helpless to stop the blade as it began to drop.

"Excuse me." A shadowed figure stepped into the alleyway. "Might I ask what you intend to do with that boy?"

The blade stopped.

"Just keep walking, slaghead, and mind your business," the shopkeeper said, still holding his blade in the air.

"My name is Landren, not slaghead. And I believe murder is against the law, is it not?" the man said. He had an odd way of talking. The words he said were completely monotonous, void of any inflection.

"The boy stole something expensive from me," the shopkeeper replied. "This is his punishment."

"Oh, do you mean this trinket here," Landren said as he pulled out the stolen bracelet from his pocket and held it up.

"Where did you get that!" the shopkeeper demanded.

"I found it in the street," Landren said, stepping closer and tossing the bracelet to the shopkeeper. Brand could see that his face was completely impassive. "Now, as this seems to be a misunderstanding, perhaps you can let the boy go and we can all go on our way."

"I'll do what I want with the boy," the shopkeeper growled. "Get lost."

"I'm afraid I must insist you let the boy go," Landren said, stepping even closer.

The shopkeeper backhanded Brand, sending him sprawling back to the ground. He crawled backward until his back was against the stone wall at the end of the alley and watched the scene unfold. The shopkeeper and his two buddies faced Landren and began to walk towards him.

"Oh yeah, and what are you going to do about it?" the shopkeeper asked.

Landren set down his pack and rolled up his sleeves to his forearms. Brand watched as he settled into a peculiar stance that Brand had never seen before. His calm, almost unnaturally still posture seemed out of place opposite the aggressive stances of the three men circling him. Landren took a breath and stood his ground. Brand must have taken one too many blows to the head because he swore he saw little trails of steam begin to rise from Landren's body.

The three men lunged at Landren with their weapons, but he disarmed and knocked each of them unconscious with quick, precise blows. The whole fight was over in less than five seconds. The stolen bracelet dropped from the shopkeeper's hand and rolled to a stop to settle a few feet away from Brand. Before Brand could even register what he'd seen, Landren was already picking his pack up and strapping it to his back again.

Then, Landren's focus settled on Brand, and he began walking towards him, stopping a few feet away and crouching down to Brand's level. Landren studied him silently for a moment.

Brand knew exactly what Landren was seeing. A starving, angry young boy with a life of misery ahead of him. Worthless. And then something surprising happened.

"Why are you so angry?" Landren asked.

"What?" Brand said, caught off guard by the sudden question. Nobody ever stopped to actually talk to him. There was something odd about this man.

"I can see the deep pools of anger in your eyes," Landren said.

"Well, why wouldn't I be angry?" Brand snapped, snatching up the bracelet that was lying nearby. "My life is just a series of beatings and stealing things like this to live."

Landren paused for a moment in thought. He stared deep into Brand's eyes, and Brand met his gaze, refusing to look away in shame. Finally, Landren seemed to come to a decision.

"I can offer you a different way of life," Landren said, standing up. "But if you accept, you leave the bracelet behind."

"This bracelet will keep me fed for weeks!" Brand said. "What could you possibly offer me that's better than that?"

"Purpose."

A piece of Brand's soul flickered back to life as soon as he heard the word. *Purpose.* That was something that he never thought he'd have. Until Landren said it, Brand didn't realize that he craved it more than anything in the world. He dropped the bracelet.

Landren held out a hand to help Brand back to his feet.

"Come with me and I'll teach you the way of the Open Path."

* * *

Present day

They'd decided to take things a little slower that morning. They were actually pretty close to Midral at this point. There was just one more night to spend on the road. After a late breakfast, they packed up their bags and started back out on the road to their destination.

The sky was cloudy and the temperature had continued to drop, the weather matching Brand's current mood perfectly. But despite the poor weather, they pressed on. The mountains of Midral were beginning to rise in the distance. It was an impressive mountain range and reminded Brand of his time in the higher altitudes back home. He'd never traveled this far north before. He was surprised how much colder it was this time of year compared to the mountains he'd grown up in.

They fell into the familiar cadence of travel, though Brand was a little less talkative today. Eventually, the conversation died down and they traveled in silence for a time, leaving Brand alone with his troubled thoughts. As much as he tried, he still was unable to repeat the feat of accessing his Chi without clearing the path. He'd even tried forcing it at one point until it began causing him some significant pain and he decided that was probably a bad idea.

He was still struggling to clear his Path through meditation, which meant he couldn't access his Chi the normal way either. He'd come to the quick conclusion during the night that the poison must have had more of an effect than he'd originally thought it would. That had to be it.

I thought Astoro said I'd be able to shake off this poison, but I still can't access my Chi. Brand thought in frustration. *What I do isn't magic, but it must affect my ability to open the Path.*

Yes, that made the most sense. Otherwise, with his training, he should be able to open the Path without any issues. He was also concerned about the rage he felt when he'd accessed his Chi momentarily the previous night along a new Path. Feeling emotion was exactly the opposite of what should happen when accessing his Chi. That must also be the poison's fault. It was the only explanation.

"Well, I suppose this is as good a place as any. What do you think, Brand?" Astoro said, snapping Brand back into the present moment. The sky had dimmed and he could barely see that the sun was setting behind some gray clouds. Soon they'd be completely in the dark.

"Uh, yeah this seems fine," Brand said, still annoyed at his predicament. "Let's make camp. You said we should arrive tomorrow?"

"Yeah, I think so. We'll have to get an earlier start tomorrow than we did this morning," Astoro said, and then quickly added, "As long as you're up for it, of course. Don't want to push you too hard after last night."

"No, that will be fine," Brand said, dumping the contents of his pack on the ground. "I feel like I've already slowed us down too much between getting beaten half to death last night and getting stabbed half to death a week ago."

"Well, you can plant a seed when Spring's in sight, but it will only grow when the weather is right," Astoro said, starting to unpack his bedroll.

"What?" Brand said, looking at Astoro in total confusion.

"Oh sorry," Astoro said, looking at Brand with a sheepish smile and scratching the back of his head. "Guess I'm a little homesick. It means things happen when they're supposed to happen. No use worrying about it."

"Yeah…" Brand said. He knew Astoro meant well, but he didn't need comforting words at the moment. He needed to figure out how to access his Chi so he could stop being so helpless. "Well, I hope the weather is right for us tomorrow."

"Me too, Brand," Astoro said. "Me too."

* * *

Brand and Astoro made their way down the increasingly populated road toward the gates of the massive dwarven city. They learned from some other travelers that there was a festival happening for the next few days. Many people were traveling to the city to set up stalls to sell things or join in on the general festivities.

"Do you think you'll stick around for the festival?" Astoro asked Brand as they walked.

"No," Brand replied. "I'm looking forward to meeting up with Pathwarden Landren and figuring out why he summoned me. How about you?"

"I'm not sure," Astoro replied. "I think I'd like to see it, but if you're not planning on going, I don't feel like going alone."

Much of the idle conversation was about the Shaping Trial itself. The fact that it was the Phoenix's apprentice who was participating in the Shaping Trial was creating quite a stir in the crowds. Brand and Astoro didn't know who the Phoenix was, but based on the chatter, he must be some local celebrity. They heard a few people call him Niradim's chosen Disciple, but others said he'd turned his back on Niradim and that's why it was a colder winter than normal.

Either way, Brand and Astoro picked up on the fact that this Phoenix person was the reason for the crowded roads. Normally, Shaping Trials weren't this popular, despite the Festival of Fire celebration that happened at the end of the Trial.

"I wish Ronan was here," Astoro said. "He always talked about how important this Trial was for his faith. Apparently passing a Shaping Trial was rare, and he was immensely proud of being the only human to ever do so."

"I'm sure he would have loved to share this with you," Brand said. "And even more so with all the excitement about this Phoenix person."

As Brand and Astoro approached the massive gates, the air buzzed with excitement. Colorful banners depicting ancient dwarven heroes adorned the city walls, setting a festive mood. The mouthwatering aroma of roasting meats wafted from the city, and Brand could hear the sounds of hundreds of people on the other side of the gates. It was even larger than he'd imagined. After a long wait, Brand and Astoro found themselves at the front of the line speaking with the guards.

"Hello, please state your business," the guard said.

"Hi, we're here to visit with a dwarf named Ginmar," Astoro said. "Do you happen to know anyone by that name? He would be a follower of Niradim."

"Aye, he certainly is!" The guard chuckled. "Sorry friend, but Ginmar won't be available any time before the end of the Festival of Fire. He's in charge of the city guard and security has been heightened due to some recent criminal activity."

"I see," Astoro replied. "Well, thank you, I'll try to contact him after the Festival."

"Please enjoy the Festival, but stay out of trouble," the guard warned. "As I said, many of the guards are on edge, and rules will be stricter this year with the increased number of people."

"Understood," Brand said. "By the way, aside from my friend here, have there been any other florians who have entered the city in the past few days?"

"We've had a handful show up in the past few weeks for the festival," the guard said. "But I wouldn't be able to pick a specific one out if you're looking for a friend."

"Ah, ok," Brand said. "Thank you."

"Have a nice day," the guard said as Brand and Astoro entered the city of Midral.

"You think the guy that poisoned you might be here?" Astoro asked.

"I don't know," Brand said. "I just have a bad feeling."

"Well, it sounds like finding Ginmar to deliver Ronan's necklace isn't going to happen for the next few days," Astoro said. "How about we focus on finding your old warden?"

Brand nodded. "Pathwarden Landren didn't tell me much in his message. Just to meet him in Midral, and there was an inn he mentioned - The Fire and Ale."

Asking around, directions to The Fire and Ale took them to a part of the city that was more run down than what they'd seen so far. The location seemed like an odd choice, but things had been going so strangely ever since he left the mountain. He wasn't about to start questioning things now.

Brand and Astoro passed several patrols of guards who were on high alert. There was a strange energy in the air, and everyone seemed to be on a razor's edge. It was as if everyone was looking over their shoulder and expecting something bad to happen at any moment.

After some time, they reached a dilapidated building with a crooked, aging sign out front showing a mug of ale that looked like it was on fire. And if there was nothing good to say about the outside of the building, the inside was somehow even worse. A musty odor mixed with stale ale assaulted their senses, while the dim light barely revealed the dirt and grime that seemed to cover every surface. The inn's patrons, only two of them at the moment, sat in opposite corners of the room, sipping from dirty mugs. Brand was astonished that this was the place he was instructed to go. Still, his warden had been clear about the name of the Inn, so he proceeded to the bar as Astoro followed him and kept his eyes on the other patrons.

"Umm, hello sir," Brand said, addressing the crusty barkeeper. "I'm looking for someone and I was hoping you could help."

"What'll ya have?" the barkeeper said without turning around.

"Oh, no, sorry I don't drink," Brand said. "I'm trying to find someone and he told me to meet him…"

"If you're not drinking, then get out," the barkeeper said, cutting him off. "Don't need nobody hanging around here without payin'."

"I'm not here to drink," Brand said. His fists clenched at his sides. "I'm looking for someone."

"What, you hard of hearin'? I said get out if you're not spending any coin." The barkeeper turned around and was holding a knife, not exactly towards Brand, but not exactly away from him either. Brand locked eyes with him, anger beginning to boil to the surface.

"Apologies my good man!" Astoro said, interjecting himself between Brand and the barkeeper. "Yes, he is hard of hearing, and a couple seeds short of a good crop if you catch my drift. We'll take some of your, uh, finest ale if you don't mind." He dropped a couple coins on the counter, which the barkeeper swiftly snatched up. He tucked them into his pocket before grabbing a couple mugs to fill up with some kind of dark thick liquid.

"A couple seeds short of a good crop?" Brand whispered to Astoro.

"Yeah, I just made that up. Sounded pretty good though right?" Astoro whispered back with a wink.

The barkeeper returned and dropped the two mugs in front of them. As he was turning away, Astoro slapped a couple more coins on the counter, keeping the barkeeper's attention.

"You know, my buddy here was looking for a friend of his. We were hoping you might be able to help us out…" Astoro said, sliding two coins forward. The barkeeper reached for them, but Astoro slid them back and raised one of his eyebrows at the greedy dwarf.

The barkeeper looked up from the coins. "What'd you say his name was?"

Astoro looked at Brand, who took his cue to speak.

"His name is Landren," Brand said. "He sent me a message and mentioned this place. Do you know him?"

"I might, or I might not," the barkeeper said with a shrug and a wry smile, eyeing the coins in Astoro's hand. "Memory's a little fuzzy and it's hard to remember every person who might've stopped by."

"Listen, if you're not going to…" Brand started, but Astoro cut him off before he could finish the threat.

Astoro slapped a couple more coins on the counter. "Name ringing a bell now?"

The barkeeper reached for the coins, and Astoro made to move them away, but the barkeeper locked eyes with him. Astoro sighed and relinquished the coins. The barkeeper pocketed the bribe and walked toward the back of the bar where a few keys were hanging. He grabbed one and returned to the two travelers.

"Room's paid for till the end of the Festival of Fire," the barkeeper said, nodding toward the stairs at the far end of the room. "Was startin' to think nobody'd show up."

"What? No, we don't want a room. We're looking for..." Brand started again.

"Thanks," Astoro said, cutting him off despite the confusion on Brand's face. He got up and motioned Brand to follow him. "We'll uh, take these drinks to go."

"Bring those mugs back when you're done!" the barkeeper called after them.

Astoro gave him a thumbs up as he pulled Brand away from the bar. After climbing a very suspect set of stairs, they made their way down the hall and found their room.

"What just happened down there?" Brand said as Astoro unlocked the door.

"Sometimes you have to speak their language," Astoro said. "Landren probably paid for this room to be held until you got into town."

"Wow," Brand said, taking a breath and running his hand through his hair. "Well thank you, I didn't pick up on any of that."

"No worries, I doubt you've had much experience with that kind of interaction up in the mountains," Astoro said, laughing.

"No, I suppose not," Brand said with a smile.

The room they stepped into, if you could call it that, was barely enough space for the cot that was in there and a spare chair in the corner. It had a moldy smell and looked like it had never seen a wash rag. Aside from the two furnishings, the room was completely empty. It was clear that despite having paid for the room, Landren certainly wasn't staying here.

"What do you suppose Landren wanted you to do with this room? Do you think he means for you to stay here?" Astoro asked.

"I don't know. This whole thing is very strange to me," Brand said as he sat down on the chair against the far wall. "I wish he'd given clearer direcTIONS!" The chair Brand sat on cracked beneath his weight and he fell to the floor. Astoro doubled over in laughter as Brand rubbed his sore backside.

"Brand, my friend," Astoro said between laughs. "You really are having a rough time of it lately!"

"Ugh, you can say that again," Brand said, embarrassed and a little angry as he got to his feet. He kicked the remains of the chair against the wall. "Stupid chair in this stupid inn. What is Landren getting at, having me come here!"

"Hey Brand," Astoro said, suddenly serious. "That paper on the ground, is that something you dropped? It wasn't there before."

Brand looked down and sure enough, there was a sealed envelope sticking out under one of the pieces of wood. He reached down to uncover the letter and found out that the letter wasn't under the wood, it was sticking out of the wood! One of the legs of the chair had been hollowed out. Brand could see the joint had been weakened so that it would fall apart as soon as someone sat in it.

"This is Landren's handwriting!" Brand said, looking at the front of the letter.

"Well at least that explains the room," Astoro said. "What does it say?"

Brand opened and began to read the letter. Yes, this was definitely from his warden and it gave a time and location for where to meet him in the next few days. After scanning the letter a second time to make sure he hadn't missed anything, Brand smiled.

"What is it, Brand?" Astoro asked.

Brand looked up, still grinning.

"Looks like we'll be attending the Festival after all."

13

Ronan

It was the morning of the Shaping Trial and Ronan had decided to treat his apprentice to a large breakfast. This would be her last meal until she finished her Trial in three days, so he took her to her favorite spot in the Earth Sector. A cozy little tavern called Heart of the Forge. She had already downed two sausages, eggs, and some bread. Now she was shoveling the last few bites of a meat pie into her mouth before they had to head to the Soul Forge.

"Now listen, Brin, many people believe the Shaping Trial is simply a matter of skill - that as long as you can forge a nice piece of metal you'll be fine," Ronan began as Brin was finishing up her meal. "But it's more than that. There's a reason so many people get to this point only to fail the Trial."

"Nice pep talk," Brin said with her mouth full. "I'm really feeling confident about my chances now."

"Sorry," Ronan said with a chuckle. "I'm telling you this because I don't want you going in there without knowing what you're getting yourself into. The Trial is not about your skill as a blacksmith, it's about your relationship with… your god."

Ronan still had trouble talking about Niradim and anything regarding his faith. But he knew he couldn't completely avoid the topic and prepare Brin properly. As she finished the last bite, they got up to make the short walk over to the Cathedral of Niradim. As they walked, he explained some more about what to expect from her Trial.

"Each person experiences something different at the Soul Forge during their Shaping Trial. What you experience is for you and you alone," Ronan explained. "Almost everyone who enters the Soul Forge for their Trial is skilled enough at forging to be there. Where people fail is during the Vision."

"The Vision?" Brin asked, furrowing her brows. "I've never heard of a Vision during the Trial."

"It's not something that you are supposed to have time to prepare for," Ronan said. "Some masters don't tell their Acolytes until just before they enter their Trial. Others believe Acolytes shouldn't know at all until it happens. But I'll do for you what Ginmar did for me - I don't want you to be caught off guard completely."

"What should I expect?" Brin asked.

They stopped in front of the doors to the Cathedral of Niradim. Behind those doors was the Soul Forge, where Brin would spend the next three days creating an offering to Niradim. She would forge the armor she'd designed and if Niradim imbued it with his Flame at the end of the Trial, she would pass. If he didn't, she would fail.

"Everyone sees something different for their Vision," Ronan said, turning to face her. "But basically, it's a test of your faith. There's no way to know what your Vision will be, so just trust your instincts when it happens."

Ronan put his hands on her shoulders and looked into her eyes. "I believe in you."

She looked back into his eyes for a long moment, eyes watering. He knew these were some of the last moments he'd spend with her before he left after her Trial was complete. He wished he could stay here with her, but he knew as soon as the Trial was over, they would be on two separate paths. She'd be even more dedicated to Niradim, and Ronan still wanted nothing to do with him.

"Thank you, Ronan," Brin said, finally breaking eye contact and stepping up to the doors. She paused, and then looked back at Ronan, "What, um… What did you see in your Vision?"

"Like I said, Brin," Ronan said, looking away. "Your Vision is meant for you and you alone."

Brin nodded and turned back to the doors. She wiped her eyes and took a deep breath before pushing her way through. As the doors shut behind her, Ronan turned and took his post. He would guard those doors for the next three days. Brin's Shaping Trial had begun.

* * *

Three years ago

"I've done everything I can to prepare you, Ronan," Ginmar said. "You're as ready as you're going to be for the Trial ahead. Remember the Visions - they will test your faith in Niradim. Believe in him, and you will pass."

"Thank you, Master Ginmar," Ronan said. "I'll be ready for whatever waits for me in there. Besides, if I don't pass this time, I can always try again when I'm ready."

"Ronan…" Ginmar said, frowning. "This will be your only attempt at the Trial."

"Wait, what?" Ronan asked, eyes going wide. "No, I've seen others attempt the Shaping Trial several times. What do you mean this will be my only attempt?"

"The decision came from the elders this morning." Ginmar looked down, ashamed. "It was tough enough to get them to agree to allow a non-dwarf to take the Trial. You are the first human ever to be able to channel Niradim's magic, so they were forced to allow you at least one chance." He looked back up into Ronan's eyes. "But Ronan, if you fail today, they won't let you take it again."

Ronan took a moment to process Ginmar's words. He knew that his membership as an Acolyte of Niradim didn't sit well with all the dwarves. Niradim was, after all, the dwarven god, and most dwarves weren't even blessed with being able to channel his magic. Ronan had been the first human to do so, though, among those who could channel Niradim's magic, he was the weakest.

"I'm ready, Master Ginmar," Ronan said. "I won't let you, or Niradim, down today."

"I know you won't, son," Ginmar replied. "Niradim's blessings, and good luck."

Ginmar stepped aside and let Ronan approach the doors to the Cathedral. Ronan had been in the Cathedral of Niradim countless times for worship, but this time would be different. He would be working the Soul Forge for the first time. Only full Disciples of Niradim or Acolytes during their Trial were allowed use of the Soul Forge. It was the only forge in existence with the ability to imbue magic into metal that was forged with its flames. The very Flame of Niradim resided in and powered the Soul Forge. It was a sacred ritual, and as the heavy doors closed behind him, he instantly knew that he was less prepared than he thought he'd be at this moment.

Instantly, the room was cloaked in darkness. A moment ago, the pews were before him on the left and right of the aisle that would have taken him straight to the Soul Forge. But now, there was nothing. He tried using his magic to create light, but he wasn't able to channel any magic at all, even the small amount he normally could. Panic began to set in.

Was this some kind of cruel joke? Did Niradim disapprove of the elders' decision to let Ronan attempt the Trial?

No, thought Ronan *I know I'm supposed to be here. My relationship with Niradim is strong, and he will help me complete my Trial.*

Ronan took a deep breath and centered himself. Keeping his feet planted forward so he didn't get turned around, he calmly looked to the left, right, and behind him. He still couldn't pierce the darkness. Finally, he looked up. There, far in the distance high in front of him, he could barely make out a tiny, flickering, pinprick of light.

He took a cautious step forward, and his foot kicked something solid. Reaching out with his hands, he couldn't feel anything, so he tried with his foot again and figured out it was a step. As he placed his foot on the first step, it began to glow with a soft flickering light that continued upward. Before Ronan was the longest set of stairs he'd ever seen. The stairs continued straight towards the light, and so Ronan began to climb.

He climbed for hours. His legs ached more than they ever had before. With each agonizing step, Ronan's muscles screamed in protest, his heart thundering in his chest like a war drum. But still, he climbed. Doubts whispered in his mind, battling with his determined spirit that refused to yield. After a while, the light in the distance began to take shape. He was climbing towards the Soul Forge where he'd finally be able to begin crafting his masterpiece. And a masterpiece, it would be.

Ronan had decided to forge two magical items for his Trial, a feat that had never been done before. The first would be a sword, to honor his father and the sacrifices he made so Ronan could have a better life. The second would be a magnificent shield, to honor Master Ginmar who had become a second father to him.

And to bring it all together, the shield would be a sheath for the sword. The two would combine as one piece, just like he was a combination of his father, Kilian, and his master, Ginmar. He was a protector of Niradim and his people, and the sword and shield would make him stand out as one of Niradim's elite. He would prove to them by the skill of his craft that he belonged. And so he continued to climb, determined to complete his Trial.

Finally, he reached the top of the stairs, and the full beauty and might of the Soul Forge towered before him. He stopped for a moment, breath caught in his lungs at the majesty of it. He had seen the Soul Forge up close before, even witnessed other dwarves crafting there, but this was different. It was covered in ornate sigils and symbols of Niradim and each detail seemed to stand out and glow with brilliant power. He could feel the intense heat radiating from the Flame of Niradim deep within the heart of the Soul Forge.

He took a step towards the forge and the Flame of Niradim shot out towards him. Ronan put up his hands to guard against the heat. About ten feet in front of him, the flame split and created a towering wall, blocking his path to the Soul Forge. The massive wall of fire encompassed his whole field of view, and the heat was nearly unbearable. Each breath he took felt like it was searing the inside of his lungs. He could see the light of the flames through his closed eyelids as if they were wide open.

Ronan fell to one knee before the blazing wall of Niradim's Flame. He somehow knew that if he were to take a step back onto the stairs he had just climbed, the Trial would end and his pain would subside immediately. The logical part of his brain screamed for him to just take that one step backward and make it stop. It took all of his willpower just to stay put.

I've come too far to back down now! Ronan screamed inside his mind. *I will prove that I belong!*

Slowly, Ronan stood, arms trying to block the worst of the heat from his face. It felt like his skin was already blistering, and the sweat pouring off his body was evaporating as soon as it touched the searing air around him. He took one step forward.

Pain

Ronan screamed as the heat only intensified. He would push forward. He had to push forward.

Step

The clothes on his body erupted in white-hot flames. He was here to prove that he belonged. He would be accepted by his people, or he would die.

Step

"I. WILL. NOT. STOP!" Ronan yelled. He reached the perimeter of the wall of holy fire and the flames consumed him.

Pain

Step

Darkness

Ronan opened his eyes a moment later, lying prostrate on the ground before the Soul Forge. The Flame of Niradim was back in the heart of the forge, and all the pain from walking through the flames was completely gone. His exhaustion remained, but at least the exhaustion was something he was prepared and trained for. All the tools and materials he needed for his crafting were before him. It was time to get to work.

* * *

Working at the Soul Forge was an absolute dream. He forgot his exhaustion as he began crafting and getting into the familiar rhythm of forging. The heat from the forge was a living thing, wrapping around him as he worked. This process is what brought him joy. Creating something from base materials and forging them into something powerful and useful was what he was meant to do, and he excelled at it.

He smiled as his masterpiece slowly began to take shape. The sword and shield were the perfect symbol of what he wanted to be for Niradim and his people. It was also something that stood out and would make people take notice of him. He couldn't afford to forge each item separately or he'd run out of time, so he danced between the two - working on one while heating the metal of the other. It was nearly an impossible task, and he knew he had already lost time from his climb.

He moved with practiced precision, the metal singing under his hammer. Sparks flew like shooting stars born from the anvil. Slowly, but surely, the pieces came together. Sweat coated every inch of him, and his body screamed at him for the marathon he was putting it through without proper nourishment. Even so, Ronan moved with a grace that belied his exhaustion, each hammer strike was a melody in the symphony of creation. He was weak from effort and hunger, but at last, it was complete. The sword and shield lay in front of him. His masterpiece.

Slowly, and with great care, he picked up the piece and attached the shield to his left forearm. He reached his right hand to the part of the shield where the sword handle protruded and drew the sword in a swift motion. Instantly, his environment changed.

The sounds of battle raged around Ronan and he found himself in a small clearing surrounded by fog. He could see figures in the fog clashing with weapons drawn and smelled the fresh blood being spilled around him. His body was still sluggish, and his mind was reeling with confusion. Before he could completely get his bearings, two shadowy figures stepped out of the fog towards Ronan.

The first figure was shorter than Ronan, holding an identical copy of Ronan's shield in one hand, and a war hammer in the other. The second figure was Ronan's height, holding an identical copy of Ronan's sword in his right hand. But Ronan noticed that their copies of his sword and shield glowed with Niradim's power, where his were dull. As they stepped closer, their features became clearer. Standing before him were Master Ginmar, and his father Kilian.

"What's going on?" Ronan asked the pair, taking a step back on sluggish, heavy legs. "How are you both here?"

"We're here to test your faith," Master Ginmar said.

"You will have to strike us down to complete your Trial and be accepted by Niradim." Kilian continued. "Now, defend yourself!"

They both rushed him, weapons swinging. Ronan was at a great disadvantage, exhausted from his trial and outnumbered, it was all he could do to keep from being slaughtered. He backed away from them and found that the dense fog moved with them. No matter which way he retreated, the fog would retreat exactly with his steps, always leaving a clearing around him and his assailants.

Ronan was battered and bleeding. The logical part of his brain tried to tell him this must be one of the visions of his trial, but it all seemed so real! The pain, exhaustion, and fear were all real to him as he defended himself against his two father figures.

He slashed at Ginmar with his sword, but Ginmar brought his shield, *Ronan's* shield, up and blocked the blow. Upon impact with the glowing shield, Ronan's sword shattered in his hand. Before he could process what was happening, Kilian swung his copy of Ronan's sword at him. Ronan put up his own shield to block the blow, but it exploded into pieces on contact with the glowing blade.

Ronan's masterpiece was destroyed.

"Your offerings are not accepted," Master Ginmar said.

"You have failed your Trial," Kilian finished.

"No!" Yelled Ronan. "This can't be it! These were the greatest items that have ever been forged in a Shaping Trial. I've earned the right to become a Disciple!"

"It's not about earning your way into Niradim's grace on your own skill," Master Ginmar said. "That's not how faith works."

"You didn't forge these great works for Niradim," Kilian said. "You forged them out of pride and pettiness. You just wanted to show you were better than the others. It had nothing to do with your faith."

The words struck Ronan like a hammer. They were right. He had only been focused on proving his worth to the others. This had never been about his faith, but his pride. He had failed his Trial.

As the realization dawned on him, the two figures before him swirled into mist and joined the fog around him. The fog closed in on him, obscuring his view for a moment, and then faded, leaving him kneeling before the dormant Soul Forge empty-handed.

"I've… failed," Ronan said. "I'm sorry, Niradim. My pride got in the way of the purpose of the Trial. But if you'll let me, I want to forge one last item to remind me of your faith when my pride takes over."

In response to his request, the forge blazed back to life in front of him. He took some simple silver and forged a necklace of a sword sheathed into an anvil and placed it around his neck when it was complete.

"Thank you, Niradim," Ronan said. "May this always remind me to put faith in front of pride. I don't need to prove myself to others, only to you."

As he said those words, the Flame of Niradim surged out of the Soul Forge once again and engulfed Ronan. But this time, there was no pain. The Flame poured itself into the simple necklace he had forged and began to glow.

CONGRATULATIONS, MY CHILD. YOU HAVE PASSED YOUR TRIAL.

The flame receded, revealing a glowing sword and shield at Ronan's feet, perfectly intact and imbued with Niradim's Flame. Ronan had created not one, not two, but three magical items to complete his Trial. Ronan dropped to his knees, held his necklace in his hand, and wept.

14

Kyros

Finally, it's time to get this over with, Kyros thought. *The Festival of Fire is set to begin.*

Kyros learned that every time someone completed their Trial, a huge festival was held for the sucker who decided to join Niradim's cult. He didn't know whose turn it was this year, and he didn't care, but he wished he could thank them for providing the best cover for his infiltration.

He sat in the same place he did a couple weeks ago when he arrived to survey the gate, but this time the Court of Fire was teeming with activity. The air was alive with the rich aromas of sizzling meats and sweet pastries from the vendors. Their stalls were a vibrant tapestry of colors with toy swords glinting in the sunlight and games echoing with the laughter of children. He leaned back, the chair creaking under his weight. Pulling his hat lower, a flicker of amethyst sparked in his eyes as he felt the familiar switch into Noct's aerial view.

He directed Noct on a circular flyover and could see his people taking their places among the crowd. Even though he knew what he was looking for, it was still difficult to pick out his men among the crowds. Continuing his flight, it was easy to tell that security had been ramped up for this event. Good. That would only play in his favor tonight. He took another moment to fly Noct to the west of the city, over the forest. After a moment, he found what he was looking for. The herd of giants he'd been luring here by using his ring would arrive soon to wreak havoc on the city. Perfect. It was nearing sundown, and that meant it was about time to get this party started.

He blinked and was back in his chair. He stood up, pulled his cloak closer around him, and strode out to the middle of the court. As he did, the evening air began to cool and he felt his left hand go numb. He could see the people around him pull their own cloaks tighter as the cold front descended on them. A light snow began to fall as he neared the center of the court and the numbing sensation moved up his arm to the elbow. The guards began to stir, sensing something was wrong. It was time.

With his left hand now a cold, numb appendage, Kyros clasped it around his staff, a surge of icy energy coursing through him. The temperature plummeted around him, frost spiraling from the staff as he focused on amplifying the ring's power. A biting cold swept through the court, frost creeping like a living entity over the buildings and cobblestones. People gasped, their breaths turning to mist, as the sudden freeze nipped at exposed skin. Sharp winds whipped up vendor stalls and sent their wares scattering across the stone. Panic was beginning to set in.

The light flurry that had begun to drop in the area thickened into snow, then hail, and then a wild blizzard centered on the Court of Fire all in mere moments. He heard what sounded like instructions being yelled from one group to another, being passed along around the court. Sure enough, he saw that the guards had spotted him and had begun to close the ground between them.

Kyros couldn't feel his left arm anymore, but he wasn't quite done yet. He had never wielded the ring like this - it was exhilarating and terrifying at the same time. He raised the staff, which had begun to emanate an ice-cold blue aura, mimicking the ring around his hand. Just as the first wave of guards raised their weapons to attack, he slammed the staff into the ground. Spires of ice shot out of the ground around him at all angles. The spires spread out like a shockwave throughout the court, rippling through the wild crowd. Sharp spikes of ice tore through some unlucky individuals, impaling and lifting them into the air. He'd transformed the Court of Fire into his own personal court of ice.

His people were positioned outside the radius of the ice spikes. As soon as the spikes were in place, they moved into the forest of icy stalagmites and used the chaos to their advantage, attacking guards left and right. Agent Viridian and a few other individuals sprinted to the center of the ring where Kyros knelt. They were wearing cloaks identical to his. His left arm hung useless at his side, and the numbness had spread up across his shoulders and through the left side of his chest. The enormous amount of energy he'd expended combined with the numbness made his breathing labored, but he struggled to his feet. This was only phase one of the plan - he still needed to get inside.

The raging blizzard created limited visibility, so he used the opportunity to begin phase two. He shed his cloak, revealing white robes that billowed around him, accented with crimson that hinted at his rank and power. After handing his old cloak to Viridian, he whispered an incantation and his features shifted. His hair turned a fiery red, and his robes tore, revealing fabricated wounds that seeped with blood. The crystal staff morphed into a bloody sword that he dragged behind himself.

Viridian and the other cloaked figures around him took up some staves of ice made to look like his crystalline staff. Each individual ran in a random direction to cause confusion among the guards. They would start to see the wielder of the Black Frost Ring all over the battlefield. They wouldn't know what was happening or how to coordinate an attack.

Kyros stumbled out of the ring of icy spikes in front of the Crucible Gate, doing his best to look like he'd been maimed in the battle. To their credit, even with all the chaos unfolding in front of them, four of the guards still stood in front of the gate. They were busy redirecting the growing number of panicked civilians to the sides of the gate instead of letting them inside. Other guards standing by were funneling them out of the Court of Fire to safety.

He'd hoped that the guards would allow civilians to flee to safety in the Earth Sector, but they must have been warned that he might try to infiltrate. Fortunately, he had decided to go ahead with his disguise to guarantee his entry. As soon as one of the guards spotted him, his eyes grew wide and he began shouting orders at two of the guards standing nearby.

"Make way! Make way!" the two guards shouted as they pushed through the crowd towards him.

"Master Ronan!" the first guard who reached him said. "Are you alright? What are you doing out here, we thought you were inside guarding the temple!"

"I'm on my way there now," Kyros said with Ronan's voice. "Let me through so I can make sure the temple is safe."

"Sir, it looks like you're injured, we need to get you to a medic…" The second guard said.

"There's no time!" Kyros yelled back. "I'm fine, I just need to get through and I can stitch myself up on the way."

"But…"

This wasn't working, he needed to try a different tactic. He was already exhausted from the magic he'd expended, but he'd have to use some more. Everything hinged on getting through that gate.

"People are dying, let me inside the gate and take me to the temple!"

Kyros laced this command with a spell. The Crystal on his forehead flashed underneath his disguise, but neither guard noticed amid the chaos raging around them.

The guard's eyes went dull for a split second, and then he turned to the guard next to him. "He's right, we need to get Ronan inside the gates, let's go"

The guards pulled Kyros back through the crowd to the gate. He flashed his counterfeit paperwork once he got there and the gate opened for him.

Kyros had successfully infiltrated the Earth Sector.

* * *

The first chance he had, he slit his escort's throat and hid the body in a nearby room. Kyros couldn't risk the guard coming out of the effects of his spell and turning on him - besides, he knew exactly where he was going thanks to Brin.

Disguising himself as Ronan meant that he could walk into the Cathedral, steal the Flame, and then stroll out. Everyone else would be distracted by the commotion in the Court of Fire. It would be simple, the only thing that could complicate things would be running into…

Wait, that guard was surprised that I wasn't guarding the temple. Kyros realized, putting a hand to his head. *Oh no. Ronan is guarding the temple. Of course, he is. That's just my luck.*

Now he was going to have to figure out how to get past that pesky human, and he definitely wasn't in any shape to keep using the ring. He couldn't use one of his arms at all. Curses, he should have kept that stupid guard alive as a hostage. He slowed down as he got closer to the temple and found a shady corner where he could see the massive doors to Niradim's holy place.

Sure enough, there was Ronan, standing vigil at the doors along with a slim, older dwarf in white and red robes. He didn't know much about Ronan, but he did remember the way Ronan reacted when Kyros almost killed Brin in their first encounter. He bet that Brin was the poor sucker undergoing the Trial and Ronan, as her master, was tasked with guarding her.

Kyros turned and leaned against the wall. What was he going to do now? He still had his staff and one of his arms. He could try controlling Ronan with a spell, but that trick didn't work on everyone, and Ronan would be on his guard as soon as he saw Kyros. He couldn't risk it. He'd have to just sit and wait.

Fortunately, he'd timed the heist to take place just after the Trial finished so the Cathedral would be empty. After a few moments, the doors burst open, and an exhausted female dwarf stumbled out into Ronan's arms. He could barely overhear their conversation.

"Ronan," she gasped. "I actually… did it…"

"I knew you could do it, Brin!" Ronan said, taking her into his embrace. Kyros could see that Ronan's face was beaming with pride. "Now let's get you some rest, you've earned it."

Brin had already passed out in his arms by the end of his sentence, so Kyros watched as Ronan gently picked her up and started carrying her away from the temple. Before he did, he turned to the slim dwarf next to him and said something Kyros couldn't hear, while pointing inside the church. The robed dwarf disappeared inside the temple for a moment and came back out holding a bundle of something in his arms. He then followed Ronan out of the area, away from the temple.

It was time for Kyros to make his move. Once they turned a corner, Kyros made his way quickly to the temple doors. They were heavy, and it took most of his remaining strength just to push the double doors open enough to slip through, but he made it.

He took a look around a room that he had seen once before, in the vision his Patron showed him when he first received the mission. The Soul Forge still radiated with a divine heat from the Trial, and the Flame of Niradim flickered at its heart. Fortunately, his ring not only kept him protected from extreme cold but also extreme heat. He stumbled up the aisle of the temple and made his way toward the holy Flame.

The door to the temple slammed shut behind him.

Kyros spun on his heels, bringing his staff up into a defensive position. A familiar human with red hair and white robes stood at the entrance, holding a short sword in one hand and an ornate shield in the other. Ronan.

"That's far enough, Kyros," Ronan said. "Drop the disguise and put down your weapons."

"Well look who it is." Kyros smiled, letting the illusionary disguise fade. "Ronan, was it? I appreciate you letting me borrow your face, but I have urgent business to attend to."

Kyros turned to make a run for the Soul Forge only to slide to a stop after a few steps. A snarl plastered his face as he looked up to see Master Ginmar standing in front of his target. Ginmar's mace was already beginning to crackle with holy energy and his shield was at the ready.

"It's over, Kyros," Ginmar said. "Listen to Ronan and drop your weapons."

He was stuck between them with no way out. There must be a back entrance he didn't know about for Ginmar to have been able to flank him while he was focused on Ronan. Normally, these two wouldn't pose a threat to him, but he was significantly drained from his theatrics in the Court of Fire. His left arm hung useless at his side and the numbness in his chest made it difficult for him to take full breaths. His staff's power was almost completely drained as well.

He couldn't afford to engage both of them at the same time, and this would be his only shot at stealing the Flame. He had to risk facing Ginmar. He muttered some words and touched the crystal on his forehead. The spiderweb of crystalline fractals spread over his body to form an arcane barrier.

Ronan and Ginmar used that moment to close the distance. Kyros spun and raised an ice wall between him and Ronan to cut the human off from the fight, causing the numbness in him to shoot down his left leg. Ronan slammed his fist against the ice, but he'd be stuck watching from the other side until they were able to melt it down. He tried to turn and face Ginmar, but the dwarf's glowing mace slammed into him with an explosion of magic. Kyros went sprawling across the ground, smashing through some wooden pews.

He struggled to his feet, his leg barely working and slightly dizzy. His arcane barrier flickered and barely stayed intact. It would fail completely with another hit like that. The ice wall had drained what magic remained in his staff, and any more usage of the ring would severely cripple him. He was exhausted and barely had any of his own magic to fall back on.

He needed to end this quickly. A plan formed in Kyros' mind, but he only had one shot. If it didn't work, he'd be completely at their mercy. He raised his staff and fired a dark blast of energy at Ginmar, but his shield deflected it as he closed in on Kyros again.

Ginmar swung his mace, but Kyros rolled out of the way, putting himself between Ginmar and the steps leading up to the Soul Forge. Before he could regain his footing, Ginmar swung with a backhand blow that Kyros was barely able to block. The force of the blow knocked the staff flying out of his hands.

Kyros was disarmed. He tried to scramble up the steps towards the Soul Forge where his staff lay, but he felt Ginmar's hands grab him by the cloak and pull him off the steps. Kyros slid across the ground until he slammed against his own ice wall about halfway down the cathedral. His arcane barrier shattered on impact. He was disarmed and defenseless. He could see Ronan on the other side, looking down at him smiling as he watched his master dominating the fight.

Well, that's about to change. Kyros thought as he returned the smile. Ronan immediately stiffened.

Kyros pushed himself into a sitting position with his back resting against the ice, facing Ginmar again. His breathing was so labored, that he could barely catch his breath. This was it, it had to be now or he was going to pass out.

"The ring, Kyros," Ginmar said, approaching. "Take it off, or I will have no choice but to finish you right here."

"Just finish him, Ginmar!" Ronan yelled from behind the ice.

"You'll deliver Niradim's justice yourself, huh?" Kyros replied, buying just a little more time. The numbness spread even further across his torso.

"I can't take any chances with you after the havoc you've wrought on the city," Ginmar said, holding out a hand. "The ring. Now."

"You know what?" Kyros said, gathering his remaining strength. "I think I'll hold onto it a little longer."

Kyros lunged forward and plunged the dagger of ice he'd formed into Ginmar's leg. As he did, he muttered a spell under his breath.

"Ginmar!" Ronan yelled, slamming his fists against the ice.

Ginmar shoved Kyros off of him and pulled the dagger out of his leg, tossing it aside. He swung his mace in a powerful arc for a finishing blow, but the mace swung through a cloud of mist where Kyros had been a moment before. Without the staff, his Mist Jump couldn't travel as far as before, but it was far enough.

He picked the staff up off the ground in front of the Soul Forge, just as he'd planned. He knew he was going to lose the staff in the fight with Ginmar, but he had to make sure it was in the right location. Pivoting himself between Ginmar and the Forge had given him the perfect opportunity to throw the staff into position when Ginmar disarmed him. He took the Crystalline Staff in his right hand and began to lower it into the Flame.

"No, stop!" Master Ginmar yelled as he limped down the aisle. As Kyros had hoped, the fresh leg wound slowed Ginmar enough for Kyros to accomplish his task. Ginmar's mace was beginning to crackle with divine energy as he approached. Kyros could see that some of the energy was also sealing up Ginmar's wound with each step.

"Sorry my friend, you're too late," Kyros said as he forced the staff into place. Even with the protection from his ring, Kyros could feel the heat from the essence of the dwarven god. The Staff radiated with holy brilliance as it drew the Flame of Niradim out of the Soul Forge and into itself. As it did, Kyros felt a surge of warmth through his body. The numbness that had crippled him faded.

"NO!" Ginmar screamed as he leapt in the air to bring his mace down on Kyros. As he did, Kyros spun and swung his staff around, knocking Ginmar back across the floor. Ginmar crashed into the same spot Kyros had been at Ginmar's mercy moments ago.

"Ginmar, get out of there!" Ronan screamed from behind the wall.

"Oh, now that was an unexpected but very welcome surprise," Kyros said, looking down and flexing his healed left hand. He looked up at Ginmar, who was getting back on his feet.

"Looks like your god is fighting for my team now, old man." Kyros gestured to his glowing staff, as he secured it to his back.

Ginmar's eyes flared with urgency and a hint of fear as he realized the staff was glowing with Niradim's energy. He looked down at his own mace, which had gone dull. The Soul Forge was empty.

"What have you done?" Ginmar whispered. "I can't access Niradim's magic."

"Some might say I've pulled the greatest heist in history," Kyros said. "Unfortunately, you won't be one of those people, as you won't be making it out of here alive."

"I'll never let you leave here with that," Ginmar said.

"Oh, I doubt you have much of a say in the matter," Kyros replied. "But I get it, you have to try. Come on then, let's make this quick, I do need to be on my way."

Ginmar advanced slowly this time, shield and mace up and ready. Kyros casually walked down the aisle towards Ginmar, as if he was out for a stroll on a nice day. The gem on his forehead flashed with amethyst light, as he raised his right hand. But Ginmar dodged out of the way as inky-black tendrils snatched at him from the ground.

"Ginmar!" Ronan yelled again.

"Ronan, go get backup!" Ginmar yelled

"I'm not leaving you!" Ronan yelled back.

As Ginmar gathered himself, three bolts of black energy shot from Kyros' hand toward him. Ginmar barely had time to get his shield up to block the blasts, but he managed to deflect them from hitting him directly. Even so, he was thrown backward into the wall of ice again. He slowly got back to his feet.

"Oh very good, old man, you've been paying attention! Now who said you can't teach an old dog new tricks?" Kyros said as he took the glowing staff in his hands again. "Now let's see what Niradim's magic can do..."

As he spoke, a ball of white fire coalesced in the air above the staff and he threw it at the dwarf. Ginmar raised his shield, but the force of the explosion sent Ginmar through the ice wall into Ronan as the holy flames melted through the dark ice. Ginmar and Ronan smashed through the gathering debris in the cathedral.

Ronan was leaning against a wall, bleeding heavily and screaming in pain. Kyros saw that a large stone had fallen and crushed one of his legs. He wasn't going anywhere. Ginmar, to his credit, struggled to his feet despite bleeding from a dozen different places.

"I'd love to stay and play some more, but…" Kyros' form burst into purple mist and he coalesced behind Ginmar

"I've really got to get going," he said into Ginmar's ear and plunged the dagger into his back.

Ginmar only had time to gasp as the dark ice spread across his body, creating a new effigy of ice in front of the Temple of Niradim.

"Ginmar!" Ronan yelled.

"And you," Kyros said, turning to Ronan, darkness filling his voice. "Sit tight and watch as everything you love crumbles."

Before he could reply, Ronan passed out from his injuries.

"Or not," Kyros said as he restored his illusionary disguise and took on Ronan's form once more. "Thanks again for the face."

15

Val'ran

"Are you sure he went this way? Maybe we could check to see if he went somewhere warmer."

"Shut up Bogg."

As they emerged from the dense thicket, the ancient trees gave way to the imposing silhouette of Midral. Now that they could see the dwarven city, she found herself wishing they were heading anywhere but there. Something strange was going on, and she knew that Zandro must be involved.

They were still a small distance to the west of the city when they began to feel the temperature plummet. Clouds began to gather over a portion of the city, and in a matter of moments, a blizzard formed. Val had never seen anything like it, she wouldn't have believed it if she hadn't witnessed it herself. As she watched, a flash of blue light emanated from beneath the storm and blue spires shot up from the ground in a shockwave.

"Val, did you see that? What is going on down there?"

"I don't know, Bogg, but whatever it is, I bet Zandro has something to do with it. Come on, let's move, and quickly!"

Fueled by adrenaline and vengeance, Val took off straight towards the front gates of the city. Bogg struggled but managed to keep relatively close. They were running too fast to talk, so she just focused on her goal. She would find Zandro, and she would kill him.

By the time they reached the gates, they were both breathing heavily. It had taken quite some time to get down to the front of the city, Now that they were closer, they could hear the screams coming from beyond the gates. It sounded like a battle was going on. The gates were barred from the other side and nobody answered when they yelled. Whoever had been on guard duty must have left the gates to deal with the bigger threat inside the city.

"We're not going to be able to get through the gates," Val said. "We'll have to find another way in."

"Can't you do your teleporty magic thing and get to the other side of the gate and open it?"

"No, Bogg, for the millionth time, I have to draw someone's blood to switch with them."

"Use my blood again, I got plenty."

"You're not on the other side of the gate!"

"Oh, right."

Sometimes Bogg could be so stupid, it was smart. But most other times, it was just the normal kind of stupid. She needed a second to think. Going through the gate wasn't going to be an option, and they couldn't wait and see if someone would come back. Zandro was up to something right now, and she needed to get in. They'd have to go over.

"Hey Bogg," Val said as she leapt in the air and grabbed a couple stones protruding from the side of the large gates. "Last one to the top of the wall buys dinner and drinks."

Bogg's eyes lit up. "Oh yeah, you're goin' down!" Bogg said, clumsily beginning to claw his way up the side.

Normally, climbing up the front gate of a city under siege would be a very good way to turn yourself into a pin cushion for arrows. But if the battle beyond the walls was serious enough to take all guards away from the gates, it would likely keep them away until they reached the top.

"Ok, listen, this isn't fair," Bogg said from below a few minutes later, still struggling to make his way up the side. "You got a head start, and plus I'm bigger than you!"

"Nobody likes a complainer, Bogg!" Val called back. She was already approaching the halfway point. "I think I'm going to order a nice big meal and several rounds of drinks. Maybe even dessert!"

Val's muscles burned as she hoisted herself up the front of the gate. The wind howled around her, carrying with it the biting chill of frost and the distant clamor of battle. She could smell the familiar scent of blood in the air.

"Bogg, seriously, you need to pick up the pace," Val called down to him. "I think the blizzard is getting worse!

"I'm going as fast as I can!" Bogg said. "You know what, why don't you just get to the other side and let me in? I'm tired!"

Just as she was going to tell Bogg that this particular idea was one of his rare good ones, a loud horn sounded from the tree line.

"Uh, Val?" Bogg said, pausing. "What was that?"

"Oh no," Val said, eyes focused on the line of trees that they had recently traversed.

Dire wolves broke through the tree line first. They began howling as they ran, working themselves up into a killing frenzy. Orcs followed shortly after, chasing after the large beasts who were heading straight for the city. Finally, Val saw the large figure of an ice giant smash through a few of the smaller trees into the clearing.

He was holding a large horn in one hand, and as soon as he was clear of the trees, he blew another long, loud note on the horn. To Val's horror, another horn joined him, and then another, and then another as more ice giants broke through the trees. Together, their horns blared a siren of impending doom far louder than the chaos she could hear inside the gates.

She had hoped running into giants on their way to Midral was a simple coincidence, but there was no way they would just happen to arrive at the same time the city was under attack from the inside. Some massive plan was at play here, and they needed to get to the other side of these gates.

"Bogg, you're not going to be able to wait for me at the bottom. Pick up the pace!" Val shouted.

She turned back to her climb. If she could make it to the top, she could throw a rope down to Bogg to help. The wolves didn't concern her. They wouldn't be able to climb up to get Bogg, but she could tell the orcs had bows on them. As soon as they got into range, Bogg would make an easy target. Fortunately, they still had a few minutes before they'd be close enough to try to start firing.

The dire wolves slammed into the gate below them, making Bogg lose his footing for a moment and slowing him down. Val barely registered it. All her focus was on climbing. Just a few more moments until she reached the top.

"Bogg, how's it going down there?" she yelled to him without looking down. The winds were beginning to pick up and the sky was quickly darkening as she neared the top of the wall.

"Not so great!" Bogg yelled back. He was only getting close to the halfway point and it was starting to snow. Whatever that storm was, it was getting closer. There was no way Bogg was going to make it to the top without some help.

"Hold on! I'm going to throw you a rope in just a second!" Val's hands reached the top of the gate and she hoisted herself to the top. She whipped out a rope and lowered it to Bogg. He would be too heavy for her to manage on her own, but fortunately for them both, she found a spot at the top of the gate to tie the rope off.

"Here it comes!" She dropped one end of the rope down to Bogg. It didn't reach.

"Ashes, Val, why don't you have a longer rope?!" Bogg yelled up at her.

"Sorry, I didn't realize I'd have to haul your slow rear end over a gate!" Val called back.

She looked up and saw the line of orcs slowing down and pulling out their bows.

"Hurry up, Bogg!" Val cried out.

"Almost there…" Bogg yelled. "Got it!"

Just as he grabbed the end of the rope, the orcs let their arrows loose. There was nothing Val could do. At least one of those arrows would find their target.

As she began to yell, the blizzard descended like a white curtain, its howling winds a deafening roar in her ears. Snowflakes that felt like needles stung her face, blurring her vision and turning the world into a shifting expanse of white shadow. She barely saw the arrows, blown off target by the wind, as they thudded into the gate about five feet to Bogg's left.

"Slag and ashes!" screamed Bogg as he almost lost his grip on the rope. "That was close!"

"They won't be able to hit you in this storm, Bogg, but it's only going to get worse!" Val yelled back through the storm. "Hurry up and climb!"

Bogg's pace increased now that he had a rope to climb. He might not be the nimblest of fighters, but he was definitely strong, and he would be able to pull himself up to the top in no time. She needed to go ahead and figure out what the climb down on the other side would look like. She could see there were ladders leading up to guard posts on either side of the gate. She would have to walk across the top towards one of those posts and then take the ladder down.

She started making her way across the top of the gate. Bogg only had a quarter of the climb left. It was time to get down into the city and find out what was going on. Zandro must have started this mess. She didn't know how the giants factored in, and she didn't care. She'd find Zandro and end this.

Another long horn blast snapped her out of her thoughts. This one was much closer, but since the blizzard had picked up, she couldn't see where it was coming from. She looked down and saw the dire wolves pulling back from the gate. When she looked up, several circular shadows appeared at the edge of her eyesight, growing larger. By the time she recognized them as boulders, she only had time to scream and dive away before they smashed through the gate Bogg was still climbing.

Several booms emanated from behind her, and she felt the shrapnel from the wooden gate rain over her as she hit the guard post hard and rolled to a stop. Dazed from the hard landing, she stumbled to her feet with a hand to her head and stumbled towards the gate. A pile of debris filled the area where the secured gate once stood. Bogg was gone.

* * *

No! Val screamed in her head.

The dire wolves, their fur matted with dust and blood, surged through the shattered remains of the gate, their howls mingling with the city's chaos. She knew the orcs and giants wouldn't be too far behind. As much as she wanted to go down and search for Bogg, it would be suicide to go down there now. She let her eyes linger for a moment, holding her breath for any signs that Bogg had survived, but she didn't see any movement.

She couldn't believe it. Bogg was gone. She'd finally opened herself up to trusting someone again and they were immediately taken away from her. She didn't know who was responsible for everything that was happening, but they would be added to her list. Bogg may have been annoying, but he was her only real friend. She didn't have time to properly mourn, so she brushed away the tears that threatened to blur her vision and focused on what needed to be done. She needed the distraction.

The wolves spread out and moved through the city, but she had a feeling the rest of the enemy force would make a beeline directly to whatever was happening in the courtyard. She had to get there first and warn whoever she could of what was coming. She rushed down the guard post to the street below and sprinted toward the center of the storm. Now that the expanding wall of the storm had passed, the visibility had improved and she was starting to be able to make out what she was running toward.

A spiral of clouds coalesced around a central courtyard in the city. Tall, dark stalagmites of ice protruded from the ground of the courtyard at differing angles. The effect created a forest of ice spears that made it difficult to see all the way to the other side of the courtyard. She could see figures adorned in white and red impaled at the top of some of the spires, and others fighting on the ground amongst the chaos. She needed to find someone in command, and fast.

Val sprinted towards a couple of guards who were surrounded by several attackers who were closing in. As they attacked the guards, she slung three throwing knives, picking off the attackers on the far side of the guards. One remained and spun with a confused look on his face. Val swung her blade and silenced the attacker before he could make a sound. She sheathed her father's scimitar and turned to the guards with urgency.

"I need to speak with someone who's in charge, immediately," Val said.

"Who are you?" One of the guards asked her.

"It doesn't matter," Val replied. "This city is in danger. More than what you all are dealing with in this area. I need to get word to your commanding officer, now!"

"Well, Master Ginmar..." The first guard started.

"No, I saw him head into the Earth Sector," the second guard interrupted. "Captain Landren is the ranking member out here right now."

"I'm sorry, did you say Landren?" Val asked.

"Yes," the guard replied. "He's the ranking officer right now."

"Where is he?" Val asked.

The second guard pointed across the courtyard and Val turned. She found herself staring at an unarmed man weaving through a large group of attackers all on his own. His movements were fluid and precise, and she swore she could see wisps of gold energy emanating from his body. Each strike sent its target flying with a flash of light. As he cleared his area, she saw him turn and start giving orders to some guards who were reporting in. He was exactly as she remembered him, except that his energy had been orange the last time she'd seen him.

"Thanks," she said and turned to run towards her old friend, but turned her head and yelled over her shoulder. "And get people somewhere safe. Giants are attacking the city!"

"Wait, what.." But she didn't hear the rest of the reply as she focused on getting to Captain Landren as fast as possible.

She had to dispatch a couple more enemies on her way across the courtyard, but she arrived at Landren's location quickly. He knocked another attacker back with a swift kick and whirled on her, prepared to deal another powerful blow. He stopped short as recognition flashed across his face.

"Burning Ashes…" Captain Landren said as a huge smile flashed across his face. "Val, I thought you were dead!"

"Yeah, I did too…" Val was cut off as he took her in a huge hug. She hesitantly hugged him back. Was this really the same man she'd traveled with? Over the weeks they'd spent together on their mission, she'd never once seen him even crack a smile, much less show so much emotion as to hug someone. "Uh, it's good to see you too, Landren. Are you, uh, feeling ok?"

"Never better! Well, you couldn't have picked a better time to show up," Landren said, gesturing to the battlefield. "We could use your help out here. Is that obnoxious oaf, Bogg with you?"

Images of Bogg on the gate as the boulders smashed through flashed through her mind and she had to shake them free before she was able to speak.

"He was…" Val started to say before getting choked up.

Landren's nod was heavy with unspoken sorrow as he placed a battle-worn hand on her shoulder, his grip firm yet comforting. "I'm sorry, Val. We'll talk later about what you've been through. Right now, we need to focus on defending the city, will you help?"

"That's actually what I came here to talk to you about," Val said, remembering the immediate threat. "You need to send any and all guards you can spare to the front of the city. A group of giants leading a band of orcs and dire wolves have destroyed the gates to the city and are on their way in. Some wolves are already prowling the streets, and the Orcs won't be far behind. It's only a matter of time before the giants join them."

"Slag and Ashes…" Landren swore. "Master Ginmar still hasn't returned from the Earth Sector, and we've got our hands full out here."

He turned to address a guard nearby. "Vorkin, you're the ranking guard while I move to secure the front of the city against an active threat. Focus on securing the courtyard and protecting the gates to the Earth Sector." Landren hesitated for a moment in thought and then continued. "Also, open up the Crucible Gate and start funneling civilians into the Protection Ward of the Earth Sector. Once that's done, send all non-essential fighters to the front gates."

"But sir, Ginmar gave us direct orders to keep the Crucible Gate sealed due to the threat to the Soul Forge," Vorkin protested.

"The situation has changed. Giants are attacking Midral," Landren said and Vorkin's eyes went wide. "I'll accept full responsibility later if Ginmar has a problem with it. Do you understand?"

"Yes, sir!" Vorkin said before turning to give orders to the guards around them.

Landren turned back to Val. "Can you help me hold off the giants while we wait for reinforcements?"

"Yes," Val said. "Besides, I have to pay them back for what they did to Bogg."

Captain Landren nodded. "Then lead the way."

16

Brand

Brand ducked under a sword and incapacitated the thug swinging it with two strikes. As he turned, he saw a flash of green light from behind an ice spire to his left. Astoro appeared from around the spire, shivering as he brushed off the snow and ice that had gathered on his clothes. Brand pulled his own cloak tighter to protect himself from the wind that ripped through the icy court.

"Well, that takes care of the three I found over there," Astoro yelled over the sounds of the storm and fighting. "How are you doing?"

"Two down over here," Brand replied, using his forearm to shield his face. The sky was still spilling snow and hail as they fought.

"By the way, this is not what I had in mind when I said I wanted to attend the festival," Astoro joked.

"Yeah, me neither," Brand said. "I wonder if Pathwarden Landren is also fighting somewhere in the courtyard."

They'd been fighting for several minutes in the aftermath of the initial attack. Brand was also trying to keep an eye out for his warden. Unfortunately, they hadn't been able to pin him down with their visibility limited by the storm and ice spires. Thankfully, he and

Astoro had been on the outskirts of the courtyard when the ripple of ice spikes radiated out from the center of the Court of Fire. Soon after, they found themselves surrounded by adversaries. Most of them focused on the city guards, but some of them attacked indiscriminately.

Two more enemies approached with weapons drawn and Brand struggled to settle into his normal stance. The emotions he normally kept under control were running wild and it was beginning to affect his focus. Excitement, anxiety, anger, everything raged inside him, mirroring the storm he was fighting through. It was all he could do to fend off the incoming attacks. Fortunately, his body remembered the appropriate movements of self-defense from years of training.

Astoro's eyes flashed a vibrant green and vines grew from his forearm to entangle one of the thugs. He pulled his arm back and stabbed the thug with a knife he'd been holding in the same hand. As Astoro was dealing with him, the other attacker closed the distance on Brand and was able to get a cut along Brand's arm. Brand's anger flared to the surface, drowning out the other emotions flowing within. A familiar fire burned in Brand and his Chi found the new Path again. Red energy streaked down Brand's arm and he screamed in rage as he swung at his assailant.

His punch connected with the man's chest with a sickening crunch and the man went flying backwards. He slammed into one of the ice spires and it toppled to the ground like a frozen tree, sending other people nearby jumping for cover.

"Brand, what in the blooming ashes was that?!" Astoro yelled as he removed his arm from the tangle of vines around the thug's body. He stepped towards Brand and stopped short. His face was a mixture of shock and concern. "Brand, your eyes…"

But Brand wasn't paying attention. The power felt amazing. It was stronger than he was used to with his normal Path. A lot stronger. The first time he'd accidentally stumbled into this new Path, it had been barely a splash of power. But ever since that night, a small part of him in the back of his mind wondered if the river ran deeper. This time, he was sure of it. Without having to focus on pushing his emotions out of the way, he was able to access a much stronger current of Chi.

He needed to hunt down more of these thugs and test its limits. But before he could locate his next victim, he saw a golden flash out of the corner of his eye that caught his attention. Two figures sprinted out of the icy forest towards the front of the city. The surprise of seeing the man who trained him shocked his system and the new Path snapped shut.

"Astoro, I found him!" Brand yelled.

"Wait, who?" Astoro replied.

"Pathwarden Landren!" Brand said. "Follow me!"

Brand took off in the direction his old warden was going, dodging between spires toward the edge of the courtyard. Landren had a big head start, but he could see his warden and the other figure moving with purpose toward the front of the city for some reason.

"Why are they heading away from the battle?" Astoro said, catching up to Brand as he exited the courtyard.

"I don't know…" Brand stopped mid-sentence as he began to see enormous boulders flying over the wall, crashing into buildings near the edge of the city. As he looked closer, he could see a gaping hole and rubble where the front gate was supposed to be.

The city was under siege.

After a few moments of running, they were halfway to the front gates and they encountered a pack of dire wolves that were roaming the streets. Astoro fared much better than Brand. Even with his extensive training, it was difficult to alternate between fighting and running. One of the wolves raked its claws across his chest before he was able to recover and finish it off.

When Astoro finished off the last of them, he turned and put a hand on Brand's chest. Vines made of a soft, green light crawled out of Astoro's hand and covered the wound. They pulsed a few times and then dissipated, revealing the healed skin beneath.

"Thanks," Brand said. "That was sloppy of me."

"Don't worry about it," Astoro replied. "You're not at full strength right now, just be careful."

Brand nodded. "Let's keep going, we've lost a little bit of ground."

Sure enough, Landren and his companion were already nearing the front gates. A small group of orcs had moved to intercept Landren as several others stayed back to clear some remaining rubble from the road to allow others through. As Brand and Astoro ran, he could see his warden's fighting a little clearer. It was definitely him. It was amazing to see him fight again, but Brand slid to a stop as he saw the color of his warden's energy.

Golden steam rose from Landren's body as he weaved through the five attackers. Not the orange energy of the Open Path or the red energy of whatever this new Path Brand had discovered, but something new and different. How many Paths were there that Brand had never heard about? What was his monastery hiding? Or did they even know that the Open Path wasn't the only Path? Brand continued to watch his warden fight in awe.

Flashes of golden light radiated every time he made a strike. Brand recognized it as a technique that opened the Chi gates only for a split second as he struck to prevent any waste of energy. It was the mark of a true Pathwarden for someone to be able to get the timing so precise. Brand, still the rank of Pathfinder, hadn't fully mastered the technique. He usually kept his gates open a little longer and relied on his high endurance to get him through tough fights.

Each strike sent its target flying away or scattering across the ground. His warden was not holding back, not a single one of the orcs so much as moved after taking a single blow, and he finished them off in a matter of seconds. While this was going on, an elven woman wearing green leather armor was climbing one of the buildings. She was the person he'd seen running with Landren. The top of the building would be a good vantage point to use the bow he could see slung around her shoulder.

As she was still climbing, one of the orcs stopped clearing the rubble and aimed a bow at Landren. He didn't have any cover or any weapons on him to try and kill the orc from a distance. Brand yelled and reached his hand toward his warden helplessly as he saw the orc loose the arrow at Landren's chest. He was too close, there was no way Landren could dodge an arrow at that range.

The next few seconds seemed to happen in slow motion. Landren's right forearm lit up like a beacon as he swept it from the left side of his body across his chest to the right. Brand watched in astonishment as Landren deflected the arrow out of the air in a smooth motion. But even if that feat already hadn't been the most amazing thing he'd ever seen someone do, what happened next easily topped it. Using the momentum from deflecting the arrow, Landren stepped forward with his left foot and took a stance that Brand had grown so familiar with.

Left foot forward. Right foot back and angled. This would anchor him to the ground. Left hand up, palm open, ready to defend. Right hand back at the waist, balled into a fist, ready to strike. Brand could see the massive amount of Chi building in both of Landren's hands. Brand wasn't sure what he was going to do, there were no enemies within striking distance.

Then, his warden's stance changed. Landren rotated slightly at the hips and brought his left hand back behind him, just below his right hand, both palms open. His arms began to fill with glowing light from his hands, now up to his elbow. Brand's eyes widened as he saw a bright ball of golden Chi begin to form between Landren's hands. His arms were glowing all the way to his shoulders.

Landren began to sweat and a pained expression flashed across his face as he let the energy build for a moment. Once Brand was sure his warden was going to burn himself out, Landren extended his arms forward toward the orcs that were still gathered. Brand's breath caught in his chest as a beam of Chi energy flew at the enemy and detonated in a large explosion. Rubble and pieces of orcs scattered in all directions.

Landren's arms stopped glowing as the last of the Chi left his palms. He held the stance for a moment, golden steam radiating off his body as he took several heavy breaths. Finally, he lowered his arms and turned to look over his shoulder. As he scanned behind him, he locked eyes with Brand, seeing his wide-eyed and open-jawed pupil for the first time.

Landren smiled at Brand and winked. "Oh hey, Brand! How do you like my new technique?"

* * *

"Pathwarden, what *was* that?" Brand exclaimed as he and Astoro finally closed the distance between them.

"Well hello to you too." Landren chuckled, embracing Brand and slapping him on the back.

Brand was shocked at his warden's demeanor. Here was the man who had trained him to always be vigilant about containing his emotions. Brand hadn't known Landren to ever even crack the slightest smile, and here he was grinning and laughing like any ordinary person.

"Sorry, Pathwarden, I mean it's great to see you, but…" Brand said, shifting his feet. "I'm not used to… this version of you I guess."

Landren held him by the shoulders at arm's length and looked him over. "It's been quite some time, Brand. You've grown a lot in the last few years. I'm very glad to see you, and thank you for coming."

"Of course, I came as soon as I received your letter at the monastery," Brand replied, trying to regain his composure.

"And yes, I'm a much different person than the one you remember. It's one of the reasons I wrote to you," Landren said, releasing Brand. "There's much to discuss, but not enough time to do so at the moment."

"Hey, Landren, nice shot but look alive, we've got more on the way!" the woman on the building yelled down. She knocked an arrow in her bow and took aim at the gates. "A lot more from the looks of it, I hope you've got another few of those blasts in you!"

Brand looked beyond the gate's rubble at about thirty orcs advancing on their position. That was going to be too much for the four of them to take on, even with his warden's new technique. Landren took a look at the orcs coming their way and frowned.

"We'll talk more later," Landren promised Brand as he turned his attention to the elven woman.

"Save your arrows for larger targets, Val!" he yelled up to her. "I'll take care of this group!"

"Alright, you got it," Val said back to Landren as she lowered her bow.

"Pathwarden, that Chi blast was amazing, but I don't think it's going to handle that many of them!" Brand protested.

"Don't worry Brand, I do have one more surprise in store," Landren said. He reached into a pouch at his waist and pulled out the handle of a sword without a blade. "You and your friend..."

"Oh, uh, Astoro," Astoro replied with a small wave. "Also, did you say something about larger targets?"

Landren nodded to him. "You and Astoro, please stand back. I'll take care of this group on my own." He took a few steps forward, holding the handle out to his side. "And yes, Astoro, larger targets are on their way. After the orcs, we'll be holding the gates against giants."

Giants? Brand and Astoro's eyes both went wide as Landren stepped toward the open hole in the wall. How could they possibly hold against giants? And how was Landren so casual about all of this? Was his new power really that great?

The band of orcs had reached the gates and began to pour through. Landren increased his pace to a brisk walk, then a jog, and finally worked his way to a full sprint, directly at the charging orcs. The orc in front swung his blade to meet Landren head-on, but his blade met air. He stumbled forward as Landren leapt towards the middle of the pack.

Landren soared in a graceful arc over the heads of the confused orcs, who backed away from where Landren landed. They hesitated as Landren held the sword handle in front of his face. A golden energy began to build in the hilt and around Landren as he began to yell with effort. Finally, Landren swung his arm out to his right side in a flourish, and with a flash of light, a golden blade of Chi ignited from the handle. The orcs took a step back in unison, and Landren charged.

Brand had never seen someone tap into the amount of Chi that Landren was using. Steam was erupting from his body in a golden aura, and it looked like the orcs were moving in slow motion compared to the speed at which Landren cut them down. The Chi Blade sliced through weapons, armor, and flesh equally without effort, and no blade was quick enough to touch Landren.

He danced, jumped, and spun his way through the increasingly panicked forces, always in motion but no movement wasted, and the orcs fell in troves. As he cut down the last orc, the Chi Blade and Landren's aura extinguished. Landren dropped to a knee, gasping for breath, and sweat dripped from his head. Brand ran over to his warden to help him up as Landren hung the Chi Blade's hilt from his belt.

"Thanks, Brand," Landren said between breaths. "I sometimes forget just how much that takes out of me. I'll need a moment to recover but should be ok to use it again when the giants get here. They can't be too far behind."

Brand pulled him back further inside the wall and Landren sat up against the outside of the building Val had been standing on. She quickly climbed down the wall to where Landren sat.

"There are three of the smaller giants making their way down here after your display with that glowing sword," Val said. "And a few other greater giants holding back at the tree line. One is enormous, he must be the leader. We need to come up with a plan, and fast. The first three will be here in the next few minutes."

"We'll need to split them up and take them down individually," Landren said. "I can take one on my own with the Chi Blade, but it may take me a few moments." He looked at Brand, "Brand, with your abilities, you should be able to handle keeping one of the giants busy. Then, once I help Val and Astoro finish off the second one, we'll come join you if you haven't already finished off the third on your own."

"Actually, Pathwarden, about my abilities…" Brand started. "I can't access my Chi at the moment. At least, not reliably."

"What do you mean?" Landren asked.

"It's a long story, but Astoro and I fought a man who used some kind of florian poison which nearly killed me. It left me without the ability to use my Chi," Brand said. Val's head snapped to look at Brand. "I would be dead if it weren't for Astoro's knowledge and healing."

"I see," Landren said. "Well then we…"

"What was the man's name?" Val interrupted, staring directly at Brand.

"What?" Brand said.

"The florian who poisoned you," Val said with a dark intensity. "Did you get his name?"

"Well we don't know for sure, but I think Astoro found something with a name on it at the hideout we cleared out," Brand said, turning to Astoro. "Astoro, do you remember?"

"Uh, Viridian, I think. Agent Viridian," Astoro replied. Rage flashed across Val's face for a moment. "Do you know him?"

"Yes I do, but I'll explain later," Val said, shaking her head and taking a deep breath. "Sorry Landren, I interrupted you."

Something like understanding flashed across Landren's face and their eyes met. She gave the slightest nod.

"It's alright, Val." He cleared his throat. "As I was saying, we'll need a new plan. Astoro, do you have any abilities?"

Astoro nodded. "Yes, like a lot of florians, I have access to Florana's nature magic, but there's no way I can take out a giant on my own."

"I can keep one busy by myself," Val said. "Landren, take care of the one on your own, here in front of the gate. I'll kite one along the inside of the wall and try to keep it from doing too much damage." She looked at Brand and Astoro. "You two distract the other one and take it in the other direction, can you manage that?"

"Yeah," Brand said.

"We can handle it," Astoro added, looking at Brand and giving him a firm nod.

"Then Landren will help you both finish off your giant once he's done and then you can all come assist me," Val finished.

"Then we meet back up at the front gate and hope reinforcements are on the way, otherwise we do it all again," Landren said. He grinned and gave Brand a wink. "No problem."

* * *

"No problem, huh?" Astoro yelled at Brand as they sprinted through the cobblestone streets, shrapnel raining down on them. Keeping ahead of the giant was, in fact, turning out to be a huge problem. They were able to weave through some alleys to gain a little ground, but they had to stay close enough to force the giant to keep up the chase. Astoro was the only one of them with any ranged attacks to keep the giant's attention from a safe distance, and it was beginning to wear on him.

Astoro unleashed a surge of green arcane energy, his hands glowing with an ethereal light as the blast spiraled toward the giant. People were fleeing in every direction, adding to the chaos. The blast to its face was enough to retain its attention on Brand and Astoro, at least for now.

Brand only hoped that leading the giant on this chase wasn't doing more harm to the townspeople than good. But this was the best plan they had, and the only hope of holding out long enough to defend the town from being overrun.

The guards back in the courtyard should be enough to take care of the initial attack, but would they be in time to help Brand and his friends? Distracted by his thoughts, Brand narrowly avoided a chimney that the giant hurled at him.

"Frost and fire!" Brand cursed at the near-miss. "Astoro, how are you holding up?"

"Oh, fresh as the new Spring!" Astoro replied between heavy breaths. "Just running for my thorning life in an unfamiliar city while poking something that will easily kill me when it catches up. You know, no big deal!"

Brand chuckled as they ran side by side, but he could tell that Astoro was slowing with each step. Brand focused inward and tested the gates to his chi, but both Paths were closed at the moment.

Slagging poison! Brand cursed to himself.

This giant would be a foe he could deal with if he had access to his usual power. Even easier if he could figure out how to use his new power. But that wasn't an option, and he hated being a dead weight that everyone had to cover for. He was tired of being weak and useless. So it was time to start only being weak.

"Astoro, I've got an idea," Brand said as they rounded another corner. "We're close to the Court of Fire. If we can lead it to the ice spires, we can try to lose it and buy some extra time for Pathwarden Landren to show up."

"Sounds good to me," Astoro replied, still gasping for air. "I'm not going to be able to keep this up much longer."

Brand turned back toward the Court of Fire, Astoro following shortly behind and keeping ahead of the giant chasing them. It towered over the shops and houses they ran past. Brand only hoped that any civilians remaining at the courtyard had fled since all the fighting began.

Finally, the ice spires that protruded from the Court of Fire came into view. Brand increased his speed and made it into the icy forest. He turned and watched as Astoro tripped on a patch of ice outside the courtyard. The giant bore down on Astoro and raised a closed fist in the air to finish Astoro off.

Fear paralyzed Brand. He wanted to go help his friend, but he couldn't will his muscles to move. He couldn't control the emotions inside of him and now they were controlling him. His heart pounded against his chest, a maelstrom of fear and shame swirling within.

Brand watched, holding his breath as the giant's arm swung down at Astoro. At the last second, vines sprung from Asoro's arms and wrapped around a nearby street pole. He pulled himself off to the side as the giant's fist slammed into the ground.

A familiar golden aura appeared on the other side of the giant. Brand heard several strikes that drove the giant backward towards the massive spikes of ice, right toward where he was standing. The giant stumbled backward as one more powerful blow sent the giant flying into the air right towards him. His fear still prevented him from moving. Instead, he crouched and covered his head with his hands and cowered as the giant's massive body plummeted towards him. Brand closed his eyes and waited for the end, but it didn't come.

"It's alright, Brand," a familiar voice said a moment later. "You're safe."

Brand opened his eyes and looked up, past Pathwarden Landren's concerned face, to the massive body of the giant suspended above him. It had been impaled on one of the massive ice spikes jutting from the ground.

"It looks like I have pretty good timing," Landren said with a gentle smile.

"A minute or two earlier would have been preferable, Pathwarden" Brand said as he gathered himself and got back to his feet. His legs felt unstable beneath him.

"Yes, but still much better than a minute or two later," Landren replied with a wink.

What is wrong with me? Brand thought.

He'd never frozen in battle like that in his entire life. And for it to happen while his friend was in danger and right in front of his Pathwarden? Brand was completely ashamed of himself. If it weren't for Astoro's quick thinking and Pathwarden Landren's timing, he and Astoro might have been dead.

"Brand, are you alright?" Astoro asked, running up to him.

"Yeah," Brand said without looking Astoro in the eye. "I'm alright. I'm sorry I couldn't be more help."

"It's ok, there's nothing you could have done without access to your Chi," Astoro said. He was still breathing heavily but was recovering. "And everything turned out fine, so don't worry about it."

"Thanks, Astoro," Brand said. "At some point, I promise I'm going to pay you back for constantly saving my life."

"Perhaps some drinks once we've finished saving the day?" Astoro said with a smile.

"I feel like I owe you a little more than drinks, but you got it," Brand replied, dusting himself off as he tried to regain his composure. "Maybe I'll even have one myself."

Brand turned to Landren and nodded. "Now let's go help Val and then get back to the gates. Then... how did you put it, Pathwarden?"

"We do it all again," Landren replied with a reassuring smile.

Brand smiled back, but it didn't reach his eyes. "No problem."

17

Ronan

"Help me move this rock off his legs so we can heal him! Hold on Ronan, just stay with us!"

Ronan wasn't sure who the voices belonged to as he struggled on the edge of consciousness. But after a moment, he felt some pressure release from somewhere on his body. The pain was overwhelming.

"My magic isn't working!" A voice said frantically. Was that Brin? He wasn't sure. "Elder Oren, what do we do?"

"I don't know, the Flame is missing… This has never happened before."

"My armor! Elder, help me get my armor on him. It's still infused with Niradim's Flame, we can use it to heal him."

He felt a couple sets of hands moving him around, and pieces of armor were being fastened to him. Whatever was being put on him emanated a familiar warmth that he hadn't felt in a long time. After a moment, the last piece clicked into place and he felt a vibration with a slight hum as the pieces of armor synced with each other.

"Ronan, you have to focus," Brin said, pulling his face close to hers. "Focus on the armor you're wearing and pull Niradim's healing magic into you."

"I've only been able to do that once before…"

"Remember it, you have to try"

"I'll try."

* * *

Four years ago

"They're here! Men, ready your weapons, we fight for Niradim!"

Ronan drew his standard-issue short sword from the scabbard at his waist. He'd only joined the Niradim Protectors six months ago and this was supposed to be a routine guard duty at a nearby outpost. This location hadn't seen battle in hundreds of years.

The outpost was a weathered stone fortress with ivy creeping up its ancient walls, empty save for the twelve Protectors guarding it this day. It stood sentinel in a small clearing amidst a dense forest to the east of Midral. The usual noises of wildlife had retreated at the sound of the impending horde.

He heard the horde before he saw them. A scout had arrived an hour ago warning about a band of orcs in the area heading their direction riding dire wolves. Orc activity had increased recently, but this was a bold move to attack so close to Midral.

"Don't worry, son. We can handle them," Ginmar said, walking up from behind him. He casually unbuckled the mace hanging next to his red and gold mark of Niradim at his waist and it began to crackle with holy energy. "Just stay close to me, got it?"

Ronan nodded. He'd feel a lot better if he was able to wield magic like some of the others. He could see the weapons and armor of three other dwarves ignite with holy flames. Only the strongest Protectors could wield Niradim's power. This was the safest outpost, so those with Niradim's magic were rarely stationed here unless they were

194

traveling through. There were only about twelve of them stationed here today.

Ginmar outranked everyone here, so Ronan knew he was in safe hands. It helped that he'd seen Ginmar's power up close since he'd been living with him from when he was a young boy. He'd learned everything from the dwarf who stood by his side.

He had his father to thank for that. Years ago, Ronan's father, Kilian, had saved Ginmar's life. In return, Ginmar asked Kilian what he could do to repay the life debt he owed Kilian. Ronan's father made one request - give his son a chance at a better life and allow him to apprentice and live with Ginmar. Kilian was a great blacksmith in his town, but he knew that the dwarves of Midral were the best in the world, and he wanted Ronan to learn from the best.

"How many do you think there are?" Ronan asked.

"A few dozen at least. We're outnumbered, but not outmatched," Ginmar replied. He pointed to a large orc at the front of the horde riding a massive dire wolf. "The war chief rides at the front of that group. Since I'm the ranking member of the Protectors at this post, it falls to me to make sure he goes down. When I fight him, I need you to stay clear. He'll be the strongest of their group. Don't be a hero."

"Yes, Master Ginmar," Ronan said.

He checked the knives he had strapped to his chest and legs to make sure they were secure but able to be drawn at a moment's notice. He selected one of his longer ones to hold in his off-hand in a reverse grip to help parry any attacks. Ginmar used a shield, but Ronan had always loved knives like his father.

"Just remember your training and you'll be fine," Ginmar reassured him. "Like I said, stay close to me until I engage the leader. I won't let anything happen to you."

The orcs closed in with their dire wolves and Ginmar began to gather the dwarves near the entrance.

"Stay together, men, and fight in pairs. If your partner goes down, join the closest pair immediately and reinforce them. Stay close and guard each others' backs. They will be unorganized, use that to your advantage."

Ginmar turned and held up his shield.

"For Niradim!" he yelled.

"For Niradim!" they all replied as they charged into the fray.

Ronan quickly found that Ginmar had been right about the abilities of the orcs. He stayed close to Ginmar for safety, but he was able to hold his own against the enemies that got too close. Sparing a quick glance around the battlefield, he could see the orc forces dwindling faster than the Protectors.

Ronan raised his knife to deflect an incoming blow and swung his sword in an arc, cutting down his attacker. Ginmar had finally fought past the opposition between himself and the war chief. He was about to engage their leader. Ronan did as he was told and joined a smaller group of Protectors nearby to stay out of his way, but he kept an eye on Ginmar as he approached the powerful orc.

The war chief cleaved through a pair of Protectors with one swing of his greatsword and spotted Ginmar. A smile crept along his lips as he recognized the challenge approaching him. He raised his massive sword above his head and charged, meeting Ginmar head-on. Despite the size difference, Ginmar raised his shield and blocked the powerful opening attack.

They began to exchange powerful blows. Ronan could tell the war chief was the most experienced fighter they had, but Ginmar was holding his own really well. It was a closer match than Ronan would have liked, but slowly, Ginmar was gaining the upper hand.

The chief made to swing his sword again, but as Ginmar raised his shield, he instead delivered a kick that sent Ginmar tumbling backward. Ginmar swiftly regained his footing, rising into a defensive stance as he expected the war chief to push his advantage. Instead, Ronan watched as the chief raised a horn hanging from his waist and blew a long, loud note through it.

A tense moment passed and then Ronan heard a matching horn from behind them accompanied by howling. He spun toward the back of the outpost and watched as a second horde of orcs as large as the first advanced from the treeline behind the outpost. They'd been flanked.

The fighting began in earnest again. Ronan could no longer watch the fight between Ginmar and the chief as his attention turned to keeping himself alive. Clashing steel rang out around him like a discordant symphony. Each swing of his sword that found its target sent tremors up his arm, the jarring impacts a stark reminder of the stakes at hand. He lost track of time as the skirmish continued and he watched as the Protectors succumbed to the orc reinforcements one by one.

The dwarf next to him fell to the swing of an axe and now three orcs were closing in on him. He was able to block the first attack, but another orc used that opportunity to press with an attack of his own. Ronan could barely keep the onslaught at bay.

A sword found an opening in his defenses and sliced a deep gash across his left arm, causing him to drop his knife. He ducked under a swing from a war hammer that would have crushed his skull, but it left him open to taking a glancing strike from an axe across his chest. If it weren't for his armor, he'd already be dead.

He needed to even his odds if he was going to survive. Ronan waited for the orc with the sword to raise it above his head and he used that moment to reach his injured hand down to the knives strapped to his thighs. With a smooth motion, he threw the knife directly into the orc's eye. The orc fell back screaming in pain, clutching at its face. Ronan removed that threat from his mind and focused on the two remaining orcs.

Unfortunately, the throwing motion left his side completely un-guarded. He screamed in pain as a war hammer crashed into his side, crumpling his armor. He heard a sickening crunch and felt at least a few of his ribs as they snapped inside him.

The pain sent him to his knee and the other remaining orc tried to come in with an overhead blow with his axe to finish him off. Ronan's training kicked in and he had the presence of mind to parry the swing and stab his sword into the orc's gut.

Before he could remove his sword, the last orc with the war hammer kicked him in the chest onto his back, sending a flash of pain through his body. Every breath radiated pain from his chest, and the blood loss was beginning to make his body weaken in a way adrenaline couldn't compensate for.

He still held his sword, but he couldn't find the strength to raise it as the orc closed in for a killing blow. He raised the war hammer over his head and Ronan braced himself.

Before the war hammer descended, a flash of holy light blasted the orc in the chest and sent him flying backward. He watched from his back as Ginmar's face appeared above him.

"Hold on, Ronan, you'll be ok," Ginmar said as he placed a hand on Ronan's chest and muttered a prayer to Niradim. Ronan felt as his bones reformed and the cuts over his body knit back together. He took a deep breath as the healing energy finished and the pain subsided to a dull throb.

"Now I need to get back to my fight," Ginmar said, holding out a hand to help Ronan up. "Just be careful…"

Ginmar screamed in pain and Ronan watched as the end of a blade jutted from Ginmar's chest for a moment and then withdrew. Ginmar fell to the ground, clutching his wound. Ronan watched as Ginmar's blood dripped from a sword gripped by an orc with Ronan's own knife still jutting from its eye.

"Ginmar, no!" Ronan screamed. He drew a knife from his chest and flicked it towards the orc, this time catching it directly in the throat. As the orc struggled to breathe, Ronan got to his feet and swung his sword, separating the orc's head from his body. He turned back to his mentor lying on the ground, bleeding out.

He knelt over Ginmar, tears streaking down his face as he rolled his mentor onto his back. Ginmar was breathing, but barely. He looked around the battlefield, searching for someone to heal Ginmar. There were such a small number of Protectors still on their feet. After scanning the battlefield, his heart sank. None that remained standing could wield Niradim's magic. There was nobody left who could heal. Ginmar was going to die.

"Stay with me Ginmar. Please, stay with me!"

"Ronan…" Ginmar struggled to get the words out. "You still have to fight."

"No, I'm not leaving your side," Ronan said. The battle raged around them, but they seemed to be in a pocket of their own at the moment. All attention was focused elsewhere, but Ronan knew that wouldn't last long.

Ronan closed his eyes and put his hands on his master's chest, just as he'd seen Ginmar do a moment ago to him. Humans couldn't wield Niradim's magic. That honor was only reserved for dwarves. The dwarven race was Niradim's created people, forged from the earth and imbued with a piece of Niradim's own soul. And only those with a piece of Niradim's soul could wield his magic.

Ronan didn't have a piece of Niradim's soul, but right now, he didn't care. He served Niradim, despite his race. He loved the dwarven people that he'd grown up with, and Midral was the only place he truly considered his home. Even if he didn't have a true piece of Niradim's soul within him, the soul of Niradim's people resided in

Ronan, and right now, that would have to be enough.

Please Niradim, lend me your power so I can save your people. Ronan prayed. *Even if it's just for a moment.*

At first, Ronan felt nothing, and then a power began to stir around him. Ronan watched as Ginmar's shield and mace which lay discarded next to his master began to radiate with holy energy. Ronan slowly reached out and picked them up in each hand.

As soon as his hands wrapped around the mace and shield, power that Ronan had never known flooded into him, lighting him up like a beacon. He watched as tendrils of that power connected him to Ginmar and his master's wounds began to heal. Ginmar's eyes went wide with surprise, and Ronan looked around to see the remaining Protectors nearby staring at him in awe.

A human was wielding the power of their god.

The display caught the attention of the war chief and he slowly made his way over to Ronan. Ginmar struggled to stand, but was still too weak, despite the healing.

"Ronan, you have to leave," Ginmar said. "He's too strong for you."

"Don't worry, Master Ginmar," Ronan said. "Niradim is with me. It's my turn to protect you."

The war chief screamed out a battle cry and came charging at Ronan with his greatsword. The entire battlefield had gone still as they watched the ensuing duel. The war chief's attacks came in a flurry, but Ronan expertly blocked each one, not losing a single step to the massive orc that was trying to push him back.

Ronan reached into the well of power he felt within him and focused it into Ginmar's shield. He swung the shield to meet the swing of the greatsword and the massive clash shattered the sword on impact. The war chief stumbled backward holding his arm which was bent at an unnatural angle.

Ronan took two steps to close the distance, now pouring the power into Ginmar's mace. He swung with all his might and connected with the war chief's face in a massive explosion of holy power. What remained of the war chief's body soared through the air and landed among a group of orcs.

That was all the orcs needed to see to give up the attack. The remaining Protectors killed off any orcs who weren't able to escape, but the rest of the orcs fled the outpost.

Ronan felt Niradim's power fade as he went back to check on Ginmar.

It was the last time he'd felt that much power from Niradim.

* * *

Present day

Until now.

Power flooded into Ronan from the armor that had been placed on him. Brin's armor. Niradim's magic spread through the core of him and connected with his soul in a way he'd never experienced before.

He felt his body knit itself back together and become stronger. He opened his eyes and saw Brin standing over him with a relieved smile and tear stains streaking down her face.

"Oh, thank Niradim," Brin said. "You're alive!"

She put a hand to her head and swayed before Ronan reached his hand out to steady her. She slumped into his arms. The adrenaline-fueled concern for his safety must have finally worn off.

"Brin, you're exhausted, you should be resting," Ronan said, sitting up.

"I think what you meant to say was, 'Thank you, Brin, you're amazing. Easily the best Acolyte I've ever seen!'" Brin said with a heavy smile.

Ronan chuckled. "I think you mean 'best *Disciple* I've ever seen.' You passed your Trial, remember?"

"Oh right," she said. "*Master* Brin. That's going to take some getting used to."

"I'm sure you'll take to it quickly," Ronan said with a smile as he helped her sit up against some nearby debris.

His smile disappeared as he remembered his recent fight. Ginmar stood frozen where Kyros left him, just a few feet away from where Ronan had been pinned in the rubble.

"Ginmar!" Ronan yelled.

He made sure Brin was steady and then ran to his master's side and placed a hand on Ginmar's frozen body. His hands glowed faintly as he channeled Niradim's magic into a healing spell, but the light flickered and died like a starved flame. It wasn't working.

"Slag and Ashes," Ronan cursed. "Come on Niradim, heal him!"

"It's not going to work," a voice said from behind. Ronan turned and saw Elder Oren carrying a large bundle in his arms through the front of the cathedral.

"What do you mean?" Ronan demanded.

"A simple healing with the power you have available to you isn't going to work," Oren said. "We could maybe save him if the Flame is returned to the Soul Forge, but it would need to be done quickly."

Ronan looked at him, and then at Ginmar. Niradim had found a way to pull him back into his conflicts, whether or not Ronan wanted it. So be it, Ronan would return the Flame, but not for Niradim's sake. He'd do it for Ginmar.

"Fine," Ronan said. "I'll do it."

"Thank you," Elder Oren said. "By the way, I must say I'm glad to see Niradim's Phoenix back on his feet."

"I wish people would stop calling me that," Ronan said.

"Master Ronan, you were quite literally reborn from the ashes just a few feet from here, or don't you remember?" Oren said. "Besides, it looks good on you." He gestured to Ronan's breastplate with a smile.

Ronan paused and finally took a moment to inspect the armor he was wearing.

It was breathtaking.

Each piece of armor was a stark white, with golden trim around the outsides and red embossing that seemed to breathe with Niradim's flame. But the most stunning part of the armor was the breastplate.

Emblazoned across his chest was a crimson Phoenix flickering with flamelight that made it appear as if it was on fire. It was completely different from the designs he'd been helping Brin with the past several weeks. He'd never seen armor more beautiful.

Ronan turned back to Brin. "Is this the armor you forged in your Trial?" Ronan asked. Brin's face flushed and she turned away but nodded.

"Why does it fit me?" Ronan asked hesitantly. "The armor we worked on was designed to fit dwarves."

She still averted her eyes. "Because I made it for you."

He slowly walked over to her, cupped her cheek in his hand, and gently turned her face to look up at him. Her eyes sparkled through the tears threatening to slip down her cheeks.

"Why would you make this for me?" Ronan asked her quietly.

"Because he promised it would protect you," she whispered.

"Who promised…" Ronan cut short as the realization struck him.

"I've been working on redesigning my armor since our fight with Kyros," Brin said softly. "After what we went through the other day, I couldn't stop thinking about your relationship with Niradim, and what that means. As long as you're not one of his followers, you won't have his protection."

She stared into his eyes. "This is my gift to you, Ronan. You gave the ultimate sacrifice in service to him. So I told Niradim if he won't protect you, then I will."

Ronan paused, looking at her and processing her words. "And what did he have to say about that?" he asked quietly.

"He said." Brin smiled. "Brin, why do you think I sent you to him?"

Ronan looked deep into her eyes and really saw her, not as the young Acolyte he'd been mentoring, but as a strong and passionate person who would do anything to keep her loved ones safe. He'd been so preoccupied with his feud with Niradim that he'd been blind to everything else happening around him. He'd pushed his feelings about her down and away to make his decision to leave easier to bear. But he couldn't ignore them now, staring into the depths of her eyes. He leaned over, took her into his arms, and kissed her.

Lightning surged through his veins, stronger even than the power he felt from Niradim. He couldn't believe he'd been ignoring these feelings for so long. It didn't matter if she was walking into a faith that he was walking away from. If she was willing to try to make this work, so was he. He pulled back to catch his breath.

"This is more than I deserve, Brin," Ronan said to her. "But thank you."

She pulled him into a longer kiss and for that moment, everything was ok. His relationship with Niradim may be complicated, but that didn't mean this one had to be. Ronan enjoyed the moment until Oren cleared his throat from behind them.

"Pardon the interruption, but Master Brin had me fetch one more thing for you while you were recovering from your injuries." He held up the bundle he was holding and Ronan noticed Brin stiffen in his arms before he turned to regard what Oren had for him.

Ronan approached Oren slowly, his heart racing. He knew what it was. He'd known it since the moment Oren had arrived with it, he'd just been pushing it to the back of his mind so he didn't have to think about it. He placed his hand tentatively on the cloth, and slowly pulled it back to reveal the one thing he hadn't been able to confront since his rebirth. He turned to look at Brin.

"Please don't hate me," she said. "I know what these mean to you and what they represent. But you need to be at your full strength to beat Kyros, and this is your full strength."

Ronan nodded and turned back to Oren. Even though he didn't know if he was ready to pick them back up, he didn't have the luxury of time to get ready. Brin was right, he needed all the help he could get right now. He carefully picked up the sword and shield that had laid untouched since his resurrection and slowly strapped them to his arm.

The familiar weight of the shield settled onto his left forearm, and he drew the short sword from its scabbard at the top of the shield. As he did, Brin's Phoenix armor pulsed with a fiery white glow and spread into Ronan's weapons. They relit with the holy power they'd once held in a previous lifetime. The armor, sword, and shield linked together with Niradim's power. He was a blazing knight for Niradim in all but his belief.

These weapons used to be symbols of his faith in Niradim. But they failed him in his time of need. They would have to be enough this time, even without the necklace that was the true symbol of his faith over his pride. As far as he knew, that was lost when he died, just like his own faith. He was fine with that, he wasn't sure if he'd be able to wear it even now with how much was at stake. He nodded his thanks to Oren.

"With that armor and those weapons, you should have access to what remains of Niradim's power, even without the Flame residing in the Soul Forge," Oren said. "But that's all that remains. Dwarves will not be able to wield the power of Niradim until the Flame is returned."

"Understood. Thank you, Oren," Ronan said, sheathing the sword back into his shield. He looked at Brin. "And thank you, Brin. For everything."

"You're welcome," she said, smiling. "Now get going. Like it or not, the people need their Phoenix. Just make sure you come back alive this time."

She winked at him and he smirked back. His city, his people, and his master needed him. It was time to get to work.

* * *

Ronan sprinted across the rugged terrain towards the Crucible Gate. The doors loomed ahead like an ancient guardian between the Earth and Sky Sectors. He needed to get beyond the gate and find Kyros.

Oren was right, even without Ronan's faith in Niradim, he could feel the magical protection coursing through the armor. Tapping into Niradim's power made him uncomfortable, but it was there waiting for him as soon as he needed it.

As he ran, heads turned, and shortly after, cheers erupted behind him. Everyone knew who he was, and now he bore the very symbol of what they proclaimed him to be. They thought he finally accepted his place as Niradim's Phoenix. Even if that was a lie, he would live that lie if it would give them the hope they needed to get through this. Besides, as Brin had said, there were worse nicknames.

For a while, he saw plenty of dwarves fleeing deeper into the Earth Sector, but after some time, it trickled down to nothing. If the guards sealed the gates shut, this threat must be pretty serious. The walls of the Earth Sector flew by as he descended the long ramp down to the ground level.

"Open the gates!" Ronan yelled to the guards as he approached at high speed.

The guards looked at him in surprise and confusion for a moment, and then they saw what he was wearing. They passed the word along and swung the gates open just as he arrived. He burst through the open doors at full speed and they closed shut behind him as he slid to a stop a few feet beyond the gates and took in the chaos before him.

It was even worse than he could have imagined. A ferocious winter storm raged, with howling winds that lashed at his skin like frozen knives. As he adjusted to the storm, he began to take in the carnage. Many of the people he'd fought beside lay wounded and dying around the courtyard-turned-battlefield.

Through the swirling blizzard, Ronan's gaze found Lieutenant Vorkin and his fellow guards fighting a losing battle against an encroaching tide of enemies. Ronan closed the distance in a flash and entered the fray. In a few heartbeats, he had downed all of the enemies surrounding Vorkin and the others. He stepped towards Vorkin and offered him his hand to pull him to his feet. Ronan looked over his shoulder to the other guards.

"Spread the word, gentlemen," Ronan said, and turned his attention back to the battle before them. "The Phoenix has joined the fight."

The guards cheered, scattering to reinforce other skirmishes happening around the battlefield. Ronan watched as his mere presence seemed to change the tide of battle. He searched the area to see if he could spot Kyros, but he didn't see the purple novaborn anywhere. He needed to get to the front gates. As he was about to begin his hunt, a vibration rippled out from the center of the Court of Fire.

Ronan took a step back as a vibrant purple light erupted from the ground in a circle around the spires of ice jutting up from the Court of Fire. Within the circle, the stone itself seemed to breathe and pulse. It transformed into a living sea of amethyst fluid that shimmered with an eerie light, casting twisted shadows on the icy landscape. Ronan's blood ran cold. He'd seen this exact thing only once in his life, but plenty of times in his nightmares after.

The spires of ice and the bodies impaled upon them sunk into the ground, dissolving into the pool of liquid like he remembered. As soon as the giant's body completely assimilated into the pool of liquid, a familiar form began to rise from the center.

Ronan stared up at the monster of starlight and death before him, at least three times larger than the one that had killed him, and drew his sword. With a roar that split the silence, the Starspawn's eyes ignited like twin suns, malevolence burning in its gaze as it focused on Ronan. The axes in its gargantuan hands radiated with a white-hot intensity.

Ronan took a deep breath and steadied his nerves. He met the monster's eyes and raised his sword and shield. Memories flashed of the last time he fought a smaller monster like this, staring up from his back as a blazing axe ripped the soul from his body. He shook his head and banished the memory from his mind.

"Not this time," Ronan said under his breath, and he charged the massive beast.

18

Kyros

Kyros watched from atop a nearby roof as the enormous Starspawn rose from the amethyst pool of the summoning gate he created. He didn't know who he had to thank for leaving such a huge sacrifice in the Court of Fire, but he certainly was grateful for it. The corpse of the giant impaled on one of his ice spires provided fuel enough to summon the largest Starspawn he'd ever seen.

He looked past the starlight monster and was shocked to see Ronan standing in front of the Crucible Gate, sword and shield in hand. His bright white armor gleamed under the chaotic light, the phoenix emblem blazing across his chest as though alive with fire. Why couldn't that human just stay dead?

No matter, nothing was going to bring down a monster the size that Kyros had just brought to the fight. And he wasn't done yet. He looked out and surveyed the city. He could see from here that the giant sacrificed for his ritual wasn't the only one drawn to the city by his repeated use of the Black Frost Ring.

Another giant was rampaging the west side of the Sky Sector and he could see three greater giants descending from the nearby tree line to join the fray. He closed his eyes and opened them high above the city from Noct's point of view so he could take a closer look. One of the giants advancing on the city towered over the other two, even larger than the Starspawn in front of him. That would do perfectly for his plans to complete his Patron's revenge against Niradim. Midral would fall today.

He closed his eyes again and switched his perspective back to his own body. Agents Viridian and Crimson had orders to meet him at the front of the city after the summoning at the Court of Fire had been completed. He needed to make his way toward the front gates.

He smiled as chaos raged around him. The hard part was over, and he could feel the immense power that his staff contained. Power that he now controlled. That made two gods whose power he had attained. Perhaps one day he'd attain the third as well.

He was a far cry from the weak man he'd been before making his contract. And now he was one step closer to walking away more powerful than he'd ever been before.

* * *

One year ago

"What have you got there, brother?"

Kyros lowered the book he was reading and looked up at his twin brother sitting at his desk. Falrose was buried in some new magical tome he'd discovered at a fancy library. His orange-red skin perfectly mirrored the color of the flames hovering around the room to provide light.

"Oh you know, just some light reading," Kyros replied, waving his hand. "Shouldn't you worry more about your studies?"

He settled back into the cushion he was lounging on and went back to reading, idly stroking Noct as she perched on his shoulder. He heard Falrose mutter some words and Kyros' book went flying out of his hand to hover directly in front of his brother. Noct screeched as Falrose snatched it out of the air with a smirk.

"Forbidden Rites: Reclaiming the lost power of the nova" Falrose read aloud. "Superstition? Really, Kyros? You're better than this," he said, tossing the book back to him. "Shouldn't you be studying something more practical?"

Kyros caught the book and slipped it into his pocket, rolling his eyes. This conversation again? It was true, the book was laced with superstition. But Kyros always believed that superstition found its origins in a kernel of truth.

"Oh, you and I both know I'm useless when it comes to learning magic from a book," Kyros said nonchalantly. "But there are other forms of power that I'm quite fluent in."

Falrose rolled his eyes. "Yes, father mentioned you've become quite the smooth talker."

"Politics is more than just smooth talking," Kyros said with a little more bite than he intended. His brother was a master at getting under his skin like no one else could. "The right words said at the right time and in the right way can sway anyone - even kings. And a carefully crafted contract can grant someone massive amounts of power."

"Not the kind of power that matters," Falrose said, crafting a ball of fire in the air above his hand to emphasize his point. It crackled and warped the air before Falrose snuffed it out. He smirked at Kyros.

"All power matters," Kyros muttered, sitting back down.

The truth was, Kyros was incredibly jealous of his brother's uncanny ability to learn magic so easily. Kyros could only manage the most minor magical feats. Falrose was already mastering things that his teachers struggled with. He'd be graduating at the top of his class in the next few months as one of the most powerful mages of their time.

Their father had quickly seen that Kyros didn't have the same talents as his brother, but he couldn't afford to be embarrassed by one of his sons. So Kyros had been given a different education. He studied politics and the ways of the court. His father brought him along as he traveled around the country, rubbing elbows with the wealthy and the powerful.

He'd made many powerful allies, even ones that his father didn't know about. But still, he was jealous of the raw power his brother could wield at his fingertips. There had to be a way to tap into that without all of that annoying studying.

He settled back into his cushion and opened the book back up to where he'd left off:

The god of stars and dreams was sealed away along with the power of the nova after the dwarven and florian gods combined their forces to repel the cursed Starspawn army from their assault on Gladen. After Celestian's defeat, Niradim and Florana destroyed the city of Lumenova and hid its location from the world, surrounding it with mountains and forests full of danger. It is said that if a novaborn were to somehow pierce the Star Prison, they could reclaim the power of the nova for themselves, for a price.

Kyros shut the book and rubbed his eyes. This book was the most historically accurate of the dozens he'd read through over the past few months. Unfortunately, it too lacked clear details on how to claim power. How was anyone supposed to pierce the Star Prison? Or even get to it? It was literally in space. Another dead end.

It was getting late, and unlike his brother, he wasn't one to stay up all night studying. Indeed, Kyros watched as his brother dropped a few leaves on the desk next to him and traced some symbols in a circle around them. Once the circle was complete, he muttered a few incantations under his breath, and the leaves sunk into the desk. After a second, a steaming cup of what smelled like tea rose to the surface. He picked up the cup of tea and raised it in the air towards Kyros with a wink before taking a sip and returning to his tome. Kyros rolled his eyes. Show off.

"Come Noct, it's getting late. It's time for you to hunt, and for me to get some beauty rest," Kyros said. "After all, I *am* the good-looking one in the family."

"We're twins!" Falrose called after him as he exited their home library.

He retreated to his private room and had a servant draw him a warm bath. As he settled into the warm water, he let his thoughts drift to the Star Prison and the god sealed within. Such massive amounts of untapped power resided within the confines of that star. If only there was a way to access it.

He continued to ponder on that power until he eventually got into bed and drifted off to sleep.

* * *

Kyros felt a sudden pull and he jolted awake. Something wasn't right. He turned to look around the room but didn't see anything out of place. His paintings were hanging right where they should be, depicting ancient battles and mystic landscapes. He could see the small stack of books and correspondences sitting on his desk where he'd left them before falling asleep. Noct's perch was empty, but that was to be expected this time of night. And there was his bed where his body was still sleeping…

Kyros' heart began to race. Well, at least he was sure that's what it would be doing if he could feel it. He was in the air looking down at his sleeping body. Was he dead? He didn't feel dead. He looked at his hands and saw that they were somewhat transparent. He found that he was actually able to float around somehow, so he moved over to his desk and tried picking up one of the books resting on top. His fingers couldn't take hold of the solid object. How strange.

Suddenly, a violet light began to pulse from outside his bedroom. He floated over to the door to his balcony to inspect the light, but couldn't see what it was from inside. Reaching a hand down, he went to unlatch the door but his hand passed through the handle.

I wonder... Kyros thought and pushed his hand through the door.

He could feel a slight resistance as his hand traveled through the wood, but there was no pain. He continued through the closed door until he was all the way through onto his balcony.

This is very interesting.

The pulsing light was coming from above. He turned his head to the heavens and saw a bright purple star flashing in rhythm with the pulses of light.

COME.

Kyros doubled over and grabbed his head with both hands. The word had vibrated through his skull and body, spoken into his mind. Kyros began to put the pieces together of what was happening to him. Words from the book he'd been reading last night flashed through his memories.

...god of stars and dreams...

...power of the novaborn...

...pierce the Star Prison...

...price.

This was it. This was his path to more power. He pulled himself together and looked toward the star again. This time he was prepared for the voice

COME.

He willed his body towards the star. The fabric of the cosmos unfolded before him and he found himself accelerating through space at an incredible speed. He didn't know how long he flew, it felt like long hours and mere seconds at the same time. The light from the star grew brighter and larger until it completely filled his field of vision.

He floated in front of a violet sea of amoebic fluid sealed into an orb covered in what he recognized as a combination of dwarven and florian runes. The Star Prison. Staring into the depths, he could see the shadowy outline of someone trapped inside.

As he got closer, the figure mirrored his actions and approached as well. It was as if the imprisoned god was a dark shadow of Kyros on the other side of the shield. He stopped a few feet in front of the Star, squinting at the violet light. The shadow stopped on the other side, the same distance away from the barrier separating them.

Kyros waited, resisting the temptation to speak first. He kept himself composed, his face a mask. He relaxed his body as much as possible and maintained eye contact with the man's face on the other side. In negotiations, it was the person who spoke first that usually lost. And this was the most important negotiation of Kyros' life. He couldn't afford to lose.

YOU CRAVE POWER.

It wasn't a question, it was a statement. Kyros didn't know the extent of this being's abilities, especially while contained within the prison. But he did know there was only one reason they would summon him here. The being knew what Kyros wanted, which meant he'd at least been paying some attention to Kyros recently.

"And you can provide it," Kyros replied. He didn't need to hear the reply, he knew it was true. He also sensed this individual wasn't one for small talk. It was best to get right to the point. "What are your terms?

Politics and deals were all about knowing who you were dealing with, figuring out exactly what they wanted, and exploiting it for your own gain. This was the power he'd always bragged about to his twin brother. Raw power was something Kyros desperately craved, but he knew it wasn't the only form of power. He didn't take for granted how much power one could wield with the right words and the ability to read people and know what they wanted. And Kyros was a master at reading people.

For example, he may not know much about this person, but he knew they wanted something from him. In fact, he knew exactly what they wanted, but he'd make them say it. It was another tactic. He wouldn't offer anything freely, including information.

MY FREEDOM IN EXCHANGE FOR POWER.

"Too much wiggle room in that deal and not enough guarantees," Kyros said. "Here's what I had in mind."

Kyros laid out his terms to the individual, being as specific as he could with what he wanted and what it would take for his part of the contract to be complete. The first thing Kyros wanted was a show of good faith - some power granted to him before he fully agreed to the deal. He wanted to make sure the individual could actually provide what he was offering for his end of the bargain. If he could provide that, Kyros would have the chance to agree to the rest of the contract or walk away.

'Freedom' was too subjective of a word for Kyros to agree to that stipulation of fulfilling his end of the contract. Instead, the contract would be fulfilled when a specific ritual was completed to summon back the individual. If the ritual didn't work, that wasn't Kyros' problem. He didn't want to be stuck in an endless contract.

And most of all, Kyros wanted a guarantee that the power would be his permanently. Once he'd completed his end of the deal, Kyros kept the power granted to him forever. The individual could cancel the contract at any time, but Kyros would keep the power no matter what.

In exchange, Kyros agreed to work towards the individual's goals to the best of his ability. This would include locating a lost city, collecting a few powerful Artifacts, and then returning to the city where the ritual would be done. The ritual would unlock the seals on the Star Prison, freeing the figure trapped within. Once that was done, Kyros had completed his end of the deal and was free to do what he wanted with the power granted to him.

YOUR OFFER IS ACCEPTED. PIERCE THE BARRIER AND IT WILL BE DONE.

This was it. He shoved his hand through the prison shield to seal their contract. His hand began to sizzle and burn as he pushed through the shield and he gritted his teeth in pain. He didn't care about the pain, as long as the power came with it. He reached his hand further into the prison and held it open towards the figure within the orb.

The figure extended his hand to Kyros. As soon as their hands met, lightning coursed through Kyros' body as a torrent of raw power surged into him. Kyros closed his eyes and screamed as the power threatened to tear him apart. He screamed until his voice hurt, and then he screamed some more.

"Kyros! Wake up!"

Kyros stopped screaming and opened his eyes, taking heavy breaths as his heart raced. It was morning and he was lying in his bed. He quickly sat up and saw his brother standing in the doorway, wearing the same robes as the night before with an annoyed look on his face.

"What in the void was that about?" Falrose asked.

Kyros looked at his hand, completely fine despite the vivid memory of it burning within the Star Prison what felt like only moments ago. Had it only been a dream? It felt so real.

Falrose stared at him. "Well?"

"Uh, nothing," Kyros said without looking up from his hand. "Just a bad dream I guess."

"Honestly, brother, you need to pull yourself together," Falrose said. "Your incessant screaming interrupted my studies just as I was making a breakthrough. Some of us actually have important things we're working on."

"Yeah sure, whatever," Kyros replied, turning his hand over to inspect the back. Nothing seemed physically different, but the burning felt so *real*.

"Hey, pay attention to me when I'm talking to you." A flash of arcane light finally captured Kyros' attention but he was too late to do anything as Falrose held him up in the air with his magic.

"Put me down, Falrose," Kyros said, barely keeping his anger in check.

"Oh, do I finally have your attention?" Falrose mocked as he toyed with Kyros by rotating him in the air above his bed. "This is what *real* power looks like, brother."

"Falrose…" Kyros growled, letting his anger seep through.

"What are you going to do?" Falrose continued. "Use the power of words to talk your way out of it? Maybe you should say please. I hear that's a magic word some people use!" he snickered.

"I said PUT ME DOWN!" Kyros reached for his brother and a ball of purple energy streaked out from his hand, slamming into his brother's chest. Falrose flew out the open door and tumbled into the hall beyond. Kyros immediately fell down onto his bed, free from his brother's spell.

Falrose slowly sat up, rubbing the back of his head, eyes wide in astonishment. The attack hadn't done any real damage, but Kyros had never manifested any magic like that in his life. His brother looked him up and down, searching for an explanation. He knew Kyros' limitations almost as much as he did.

"Kyros," Falrose said, all amusement and mocking gone from his voice. "What was that power?"

Kyros looked at the smoke rising from his hand as a grin slowly spread across his face.

"The power of words, brother," Kyros replied, looking up at Falrose. "Let me tell you about my dream."

* * *

"You'd better be sure about this, Kyros," Falrose muttered for what felt like the hundredth time. As they descended further into the caverns, the air grew cooler and more stale. Kyros placed his hand against the rocky wall to steady himself as he stepped over a crack. It was slick with moisture and veined with minerals that glinted in the torchlight. All they could hear were drips and echoes of their own footsteps in the dark.

They'd been delving for days, and the caverns continued deeper and deeper into the earth. The night after he'd made the deal, his new Patron contacted him again with instructions on how Kyros was to accept the rest of the contract. He'd proven he was capable of bestowing the power that Kyros craved, so he set out with a small party to ratify the rest of the deal.

Kyros needed to find a suitable conduit to access the rest of the power his Patron had promised him. But it hadn't been as easy as Kyros hoped. There was something that would do the trick at the end of what had turned out to be a dangerous trek into the earth.

"What, don't tell me daddy's powerful mage can't handle the challenge," Zandro said from behind.

"Shut it, Zandro, I can't believe you agreed to this in the first place," Falrose snapped back.

"Let's just say your brother can be very persuasive," Zandro said.

"So I've heard," Falrose said, rolling his eyes. "Are you really that greedy?"

"Oh, I'm not in this for the money, my dear," Zandro said. "Your brother offered me something so much more delicious than simple coin. But that's all I'll say about that."

Falros turned his attention to the fourth member of their little group. "And why are you here, Scarlet? Did my twin brother use his powers of persuasion on you as well?"

A draken woman dressed in black trousers and a tight-fitting shirt with a red sash around her waist stepped out of the shadows. Her red scales reflected the firelight of their torches in the dark.

"We all know I'm the persuasive one here, Falrose," She said with a slight tilt of her lips. "But in this case, yes, Kyros promised me something that nobody else has been able to deliver, courtesy of his new partnership."

"I told you words held more power than you knew, dear brother," Kyros said, putting a hand on Falrose's shoulder and stepping past him to the front of the group. "Now get behind me and step carefully. There's only one safe path through this room."

The floor before them was a mosaic of ancient runes. Kyros recognized some of them as similar to the ones found on the outside of the Star Prison - dwarven and florian runes of power. It was a death sentence for anyone who stepped on the wrong square crossing the room.

Fortunately, the power granted to him by his Patron allowed him to see invisible novaborn runes overlaying some of the other symbols. They marked a safe path through to the other side. It was only because he had access to his Patron's power that he could see the correct path. The others were blind to it. They'd have to follow his lead closely.

He carefully made his way through the hidden maze, following the invisible path. Zandro went next with no issues, and Scarlet followed quickly behind him. It was Falrose's turn.

"As much as I'd love to take the hard way across, let me show you what working smarter and not harder means," Falrose said.

Before Kyros could protest, Falrose traced a teleportation symbol in the air and his body phased out of view for a moment. But instead of appearing on the other side next to them, he appeared in the air above the runes and dropped face-first into the middle of the room.

"Frost and fire, Falrose, what in the void were you thinking?!" Kyros yelled. But his brother had been knocked out from the fall and wasn't moving.

They heard an audible click and a stone wall began to descend to cut off their path into the next room. Scarlet roared in rage as she leapt into the doorway and caught the stone as it descended. Kyros watched as her eyes flashed with crimson energy. Red steam began to rise from her body as she held the massive stone up to keep it from cutting off their path.

"Zandro, help me get my brother out of here!" Kyros said. He began crossing the safe path to the middle of the maze where his brother lay unconscious.

"Sorry, but I'm preoccupied at the moment," he heard Zandro say from behind. Kyros looked back over his shoulder to see Zandro had moved into a defensive position by the door Scarlet was holding up.

Three stone golems were advancing from the walls towards the door that was their escape. Zandro squared off against them to make sure they couldn't get to Scarlet and cause her to drop the door. Kyros could see the same runes covering various parts of the golems, and he thought he could see a faint novaborn rune on each one as well.

"Zandro, each one has a weak point that should deactivate them, but they're all in different spots. You'll have to use some kind of magic weapon to hit each point," Kyros said as he bent down to pick up his brother. "The one to your right has a weak spot on top of its left shoulder. The one on your left is behind its right knee. And I can't see the weak spot on the one in front of you, so it must be somewhere on the front of it."

Kyros started the slow trek back through the maze with his brother. He didn't want to risk setting off any other potential traps by taking a wrong step, so he'd have to trust Zandro and Scarlet to buy them the time they needed.

He saw Zandro take out a small vial of pale green liquid and coat one of his knives in it as he muttered some words under his breath.

The knife pulsed with energy and he slid it back into its sheath. As he did, the sickly green energy spread around him to the other knives he had sheathed at various parts of his body.

Kyros watched Zandro flick two knives into the front of the middle golem, one in its chest and another into one of its legs. Nothing happened, so he moved to engage the one on his right at close range. After dodging under an attack, he grabbed hold of the golem and used the momentum of its punch to swing himself up to the top of it. In one smooth motion, he drew a knife from somewhere on his chest and slammed it into the weak shoulder. The golem crumbled back into scattered stones.

Before the stones hit the ground, he'd already thrown two more knives at the middle golem, this time one into each arm. He passed close to the center golem and struck at both of its calves as he dodged another attack. Still, nothing happened, so he moved to engage the golem with the weakness on the back of its knees.

He must be trying to figure out where the weak spot is on that middle one even while he takes out the others, Kyros thought to himself. *Incredible.*

Kyros was almost to the other side. He watched Zandro roll past the far golem's legs and throw a knife behind his back into the weak spot Kyros had described. The golem crumbled like the first. Only one left, but it was getting dangerously close to Scarlet.

"This door isn't getting any lighter!" she yelled as the door fell to her shoulders. Massive amounts of red steam were pouring off of her. Kyros wasn't sure exactly how long she could use her power like that, but he knew it wasn't limitless.

Zandro ignored her and moved into close combat with the final golem. He was a whirlwind of attacks and dodges, but the golem stayed intact despite being riddled with cuts all along its body. Kyros finally reached the end of the maze with his brother.

"Kyros, I know where its weak spot is, but I need it to be prone!"

Zandro yelled between a flurry of attacks. "Is your idiot brother awake so he can knock this thing over with his magic?"

"No, he's still out cold, but I have an idea," Kyros called out, lowering his brother to the ground. "Be ready!"

Zandro nodded and rolled out of the way of a massive slam. Kyros watched as Scarlet dropped to a knee, still holding up the door, but it didn't seem like she could hold out for much longer. Kyros held out both of his hands and focused his new energy into each one. He took aim and fired two powerful blasts at the back of the golem's legs, knocking them out from under him and toppling it to the ground.

As soon as it was prone, Zandro slammed a knife into the bottom of both its feet, and it crumbled back into inert stone like the others. He didn't waste any time running over to Kyros and helping him pick Falrose off the ground. They hurried to the door, shoved Falrose through, and then dove through themselves. Scarlet roared and rolled into the room with them as the stone door slammed shut behind them.

"How did you know the weak point was on the bottom of its feet?" Kyros asked between catching his breath.

"It was the only logical place left I hadn't attacked and that you wouldn't be able to see easily. Simple really," Zandro said as he shrugged. He didn't even seem winded.

Scarlet, on the other hand, had collapsed with exhaustion, and Falrose was only beginning to come back to consciousness. Fortunately, this was the room they'd been searching for. He could see the hidden novaborn runes adorning the walls, and a small diamond-shaped crystal hung in the air in the center of the room.

"This is it, Zandro," Kyros said. "We made it."

Kyros began to step forward but Zandro grabbed his arm to stop him.

"Remember our deal, Kyros," Zandro whispered with fierce intensity. "I help you with whatever contract you've signed, and you deliver me the girl."

Kyros nodded. "I've already located her. She'll be involved in the next phase of our plan. I'll need someone with her kind of experience anyway."

"Good." Zandro smiled and released Kyros' arm.

Kyros walked to the small crystal in the center of the room and stopped about a foot away.

DO YOU ACCEPT THE CONTRACT?

"I accept," Kyros said.

Violet light exploded from the crystal and it streaked forward to embed itself into Kyros' head. His forehead burned and sizzled. The shadows around the room coalesced and rushed into him. Pain jolted through his body like strikes of lightning, just as it had in his dream, and he screamed at the massive amount of pain.

He didn't know how long it lasted, but the next thing he realized was that Zandro was helping him to his feet. He put a hand to his head to steady himself and felt the crystal embedded there. This was the conduit to his Patron's power that he sought, and he could feel it thrumming within him.

"Did it work?" Zandro asked.

"It worked," Kyros said with a smile.

"Great, so how do we get out of here?" Scarlet said. Kyros could see she was still recovering from the tremendous amount of Chi it must have taken her to keep the door open as long as she did.

"I can take care of that," Kyros said. The crystal on his forehead flashed with violet light and his eyes turned black. Shadows streaked out from Kyros along the ground and inky black tendrils snaked their way below the stone door. With the sound of stone grinding against stone, the heavy door rose from the ground, being pushed up by the tendrils controlled.

"Come along everyone," Kyros said, strolling through the door back into the room with the runic maze. "And this time, Falrose, let's follow directions. It would be a shame to lose you before we rediscover the lost city of Lumenova."

* * *

Kyros climbed to the top of a building close to the gates of Midral after seeing the debris and carnage and deciding he needed a better viewpoint. Below him, the once-majestic gates of Midral lay in ruins, crushed under the might of the giants' assault. Glancing around, he also noticed a rather large number of orcs and even some dire wolves that had been slaughtered inside the city as well.

He heard a crash off to his right as the lone giant inside the city walls rampaged through the streets. He climbed back down from the building and proceeded towards the decimated city gates. As he got close, three looming shadows approached the city from outside the walls and blocked Kyros' exit.

"You have what is rightfully ours," the biggest of the three giants said to Kyros. "Give it back and we will make your death painless."

"And if I don't?" Kyros replied with a smile.

"We will strip the flesh from your bones while you still live, and consume it as you watch," the giant boomed down at him.

"Oh that does sound tempting, but I'm sorry, I'll have to take a rain check. I have a previous engagement."

Kyros held the staff still radiating with Niradim's Flame in front of him and began to draw the holy fire out of it.

This was going to be *so* much fun.

19

Val'ran

Val couldn't help but think of her fallen comrade as she dodged between houses and fired another arrow over her shoulder. He probably would have said something stupid about trying to lead the giant for a nice cold drink and she'd be telling him to shut up for the millionth time.

She turned another corner, intending to lead the giant back in a circle to get him closer to the others. Val's heartbeat pounded in her ears, and her heavy breath left clouds of fog trailing behind her as she ran. They must be finishing up with their targets pretty soon, and they needed to get back to the gates for the next round of giants. She couldn't imagine the damage that one of those greater giants could do if let loose in the city, much less three.

She turned a corner a little too sharply and her feet slid out from under her. Ice had already formed on the cobblestone streets from the sudden winter storm. The giant advanced and swung his wooden club down at her. She pushed off a nearby rock and slid on her back a few feet, narrowly dodging the attack. She used the momentum from the slide to tuck into a roll and get her feet back under her.

While the giant was preparing his next attack, she sprinted forward, drawing her scimitar which roared to life with blue flame. She slid under the giant's attack and through the giant's legs, slicing a deep cut with her blade as she passed through. The giant roared with pain and stumbled forward before regaining his balance and turning around.

She turned and skidded to a stop on one knee and took a look at the giant. He tested the foot back on the ground and looked up at her, face contorted in rage. In a movement quicker than she expected, he flung a nearby carriage at her. Her reflexes reacted quickly, but the ice on the road betrayed her again. Heavy wood slammed into her, and the impact sent her sliding across the ice and dislocated her shoulder.

"I finally caught you, you annoying little gnat," the giant snarled in her face as he reached down and scooped her up in one hand. "I am going to enjoy squeezing you until you pop."

He squeezed and she screamed as her body began to bend. Nothing had broken, but the pain was immense. She was beginning to get lightheaded and she couldn't breathe, as the giant's grip tightened around her. He began to laugh, but she barely registered it as the edges of her vision began to darken.

Suddenly, the giant bellowed in pain and dropped her to the ground. Confused and dazed from the fall, she looked up as the giant clawed at his face. Two large arrows protruded from between the fingers of each hand, deeply embedded into each eye. A figure ran across the rooftop to her right and jumped toward the giant.

Steel flashed and deep crimson poured from the clean wound that appeared at the giant's throat. Its screams turned to gurgling as it choked on its own blood. It fell backward in the street, slamming into the ground across from her.

"Hey Val, I've been thinking," a familiar figure said as he casually cleaned off his blade and walked toward her out of the shadows. "*Technically*, I never made it to the top of the wall since it broke while I was climbing. So that means you were actually the last one to the top."

Bogg smiled as he reached out a hand to help her up.

"I think you owe me dinner and drinks!"

* * *

It took her a few minutes to shake off both the damage she had taken and the fact that Bogg was, in fact, still alive. He helped her pop her shoulder back into place and she rotated it to test it out. That was really going to hurt tomorrow if they somehow made it to the end of the day alive. It was time to meet with Landren and the others.

"Bogg, how in the world are you alive?" Val said. "I saw the boulders hit the gates while you were still on them!"

Bogg was pretty banged up, with cuts and bruises covering every inch of his body. She was still impressed with how much of a beating he could take without seeming fazed at all.

"Well yeah, they hit the *gate*, they didn't hit *me*," Bogg explained with a shrug as they ran. "Although to be fair - after the boulders hit the gate, a whole lot of the gate hit me and knocked me out real good for a while. But then I woke up and started wanderin' around."

"You just wandered around?" Val asked.

"Well I killed a few wolves and orcs, but then I got lost," he said, gesturing around himself. "This is a pretty big city, you know? Then I heard some commotion and thought it sounded like fun and then there you were gettin' squeezed like a pimple. So I shot that big oaf in both eyes and cut his throat."

Val was dumbstruck by how casual Bogg was about his near-death experience. But then again, Bogg was a simple man, and he didn't see it as *near death* as much as *not death.* He didn't die all the time, so why should this time be any different? She shook her head and smiled. Yeah, she'd missed this big dummy.

"So that shot in the eyes, that was one shot with two arrows knocked?" Val asked.

"Yeah, I saw you do it before and it looked fun," Bogg said. "Twice the killin' for just one shot? Sign me up."

Never mind the fact that the shot was close to where the giant held her, which means either arrow could have hit her instead. *Or* the fact that technically he didn't even get one kill from the double-arrow shot since he had to finish the giant off with his sword. It was still very impressive.

"Well, thanks again, Bogg," Val said. "And congrats on spontaneously learning logic when food and drinks are involved. You're right, technically since I was the last one up the wall, I owe you dinner and drinks."

Val searched the streets for any signs of the other giants, but it sounded like the threat was neutralized at the moment. She steered them towards the main road that led to the gates.

"By the way," Val said. "You'll never guess who I ran into today."

"Oh yeah, who?" Bogg asked.

"Landren."

"Really? That old fart is here?"

"Bogg, that 'old fart' is a powerful martial artist, and I watched him literally shoot energy out of his hands and blow up a ton of orcs," Val said. "Plus, I think he's already killed two giants on his own."

Bogg let out a long whistle. "Well I have to admit, that is very impressive for an old fart."

"Yes, it is," Val replied. "And hopefully it will be enough to defend the gates against the next wave of giants. The next ones coming are much larger and more powerful than the one you just killed. We need to meet up with him and a couple of others who have been helping us defend the city."

"Sounds like more fun," Bogg said with a grin.

"It always does, to you," Val said, but couldn't help returning his grin.

"It's good to have you back."

Her face turned more serious as she remembered that Zandro was still somewhere out there in the city.

"What's wrong?" Bog asked.

"It's Zandro," Val replied with a grimace. "I don't know what his part in all this is, but I know he's involved."

"What's your deal with this guy anyways?" Bogg asked. "I know you want to kill him, but why?"

"It's simple really," Val said, her voice lowering as the memories flashed in her mind.

"He killed everyone I loved."

* * *

Four years ago

"Seriously Val, great shot!"

"Thanks, Vix!"

Val and the white-scaled draken ducked down behind a boulder to obscure themselves from view. The rest of their squad would be infiltrating the enemy camp on foot, now that Val had taken out the guards at the gate. She and Vix had been tasked with providing the other Arcane Knights a way in. Her main objective was already complete, now it was Vixia's turn.

Val watched as Vix's scales began to emit a soft, ethereal glow. Moments later, a dense, creeping fog rolled down from the cliffside, enveloping the encampment in a thick, misty blanket. Val could barely make out a few shadowy figures entering the front of the camp. Here and there, she'd see an arcane flash of light in the fog, but no sound. Zandro must be using his sound-dampening magic to cover their infiltration.

"Do you think he'll actually be here this time?" Val said as they climbed down the steep rocks to join their team.

"Who knows?" Vix replied. "This is what, the fifth camp we've infiltrated over the last several weeks?"

"Yeah, and he keeps getting away," Val said. "It's almost like he knows we're coming."

"They probably keep him moving around because of attacks like this," Vix said.

"Don't worry, Val, we'll pin him down one of these days. Now focus on the climb."

They finished their descent and closed in on the back of the enemy camp. Their mission was to capture or kill one of their enemy's nobles who commanded a large number of their forces. The problem was, every time they got close he slipped through their fingers, usually departing a day or two before they attacked. But this time, their intel was fresh. He had to be there.

They reached the bottom and scanned the area to be sure they hadn't been spotted. Everything was clear around where they were. Their next orders were to stay put and wait for Zandro and the others to finish clearing out the camp, but Val was restless. She needed to be out there fighting.

"You know, it really only takes one of us to keep watch in this area..." Val said.

"Those weren't our orders Val, you know that," Vix said.

"Oh come on, what if our target tries to sneak out the back?" Val pleaded. "Doesn't it make more sense for one of us to be covering the back exit?"

"Ugh, fine, just don't die, got it?" Vix said.

"Got it!" Val said with a sly wink. She waved as she left Vix to stand watch.

Val picked a nearby tree and quickly scaled it to the top. From her vantage point, she could barely make out a lone guard well out towards the back of the camp keeping watch. He was far enough away from the camp that nobody should notice right away if he went missing.

She sighted him with her bow and steadied her breathing. She focused her magic into her arrow and waited for the perfect moment for the man to peek out around a tree... Now!

She let her arrow fly. It sliced through the night air with a whisper, finding its mark deep in the man's neck. She felt a familiar jolt as she switched locations with the man and found herself at the back of the camp. She wasn't worried whether or not her shot had been fatal. Vix would make quick work of the guard if he still had a pulse when he fell out of the tree.

She took in her new surroundings and noticed another person standing guard opposite of her. Before he could process what was going on, she threw one of her knives and silenced any potential alarm he could raise. Val moved into the camp with silent steps, her eyes scanning the shadowy outlines of the camp. Her every sense was attuned to the hidden dangers that lurked in the obscured night.

Visibility was still limited because of Vix's fog, so she made sure to be on high alert for any potential dangers. Most people would be sleeping this time of night, but you never knew when someone might exit their tent to relieve themselves. The path to the target's tent was clear, so she approached from the front.

After listening for a moment and not hearing anything, she slipped inside. The tent was massive and had been sectioned off almost into what could be considered different living areas. A desk with a stack of papers and maps strewn about its surface sat empty in the center of the main part of the tent. She ignored that for the moment as she approached the smaller section at the back of the tent and pulled out a knife. She swung the flap open and prepared to attack.

It was empty. He'd gotten away. Again.

Frost and Fire!, Val cursed to herself, sheathing her knife.

What was it going to take to catch this guy? She couldn't tell exactly, but the way the tent was put together and felt lived in made it seem like he'd left in a hurry. In fact, she didn't recall ever seeing him leave behind intel like papers or maps in any previous of their attempts. Maybe she could find out more.

She retraced her steps to the desk and began to investigate. The letters on the desk were updates from other troops on their movements, and the map showed their camps and plans for future movements. This intel would prove invaluable. Even if they hadn't been able to catch their target, this intel would almost completely make up for it, though it didn't make her feel much better.

She was about to head back out of the tent when a charred piece of paper caught her eye. It looked like someone had left it to burn, but the fire had blown out before the entire paper had burned up. The top had been completely burned away, but the bottom was still legible.

...tonight. By the time you receive this letter, you have less than an hour to get out. Don't bother packing.

-V

Val's heart skipped a beat. This couldn't be what it looked like. Something had been bothering her about how their target kept slipping through their fingers. Now she knew why.

Someone in the Arcane Knights was a traitor.

* * *

"Zandro, can I talk to you in private for a moment."

"Of course, my dear. What's troubling you?"

The rest of the Arcane Knights had cleared the enemy camp without resistance. It was to be expected, they were an elite group of specially trained soldiers. Now they were back at camp, drinking and having fun, not focusing on the fact that their target hadn't been at the location for the fifth time in a row.

And now she had something indicating that one of their own had been betraying them the whole time. Even worse, the evidence suggested it was the person who was like a sister to her.

But even if it wasn't her, the Arcane Knights had always been like family to her. She was the youngest member, but she'd grown up around all five of them since her father had founded the Arcane Knights almost a decade ago. After her father's death, she'd worked her way into their elite group under Zandro's tutelage. She'd be devastated to find out any one of them had turned to the other side.

Zandro led her through the whispering trees, their leaves rustling like quiet secrets in the twilight. Shadows lengthened, transforming the familiar woods into a realm of shadows, mirroring the uncertainty and fear knotting in Val's stomach.

"What's wrong?" Zandro asked her again.

She didn't know where to begin. So she did the only thing she could think of. She pulled the note out of her pocket and handed it to Zandro. He tilted his head as he took the charred note and read through the small amount of text that remained.

"What is this?" he asked her.

"I found it in Lord Syndalin's tent," she said. She picked her next words carefully. "I think the reason we haven't been able to pin him down is because someone has been tipping him off."

Zandro raised one of his eyebrows at her. She held her breath. What she was suggesting was something that would tear their close-knit group apart at the seams. She hoped Zandro could provide some kind of plausible explanation as to how it was impossible the most logical answer was true. That one of the few people she considered family was betraying them.

Zandro studied her for a moment as if considering what he should say. She could hear her heartbeat pounding in her ears. Each second felt like an eternity as she waited for Zando to say something.

"I've been thinking the same thing for a couple weeks," Zandro finally said, and her heart dropped. "This only seems to confirm my suspicions."

She nodded, tears forming in her eyes.

"I don't want it to be true," she whispered.

"Neither do I," Zandro said with a sad smile. "But this is the harsh reality we live in. This is a hard lesson, but a valuable one. You can't ever fully trust anyone."

But she did. She trusted all of them, even knowing that everything pointed to one of their betrayals.

"Do you have any suspicions who it could be?" she asked him.

"I didn't," Zandro said. He turned the paper around and pointed at the signature at the bottom. A single letter 'V'. "But there are only two people in the Arcane Knights whose names begin with the letter 'V'. One of them brought me this evidence. That would be a rather stupid thing to do if they were betraying their comrades and wanted to keep it a secret, don't you think?"

She nodded again. She hated this. Not Vix. Vix had been the youngest in the squad before Val joined, and they were already close before Val even joined the Arcane Knights. Vix was her absolute best friend in the world, could it really be her?

"I just can't believe she would do this to us…" Val said. "I've known her almost my whole life. I can't imagine her ever doing anything like this."

Zandro nodded. "It always hurts the worst when it's the ones closest to you."

"What do we do?" Val asked.

Zandro paused for a moment to consider.

"Nothing for now," Zandro said. "Even with such strong evidence, we haven't proven anything without a shadow of a doubt. Perhaps we'll discover that these warnings are coming from somewhere else, and we don't want to be premature in our actions."

Val's spirits rose. It was selfish of her, but she didn't want to take an action that would split apart the little family they'd become.

"Ok," Val agreed.

"But," Zandro said. "I will watch her more closely, and so will you. Two sets of eyes are better than one, and if she is in fact a mole, it will be more difficult for her to send warnings out from now on. Stick to her and watch her every move. That's an order."

"Yes, sir," Val said.

Zandro started to walk back to the camp but turned after a few steps.

"And Val," he said. "Thank you for bringing this to my attention. It was the right thing to do."

She watched as he walked back to the others and wished she felt the same as he did.

* * *

"Night Val!"

"Good night Vix."

Val entered her tent and settled in. Ever since their conversation a couple weeks ago, Val had been keeping a close eye on Vix, as ordered. She hadn't discovered anything definitive, but it did seem like Vix was keeping a closer eye on Zandro than normal. Maybe that was how she got her intel out to the enemy. She might be able to learn something by spying on him and then send out a warning.

Now, they were on the verge of infiltrating a sixth camp, and Val was losing sleep each night as she made sure she didn't miss anything Vix might be up to. So far, she was as certain as she could be that Vix hadn't been able to send any warnings out from their camp. If she was going to do anything, it would be tonight.

Unfortunately, the sleep Val had been losing was catching up to her. She found it difficult to stay up and soon nodded off to a light sleep. About an hour later, she startled awake at the sound of Vix's tent flap rustling. They took turns keeping watch each night, so it wasn't completely unusual for Vix to be waking up this time of night.

But it wasn't her turn to be on watch.

Warde should be the one currently on watch, but she didn't hear the novaborn make any comments about Vix being up so late. Well, maybe he just didn't have anything to say. He was the quietest of the bunch, always lost in thought. But something didn't feel right. Val waited a couple more moments, but when Vix didn't return immediately to her tent, she knew she had to investigate.

She crept out of her tent and made her way to the front of the camp where Warde would be. Maybe she'd find Vix keeping him company on the night before a mission. She could see Warde sitting up against a tree but could tell immediately that something was off.

She hurried over to him and found him completely unconscious. He was still alive, but in a deep sleep that she wasn't able to shake him out of.

Vix had to have done this with her magic. Val's heart started to race with anger. Vix had been betraying them this whole time, right under her nose. She should go back and wake the rest of the group, but she could make out a light getting further out of view heading toward the river. No, she'd hunt Vix down herself right now and end this.

She sped down the path, thankful that she had thought to grab her bow and arrows and her father's scimitar before leaving. They had camped up on a ridge and there was only one path down that led toward a river. Once Vix got to the river, the path branched in different directions so it would be difficult to keep tracking her.

Val caught up just as Vix approached the river and turned to head downstream. Fortunately, the sound of the river allowed Val to sneak a lot closer than if it had been quiet. Vix crouched at the edge of a small cliff that overlooked the other bank, about twenty feet above the river. She was staring at something on the other side.

Val followed her gaze and her jaw dropped as she saw Lord Syndalin with a small personal guard standing on the other side of the riverbank. So it was true. Vix was meeting with him to warn him of their attack.

Rage boiled in her veins as she slotted an arrow into her bow. As much as she wanted to end Vix right then and there, she would subdue her instead and bring her in for questioning. If she took Vix out quickly, she may even be able to finish off Lord Syndalin here as well.

Val poured her arcane energy into her arrow and took aim. Vix turned and began to walk in Val's direction. She looked up and met Val's eyes and her own widened in shock as Val let loose with her arrow. The arrow struck Vix in the left shoulder, erupting into a cascade of thorny vines that spiraled outward. They bound her tightly, biting into her flesh as she fell with a muffled cry. Val closed the distance between them and held a knife to Vix's throat.

"How could you, Vix?" Val said

"What? Val, what are you doing here?" Vix asked, visible confusion playing across her face.

"We trusted you, and you've been working for Lord Syndalin this whole time," Val said. "Now I'm going to finish him off and bring you in."

"No, Val, I'm not the one working for him," Vix said. "It's Zandro!"

"You can't possibly expect me to believe that," Val said. "Zandro would never do that to us."

"No, it's true," Vix said. "I started suspecting something was off after the third failed assassination mission. It was too much of a coincidence that Syndalin kept getting away before we even got there."

"You told me they kept him moving from location to location," Val said.

"I didn't know who I could trust at the time," Vix said. "But think about it, Val, really think about it. Zandro was the only one of us who knew the location of our last mission early enough to have gotten word out to someone."

"A good attempt at lying your way out of this, my dear, but I'm afraid Val's not buying it."

"Zandro!" Vix growled.

Zandro walked up from behind a nearby tree, standing next to Val, facing Vix on the ground. He muttered some words and the forest and river went silent around them. He had them within a sound-dampening barrier.

"Val, you have to believe me, he's the traitor!" Vix said.

"That's enough, Vix," Val said. "We know it's you. We found a letter in the enemy camp to Syndalin signed 'V'. And now he's waiting across the river you happen to be standing next to."

"I'm here because I was following *him!*" Vix said. She muttered a couple words under her breath, but Zandro flicked one of his throwing knives at her. His knife cut into her throat as the sound of the river and forest came crashing back in around them.

"No! Vix!" Val cried.

"I'm so sorry," Zandro said. "She cast a spell to drop my barrier, likely to call for help. I couldn't let her."

Val was in shock. She couldn't believe Vix was dead.

"Viridian! I'm not going to wait here all night!" She could hear Lord Syndalin calling out from across the river.

Viridian? Was that Vix's code name or something? She didn't care at the moment. Her best friend was dead, and a traitor. Her hands covered her eyes as she began to weep. She knew she shouldn't cry for a traitor, but it felt so wrong that her best friend was dead.

"It's all right. Let's get back to camp, there's nothing more we can do here," Zandro said, taking her by the arm.

"I'm serious, I won't be kept waiting!" Syndalin called again.

"But… Lord Syndalin…" Val started.

"Has nobody to warn him we're coming tomorrow," Zandro said, trying to lead her away. "You're in no shape to fight right now. We'll take him out after we've rested and spoken with the rest of the team."

She began to let him lead her away. Vix. Why did it have to be Vix? But the more she thought about it, the more doubt began to creep into her mind. Was she sure it was Vix? She stopped walking. What if she'd been telling the truth? She'd been getting closer to Zandro recently, but if she thought he was the traitor, that checked out. She said she'd been following Zandro, and then he appeared just after Val had confronted Vix. And Warde… That could have been the work of one of Zandro's many poisons and not a spell.

"That's it, consider your next payment cut in half for making me wait, Zandro!" Syndalin yelled.

Val stopped cold in her tracks.

"Thorns," Zandro said. "I've told him a thousand times never to use my real name."

Val spun, only to meet Zandro's cold gaze as his knife slid into her stomach. A sharp, searing pain erupted from the wound, spreading like wildfire through her veins. Poison.

"I truly hoped it wouldn't come to this," he said to her. She was in an immense amount of pain, but Zandro's betrayal was more agonizing than his blade had been.

She couldn't make sense of what was happening. Zandro was the traitor. And he'd played her and made her think it was her best friend. He'd practically raised her, how could he do this to her? She placed a hand over the wound in her stomach and felt the magical energy drain out of her. It was Zandro's signature poison, then.

She began to feel dizzy and started to slump to the ground.

"Why?" she asked.

"There's a lot of profit selling intel to the highest bidder, and the commander of the Arcane Knights is privy to a lot of very expensive intel," he said. "I tried convincing your father once, but he didn't agree. He put up more of a fight than you did though, as you can see." He gestured to the burn on his face.

Zandro had killed her father. She hung onto that thought even as she fought for consciousness. She would make him pay.

"I tried to tell you, my dear," Zandro said as she finally succumbed to the darkness.

"It always hurts the worst when it's the ones closest to you."

* * *

Present day

"When I finally woke up, I went back to our camp to find the rest of my squad completely slaughtered," Val said. "Zandro had slit all their throats."

"That's terrible," Bogg said. "I'm confused though, how did you survive the poison?"

"Ironically, it was because of Zandro," Val answered. "Since he trained me after he killed my father, he taught me about poisons, so I thought it would be a good idea to build up my own immunity to as many as I could. I took several micro-doses of Zandro's signature poison over a long period of time, which was awful, by the way. But the tolerance it gave me was enough to keep me from dying."

"Well, sounds like he made a huge mistake," Bogg said.

"What mistake?" Val asked.

"Underestimating you," Bogg said with a smile.

Val returned the smile. She was glad her walls were starting to come down. She missed having people close to her. She still struggled with trusting anyone, but hopefully, that would get better with time.

After Val and Bogg turned onto the main road, she could see the aftermath of Landren's second giant kill a few blocks down in the direction of the front gates. Bogg and Val picked up the pace and arrived as the others were preparing to head in the direction she had led her giant.

"Val!" Landren said, then noticed her companion. "And Bogg! My goodness, it's great to see you alive!" He took Bogg in an embrace, confusing Bogg at the sudden display of emotion from the historically stoic monk. "What are you two doing here? What of your giant?"

"Yeah, I got myself into a little bit of a mess," Val said. "Fortunately Bogg took advantage of me distracting the giant as a squeeze toy and was able to take him out."

Bogg beamed. "Yeah, I did the double-shot right into his eyes and then cut his throat."

"I... see," Landren said with a confused glance at Val. She shook her head to signal don't worry about it. "Well, we can take all the help we can get. We don't have time for full introductions right now, but this is my pupil, Brand, and his friend, Astoro. We'll catch up over drinks later, which I think Brand has agreed to pay for." He winked at Brand, who put a hand to his head. "For now, we go to defend the front gates. Let's go!"

Landren took off at a sprint, and the rest of them followed behind. As they ran, Val assessed their current state. They were quite the beat-up crew, but right now they were the city's best and only line of defense. It would have to be enough.

They had a decent plan, and one more person than they did the first time around. Greater giants were faster, stronger, and smarter than normal giants, so this would still be difficult even with an extra person to help. Simple tricks to keep them distracted wouldn't be as effective and they weren't at full strength. Their situation was dire at best.

She was deep in the process of seeing if there were any better ways of attacking their problem when Landren yelled "Look out!" and dove in front of her, snatching a knife out of the air that had been looking to find its home in the middle of her chest. She snapped out of her thoughts, skidding to a stop and taking in her surroundings.

A figure leapt off of a nearby roof in a large arc and landed on the road before them. She stared as a familiar florian with a burn scarring the side of his face stepped out of the shadows.

"Zandro!" Val yelled.

"Yes, my dear, it's me," Zandro said, scanning the battle-worn group before him. "My my, while I may not know all of your names, it seems as if I've met most of you before, how delightful!" He clapped his hands together in mock glee.

"How's that wound treating you, my friend?" he said, looking at Brand. "Bit of a tricky little thing, that poison is, isn't it? It's truly one of my favorites, and I'm surprised you survived. Most don't." He shot a knowing glance at Astoro. "What a shame." He chuckled as he turned his attention to Landren.

"And you! We haven't met, but I've been watching you for a while now," he said. "Your Golden Chi is impressive, but not quite as impressive as what I've seen from Crimson."

Val noticed Brand's eyes widen and he shifted uncomfortably.

"I still have a few minutes before I need to meet Kyros at the front gates," Zandro said. "Maybe the five of us could have some fun before I depart?" A wicked smile spread across his face.

She'd almost forgotten in all the excitement that they were working together. No wonder the city was in chaos. Zandro and Kyros working together would be a force to be reckoned with. It was unfortunate that Midral was suffering so much collateral damage from whatever their plot was. She didn't know how the two of them had connected, but that would be bad news for anyone unlucky enough to be in their way.

"Listen, everyone," Landren said under his breath without turning around. "It's clear we're not going to be able to leave him here, but we also need to get back to the front gates to deal with the giants."

"Did he say he was meeting Kyros?" Val asked.

"Yes," Landren said. "And that worries me, knowing what I do about Kyros."

"Agreed," Val said. "Leave Zandro to me, he's my responsibility."

"I understand why you want this, Val, but you and I both know this man is incredibly dangerous," Landren said to her. "Use the advantage of numbers to take him out. He's at full strength, and we're not. You'll need assistance. Don't let your bloodlust for revenge get you killed."

He was right. She nodded. She had already seen what kind of person she was when she focused only on revenge. She didn't want to be that person anymore.

"You're right, Landren," she said. "What do you suggest?"

"The four of you work together to take out Zandro," Landren said. "I'll rush ahead to deal with the giants. Finish Zandro quickly if you can, and I'll keep the giants and Kyros busy until you get there."

"Just save some giants for us, old man," Bogg said with a smirk.

Landren nodded and gave them a quick smile. "Good luck." He darted to the side down an alley that would take him to an adjacent street and disappeared from view.

It was them and Zandro now. Brand took a stance that Val had seen from Landren countless times and nodded at his Pathwarden. Astoro took a deep breath and steadied himself. Bogg just grinned as he drew his sword. Val didn't take her eyes off her prey but nodded.

"What a shame, I was looking forward to testing myself against him," Zandro said, watching Landren take off towards Kyros. "Oh well, you four will have to do."

He took a small glass vial and muttered something under his breath as he poured it over a knife in his other hand. Once the liquid coated the blade, it began to glow a sickly pale green color. He sheathed the knife, and the glowing energy traveled in currents around his body, slowly pulsing.

"Ok, listen up everyone," Val said. "About that spell he just used - every time he sheathes and then draws a knife from anywhere on his body, poison will be applied to the blade. The poison only lasts about five seconds before it wears off and he has to re-sheath the weapon to apply the poison again."

"How long does this spell last?" Astoro asked.

"About an hour," Val replied. "So there's no stalling for time here and waiting for the spell to wear off."

"And I'm sure most of you know," Brand cut-in. "But that poison will incapacitate you quickly."

"But not us," Val explained. "It's a long story, but his poison won't work on me, and because you've already recovered once before, your body will fight it off better than before. Though it'll still be a heck of a recovery." Val shook off the memories that began to broil under the surface.

She looked at Astoro and Bogg. "But for the two of you, don't get cut by a glowing blade. I have an antidote, but only enough to save one person."

"I'll hang back then," Astoro said. "I can draw the poison out with my magic if one of you gets hit, but the poison will nullify my magic immediately if I go down. Besides, I'm not in the same league as all of you in close combat, I would only get in the way."

"Ashes!" Brand cursed as he dodged a glowing knife that Zandro had flicked in his direction. He glared at Zandro.

"What? You expected me to just sit here and wait for you all to finish having a nice chat?" Zandro asked. "I'm on a timetable here, if you didn't notice." He gestured to the glowing spots dotted around his armor. "Now please, stop wasting my time."

"Let's go," Val said, calmer than she felt. She drew her father's scimitar which flared to life with a blue flame and charged into battle, Bogg and Brand followed her.

Zandro was as dangerous as she remembered, perhaps even more so. The first few minutes of fighting were a slew of testing strikes and dodges. The three of them had to get the hang of fighting together and figuring out how Zandro attacked, all while staying out of the reach of his blades.

Val could see that Brand was very cautious about getting too close. She was a little more brazen about her attacks, but she was worried about Bogg. He tended to lose himself in battle and didn't care too much about getting injured, but it was critically important he didn't take any cuts in this fight. So far, he was remembering the instructions, but she could tell he was beginning to press more and more as the fight went on.

Zandro dodged in and out of their attacks, parrying everything the trio threw at him. He kept forcing them into situations where they almost hit each other. He was toying with them. There were a few times that Val noticed Zandro would let the poison run out on his blade and then score a shallow strike on Bogg or Brand to make a point. He was in complete control of the fight.

He had a more difficult time with Val. She was focused and knew his tactics from fighting side by side with him for years. As she saw Brand lose steam after taking a few non-poisoned strikes, she pushed. Zandro became more focused on defending against her attacks than playing with his prey. Even so, she still couldn't land a solid hit on him.

Zandro parried one of Brand's punches and used the momentum to throw him into Val and Bogg, knocking the three of them down into a heap.

"Val, I do believe you've gone rusty since the last time I saw you fight," Zandro taunted. "Good thing Do'ran isn't here to see how much his daughter has fallen."

Val saw red at the mention of her father. "You keep his name out of your mouth!" she screamed and rushed Zandro, unleashing a flurry of attacks. Bogg and Brand were untangling themselves from one another and Astoro rushed over to heal Brand, who was bleeding from a wound at his shoulder.

Val swung and swung in fury, pushing Zandro away from the others. The sudden flurry caught Zandro off guard for the moment. She finally landed a clean strike across his chest, opening a shallow wound and burning the armor and some of the flesh below. Zandro screamed in pain and managed to push Val back with his open hand a few paces.

"Oh, now that's the fiery spirit I remember!" Zandro said. He took one of his fingers and traced the slash across his chest and pulled away some blood. He licked his fingers clean of the blood while staring at Val, a wild look in his eyes. "It's been a long long time since someone has been able to make me feel pain, Val. But now I need to return the favor."

He began to circle to his right a few paces, putting her between him and Bogg, who was getting back to his feet to rejoin the fight.

"There's nothing more you can do to me to inflict more pain. I've already suffered enough at your hands," Val said. Her limbs were beginning to feel the strain of all the fighting.

He drew one of the knives, which pulsed with that sickly green color. "Oh, I wouldn't be so sure, my dear. There's always room for more pain when one forms attachments." He threw the blade at her chest, but she dodged to the side and smirked at him.

"Argh, burning ashes!" Bogg cursed from behind as she heard him clatter to the ground. She spun around and saw Zandro's knife, still pulsing green, sticking out of Bogg's thigh as he struggled to stand back up.

"No!" she screamed and ran over to Bogg.

"Slag and ashes!" Bogg cursed as she slid up to him. "Sorry, Val, I didn't see him throw that one."

Zandro had put Val between him and Bogg to create a blind spot so Bogg couldn't see Zandro's movements. He threw the knife knowing Val would dodge and that Bogg wouldn't have enough time to react before being hit. Val had saved her own life but doomed her friend. Fortunately, she had the antidote.

"Hold on Bogg, let me get the…" Val said as she frantically searched her pockets for the vial.

"Looking for this?" Zandro said. She spun and terror gripped her as she saw him holding her one vial with the antidote. "I'm afraid you must have dropped it in the scuffle. It was a calculated risk to let you get close enough to hit me, but I must say it was worth it. The pain in my chest will be temporary, but this memory of the look on your face will last a lifetime. And it is absolutely *delicious*." His face morphed into a sinister smile.

That one strike she landed was all a part of Zandro's twisted little game to toy with her. When she'd cut him across the chest, he'd pushed her back. He must have used that opportunity to pick her pocket and come away with the antidote. He'd also made sure to not hit anyone with a poisoned blow until after he stole the vial away from Val. He waited until a situation came up where he could fight her one-on-one for a moment. He was right, there was one more way he could cause her pain…

She fell back and couldn't breathe. Bogg was beginning to fade as the poison took hold. It would take only a few minutes for the poison to work completely into his body and start shutting organs down.

Astoro ran to their side and his hands lit with a bright green glow. He yanked the now dull knife out of Bogg's wound, the pain helping

Bogg stay conscious for the moment. Then he placed one glowing hand on the wound, and the other on Bogg's chest and told him to relax and lie back.

"Weeds and rot!" Astoro cursed under his breath. He turned to Val "I'm too weak at the moment to heal him completely from something like this. The best I can do is stabilize him for as long as I can to give you two more time."

Val nodded. "Thank you Astoro." She looked at Brand. "Are you ready, Brand? It's just us now."

"Uh, yeah… I'm ready," Brand said, but his breathing was erratic and he had a distant look in his eye.

He didn't look ready, he looked scared. Val had seen that look many times in battle. Brand had reached the limit of what his mind could take. Now that they were down another person, taking a hit from Zandro's poison blades terrified him.

"You know what's so interesting?" Zandro said to them. "The only two people who have ever survived my poison are now standing before me. It's almost as if the universe is giving me a second chance to fix my clumsy mistakes."

Val saw Brand swallow hard at that statement. Zandro had seen the fear in Brand's eyes and was playing into it and making it grow.

"Don't listen to him, Brand," Val said. They didn't have time to waste, she needed to get that vial back and save Bogg. She moved to attack, and Brand, despite the obvious fear, moved in to attack with her.

Zandro continued to feed that fear in Brand. He used the same tactic as before, letting the green pulse extinguish from his blade before landing a strike on Brand. But this time the wounds were cutting deeper. Val was able to hold off any strikes from hitting her, but Brand's wounds were piling up and he was becoming more and more unfocused.

Finally, Zandro kicked Val back a few feet, creating some separation as she tumbled across the ground and he focused on Brand. Brand's eyes grew and he tried throwing a feeble strike. Zandro caught the punch, twisting Brand's arm and turning him around to face Val, who had only gotten up to her knee. He was bound in an arm lock, with Zandro standing directly behind him.

"This has been the most fun I have had in a long time, but I think our time is now coming to an end, my dear," Zandro said. "I need to get back to Kyros and get out of here, so this is where we finish." He pulled a blade out, pulsing green, and held it up to Brand's chest.

"Now, if I remember correctly, last time I hit you in this shoulder over here," he taunted as he tapped the point of the knife on Brand's left shoulder, causing Brand to flinch. "Perhaps a matching hole on the other side would be good?"

Val couldn't save him, there was no way to get there in time. She knelt among the blood splattered during their fight, mostly Brand's, and tried to think. There must be something she could do, she couldn't watch as Zandro killed another person in front of her. As she racked her brain, a memory popped into her mind of the plan she and Bogg had enacted to escape the prison. She had no time to think as Zandro's arm plunged towards Brand's chest. She reached down and touched the blood-soaked stones around her. A blue flash of light emanated from her hands as she felt the familiar jolt from her spell.

Zandro slammed the knife into Val's shoulder, as she used her Arcane Switch to trade places with Brand. She grunted in pain but was ready for it. She grabbed Zandro's hand which still held the knife in her shoulder and pulled it out. At the same time, she threw her head back and slammed it into Zandro's face.

He cried out in pain as she heard his nose crack and break from the blow. While he was stunned, she twisted his arm around and put him in the exact same arm lock he'd been holding Brand in a moment ago. In a fluid motion, she snatched one of Zandro's knives and held it up to his neck.

"This is for my father, *my dear,*" she whispered to him.

"No, please wait…"

That was all he was able to say before she drew the blade across his neck, finally silencing Zandro forever.

She took her vial back from Zandro's body and stumbled past a stunned Brand over to where Bogg lay. She uncorked the vial and poured the liquid down Bogg's throat.

He choked as the liquid went down, but his body knew what to do and he swallowed. In a moment, some of the color returned to Bogg's cheeks, and Astoro finally fell back in exhaustion. Bogg's eyes opened and she let out a breath she didn't know she'd been holding.

"What's going on? Did I get him?"

She chuckled.

"Shut up, Bogg."

20

Brand

Brand watched as Astoro finished up healing Val'ran's wounds. The most recent one in her shoulder had taken Astoro several minutes to knit back together. Astoro took a deep breath and wiped the sweat from his brow before getting back to his feet. He trudged over to where Brand was sitting up against the stone wall of a nearby home.

He was still bleeding from more than a dozen lacerations around his body. Zandro had started to cut him deeper and deeper as the fight wore on, and the mounting amount of blood loss was starting to make his head swim.

"Hey Brand, hang in there, I've got you," Astoro said with a smile as he knelt down next to Brand.

Brand felt a cool, tingling sensation as the green energy emanated from Astoro's eyes. Magical vines wrapped his wounds in a cocoon of warmth and light and began to heal them. The scent of fresh earth and spring leaves filled the air, a tangible manifestation of Astoro's nature magic. He was quite familiar with the process since Astoro had needed to heal him on several occasions since they'd met. He hated being such a burden.

"It's ok, I'm fine," Brand started.

"Brand," Astoro said with a tired smile. "I could paint the side of this house red with the amount of blood you've lost here. Let me at least make sure you're stable."

Brand nodded. He watched as his worst cuts closed up and his head began to clear. He took a deep breath and let it out.

"Thank you, Astoro."

Despite the clearer mind, Brand was still reeling from the last few moments of their fight with Zandro. He had been so sure he was going to die, and now he was ashamed of what a liability he'd been in their fight. His fear had caused him to be unfocused, and he couldn't look Astoro in the eye as his friend did what he could to patch him up.

Brand went over the fight in his head. Zandro had him completely outclassed the entire time. He'd never been so scared of an opponent before. If Zandro had wanted to, he could have put an end to Brand's life at any point in the fight.

He was fortunate that Zandro was just having fun torturing Val'ran long enough for her to finally figure out how to beat him. No thanks to Brand. She would have done better if he'd sat the fight out entirely.

"That's about all I can manage for now, but I've stopped the majority of the bleeding," Astoro said, interrupting his thoughts. "We need to get over to Landren and help him face the remaining giants."

"I can't, Astoro," Brand said. "My Chi still hasn't recovered from Zandro's poison. I'm only getting in the way and it's getting everyone else hurt." He gestured over to Val and Bogg who were sitting up against a wall, only stable because of Astoro.

There was more to it than that, but he wasn't ready to admit it to anyone, especially Astoro. The real truth was that Brand was terrified. He'd already almost died because of his fear when he fought Zandro. If he went straight into another battle right now, that same fear would actually get him killed this time.

Astoro's eyes sank, but he nodded. "I understand, Brand. You've done a lot today without access to your normal power." He looked toward the front gates. They could see the top of the giants towering over everything around them. For some reason, they'd stopped at the gates and weren't advancing yet. "I need to get to Landren and see if there's anything I can do to help."

Brand nodded, and even more shame filled him. He knew Astoro must be completely tapped out of magic at this point. He was breathing heavily, coated in sweat and small wounds, and even the ends of his leafy hair looked withered. Using all this magic was taking a serious toll on him, but he was still going to risk his life to save the city. Brand couldn't even look him in the eye.

"Good luck, Astoro," Brand said as Astoro got up to go. "Please stay alive."

"I'll do my best," Astoro said with a weak smile. He gave Brand one last pat on the shoulder and then took off to the front gates.

Brand watched as Astoro ran towards a fight he knew he couldn't win. He leaned his head back against the stone wall and closed his eyes, trying to keep from crumbling under the weight of his cowardice.

"Hey, uh, Brand, was it?" he heard from the other side of the road. He opened his eyes and saw Val'ran was talking to him. "Yeah, I overheard your conversation with Astoro. That's not how the poison works."

Brand gave her a confused look. "What do you mean?"

"That's not how Zandro's poison works. It can't block your Chi," she explained. "The poison Zandro uses blocks a person's ability to channel magic from an external source. For example, the nature magic that Astoro uses, or the magic of Niradim that the dwarves use. But your Chi comes from inside you."

That was basically correct, Chi was an internal form of energy. He'd assumed since Astoro said it blocked magical ability, that it included Chi, even though the source of the power was different.

"But I haven't been able to access my Chi since my battle with Zandro," Brand said.

"Not once?" Val'ran asked, raising her eyebrow.

Brand hesitated. While it was true that he hadn't accessed his Chi along the normal Path he was used to, he couldn't honestly say he hadn't accessed his Chi at all. In fact, he'd accessed it twice since his previous encounter with Zandro, but he still wasn't sure how.

"Ok," Brand admitted. "I did briefly a couple times, but not in the normal way."

"Well, then I suspect something else is the problem." She looked him in the eye, but it felt like she was looking right through him. "And I think you know what it is."

"You don't know what you're talking about!" Brand snapped back, a little angrier than he meant to. He didn't want to confront this. He didn't want to admit to another person or to himself that it was his own lack of self-control that was the problem, not Zandro's poison. That had been a convenient excuse to avoid the real problem. He couldn't access the Open Path in the real world.

"Actually I do," Val'ran said, not breaking eye contact. "You see, Landren tried to convert me to the Open Path when we traveled together. It's all about pushing your emotions out of the way, but you've got one emotion written all over your face, Brand. Want to know what I see?"

"Fear," Brand whispered. Val'ran nodded and her expression softened for a moment. He was the problem. He hadn't trained hard enough, he wasn't ready to rejoin the world like he thought. He was a failure.

"Want to know why he never got me to convert?" Val'ran asked.

"Why?" Brand asked.

"Because it's a hot load of slag." That caught Brand off guard. "You monks sequester yourself in the mountains, never having to deal with the complexities of the real world. It's easy to push emotion out of the way when there are no strong emotions to deal with in the mountains. The real world is messy, there's no avoiding emotions down here. So where is the real strength? Hiding away in the mountains, taking the easy path to power? I don't think so."

"Landren seems to have figured it out," Brand shot back. "Or haven't you seen him fighting today? He took the same Path I did."

"Did he?" Val'ran asked him. "Because if you'd just get out of your own head for a second, I think you'd realize that he's found a new Path. The Landren I used to know was as emotionless as you're failing to be. The Landren we've been fighting alongside today has been full of emotion. Heck, even the color of his Chi is different."

She was right. Landren's demeanor had caught him completely off guard when they first reunited. They'd been fighting so much that Brand didn't have time to process what that meant. His warden was showing plenty of emotion but was still accessing his Chi.

"And if you ask me," Val'ran continued. "This new Path he's found seems to be working out pretty well for him."

It finally clicked. This was the reason Landren had asked Brand to meet him in the city but didn't tell the Elders of the Open Path. Landren had found a new Path, one that went against all the tenants they'd been taught. And of all the people Landren could have brought this to, he trusted Brand.

"You're right," Brand said. "I can't believe I hadn't seen it yet. Thank you."

"You're welcome," Val'ran said. "Now what are you going to do about it?"

Brand considered for a moment and then willed his body to stand up. Instead of trying to push away the fear the hard way, he let his determination wash over and override the fear. His body was still sore, but he knew what he had to do.

"I'm going to do what my Pathwarden did," Brand said.

Brand stretched his muscles as he prepared to join his warden in battle.

"I'm going to find a new Path."

21

Ronan

"Evacuate everyone into the Earth Sector, now!" Ronan yelled to Vorkin as he charged the towering Starspawn.

He rolled right as the monster's axe slammed into the spot he'd vacated, spraying burning shards of stone at the impact. He could feel the intense heat scorching his skin at such a close distance. He continued running in a large circle around the Court of Fire. He needed to get that thing away from the gates, so anyone remaining in the area could get to safety.

The Starspawn kept its attention on Ronan as he circled. An axe cleaved through the air with a thunderous roar, slicing over Ronan as he slid under its path of destruction. The axe tore through a nearby tavern, crumbling its walls like a fragile stack of pebbles and reducing it to rubble.

Ronan couldn't believe this was happening to his home. He'd always thought of Midral as invincible. The city was in an amazing defensible position, and the Niradim Protectors were elite forces. That this much damage could be done in such a short amount of time seemed impossible to him.

Ronan ducked into the rubble to buy a moment to come up with a plan. As he did, the monster turned its attention to another group of guards who were valiantly trying to defend their city. The Starspawn kicked at them with one of its massive feet and sent them through the stone walls of a shop on the other end of the courtyard.

Ashes! Ronan thought. *I can't just sit here, I have to do something!*

But that was easier said than done. When he exited the Earth Sector, he hadn't wanted to use any of Niradim's magic. He still didn't trust Niradim after what he'd let happen to Ronan. But Ronan didn't have a choice. This enemy was too large to defeat with sword and shield alone. He'd need to tap into that holy energy he'd sworn to leave behind.

He focused on the subtle hum of energy radiating from his armor and weapons, a well of power that seemed to vibrate against his skin. As he reached out to tap into that power, the familiar warmth of Niradim's Flame engulfed him, far more potent than he'd ever experienced before. He'd only ever accessed a fraction of what was possible with Niradim's magic, but now he had access to the full conduit of his power.

Ronan secured his sword within the grooves of his shield, stepping from behind the shattered remnants of once-sturdy walls. He extended his hand, palm facing the behemoth, and focused Niradim's energy into it. A massive ball of holy energy blasted out of his hand and exploded against the Starspawn's back, sending it toppling to the ground. The recoil from the shot forced Ronan back a few steps and he stopped for a moment and stared at his hand.

That was far more energy than he'd ever channeled from Niradim before. Was this how the most powerful of Niradim's Disciples felt when they utilized Niradim's magic? He'd never felt anything like it, not even when he'd saved Ginmar from death years ago.

Ronan shook off the awe of the moment and drew his sword again from his shield. That shot may have done some damage, but the fight wasn't over yet. The ground shook as the Starspawn climbed back to its feet and focused its starfire eyes on him. Ronan had its undivided attention. Good.

Ronan reached back into that river of power and poured it into his sword and shield, which both lit up with white holy energy as he charged again. The Starspawn took a step forward and swung down to try and smash Ronan. This time, instead of rolling out of the way, he raised his shield to meet the attack head-on.

It was a massive amount of trust to put back into the god that had betrayed him, but he wasn't going to win this fight without Niradim's help. He needed to try to end this before Niradim changed his mind again and abandoned Ronan to a second death.

The falling axe met Ronan's shield with a massive explosion, sending a shockwave of power radiating outward from the center of the Court of Fire. All the debris scattered to the outside of the Court, and a few of the guards in the area were sent flying off their feet out of the nearby vicinity.

Ronan grunted under the weight of the axe, but he pushed more power into his shield and shoved the axe to the side. Focusing on his sword, he swung in an arc, and a crescent wave of holy energy cut through the air, severing the Starspawn's hand. It screeched in pain and reared up as its axe fell to the ground.

The axe cooled from white hot back to a normal temperature as it rested on the ground. Once the heat dissipated, the severed appendage dissolved into pinpricks of starlight from the tip of the axe to the severed part of the hand. They gently floated into the air before flickering out of existence.

Recovering from its initial shock, the Starspawn swung its second axe at Ronan. He was barely able to twist his body and block the incoming blow with his shield, but the force of this attack sent him tumbling across the ground. He let his momentum carry him, and he turned the tumble into a roll and regained his footing, sliding back a few feet.

Ronan took a moment to double-check to make sure he hadn't been injured. Sometimes the adrenaline from a fight could hide serious injuries. But he was fine. Brin's armor was truly fantastic and true to her word and Niradim's, it was doing a great job of protecting him at the moment.

He stood up and dusted the dirt off himself and prepared for the next clash, but the Starspawn had turned away from him. It had finally spotted the evacuees making their way through the Crucible Gate to the safety of the Earth Sector.

Ronan watched in horror as the Starspawn lifted the arm that now came to a stump and dark purple energy gathered in front of it in a massive orb. It was aiming at the gate. Ronan took off in a sprint, but he was too late.

The monster released the gathered energy and launched it at the Crucible Gate. It exploded on impact, blowing a massive hole in the center of the once-invincible gates. One of the doors broke off its hinges and toppled forward into the Court of Fire. It crashed to the ground and created a huge plume of smoky debris of stone and dirt.

The Crucible Gate had fallen for the first time in history.

Ronan's heart dropped. His home was suffering at the hands of Kyros and his monsters like it never had before. It was time to put an end to it.

Ronan sheathed his sword again and began firing several blasts of energy at the imposing beast. He didn't care about doing much damage at the moment, he just needed its full attention again. He wouldn't have any more innocents dying at its hands today.

It held up a hand to defend against the blasts, taking a step back at first and then focusing on Ronan. Its attention was back on him, so Ronan began to run at the giant starlight monster. It took two bounding steps toward him and swung across for another attack to send Ronan flying. Ronan kept running.

Before the attack landed, Ronan jumped and then kicked off the glowing axe as it passed under him. Steam hissed from his boot at the momentary touch, but he soared through the air at the monster's chest.

Ronan grabbed his sword as he flew through the air and poured as much of Niradim's power into it as he could muster at the moment. Beads of sweat turned to streams, and the torrent of power he wielded threatened to tear him apart. Even still, he continued. He let the love of his city and the need to protect his people fill his blade. He drew his sword and a massive arc of light extended from the earth to the sky, splitting the starlight monster in two.

Ronan hit the ground on the other side of the Starspawn and rolled into a crouch. The Starspawn was frozen in the moment, its two halves slowly separating from one another. As they fell away, they dissolved into the same pinpricks of starlight as before, floating away and flickering until it was no more.

Silence filled the Court of Fire. Ronan wasn't sure if the people were stunned by seeing the Crucible Gate fall or watching him defeat a monster. The blizzard had died down during their fight. He hadn't even noticed. Finally, Vorkin ran up to him, breaking the momentary silence.

"Phoenix," Vorkin said. "What are your orders?"

Orders? Couldn't they see that he'd failed them? The most secure place in the city, maybe the whole continent, had fallen on his watch. He hadn't been able to stop it in time. Not to mention he'd abandoned his faith. He shouldn't be giving anyone orders.

But one look at the terror plastered on Vorkin's face made Ronan bite his tongue. He may not be worthy to command these people, but they needed him to be the person they thought he was. He needed to be Niradim's Phoenix. He cleared his throat and addressed Vorkin.

"Clear as much of the debris around the gate as you can and continue allowing people in," Ronan said. "Usher them deeper into the Earth Sector, the Protection Ward isn't safe enough right now that the gate has fallen."

"Understood, Phoenix," Vorkin said. Determination and purpose replaced the terror on his face. The guards needed to stay busy to keep themselves from falling into despair. This task Ronan gave them should give them enough direction to keep going.

"What are you going to do?" Vorkin asked.

"The Flame has been stolen, Vorkin," Ronan said.

"I'm going to go get it back."

22

Kyros

The two giants on either side of the chieftain stepped forward. Kyros raised his staff, and a surge of power coursed through his veins, sending shivers down his spine and igniting a fiery sensation in his palms. The staff pulsed with energy in harmony with the beating of his heart. He could feel the fount of power at his control and he began to laugh. Never in his wildest dreams did he think he'd ever have access to such raw power!

Kyros' eyes became pools of darkness as shadows radiated from the ground around him. The shadows formed into massive inky tentacles as they rose from the ground. It was as if a dark Kraken was surfacing from the deep to claim its prey. The ropes of darkness wrapped around both of the giants that had stepped forward and lifted them into the air above the city's entrance.

The giants struggled against their bonds as he held the staff aloft, lit like a holy beacon as it housed the Flame of Niradim inside. He began to rotate it in a circle above his head. The clouds in the sky above began to circle in cadence with the staff, slowly at first, and then quicker and quicker. The winds around them picked up and began to swirl as a funnel in the clouds began to form above the trapped giants.

He brought the staff down in a quick movement. A cyclone of holy fire descended from the clouds with a deafening roar, engulfing the two giants and painting the sky with hues of crimson and gold. The air crackled with intense heat, carrying the acrid scent of burning flesh and the wails of tortured screams. When the screams finally subsided, Kyros snuffed out the tornado of flame. Lifeless husks and a mountain of ash occupied the ground where the towering giants once stood, surrounded by a dark circle of scorched earth.

His laughter echoed across the battlefield. It was a chilling crescendo of madness that mingled with the swirling wind and crackling flames. His eyes danced with manic glee, their depths obscured by an abyss of darkness as he reveled in the intoxicating rush of power. He could get used to this.

The giant chieftain's eyes went wide with shock, mixed with terror. Kyros reveled in the knowledge that he was able to cause such a gargantuan creature to fear him. The chieftain was almost twice the size of the Starspawn he'd summoned in the Court of Fire. He could only imagine the destruction such a beast could rain on the city if given the right incentive. Or command.

The chieftain shook off its momentary surprise and reached back to pull out a massive war hammer strapped to its back. As it did, Kyros' eyes and the crystal on his forehead flashed a bright purple as the chieftain's eyes met his. The giant recoiled as if struck by some invisible force and it reached up to grab its head and doubled over. Whatever resistance the giant was trying to put up, it was quickly overcome. It lowered its hand back to its war hammer and stood straight up. Its eyes flashed with the same purple light that had come from Kyros a moment ago signaling that Kyros' spell was successful.

The giant was his.

"Kyros!" A familiar voice yelled from behind him.

Kyros turned as Landren emerged from the haze of battle, his clothes ripped and bloodied. Kyros could see that each step carried the weight of the trials Landren had already endured. Despite the state his body was in, his weary gaze flickered with resolve.

"Landren, my old friend, it's so good to see you!" Kyros said with a practiced smile. "What a fun little reunion! How have you been?"

"Cut the pleasantries, Kyros," Landren said. "This whole mess is your doing, isn't it?"

"Why, yes," Kyros said with a smile. "I do believe it is."

"What game are you playing, Kyros?" Landren said. "First, you hire us to find an ancient city for you, and now you attempt to bring another to the ground?"

"Well, razing this city was really only my secondary goal," Kyros explained. "Although you have to admit, it's going quite well!" He chuckled. "No, my old friend, this right here was the main prize." He held his glowing staff up for Landren to see.

Landren stared for a moment in confusion before realization struck him.

"The Flame..." Landren said in shock.

Kyros' smile deepened in confirmation.

"Now, I have a few minutes while I'm waiting for my associates to show up. Why don't you play with my newest friend here," Kyros said, gesturing to the massive giant looming behind him. "Heck, if you last long enough, you may even get a second reunion today. With your old Pathwarden."

Landren took a step back and his eyes went wide. "What is *she* doing here?"

"Oh, it's none of your concern," Kyros said. "Besides, I'd say you've got much *bigger* things to worry about."

Kyros casually raised a hand in the air over his head and then pointed it at Landren. Immediately, the chieftain under his control stepped forward over Kyros and engaged Landren in battle.

Landren's Chi flared to life and Kyros was surprised to see a Golden aura as opposed to the Orange or Crimson he was familiar with. It blazed like a roaring fire amidst the carnage. So, Agent Crimson's suspicions were correct, Landren *had* found a new Path in the ancient city. He watched as Landren ignited a blade made of pure Chi energy from a silver hilt. Oh, he'd discovered an Artifact as well! How interesting. Agent Crimson was going to love hearing about this.

Kyros stepped back to watch the fight unfold. He didn't know what kind of power this Golden Path held, but he'd seen the Crimson Path up close. Even with his newfound power, he didn't want to tussle with someone with those particular skills at the moment.

Landren fought admirably, but it was clear that he'd already been going a few rounds before he'd arrived. He was barely dodging the giant's massive hammer and the large amounts of debris being tossed about as buildings crumbled at each strike. Any normal person would have been dead within seconds, but Landren held on.

The giant wasn't letting Landren get close enough to use that Chi Blade, so he extinguished it. Kyros watched as Landren began *throwing* Chi at the giant in bursts of energy. It wasn't doing much damage to the giant, but Kyros had never seen anything like that kind of attack from a Chi user before. This Golden Path had some surprises, it seemed.

Landren ducked in and out of cover, blasting away as much as he could, but the Chi blasts just weren't doing enough damage to the giant. After a few moments, Kyros watched as Landren held out his hand as if to fire another blast, but nothing happened. It looked like Landren had reached his limit.

Landren visibly sagged as the last bit of his Chi finally ran out. It must have been incredibly taxing to have such a large flow of Chi coursing through your body for such a long period of time. Landren looked exhausted. The giant seemed to notice too. It used that moment to backhand Landren with one of its massive hands, sending him tumbling across the rubble. Landren finally skidded to a stop a few paces from Kyros.

Landren tried to stand, but it was clear his body was too broken to manage it. The giant went for a finishing blow, but Kyros held up his hand and the giant lowered his hammer and stepped back behind Kyros.

"That was quite the show you put on, it was delightful to watch," Kyros said. "Unfortunately, it seems that you won't get to see your old Pathwarden again after all." Kyros raised his arm and pointed it at Landren as dark energy gathered in his palm. "I'll give her your regards. Goodbye…"

Kyros was cut off as a ball of green energy hit him in the chest, causing him to stumble back a few feet.

What in the void was that?! Kyros thought as he regained his composure and scanned the area.

A short florian ran up and stood between him and Landren. This one had also clearly been dealing with the threat to the city. He was breathing hard and it looked like the leaves that made up his hair were withering considerably, likely from exhaustion.

"Astoro… get out of here," Landren said between gulps of air, but the small florian ignored him and stood his ground.

"Well, that was certainly a surprise," Kyros said in annoyance. "You're not exactly the florian I was expecting."

"Zandro won't be coming," Astoro said. "He's dead."

Kyros raised his eyebrows and he noticed Landren smiled despite his pain. Well, that was unexpected.

"And you mean for me to believe that *you* killed him?" Kyros asked.

"I… helped," Astoro replied, tentatively.

"Ah, so you watched, that makes more sense," Kyros said. "Well, as unexpected as that news is, it doesn't matter. This is a rather pointless way for you to have wasted your life, but to each his own I guess."

Kyros raised his arm again and fired a dark ball of purple and black energy at Astoro and Landren. Astoro screamed as he tried to raise a green barrier of energy, but it flickered and failed as soon as Kyros' energy exploded against it. The force of the blast sent the two flying away from him.

He couldn't see where Astoro landed, but Landren was lying in the rubble across from him, impaled on a spike. Agent Crimson would probably be annoyed that Landren's secrets of this new Golden Path would die with him, but he didn't care. She could figure it out on her own if it was that important to her.

So, Agent Viridian was dead. That was unfortunate. Not because he cared about his father's double agent in any way. No, it was unfortunate to lose such a powerful tool in his arsenal. Agent Crimson would have to take a more central role in his plans going forward and take over operations at their new hidden base in the city of Lumenova.

Looks like she's getting a promotion, he chuckled to himself.

He needed to find out where she was. Noct could help him do that, but he wanted to get to a safer place before switching into Noct's eyes. He turned and walked away to leave Landren to die among the wreckage.

It was always nice to see old friends.

23

Val'ran

"That was a nice pep talk, Val. Got me right in the emotions."

"Shut up, Bogg."

She smiled as she watched Bogg push himself up against the side of a building into a sitting position. She thought he'd be out longer with what he'd been through. He was a lot tougher than anyone gave him credit for. Not that he was in any shape to continue fighting, she noted as each movement brought a grimace of pain to Bogg's face. Even he had his limits.

"Finally decided to wake up, huh?" Val teased. "Have a nice nap?"

Bogg groaned and placed a hand on his head.

"Ugh, no," Bogg said. "I got a mean headache, but didn't even get the pleasure of drinking first."

"Now that is sad," Val said, sitting down next to him. She handed him a flask filled with water for him to drink.

As he finished off her water, Val's gaze shifted to Zandro's lifeless form, her eyes tracing the stillness of his chest, a sight both surreal and final. She took a deep breath and slowly let it out. She couldn't believe she'd finally killed him. She kept expecting him to pop back up and attack again. Like a snake playing dead for the moment, waiting for her to lower her guard before it struck with its venom. But he wouldn't. He'd never torture her again. She was finally free of that monster.

She didn't know what to do with her life now that he was gone. Her vengeance was her primary motivation for surviving these long years since his betrayal. She kept honing her skills, getting stronger, and searching for the florian who had murdered her father and friends. Now she had to start over and figure out life without a mission. It left her feeling a little uncomfortable at the prospect. She looked over at Bogg who had stopped drinking and was also staring at Zandro with a distant look on his face.

"What's on your mind?" she asked.

He blinked and looked at her like he was confused by her question. "Umm…"

"What?"

"Well, nobody has ever asked me that before," Bogg said, scratching his chin. "It just caught me off guard, is all."

She chuckled. "Well, I assume it's usually constant white noise unless you're staring at an enemy. In which case you're probably thinking about how the most fun way to kill them would be."

"Oh, Val," Bogg said, faking a sniffle as he wiped an imaginary tear from his face. "You know me so well!"

"Ha ha, very funny," She said, nudging him with her elbow as he snickered. "Well, you're clearly thinking about something, and since Zandro's already dead, it's not about what fun way you'll imagine up to kill him," Val said. "So what's going on?"

Bogg took a deep breath and let it out. "That was the first time in my life I actually thought I might die," Bogg finally admitted. He brushed his hand over his bald head. "It was a strange feeling."

"Yeah, I remember the first time I felt the same way," Val said, gesturing over to Zandro with her head. "Also courtesy of our florian friend over there."

Bogg nodded. "Thank you for saving me again," Bogg said, more sincere than she'd ever heard him speak. "I know you wouldn't have risked yourself like that unless you were trying to get the antidote from him to save me."

Sometimes she forgot that Bogg knew her just as well as she knew him. They'd traveled together for a long time as a part of Kyros' party before this most recent fiasco. True, they'd been on each others' nerves basically the entire time, but still. There was an understanding they had of each other through the several battles they'd fought along the way.

There was something about fighting side by side with someone that helped you get to know them in a way you couldn't replicate in a peaceful life.

"Well, maybe I was just trying to save Brand, ever think of that?" Val offered with a smile that didn't reach her eyes. "Or maybe it was my grand plan all along. I knew I'd be able to kill Zandro by switching places."

"No," Bogg said, meeting her eyes. "It wasn't either of those things."

Val froze for a second, but then nodded and let her fake smile fall. "You're right, Bogg. You're the first friend I've had in a long long time, and when I thought I might lose you, I just acted," she said. She lowered her voice to a whisper. "I don't think even Brand knows that if your life wasn't on the line, I would have let him die."

She was a little ashamed at that last admission, but it was the truth. If Bogg's life hadn't depended on her getting the antidote from Zandro, she would have tried to find a far less risky way to end Zandro's life. Even if it meant sacrificing Brand. She was lucky the blood on the ground had been Brand's, and lucky the move had startled Zandro long enough for her to finish him off. She'd only saved Brand because it saved Bogg.

"Well, it was his own fault," Bogg said, shrugging. "He was fightin' scared."

"Hey, you took a fatal blow in that fight too, remember?" Val replied.

"Yeah, but that's because I got tricked!" Bogg protested. "It's different."

She knew what he meant. Bogg took a hit because their enemy was skilled enough to land it. Brand almost got himself killed because he was too scared to fight properly. It definitely made a difference, and a difference like that could have cost them a lot more than some injuries they'd heal from.

"You know," Bogg said, looking at nothing in particular in the sky as if they were just having a casual chat outside. "He'll probably get himself killed if you don't go babysit him again."

Her head snapped over to stare at him. He'd just complained about Brand, but still wanted her to go help?

"Are you telling me to go fight?" Val asked, raising an eyebrow. "*Without* you?"

"Well, there's no reason both of us should miss out on the fun," Bogg said with a smile. "Besides, you need to give Kyros a proper beating for lockin' us up."

Landren, Astoro, and Brand had all gone to the front gates to deal with Kyros and the threat of the giants. It would be a tough fight even if they were all at full strength. And she could tell from the noise that there was some kind of chaos still going on back at the Court of Fire. She doubted reinforcements would be arriving any time soon at the front gates.

Well, she had been considering what kind of mission could keep her going now that Zandro was gone. Save the city of Midral. It was a short-term mission, but it was a start. She'd worry about the next one if she survived this one.

She grunted as she got to her feet and checked that each of her weapons were strapped in place. She drew her father's Flame Scimitar and held it in front of her, its blade catching rays from the sun and setting them ablaze. It reflected a face sporting several cuts and bruises, but she still had the fire in her eyes that kept her going. She'd inherited that spirit from her father.

"Beautiful..." Bogg said.

"Now listen, Bogg, don't go falling in love with me just because I saved your life a couple times," Val joked.

"Hah!" Bogg laughed hard, slapping his knee and then grunting in pain. "I was talkin' about your sword! I need to get me somethin' pretty like that. This one does the job fine," he said, gesturing to the longsword lying on the ground next to him. "But sometimes I wish I had something fancier to behead people with, ya know?"

"Besides, you're not my type," he added with a wink. "I like 'em with a little more meat on 'em!"

Val rolled her eyes and sheathed her father's sword. It was just like Bogg to be more interested in a weapon than a woman. But good, she hoped he meant it. She was barely getting used to having a friend again, she didn't need romantic entanglement muddling that up.

She finished checking all her weapons and prepared to join the others at the front gates. She still didn't know what was waiting for her there, but she had a purpose again, and that was enough for her at the moment. It was time to go.

"I'll be sure to tell Kyros you said hi," Val said.

"Yeah, make sure you give him my best," Bogg replied.

"And make sure it hurts."

24

Brand

Brand arrived at the front gates, but the fighting he'd heard a few moments ago on his way there had ceased. On his way to the gates, he'd seen a pillar of fire descend from the clouds, which disappeared after a few moments. Then he watched as the largest giant he'd ever seen battled with someone or something. What he saw now was a wake of carnage.

Two colossal husks, the remnants of giants charred beyond recognition, rested ominously atop a vast circle of blackened earth. Wisps of smoke spiraled up from their smoldering remains, blurring the air with the acrid scent of destruction.

That must have been the pillar of fire he'd seen before. He didn't know who summoned that, but he had a sinking feeling it wasn't someone friendly. The last giant, the tallest one, stood very still at the front gate facing the city. He wasn't moving for some reason.

Brand's gaze swept over the destruction, finally resting upon a solitary figure perched high upon the remnants of the city's wall. The novaborn's long white hair whipped around in the gusty wind. His eyes and the jewel on his forehead shimmered with an unearthly violet glow mixed with wisps of white.

Landren and Astoro should both be here by now. Brand thought. *What happened to them?*

He picked his way through the rubble-strewn streets, careful to stay as quiet as he could so he didn't alert the giant or the man with the glowing eyes. He couldn't believe the amount of destruction around him. He didn't see a single building that hadn't sustained at least some damage. Many were completely leveled, but those that weren't had pieces of walls or roofs that had caved in.

Fear began to creep back into his mind. How was he supposed to take on an enemy that could do this? He was trying not to think about the fact that Landren and Astoro weren't currently fighting the giant. He didn't want to consider what that meant about their condition.

Landren seemed invincible in their fights leading up to this, but even his Pathwarden's impressive abilities must have some kind of limit. And he knew Astoro had already pushed past his own limits. His thoughts were interrupted by a grunt of pain coming from behind a large piece of stonework on his left.

He rushed around the massive stone and found Astoro partially crushed underneath it.

"Astoro!" Brand cried.

"Oh, hey Brand," Astoro said, grimacing through the pain. "Nice to see you made it."

He rushed to Astoro's side. The stone had crushed Astoro's right arm and leg, but none of his body was under the stone. He'd be in a ton of pain, but he should be able to live through this injury.

"Astoro, I'm going to lift the stone off of you," Brand said. "Are you ready?"

"How are you going to manage that?" Astoro said. "This thing weighs a ton, and you can't use your Chi because of Zandro's poison."

"I'll explain later, but I think I can access my Chi, at least long enough to get this off of you," Brand said with more confidence than he felt.

Brand turned inward and began to wade into the Path. It was a vast river of emotion at the moment, mostly fear, and surprisingly a large amount of anger. Still, he could tell there were other emotions as well, even if he couldn't identify them at the moment. Mentally, he took out the largest bottle he could imagine and began diverting the streams of emotion into it.

Little by little, the river began to empty. Brand concentrated harder, blocking out everything external at the moment. The world was a void. All that existed was him and the Path. Finally, the river was empty. The Path was open again.

Chi rushed down the Path in a torrent and Brand threw open all the Inner Gates to allow the Chi to fill his body and strengthen him. He missed this feeling.

Brand opened his eyes and saw the familiar Orange steam rising from his body. This was his normal Chi, not that strange Crimson Chi he'd accidentally accessed a few times. He could instantly tell that the Orange was not as potent as the Crimson had been, but it would be plenty for what he needed to do here.

He placed his hands on the stone and let the Chi build in his muscles for a moment. He braced his legs and began to lift. Slowly, the stone rose from the ground. Astoro tried to stifle a scream of pain as the stone released his trapped limbs and he managed to roll away and out from under the stone.

Brand gently lowered it back to the ground and released the Chi flooding his system. Focusing, he closed the Gates until his Chi was comfortably back at his center. He took a deep breath and felt a more metaphorical weight finally lift from his shoulder. His Chi was back.

He turned his attention to Astoro to assess the damage. His arm and leg had broken in multiple places, but they were intact. Astoro had some herbs that Brand fed to him to ease the pain, but there wasn't much else Brand could do to help at the moment.

"Just hang tight, Astoro," Brand said. "I need to find Landren and make sure he's ok too."

"Brand, Landren completely ran out of Chi in his fight against the massive giant," Astoro said. "When Kyros blasted us, I flew this way, but Landren flew in the opposite direction. I don't know what condition he's in, but he definitely can't fight anymore."

"I'll find him and then we'll come up with a plan," Brand said. "He'll think of something to get us out of this mess."

Brand focused inward again and opened the Path. This time, he only released the Gates to his legs to increase his speed. He took off in the direction Astoro had indicated to find his Pathwarden.

In moments, Brand had made it to the area Astoro had pointed out. He spared another quick look at the giant and Kyros, but they hadn't moved from their positions.

This area was even more broken than the last, it was impossible to see anything from the ground level. He located a nearby building with a roof that seemed like it was stable enough and made a Chi-enhanced leap to the top of the building.

Brand scanned the area, but nothing stood out to him at first. Then, the smallest movement out of the corner of his eye caught his attention. A hand had reached out of some rubble. That had to be Landren!

He leapt down from the building and sprinted towards the hand. He began pulling rocks off, one by one, and Landren finally came into view. He was in bad shape, much worse than Astoro.

Landren winced in pain and held some kind of metal to his chest. Brand reached to see what it was, but pulled up short. He wasn't holding metal to his chest. He was holding some kind of spike that pierced his back and exited through his chest. A flower of bright red blood was blossoming from the metal and spreading across his Pathwarden's torso.

"Landren…" Brand whispered. He didn't know what to do. There was nothing he *could* do. His brain refused to process the obvious. Landren was going to die.

"Brand…" Landren said. "I'm sorry I didn't have a chance to teach you the new Path that I found." He coughed blood and winced in pain at the motion.

"It's going to be ok, I'll… I'll figure something out. It's going to be ok, Pathwarden," Brand said, tears welling up in his eyes.

"No Brand, I don't have much longer," Landren said. "Listen to me - what we were taught at the monastery of the Open Path, what I taught you, is only the beginning. It was never meant to stop there."

Brand nodded. He may not be able to do anything to save his Pathwarden, but he could at least hear his last words.

"Emotion is the key to strength, not its adversary," Landren said. "But you have to focus the emotion, not let it control you… Never let it control you…"

Brand could see Landren was beginning to fade.

"When you access your Chi in this way… you have to… choose an emotion," Landren said, his breaths becoming more labored with each sentence. "Only the strongest emotions… will make a Path strong enough for your Chi to flow through…

"What emotion did you choose?" Brand asked.

Landren reached up and placed his hand on Brand's shoulder. Brand could see the light beginning to fade from Landren's eyes. He needed to know what emotion his Pathwarden chose. What emotion brought out such raw power and made him fearless in battle?

"I chose…"

But that was the last he could manage to get out. Landren's hand fell away from Brand's shoulder. He was gone. His Pathwarden was dead.

Brand's tears fell like a river carving down his cheeks. Why couldn't he have been strong enough to stop this? Landren said emotion was the key to strength, but why did it seem like emotion was the main thing getting in his way?

"Oh my, we have a new visitor!" he heard a voice say from behind.

He turned to see Kyros staring at him from atop the stone wall, eyes and jewel no longer glowing. Whatever he had been doing, he'd finished it. He motioned to the massive giant and pointed over at Brand. Its head snapped to focus on him as it pulled out its mighty war hammer and held it with both hands. The head of the hammer was the size of a home. It began to slowly walk towards him.

Brand tried to open his Path, pushing away emotion and opening the Gates as the giant closed in on him. An orange glow flickered around him, but he couldn't hold it in place. He was having trouble keeping the Path open. Fear was creeping in and taking its place. Fear and one other emotion that was building.

How did Landren access the Golden Chi? It was far stronger than the Orange Chi of the Open Path. He needed that strength. Even if he could manage to keep the Path open, Orange wasn't going to be enough to win this fight. What had Landren said? Only the strongest emotions will make a Path strong enough for your Chi to flow through? How did he access Gold?

Your Golden Chi is impressive, but not quite as impressive as what I've seen from Crimson.

Zandro's words echoed in his head. Landren's Golden Chi hadn't been enough to win this fight, Brand realized. But maybe Crimson would be. Finally, it clicked. Brand figured out what emotion fueled the Crimson Chi, and he had plenty of it right now. He realized he always did.

Brand always pictured bottling his emotions and putting them on a shelf when he meditated, but there was one bottle that was always the largest. One bottle that contained the strongest emotion he'd had since he was a child. Brand looked inside himself and picked up the familiar weight. It was finally time to let it out. He smashed the bottle inside him.

Rage flooded down the Path as the giant's hammer fell.

Brand caught it, and erupted in an explosion of Crimson light.

25

Everyone

As Ronan neared the once-majestic front gates of the city, a heaviness settled on him. They were gone, and everything within a few blocks of the entrance to the city had been leveled. The destruction continued in each direction down several streets. Whatever had happened here was even worse than the attack at the Court of Fire. He needed to find Kyros and put a stop to all this.

He crested the hill of rubble surrounding the front gates in time to see a blonde-haired man catch the downfall of an enormous giant's hammer. Then a massive blast of crimson energy sent the giant tumbling backward.

He watched in awe as the man, cloaked in a shroud of crimson light, advanced towards the giant and engaged it in a direct fight. It was incredible. He didn't know who this person was, but he was grateful the man was defending the city.

His eyes drifted back towards the area where the man had been standing. He saw Captain Landren lying motionless, impaled on a metal bar and covered in debris. He could tell from this distance that Landren was dead. He was a good man, and capable. No doubt Landren had given his life defending the city as well.

The battle between the crimson man and the giant raged on. Ronan could tell by the way the man fought that he must be Landren's student, Brand. Landren had bragged about Brand before, and now Ronan could see that the words of praise were more than deserved. Brand's every attack unleashed torrents of power as he pushed the giant back with each strike.

He surveyed the area looking for other survivors and heard someone yelp in pain to his left. He couldn't put his finger on it, but the voice sounded familiar, from his previous life. He began running toward the source, growing more worried with each step about who that voice belonged to.

Ronan finally spotted a small green florian with familiar leafy hair, lying on the ground next to a large stone. His arm and leg looked like they'd been crushed, but he was trying to scoot himself into a safer position, despite the pain he was in. Ronan felt his heart skip a beat in his chest.

"Astoro!" he yelled and began to slide down the debris. This couldn't be happening. He had to make sure Astoro was alright.

As Ronan neared Astoro, a purple flash caught his eyes. He instinctively raised his shield in time to block an incoming blast of energy from Kyros.

"Why do you keep showing up right when I'm trying to accomplish something?" Kyros yelled as he landed on top of a pile of rubble across from Ronan's position. "It's very annoying. This time I'll make sure you stay down, permanently."

"I think you'll find it a little more difficult this time," Ronan said, walking towards Kyros as he drew his sword out of his shield.

"Yes, you do seem to have some fancy new toys, don't you?" Kyros said, noticing the impressive display of armor and weapons Ronan wielded. "But as you remember, I have some new toys of my own."

Kyros raised the glowing white crystal staff over his head and conjured a large ball of fire. It hovered above the top of the staff before Kyros swung the staff forward and sent the small supernova racing towards Ronan.

Ronan raised his shield again and the ball of fire detonated on impact, creating a small crater around where Ronan had been standing. The smoke cleared and Ronan lowered his shield, which had created a forcefield around him. Kyros had the decency to at least look a little surprised at the human still standing before him unscathed.

"Like I said," Ronan said, locking eyes with Kyros. "I think you'll find it a little more difficult this time."

* * *

Kyros gathered himself as his adversary charged him with his sword and shield raised. He was shocked that Ronan hadn't been completely incinerated by the ball of fire he'd conjured. And now he was finally starting to feel the toll on his body that wielding such enormous powers was taking on him.

He'd had his fun, but now it was time to go. Celestian would have to be content with the amount of damage he'd rained down on Midral in the past several hours. And if that giant finished off the new martial artist, he would command it to destroy as much of the city as possible. It would continue until it dropped dead from exhaustion or someone finally managed to kill it.

He wasn't sure where Agent Crimson had gone off to, but he suspected she'd be very interested in this new fighter using Crimson Chi. As far as he knew, she was the only person who knew how to use it. Looks like the secret was out.

Focusing back on Ronan, Kyros began firing off attacks left and right as Ronan advanced. Somehow, Ronan's shield was deflecting even the strongest of Kyros' attacks.

Ronan closed in on him and Kyros took a few steps back while summoning the tendrils of darkness to entangle Ronan. Ronan rolled to the side as the tentacles grabbed for him and missed. While he was distracted, Kyros fired an icicle at him, which shattered on impact when it hit Ronan square in the back, but it at least sent him tumbling.

I'm wielding two of the most powerful Artifacts in existence and the power of two gods in my arsenal. Kyros thought to himself. *How is this man able to withstand my attacks without breaking a sweat? I've beaten him easily twice before!*

It was time to get more aggressive. Before Ronan could get his feet under him, Kyros mist-jumped up on top of the city wall to put more distance between himself and Ronan. He began raining down staff-enhanced blasts of energy down on Ronan. Ronan's shield was up with that annoying forcefield, but he could see it was beginning to crack. So it seemed there *was* a limit to just how much punishment his defenses could take. It was time to find out what that limit was.

Kyros' robes fluttered with the surge of power as he pushed his attack. The air vibrated, charged with magic as he watched Ronan's forcefield spider-web with cracks. Its once impenetrable glow began to flicker under his relentless assault. Gathering his strength, he raised his staff high above his head, conjuring another large fireball above him.

Goodbye Ronan.

Before he could launch the fireball to finish Ronan off, an arrow struck his shoulder. Thorny vines wrapped around him, causing him to drop his concentration. The fireball exploded in the air above him and the blast sent Kyros skidding across the top of the wall.

It took him a second to rip the vines off and climb to one knee. He yanked the arrow out of his shoulder, grunting with pain at the effort. He looked up in time to see another arrow flying at him and he was barely able to raise a magical barrier in time to deflect it. He followed the trajectory to find out where the arrows had originated from.

There across the battlefield was Val'ran Nisanthar, reaching for another arrow.

***

Burning Ashes, I thought that the last one was going to land. Val thought to herself as she reached for another arrow and knocked it into her bow. *At least I bought us some time.*

The man in the magical armor had taken some damage from Kyros' last volley of attacks, but he was picking himself back up. Kyros had disappeared for the moment, so she put the arrow back into her quiver.

He was unlikely to show his face again until he had relocated - he knew from firsthand experience how good of a shot she was. He wouldn't risk showing himself while he knew she was hunting him, so she turned her attention to the other massive battle that was happening.

Brand had completely changed. He was glowing in the same way Landren did, but with a Crimson aura instead of Landren's Gold or the Orange she'd seen before. And his fighting was like nothing she'd ever seen from him. He was quick, decisive, powerful. There wasn't a hint of that fear or hesitation he'd shown in their fight against Zandro. She didn't know what changed, but she was happy about it.

He was jumping through the air and striking the giant in different places, knocking him around while dodging every strike the giant threw at him. It was incredible. She didn't think he'd be able to keep up that pace for very long after everything they'd already gone through, but for now, he was holding his own. It was time to press their advantage while they still had it.

Grunting with the effort, she got up and made her way across the rooftop she was on and leapt to the one next to it. She was pretty beat up herself, and still sore from where Zandro had stabbed her, even though Astoro had been able to stop the bleeding. Despite being immune from the worst effects of Zandro's poison, it still made her body feel horrible and sore like a bad sickness coming on.

She pushed through the body aches and knocked another arrow into her bow. She was getting low on arrows. Plus, she was completely tapped out of her blood magic after that last shot on Kyros. The only thing she could do was try to distract the giant while Brand fought.

She knocked another arrow into the bow, steadied her breath, and fired.

The giant roared in pain in front of Brand as her arrow struck him in the temple. She was winded but still fired shot after shot at the giant to distract him. Brand looked up at her and made a powerful jump up to the roof to join her. They both ducked behind a wall to hide from the giant momentarily.

"Are you out of magic or something?" he snapped at her. Was he angry? "We need to finish this guy before my Chi burns out."

Val shook off her surprise at his tone and nodded. "Yeah, I'm all tapped out of magic at the moment. Any ideas?"

"I need to knock him down to finish him off," Brand said, standing back up. "Annoy him with your arrows if you must, but stay out of my way."

Val watched as he leapt back into the fight.

* * *

Brand hurdled the short wall they'd been behind and flared the Crimson Chi back through his body. Power and rage filled him. Had he been too short with Val? It didn't matter, the power he was wielding would end this fight. She was useless with her arrows if she couldn't use her magic. He watched Val lay down some cover fire for a moment

287

while he got into close range again and could occupy most of the giant's attention.

He was using every bit of Landren's training he'd ever learned to attack the giant. He stayed in constant, fluid movement. He flowed from attack to attack and never let the giant regain his full balance to counter. He was a deadly acrobat, soaring through the air. He launched off of buildings, walls, limbs, and laid into the giant with strikes carrying the force of hammers.

But he couldn't keep it up forever. He hadn't been lying to Val, they needed to end this pretty soon. It probably wasn't noticeable to his enemy yet, but Brand's movements were beginning to slow, and his strikes were beginning to weaken. The Crimson Chi was powerful, but he couldn't wield it forever. He was going to need to go for the legs to knock this giant down.

The giant retreated a bit to put some distance between him and Brand. He was seething mad. There was no way this leader of the greater giants had ever been made to feel inferior to anyone, much less such a tiny creature. Brand could see the fury build in his eyes, but it was nothing compared to the fury coursing through Brand's veins.

The giant roared and came at Brand with a new level of speed he hadn't shown before. The giant's strikes shook the ground and demolished buildings. Brand dodged the attacks, but he was unable to avoid the sheer amount of debris that exploded from each downfall of his enormous war hammer. Finally, a loose stone slammed into Brand mid-flight. Brand went sprawling backward and the giant pressed his attack.

Before the giant could fully engage, Val appeared on a nearby roof and unleashed a volley of arrows at the giant, causing him to turn towards her. The giant swung his hammer across his body to knock over the building Val was on.

Brand watched as she leapt off of the building before the giant's blow connected. She twisted in the air, upside down over the hammer as it rushed by under her. As her body spun, she pulled out the last two arrows from her quiver and fired both directly into the giant's eyes. The giant's hammer connected with the building, and the force of the blow sent Val careening away.

Brand didn't see where she landed, but he didn't care. The giant roared in pain and stepped backward, tripping on the debris littered about from its last frenzy of strikes. The massive war hammer flew through the air above the giant as it grabbed at its injured eyes. This was the moment. It was Brand's chance to end this.

Brand felt the last reserves of his strength waning, but he willed the Crimson Chi within him to burn brighter. With every Gate within his body flung wide open, Brand's aura erupted into a raging crimson inferno in the dimming light of the battlefield. His muscles coiled as he crouched low, the ground beneath him cracking with the sheer force of his energy.

He launched himself skyward, a comet streaking up above a battle-torn city. The wind howled in his ears as he ascended, drowning out the sounds of the world around him.

Brand reached out, his arms encircling the massive war hammer as he met it in the air. His muscles screamed as the war hammer's weight fought against his control. Brand twisted his body, aligning the weapon with the giant below as the earth rushed up to meet them. The moment stretched, time seeming to dilate as he descended.

This is for Landren!

The world exploded in sound and fury as the war hammer met its mark. He drove the giant into the ground with a force that reverberated through the streets of Midral. Brand was flung away by the ensuing shockwave, sending him tumbling across the ground. As he came to a rest, his Crimson Chi finally flickered out like the last ember of a great fire.

* * *

Ronan braced himself as the shockwave of Brand's final attack slammed into him. He'd never seen anything like that display of martial arts, even out of Landren. But he didn't have time to reflect on the battle as he scanned for Kyros, who was nowhere to be seen at the moment. He didn't exactly see what had happened to cause Kyros to lose control of the ball of fire that might have spelled Ronan's doom, but he was glad for it.

"Ronan?" A small voice said behind him. "Is that really you?"

Ronan spun toward the sound. Astoro! He was here! Ronan ran to his friend's side and knelt next to him.

"Astoro, what are you doing here? Are you ok?" Ronan said.

"I mean, I feel like an apple that fell out of a tree and hit every branch on the way down," Astoro said with a weak smile. "But other than that, yeah I feel great. Hey, can you answer a quick question for me? *How are you alive?*"

Ronan chuckled. "That is a long and complicated story, my friend. One that I will happily tell you after I finish dealing with Kyros. Just rest and wait here."

"Wait," Astoro said, pulling Ronan back down to him. "I brought something for you." Astoro reached into his pocket and pulled out Ronan's necklace. "I hunted it down after you died. I thought I was coming here to lay it to rest with you, but maybe I was sent to you to give it to you when you needed it most."

My child, why do you think I sent you to him?

He remembered Brin's words to him earlier, eerily similar to Astoro's now. Could this really be a coincidence? Astoro just handed him the most important piece of his faith. The piece that was lost. He didn't know, and he didn't have time to process it at the moment. He pocketed the necklace instead of putting it on.

"Here, let me heal you a bit to take away some of that pain," Ronan said. He placed one hand over Astoro's arm and the other over his leg and focused. White energy poured out of his hands, enveloping Astoro's broken body. The energy sunk into the emerald skin and he watched as Astoro's limbs rearranged themselves into their correct positions. Astoro grunted at the pain of the healing and fell back to the ground, passed out, but breathing. He would be ok.

"Oh sorry, was he a friend of yours?" Kyros taunted, emerging from behind a shattered wall.

Ronan rose to his feet and faced his adversary. Kyros' clothing was singed and torn. It was the first time he'd seen Kyros anything but perfectly put together.

Ronan knew that his shield and armor had been almost completely depleted of energy after Kyros' last barrage. There was no way he'd be able to hold off another onslaught like that. He had to get in close and take control of the battle.

Ronan sprinted toward Kyros, his movements still empowered by Brin's armor. Kyros backed away and began firing energy at Ronan again. He raised his shield and deflected the blows, but as soon as he got within a few feet of Kyros, his legs slipped out from under him. He found himself sliding on his back toward Kyros. He must have laid down a sheet of ice on the ground as soon as Ronan raised his shield. The energy blasts were just a distraction.

The staff in Kyros' hand flashed with a twisted white and purple power and he slammed it down into Ronan's chest. The blow knocked the wind completely out of Ronan's lungs and he struggled to breathe. While he was still dazed, Kyros stepped back and his shadowy tentacles wrapped around Ronan's limbs and held him up in the air. Ronan struggled, but the tentacles had a firm grip on his limbs.

"There, that's better," Kyros said. "Now it's just the two of us. There's nobody left to save you."

Kyros struck Ronan with the staff again, making Ronan see stars. Ronan spat out some blood. It was happening again. He was going to die.

What was the point of it all? Why had he been brought back, if only to die again without accomplishing anything? Was his purpose only to help Brin complete her Trial? What did Niradim want?

An ice shard formed in Kyros' hand. "You know, this reminds me of a moment I had earlier outside the Soul Forge with your old master. Ginmar was it?"

Ronan's eyes focused on Kyros. "Keep Ginmar's name out of your mouth!" he growled.

"You know, the Soul Forge has a nice new ice sculpture in front of it," Kyros said, stepping up to Ronan. "Midral should have a matching one at its front gates, don't you think?

He plunged the shard of ice into Ronan's stomach and then let the tentacles drop Ronan to his knees. Pain that Ronan had only felt one other time in his life exploded in his stomach and ice began to spiderweb out from the wound to cover his body.

"You know, they say only the Flame of Niradim can melt the ice from the Black Frost Ring." Kyros leaned down and whispered into his ear. "Too bad I have the Flame." Kyros laughed as he turned and casually walked away from Ronan as he let the ice continue to spread across his body.

I'm sorry Ginmar...

Ginmar had been like a father to Ronan, but more than just a father. He had brought Ronan into Niradim's faith. It was Ginmar's near death that had been the catalyst for Ronan to become a follower of Niradim in the first place. And now, he had been killed. The only thing that could save him was either the Flame of Niradim or maybe...

Ronan closed his eyes as the ice spread across his torso.

Pain

Ronan prayed. For the first time since his resurrection, he prayed to Niradim.

Niradim, if it's your will, give me the strength to once again protect you and your people.

Pain

The ice spread across his arms and legs. He was stuck in a kneeling position, perfect for all he had left to do. He lifted his head up and looked to the sky. He continued to pray.

I may not know why you allowed all of this to happen, but I believe that you have a plan.

Pain

The ice covered his head. He could no longer breathe, yet he prayed.

I'm sorry I lost myself.

Pain

I devote myself again to you, even if it's just for these last few moments.

Pain

LIGHT

A white light flashed from the pocket that Ronan had put the necklace into and began to spread across his body. The ice encapsulating him began to melt and puddle at his feet. As it did, the wounds on Ronan's body closed up and healed. He raised to his feet and reached into his pocket.

"Thank you Niradim," Ronan whispered, holding the necklace tightly. "For never giving up on me, even when I had given up on you."

He put on the true symbol of his faith and watched as Kyros turned around wide-eyed. Ronan stood before him, blazing with a searing white light.

"That's impossible!" Kyros yelled. "Only the Flame of Niradim itself should be able to melt that ice!"

"The Flame of Niradim or…" Ronan said. "A Phoenix."

Ronan's hands came together in front of him as wisps of white power began to stream from his body. Ten glowing knives slid out from their sheathes and unfurled into a pair of phoenix wings wrought from steel and flame.

The deadly wings shot forward toward Kyros. This time, they did not flicker. The knives found their target, creating a vortex of fiery blades that engulfed Kyros, tearing into and searing his flesh again and again.

Kyros screamed in pain, but before the blades could finish the job, Kyros puffed into mist and reappeared at the top of the wall. He was panting and bleeding from hundreds of cuts on his body. He looked down at his hand, where the Black Frost Ring was melting off of his finger. Melted by the fires of the Phoenix.

"My ring!" Kyros roared as the knives all snapped back to Ronan, sliding back into their sheathes. "I've had it with you, and I'm done playing games! If you want your Flame back so much, here, you can have it!"

Kyros spun the staff around his head, creating a tornado of fire in the sky. He pointed the staff down at Ronan and a pillar of holy fire roared down from the heavens. Ronan started to raise his shield to block the attack, but before he did, he heard a voice of fire.

TRUST ME.

It had been a long time since he'd heard that voice, and he was finally glad to hear it again. Niradim said to trust him. So he did. He lowered his shield and sheathed his sword back into it as the pillar descended, centered on him.

The holy fire blazed around him for a long time before it stopped descending from the sky. When the smoke cleared, Ronan was still standing. His armor, sword, shield, and necklace shone with holy radiance. His weapons and armor had absorbed the holy fire and left Ronan completely unscathed.

Ronan watched the terror spread across Kyros' face as he drew his sword from his shield. Ronan crouched, gathering the holy energy around him, and launched himself at Kyros high up on the wall.

Phoenix wings made of pure white energy sprouted behind him and propelled him forward. What was left of the Flame flashed in the staff and also in the crystal embedded into Kyros' forehead for a split second. He held the staff in front of him to defend the oncoming blow and Ronan swung his sword with all his might.

The two weapons clashed together, but Ronan had the Flame of Niradim on his side. The crystalline staff shattered in a massive explosion, sending Kyros soaring away from the city into the night. The energy from the explosion expanded, and then retracted back, gathering into Ronan's shield to combine with the rest of the energy. The Flame of Niradim was finally safe.

He landed on the city wall, glowing as a beacon of hope for the city of Midral on its darkest day. Niradim's Phoenix had retrieved the Flame.

Now it was time to return it to the Soul Forge and save his master once again.

* * *

Kyros soared through the air towards the dense forest to the west of the city, wind whipping past him with a ferocious howl. He crashed through the tree line, smashing through branches like cracks of thunder until he landed hard in a small clearing.

He had never been beaten so thoroughly in his life. Every movement and breath was agony as he struggled to sit up against a tree. He had several broken bones and more lacerations than he could count, but somehow he was still alive. He needed to make sure he stayed that way.

Kyros' eyes flashed purple and his view shifted to Noct's, still flying high above the city. He watched as Ronan went to each of his friends in the area and healed them. Astoro first, then Val, and finally Brand.

Landren was beyond his help. He imagined Ronan would be able to restore his master at the Soul Forge as well. He did a final sweep of the area with Noct to ensure nobody was coming to look for him and then shifted back to his own senses.

That had gone horribly, horribly wrong. He should have just taken the Flame and left. He'd be long gone, and feeling much better by now. Probably taking a nice bath in a fancy inn and drinking expensive liquor. But his Patron had wanted Midral to suffer, and Kyros had paid a heavy price for it.

Kyros groaned as he picked himself up off the ground. They may not be looking for him now, but at some point, they'd want to verify he'd been killed, and he didn't want to be here when they found out the truth. He was far weaker now that he'd lost not one, but both of his Artifacts in the battle with Ronan. His Patron was not going to be happy with that setback.

But he didn't think Celestian would be too upset. Kyros held up his hand and the crystal embedded into his forehead flashed white instead of the normal purple. A white holy energy gathered in his hand and began to knit his broken bones back together. It had worked just as he'd hoped. Kyros may no longer have the entire Flame, but in the last second before Ronan sent him flying, he'd stolen enough of Niradim's energy for his Patron's needs.

His next meeting with Celestian might go poorly, but at least his hopes for fulfilling the contract remained alive.

* * *

Val was feeling a lot better since Ronan had used his power to heal her. A human wielding the Flame of Niradim. It was supposed to be impossible for anyone but dwarves to channel that power.

He'd been very impressive in his fight, but she had a suspicion that it wouldn't be the last time they heard from Kyros. Ronan had sent him flying, but until she saw a body, she didn't trust he was truly gone.

Speaking of bodies, she was approaching the spot where she'd left Zandro. Bogg would be nearby and she needed to help him get somewhere he could recover. Hopefully, he could carry at least some of his own weight. He was bigger than her.

She turned the corner and started at the spot where she'd left Zandro's corpse.

It was gone.

She froze for a split second and then drew her Flame Scimitar as it roared to life.

"Bogg!" she yelled. "Bogg, where are you!"

She saw him poke his head out of a doorway nearby. "I'm over here, why are you yelling? And why is your sword on fire?" His face lit up. "Is there a fight?"

"Where is Zandro?" she asked, frantically.

"He's right here, chill out." He held up Zandro's decapitated head next to his own. "It was creepin' me out with him just sittin' in the middle of the road, and I wanted to make sure he stayed dead, so I cut off his head and pulled him in here."

Val let out a huge sigh of relief as she sank to the ground and extinguished her sword. She put a hand to her head. He was still dead.

"Wait." Bogg smirked at her. "Did you actually think for a second that he'd gotten back up and walked away?"

"Shut up, Bogg."

* * *

Brand awoke with a start at the sound of voices around him. His body was sore *everywhere* and he had a huge headache to go with it. He opened his eyes and looked around.

A man in some fancy armor with a phoenix on the front was talking to Astoro in a makeshift bed across the room from him.

"Oh hey, Brand, you're finally awake," Astoro said, smiling.

"Unfortunately," Brand groaned, sitting up slowly.

"Don't push yourself, you must still be exhausted from the amount of energy you expended in that fight," the armored man said. Wait, was he *glowing?*

"Brand, this is my best friend I told you about," Astoro said. "Ronan Flamestriker."

"Thought you said he was dead," Brand said to Astoro.

"I was. But I got better," Ronan replied with a chuckle. "Listen, Brand, I wanted to thank you for everything you did. Astoro filled me in on what happened in the city before I arrived."

Images of the battle flashed through his mind. To be honest, the fight with the giant was mostly a blur. But he vividly remembered the moments before.

His Pathwarden was dead, and the secret to the Golden Chi went with him. He would never know what strong emotion his Pathwarden used to fuel his Chi. But he supposed it didn't matter. Brand had found his own Path and it was strong enough.

"Wish you would have arrived sooner," Brand said. "Then Landren might still be alive."

"Brand!" Astoro said.

Ronan frowned. "I'm truly sorry about your Pathwarden. Captain Landren was a great man and a friend. He spoke very highly of you."

Brand swung his feet off the side of the bed and stood up, meeting

Ronan face to face.

"And now he'll never speak again," Brand said and stormed out of the room.

He didn't care if Ronan had saved them all. He should have saved one more.

26

Epilogue

Ronan watched as the ice melted off of Ginmar's body. The knife wound from Kyros also healed as Niradim's holy energy washed over him. Ginmar coughed and Ronan released a breath he didn't know he'd been holding. He was alive. He'd recovered the Flame in time.

"Ronan," Ginmar said, shivering. "What happened?"

Ronan took a blanket from Elder Oren and wrapped it around Ginmar's shoulders.

"Long story short," Ronan said. "Niradim and I are back on speaking terms."

Ginmar smiled. "Glad to hear it, son."

"And I'll fill you in on the rest of the details later," Ronan continued. "For now, I need to return the Flame to its rightful place."

Much like the rest of the city, the Cathedral was a mess from Kyros' attack. Even the Great Anvil in front of the Soul Forge had cracked down the middle. Fortunately, the Soul Forge itself hadn't sustained any damage.

Ronan slowly walked up the steps and focused on concentrating the Flame into his sword. Once it had completely gathered there, he

300

stepped up to the Soul Forge and plunged his sword into the heart of it. He felt the Flame transfer back into the Soul Forge.

The effects were immediate. Some of the dwarves around him gasped as they felt Niradim's magic return to them. He could feel Niradim's magic spiderweb out through the Earth Sector to fuel the other forges within the mountain.

The Flame of Niradim was home.

Ginmar returned to full strength over the next few days and Ronan settled back into his place as a Disciple of Niradim. Between Niradim's Cathedral, the Crucible Gate, and the front gates of Midral, there was a lot of work to be done to repair the mess Kyros had made. Ronan found that the days passed quickly as he worked to fix his city.

He'd also decided he wouldn't be leaving Midral as he'd planned. The attack on the city reminded him just how much he loved the people of Midral and how much he still considered it his home. He found he wasn't ready to move on just yet.

His feelings for Brin were another big reason he'd decided to stay. His decision to leave in the first place had a lot to do with her - he didn't want his deteriorating relationship with Niradim to drag her down. But she'd shown him that she cared for him more than what his status with Niradim was. He and Niradim had made up in a way, but his faith was a far cry from what it had been before his death and resurrection. There was still a lot of work to do there, but at least the door was open again.

"Knock knock," Ronan said as he entered Brin's new residence in the Earth Sector. "I brought you something, hope you're hungry." Ronan held out some food he'd purchased from Heart of the Forge.

"Yes!" Brin snatched the bag out of his hands and pulled out a soft roll filled with meat. She immediately started stuffing it into her mouth. "Thank you, I was starving!"

She was going to need to purchase new furniture since her previous home burned down, but for now she plopped down onto the edge of her bed and rummaged through the bag of food.

"Hey, save one for me!" Ronan sat down next to her on the bed and grabbed one of the meat rolls before she could finish them all off.

Brin was still recovering from her Shaping Trial, so Ronan had been coming to visit each day after helping repair various parts of the city. It was going to take them months, maybe years to repair all the damage Kyros and his makeshift army had done to Midral.

"How did things go today?" she asked him through a mouth full of food.

"We've just barely finished clearing the rubble from around the front gates," he answered. "Now that it's clear, we can start to repair the wall itself before moving on to the gates. We need to get that taken care of as soon as possible to secure the city."

She nodded and swallowed the food she'd been chewing on. "I wish there was something I could do to help."

"Give it a few more days, Brin," Ronan said, placing a hand on her shoulder. "There will still be plenty of work to be done once you're fully recovered. For now, your job is to rest and enjoy these delicious meat rolls."

He started to take a bite, but was interrupted by a knock at the door. They both looked up to see Elder Oren in the door frame.

"Excuse me, Master Phoenix," he said. "May I speak with you outside for a moment?"

Ronan lowered the roll and placed it back into the bag Brin was holding.

"That better be waiting for me when I get back," he said to her with a mock-serious look on his face.

"No promises," she shot back, sticking out her tongue.

He kissed her on the forehead as he got up and then joined Oren outside. He shut the door behind him and turned to see all of the

Elders gathered around the front of Brin's home. A knot began to form in Ronan's stomach.

"Ok, you have my attention," Ronan said. "What is this about?"

"Now that the Flame is returned, we have an important matter to discuss with you." Oren turned to one of the other Elders and took something from him covered in cloth. He was about to uncover it, but Ronan held up a hand to stop him.

"Before we discuss whatever we're going to discuss, let me ask you one question," Ronan said. "Why me?"

Oren's hand paused, hovering over the cloth. "What do you mean?"

"I'm not an Elder," Ronan said. "And until a week ago, I wasn't even a Follower of Niradim anymore. Even now, I barely qualify. Niradim and I still have issues we have to work out, like why he let me die and why I was resurrected," he explained. "I finally believe it was part of his plan, but I still have questions I need answers to."

"Your resurrection is precisely why you're included in this discussion," Oren replied. "Niradim has clearly chosen you for something. Maybe it was simply for the trials you went through a week ago, but we believe it may be more. And something has resurfaced from the past that needs to be investigated."

"From the past?" Ronan asked, raising an eyebrow.

He removed the cloth to reveal a metal orb engraved with ancient dwarven runes, about the size of his palm.

"After the Great Anvil was split, this was recovered nearby," Oren said, handing it to Ronan.

"What is it?" Ronan asked, taking it in his hands. It was heavier than it looked and it had a slight vibration to it.

"It's called a Mythril Soul," Oren said. "We don't know what they were used for, but we have scrolls that mention ancient dwarves who wielded them for some purpose. However, the few records that remain from that time all agree that the Mythril Souls were completely destroyed long ago."

"So why was a Mythril Soul hiding in the Great Anvil?" Ronan said.

"Exactly our question," Oren replied.

This was interesting. Ronan had been a member of Niradim's faith for most of his life, and he had never heard of these Mythril Souls Oren spoke about. What other secrets were the Elders hiding?

"I don't understand the problem," Ronan said. "There must be more to this than just a simple discovery."

"You may have noticed that the Flame has been acting erratically since you returned it to the Soul Forge," Oren explained. "People can channel Niradim's magic, but not with the same amount of power as before it was stolen. Also, some of the forges powered by Niradim's magic flicker in ways they never did before."

"I just assumed the Flame needed time to build back up to its previous strength."

"We did too, at first. But it doesn't make sense. The Flame is Niradim's essence, there's no reason it should need time to build up its strength," Oren said. "We believe the sudden appearance of the Mythril Soul is responsible for the Flame's condition."

That couldn't be good.

"Ok, out with it," Ronan said. He was tired of talking around the problem. They clearly wanted something from him. "What do you need from me?"

"We want you to delve into the mountain," Oren said. "And locate the ancient archives to learn as much as you can about Mythril Souls."

"Why?" Ronan asked.

"Because the Flame," Oren said, "is dying."

* * *

YOUR MISSION WAS A COMPLETE DISASTER.

"I think that's a little harsh," Kyros said. He hadn't been looking forward to this meeting since he left Midral. At least Celestian had been gracious enough to wait until he made it back to Lumenova. "I got enough of the Flame for what you need, and Midral suffered quite a bit."

YOU MADE IT OUT WITH A BARE FRACTION OF THE FLAME AND YOU LOST TWO OF THE MOST POWERFUL MAGICAL ITEMS ON THE CONTINENT IN THE PROCESS.

Kyros sighed. "Fair point."

He couldn't believe just how sideways everything went there at the end. All because of Ronan, Val'ran, and Brand. Up until their intervention, he'd had everything in complete control. He still didn't know how Ronan managed to survive the attack in the Cathedral and come back stronger.

I NO LONGER TRUST YOU TO COMPLETE YOUR MISSION ON YOUR OWN. THERE IS ONE MORE ITEM YOU NEED TO RETRIEVE, BUT I AM SENDING SOMEONE TO ASSIST YOU TO MAKE SURE YOU DON'T FAIL.

"I don't need a babysitter," Kyros said indignantly.

This was ridiculous. Even with all that had happened, he'd still retrieved what was needed. He didn't need someone coming in here and disrupting his operation, especially someone he didn't get to vet in advance.

IT'S NOT NEGOTIABLE. I RECOVERED HIM WHILE YOU WERE TRAVELING BACK FROM MIDRAL AND HE WILL MEET YOU IN THE MORNING.

"Recovered him? What does that mean…" Kyros was cut off as he was flung away from the Star Prison and back into his own body in Lumenova.

Kyros hated that Celestian had that power over him. Sleeping was always a surprise. He never knew when he'd be taking a visit to the voiding purple star in the sky for what always turned out to be an unpleasant conversation. It was still the middle of the night, so he settled back in for a few more hours of sleep.

The sun was barely cresting the horizon when someone banged on his door. Great, this must be the *help* Celestian sent him. He took his time getting out of bed and stretched his muscles that were still sore from traveling. It was time to get this over with. He walked over to the door and slowly opened it. Who could Celestian have possibly sent to him that was supposed to help...

Kyros took a step back as he recognized the figure on the other side of the door. "How are you alive?"

"Well hello to you too," the familiar orange-red novaborn said, stepping into the light.

"Brother."

* * *

"I'm tellin' ya, I woulda been able to hit him in the head at that distance."

"Shut up Bogg."

It took Bogg a few days to fully recover from Zandro's poison, but as soon as he did, she treated him to that dinner and drinks she owed him. And boy did he know how to put away the food and drinks. She was going to need to find some work soon because she was going to be broke after this meal.

"No really, I can't believe you hit him in the shoulder, it wasn't even that far," Bogg said. He'd been bugging her about this since she told him about their showdown with Kyros and the giant chieftain.

"Well maybe if you hadn't let yourself get slaggin' poisoned, you could have shown me how it was done!" she shot back.

Bogg laughed and downed his current drink as a barmaid brought him another. She'd lost count of how many that was. Ashes, this was going to be expensive!

"Oh, before I forget," Bogg said. "I was going through my bag and found some of the stuff I took off Zandro after we killed that slaghead. Here you go."

He slid a satchel over to her and downed his latest drink all at once.

"Now, if you'll excuse me, there's a different kind of celebrating I'd like to do and you're not invited," he said.

Bogg stood up and stumbled over to a very muscular dwarf with a long white beard who was looking their way. After just a few seconds, Bogg put his arm around the dwarf and began leading him upstairs to his room. He looked over his shoulder at her and gave her a wink.

Huh, she really *wasn't* his type. She chuckled to herself and then turned to investigate Zandro's satchel.

She had done a pretty good job of keeping her mind off him the last few days. It was wonderful to finally begin to heal from the betrayal he put her through. She and Bogg were becoming close friends, but she still didn't know where to go from here. Maybe soon she'd ask him what he wanted to do. He'd come with her on her mission, after all. She should return the favor.

She opened the satchel and began rummaging through it. She wasn't surprised to see various poisons and antidotes organized in the small bag. He liked to keep a stock of different concoctions on him depending on what the situation called for.

There were also various letters folded neatly near the bottom of the bag. She began to take them out one by one, scanning them to see what they contained. Most of them were correspondences with members of their cult, telling them to begin moving their operations to Lumenova. Turns out, the lost city had been rediscovered.

Sure has, Val thought to herself, shaking off the memories.

Then a name caught her eye on the last letter and she froze. *Syndallin*. That was the name of the Lord they were supposed to kill before

Zandro betrayed her. Her fingers trembled as she opened the letter and read its contents.

Dear V,

I have received your previous correspondence and request for transfer. My agent has returned and verified your claims that the lost city of Lumenova has indeed been rediscovered. Enclosed are documents that give House Syndalin exclusive rights to search the city for rare Artifacts. As soon as those documents are signed and returned to me, I will arrange transfer of the prisoner to my son, Kyros, in Lumenova.

I have also received reports that you let the daughter slip through your fingers. This is disappointing, as we were hoping to use her as leverage. Do'ran Nisanthar of the Arcane Knights will not break unless we have his daughter. I trust you will remedy the situation before the transfer.

Signed,

Lord Elandrose Syndalin

Val read the letter again. And again. And again. She was on her fifth read-through when Bogg returned to their table.

"Sorry, forgot my sword. Don't ask, you don't want to know…" He stopped as soon as he saw her face. "What's going on, you don't look so good."

She looked up at him, tears forming in her eyes.

"My father is alive."

* * *

Brand slammed his glass down on the bar. "Another."

"Sir, you've already had…"

"I said, another!" Brand threw the small empty glass at the wall behind the barkeeper, shattering it.

The barkeeper let out a small yelp. He grabbed another small glass and filled it with some kind of liquor that made Brand's eyes water when he held it up to his lips.

"You can put that on my tab," a feminine voice said from the other end of the bar.

Brand looked over at a hooded figure holding a similar drink in a clawed hand. She downed her shot and stood up to approach Brand.

"I don't know who you are, but I'm not interested," Brand said, turning away.

The draken woman ignored him and took the seat next to him. He really wasn't in the mood to talk to anyone, which is why he'd come to this mostly vacant bar in the first place. They were the only two people there besides the barkeeper. He downed his shot and rose to leave, but she grabbed his arm.

"Let me go," Brand said. Her grip was surprisingly strong for her size.

"Or what?" she asked playfully.

The barkeeper slowly backed into the kitchen, not wanting any part of what was about to happen.

"Let me go. Now," Brand said. "I'm not going to ask a third time."

"No," she replied.

He swept his leg out and then twisted his arm to try and break her grip, but she hopped over the minor attack and kept her grip on him. He was feeling some of the effects of the liquor, but that would have been enough to dislodge him from any normal person. She had some kind of training.

So she wanted to play games? Fine, he needed to let off a little steam anyway. He pulled her in close and tried to strike with his free hand, but she caught his blow. He looked her in the eyes, anger beginning to bubble to the surface and she smiled at him, baring her teeth.

He drove his knee upward to try and knock the wind out of her, but she used his momentum to spin him around and push him away from the bar to the middle of the room. He stumbled before catching himself. He was tired of this, and his anger began to take control.

He seized the rage inside of himself and opened the Inner Gates to let his Chi fill his body. Crimson steam began to rise off of him as he stared down the hooded draken woman.

"You're going to regret this," he said.

"I don't think I will," she simply replied.

He advanced quickly, fueled by his Chi, and began his attack. But even with his Chi, he wasn't able to land a blow. He kept attacking, but she dodged everything. It was like she knew his every move before he made it.

His anger finally flickered out and so did his Chi. She knocked him to the ground.

"It's not so easy to keep it going after the first time, is it?" she said down to him. "You're not angry enough."

"What would you know about it?" Brand snapped.

He watched as Crimson flashed in her eyes for just a moment. "More than you."

Brand's eyes went wide. "How?"

"I've been studying it for quite some time, actually," she said. "And as it so happens, I'm looking for students."

"Who are you?" he asked.

"You can call me Scarlet," she said, lowering her hood to reveal her red scales.

She held out a hand to help Brand to his feet.

"Come with me and I'll teach you the way of the Crimson Path."

About the Author

Danny Colmenares is a Project Manager by day and fantasy author whenever time allows. Long time reader and first time writer, Danny loves fantasy and sci-fi in all forms of media - from books, to TV, to games. Born and raised in Texas, he currently lives in a small town north of Dallas with his wife, two daughters, and schnauzer.

You can connect with me on:
- https://flamestrikerbooks.com
- https://www.facebook.com/FlamestrikerBooks
- https://www.instagram.com/flamestrikerbooks